gac

In Close

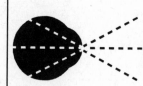

In Close

Brenda Novak

THORNDIKE PRESS
A part of Gale, Cengage Learning

GALE
CENGAGE Learning

Detroit • New York • San Francisco • New Haven, Conn • Waterville, Maine • London

GALE
CENGAGE Learning

The Bulletproof Trilogy.
Thorndike Press, a part of Gale, Cengage Learning.

Thorndike Press® Large Print Romance.
The text of this Large Print edition is unabridged.
Other aspects of the book may vary from the original edition.
Set in 16 pt. Plantin.

LIBRARY OF CONGRESS CATALOGING-IN-PUBLICATION DATA

Novak, Brenda.
In close / by Brenda Novak. — Large print ed.
p. cm. — (The bulletproof trilogy; #3) (Thorndike Press large print romance)
ISBN-13: 978-1-4104-4358-8(hardcover)
ISBN-10: 1-4104-4358-2(hardcover)
1. Large type books. 2. Single mothers—Fiction. 3. Missing persons—Fiction. 4. Sheriffs—Fiction. 5. Law enforcement—Fiction. 6. Families—Fiction. I. Title.
PS3614.O926I5 2011
813'.6—dc23 2011037754

Published in 2011 by arrangement with Harlequin Books S.A.

Printed in the United States of America
1 2 3 4 5 6 7 15 14 13 12 11

To Louise (LouBabe) Pledge,
a reader I knew only via email
for a long time, who has turned
into a cherished friend.
Thank you for all your enthusiasm
for my books and the massive support
you have given my efforts to raise
money for diabetes research.
You're one in a million!

Dear Reader,

I *love* old mysteries. Maybe that's why I'm such a fan of cold case programs. I can't stand unanswered questions, so I enjoy vicariously experiencing the resolution of such cases and the satisfaction that resolution brings to all the people involved. If something mysterious happened to my friend or loved one, I'm the type of person who'd dig and dig and dig and never give up, never be able to let go. So I completely identify with the heroine of this novel, Claire O'Toole, whose mother, Alana, went missing while Claire was in high school. I enjoyed exploring how that event shaped Claire's life. I also found it fascinating to consider what might've happened to Alana and to come up with a list of possible suspects, including Claire's stepfather, who was so good to Claire while she was growing up; her crippled sister, with whom she has a strained relationship; the man with whom Claire's mother might've had an extramarital affair; even a few surprise contenders. This case is particularly hard to solve. It's quite a challenge for Claire — and so is the man who decides to help.

Isaac Morgan has overcome great difficulty himself, which is partly what makes him a perfect match for Claire. She's exactly what he needs, if only he can figure out how to open his heart again.

Part of the fun of creating this novel was imagining the small town of Pineview, Montana. This area is unique — so different from where I live in California. I'd love to own a cabin in the Chain of Lakes area, where I placed my fictional town. Maybe someday I will (if I can ever talk my husband into leaving suburbia).

I would like to extend a special thanks to Becky Kranz for purchasing the chance to name a character in this book via one of my annual online auctions for diabetes research. She chose the name Carrie Oldman, which you will see in the story. Like every other person who's helped me raise money for this important cause, Becky is a hero to me.

For more information about me or my work, please visit www.brendanovak.com. There, you can enter my monthly contests, see what's coming out next or participate in my annual online auction for diabetes research, which runs for the entire month of May. To date, we've raised over $1.4 million!

All the best,
Brenda

1

The tiny cabin Claire O'Toole's mother had once used for painting had been shut up for years. Claire was the only one who came here, and even she didn't return all that often, maybe every six months or so.

Braced for the torrent of memories that hit her every time she walked inside, she dropped the key into the pocket of her jeans and forced open a door warped from too many Montana winters. Before she crossed the threshold, however, she looked behind her, suddenly feeling she might not be as alone as she'd thought.

A gentle wind swayed the pine trees. She could hear the rustle as it traveled through the surrounding forest, but she couldn't see any movement. She couldn't see anything at all, except for what fell inside the beam of her flashlight. There were no city lights up here, no glassy lake to reflect the moon's glow, the way there was closer to town, nothing but thick forest carpeted with pine needles, cloaked in darkness and topped with a canopy of stars.

No one was sneaking up behind her. How silly to even check. There were other cabins in these mountains, but only one in the immediate vicinity. Her parents had owned it as well as this studio from when they were first married to the summer before she started school. Then they'd sold the main house and moved to town. She could still remember her mother cooking in that kitchen, the little tree house her stepfather had built in the backyard.

The house had changed hands more than once, but Isaac Morgan owned it now, so she stayed clear. Avoiding it minimized the number of times she and Isaac ran into each other. He filmed wildlife all around the world and was often gone, which helped. Although he lived closest to the studio, she couldn't imagine any reason *he'd* be lurking in the trees. They were too busy trying to prove to each other that what they'd had ten years ago had been as easy to leave behind as it should've been.

So who else could it be? Her sister, her stepfather and his wife, her best friend and her best friend's sheriff husband — in fact, nearly all of Pineview's 1,500 residents —

were watching Fourth of July fireworks in the city park across the street from the cemetery. She could hear the distant boom of each explosion, smell the smoke that drifted up against the mountain.

No one had noticed when she slipped away.

Drawing a deep breath, she turned back and focused on the dusty interior. Cast-off furniture from her stepfather, her stepfather's wife and her maternal grandparents crowded the living room. Cobwebs hung from the rafters; rat droppings littered the floor. Pack rats built nests everywhere in this part of the state, even in the engines of cars.

This wasn't the magical place it'd been when she was a child. The good memories had been conquered and overrun, broken by tragedy, but she returned, anyway. She couldn't ignore the studio's existence and move on, like everybody else. Invariably, the past dragged her back.

As she stepped inside, she paused to listen. She'd expected silence. But she could hear the engine of her old Camaro ticking as it cooled in the overgrown drive. Then a creak, coming from the loft above. When other creaks followed, it almost sounded as if her mother was walking around up there like she used to.

Obviously, Claire's imagination had kicked into overdrive, reacting to the isolation and the spookiness of coming here after dark.

Or maybe it was her subconscious, trying to get her out before she could come across something that might disrupt what little peace of mind she had left. Her mother had been missing for fifteen years and in all that time they'd never found a trace of her. Her sister had broken her back sledding two years later and been confined to a wheelchair. And David, her husband, had died only a year ago in a terrible hunting accident. She couldn't tolerate another loss.

And yet she kept digging for the truth.

What if she discovered that her stepfather had killed her mother, as so many others believed? Or what if her mother had run off with another man, willingly left them for a new life somewhere else, as the previous sheriff had suggested?

She'd be devastated. Again. But she couldn't accept either of those possibilities. Her stepfather was a good man; he would never have hurt Alana. Alana was a loving mother; she would never have abandoned her children. That meant someone had kidnapped her, maybe killed her, and would get away with it unless Claire made sure that didn't happen. Who else would fight for justice?

Not Leanne. Claire's sister battled enough challenges. Leanne didn't even want to think about the day they'd lost their mother, let alone look into it. And her stepfather — Tug, as his friends called him — had moved in with the woman who'd eventually become her stepmother only six months after Alana went missing. At this late date, he wouldn't have known what to do with Alana even if she reappeared.

Only Claire held on. She was all her mother had left, and that made it impossible to give up, no matter how many people told her she should. Her mother deserved more than that.

At least obsessing about the mystery that had tormented her for half her life kept her from dwelling on David, a loss that was far too recent and still too raw.

Another creak. She almost lost her nerve. Maybe she should've waited until tomorrow. But her sister lived in the house right next door to hers and was constantly dropping by. It was difficult for Claire to get away without divulging *something* about where she was going and what she was doing. And because Claire ran her business, a hair salon, out of her home, if it wasn't her sister, it was one of her many clients, who paid more attention than Claire wanted. Thanks to her mother's disappearance, she'd always been watched a little too carefully. Everyone was waiting to see whether she'd recover or fall apart. That was the reason she wanted to move away — so she could be anonymous for a change, start over — a desire that had only grown more intense after David died. Except for two years when their relationship had faltered while he was in college, they'd been together since they were sixteen. Losing him meant becoming the object of everyone's pity once again.

How are you? You hangin' in there, kiddo?

She got questions like that, spoken in low, somber tones, all the time. She wouldn't have minded so much if the people who asked were as sincere as they sounded and not just inviting her to provide them with a bit of tantalizing gossip for the next community gathering or church event. *Poor Claire. She's suffering so. I talked to her last week and . . .*

Claire didn't need anyone gabbing about her efforts to solve the mystery. Or conjecturing on what she might or might not find at the studio. Or confronting her family with the fact that she'd been here. That was why she kept whatever she could to herself. Why create more curiosity? It would only upset those who'd rather forget. . . .

So, frightening though it was, she liked the cover of darkness. It made her feel as close to anonymous as she could get in the place where she'd grown up. The noises she heard were nothing to worry about. No one would have any reason to hang out in an abandoned studio that didn't have electricity or running water. If some vagabond had moved in, there'd be proof of occupancy.

Knocking the cobwebs out of the way, she followed the beam of her flashlight through the cluster of furniture. Then she climbed up to the loft, where her mother used to paint. She'd loved watching Alana work, had never felt more at peace than here, with the sun pouring through the floor-to-ceiling windows of the second floor, her mother standing in the light, concentrating on her latest masterpiece.

Several unfinished paintings perched on easels covered with sheets, looking like ghosts floating a couple of feet off the ground. The sight of them made Claire sick with loss, a loss rivaled only by David's death. Whoever had taken Alana had robbed the world, and Claire, of so much.

Was it someone she knew? Someone she

passed on the street, spoke to, cared about? One of those people who always asked how she was?

It had to be, didn't it? Alana went missing from their house in town in the dead of winter. Although this part of Montana saw an influx of hunters, fisherman and recreationists during the spring, summer and fall, it was not a place to visit in the cold months. Libby, thirty miles away, was the closest town. Notorious for the asbestos mine that'd made everyone sick and caused the death of two hundred people, Libby had been in the news a lot in recent years. But on the day Alana had gone missing, it was still just a spot on the map, and an overturned truck carrying vermiculite ore had blocked traffic on the highway for hours. The sheriff himself hadn't been able to get through until it was cleared.

Claire supposed some "bad man" could've come from the other direction, from Marion or Kalispell, but no one had spotted any strangers that day. Even more significant, there'd been no sign of forced entry at the house. Whoever had taken Alana was most likely someone she trusted. She'd opened her door, never expecting to be harmed.

The betrayal inherent in that scenario made Claire more determined than anything else to solve the mystery.

Dragging a chair from the corner, the very chair in which she used to sit and daydream while her mother painted, Claire climbed up to reach the handle that would open the attic door. Just shy of five foot three, she could barely grab hold, but once she caught it, the pull-down ladder lowered easily enough.

It was warmer in the small space above Alana's studio. Dustier, too. Claire coughed as she poked her head through the opening and used her flashlight to reacquaint herself with the contents.

Boxes stacked floor to ceiling left little room in which to maneuver. She hadn't remembered it being quite so crowded. But when it became clear that her mother wasn't coming back, Claire had insisted that everything Alana owned, down to the razor she'd been using in the shower, be preserved. The sheriff's department had confiscated the contents of Alana's desk, her computer, any recent letters she'd written or received, the photos she'd snapped in the months prior to her disappearance, her journal, the things left in her car — anything they thought might help them find her. Claire and Leanne had taken possession of any sentimental items that remained. And the rest had been packed up and stored here years ago, just after Claire graduated from high school and moved out — and her stepfather and his wife bought the luxurious home they currently enjoyed, the home they'd bought with the inheritance Alana had received when her parents died in a plane crash only a year before she disappeared.

Riddled with guilt for even thinking that her mother's misfortune had provided such a spectacular living for the woman who'd replaced her, Claire steered her mind away from that direction. She liked her stepmother. It wasn't Roni's fault that Alana was no longer around.

But it bothered Claire that Roni acted as if Alana had never existed. Tug and Leanne preferred to handle the situation the same way. They'd both asked Claire to forget the past. Learning what happened wouldn't bring Alana back, they said. And it was true. It was also true that Leanne seemed to do better if she didn't have to be reminded of that fateful day. Which was why, after pleading for the new sheriff to reopen the case a couple of years ago, Claire had gone back to call him off. Her family had been too upset about the questions he was asking. They couldn't tolerate the assumptions and suspicions that were inevitable in such a small community.

Claire respected their position. But she couldn't stop digging entirely. She needed resolution as much as they needed to forget.

What she was hoping to accomplish by coming here tonight, however, she didn't know. She'd been through all this stuff so many times. Her stepfather, his wife and Leanne had seen it, too. The three of them had packed it together.

But Claire couldn't help hoping that she'd see something she'd missed before, that some clue would emerge and solve the mystery. That happened all the time on those forensics shows.

Squeezing through the narrow pathway, she moved toward a box that contained her mother's childhood memorabilia — Alana's report cards, her early journals, pictures of her family and friends. Claire loved looking through that box because it made her feel closer to the woman she missed so terribly. And it was as good a place to begin as any. She planned on going through every last box, even if that meant frequent trips to the studio over the next few weeks.

She bent to lift it, then saw some boxes that had been packed *much* more recently. They stood out because they were labeled in her own handwriting. *David's Clothes, Da-*

vid's Things, David's Yearbooks.

Her hand flew to her chest as if she could stop that familiar lump from growing in her throat, but she couldn't. What were her late husband's personal belongings doing here? She hadn't expected to find them, wasn't ready for such a powerful reminder.

One day several months ago, her mother-in-law had come over and packed up everything of David's, insisting it all be taken from the house. She said that Claire couldn't get over his death if she was living with his ghost, still sleeping in his T-shirt and crying over the fact that it was beginning to smell more like her than him.

Claire had assumed those things of David's, except the few she'd managed to retain, had gone into his parents' garage, but Rosemary must've asked Claire's stepfather to put them here. The two often talked, usually about their concern for her and how she was or wasn't "coping."

No one had mentioned that David's belongings had been moved to this attic, but Claire supposed it was understandable that they would be. Rosemary had a large family and a crowded house. She probably didn't want to encounter her dead son's possessions every time she retrieved the holiday decorations. The studio already held what remained of Alana's life, and nobody ever used it. This must have seemed like the perfect solution.

Closing her eyes, Claire reached out for the warm presence she'd occasionally felt since David's death. She wasn't a superstitious person, certainly didn't believe in ghosts that rattled chains and haunted people, but she did have faith in the power of love to create a bridge between this world and the next. She'd felt some comfort since he died. It was almost as if he visited her now and then to make sure she was all right.

She wished she could feel him now, but the pain was too sudden and too acute. Grappling with it required all her focus.

"Why'd you leave me?" she whispered. The tears that rolled down her cheeks were nothing new. She cursed them, wished she could get beyond them, but the senselessness of his death, the fact that she'd lost David so soon and couldn't imagine ever loving someone else in quite the same way, didn't help.

She almost shoved his boxes out of sight, pushed them to the back so she wouldn't have to see the thick black letters that seared her to the bone: *David's.* They were only inanimate objects he'd once owned. As badly as she wanted him, David wasn't here anymore, and he never would be.

But she didn't push the boxes away; she pulled them closer. She'd spotted something that struck her as odd. On a two-foot-by-two-foot box, third from the bottom, David had scrawled his own name. She recognized his writing — but not this particular box, which she would've noticed since it was white and all the ones she'd used were brown.

Why had she never seen this before? She was positive it hadn't come from her house. . . .

Once she opened the flaps, she knew why. He must've stored this above his parents' garage before he went to college. If she had her guess, it'd been brought here in an effort to keep all his possessions together.

Fresh longing filled her as she touched the soccer and basketball trophies, the varsity letters he'd never sewn on a jacket, a pen set he'd made in wood shop. Then there were the cards she'd given him when they first started dating. They'd gone to high school together, were an item for two years before he left for college, so she had the same homecoming and prom pictures.

Unable to spend any more time with those memories for fear she'd undo the progress she'd made in the past few months, she began to close the box when she decided to see what was inside a fat accordion-style file folder tucked between some old sweaters. It looked far too businesslike for the seventeen-year-old David who'd packed up the rest of these things. . . .

When she opened it, she realized why. This folder wasn't from that early period. It was from after they were married. And what it contained shocked her so badly, she had to put her head between her knees so she wouldn't faint.

Jeremy Salter hung back in the trees, watching. It was pitch-black, but that didn't matter. The night-vision goggles his father had given him for Christmas worked beautifully. He'd also received a Swiss Army knife — he loved collecting things that would help him survive in the wilderness. He imagined himself as the next Rambo.

But Claire had no survival skills. She didn't belong out here, especially after dark. If she wasn't careful, a bear or a pack of wolves could attack her. Or even a man. Men were by far the most dangerous animals on earth.

His father used to say that; his father had also proved it.

She must like it here, he mused. She came

often enough. But not so much lately. Not once David was killed. Since David's death, she didn't do much of anything, except cut hair all day. Then she'd curl up on the couch, eyes glued to the TV. But he usually got the impression that she wasn't watching the program. She'd stare at the screen without blinking and soon the tears would start.

She missed David and didn't know how to go on without him.

Jeremy understood how that felt.

So what was she doing in her mother's old studio? Trying to get herself into the same trouble David had? Didn't she know that some secrets should be buried and forgotten?

She'd be fine if only she'd let the past go. Then he'd be fine, too.

Sometimes he wished he could tell her that. Promise her that everything would get better if she could just go on her way. She was so beautiful and smart and nice. Everything a woman should be. Any guy would love to be with her.

Including him. *Especially* him. Not that he'd ever have a chance. He was too . . . different. He'd always been different.

Her flashlight had made it possible for him to track her movements to the loft, but then the light disappeared.

Had she turned it off? Was she sitting on the floor, crying? Missing her mother the way she missed David?

Or did she have some other reason for being here? She'd slipped away from the park so cautiously, it'd certainly felt as if she had a purpose.

He needed to get inside the cabin to find out. But he hesitated to go that close. What if she caught him?

That could be dangerous. For both of them.

But if he was quiet enough, she'd never have to know. He'd been watching her for years, hadn't he? And she'd never caught him yet.

2

David had a copy of the case files on her mother. Everything was here, from the missing-persons report to the last interview. Claire had seen some of this before, but even she hadn't been privy to all of it. How had he come by this much information?

He must've gotten it from Sheriff King. Either that or he'd called in a favor from his old hunting buddy, Rusty Clegg. Rusty had been a deputy for the past six or seven years. It helped to have a friend on the force.

But what felt so strange about finding this was that David had made his own notations on many of the reports and interviews. It was almost as if he'd picked up the investigation where the sheriff had left off.

Why hadn't he told her what he was doing? The dates on the log he'd kept correlated with the first year of their marriage and included a number of entries in the months leading up to his death. The last time he'd written anything was two days before the accident. She found detailed information on her stepfather and Leanne, plus her mother's only sibling — a sister living in Portland, Oregon — and a complete chronology of Alana's last movements.

Some of it Claire didn't want to read. It brought back That Night, the longest night of her life, during which every adult she knew, including her stepfather, was out searching. She and Leanne hadn't been allowed to leave the house. They'd waited for their mother, or some word of her, praying all the while for her safe return — to no avail. When the sun came up, their stepfather and one friend after another checked in with the bad news that they hadn't been able to find any sign of her.

Reluctant yet determined, Claire's eyes skimmed the handwritten log fastened to the left side of the thickest folder.

> May 10: Spoke to Jason Freeman. Claims he saw Alana at the bakery between 8:00 and 9:00 a.m. Watched her go in and come out carrying a bag of doughnuts while he drank a cup of coffee in the cab of Pete Newton's truck. Jason says she got in the car with Tug and drove away. Tug confirms this in

original interview. Other than Tug, Jason is the last person to see Alana.

May 12: Tried to reach Joe Kenyon.

Now *there* was a name, the one most often mentioned by those who theorized that Alana had been unhappy in her marriage and had gone looking for fulfillment in the arms of another man. If she'd had one affair, it was plausible she'd have more and might even have run off with whatever new lover she'd taken, right? That explained the mystery to some. But it explained nothing to Claire, who couldn't believe her mother had ever cheated.

He wouldn't open his door when I knocked, but Carly Ortega across the street told me Alana stopped at Joe's house quite often. She even saw her car parked in his drive once, late at night.

Late? How could that be possible? Tug was always home at night. Alana would've had to slip out of bed without his noticing in order to leave the house. And why would she do that? Joe had come to cut down the diseased cottonwood tree that was about to fall onto their roof, but other than the few hours they'd spent together then, Claire couldn't remember them ever speaking.

May 13: Tried again to get an audience with Joe Kenyon. Refused to speak to me. Prick.

David's log went on for several pages. Figuring she'd read the rest at home, Claire switched to the other side of the folder and skimmed several interviews originally done by Sheriff Meade.

Carly wasn't the only one who believed there was something going on between Joe Kenyon and Alana. Joe's twin brother, Peter, thought they were involved. He insisted that he'd heard his brother take a call from Alana while they were at work one day. He said he couldn't hear what was being said, but he could tell by the tone of Joe's voice that it wasn't a simple request for tree-trimming services.

Cringing, Claire dropped her flashlight in her lap. Did she *really* want to continue reading? This was making her sick, making her wonder if she'd really known her mother. Had Alana been leading a double life?

Claire didn't want to suspect her, but . . . how much more about Joe, about *Alana* and Joe, could she endure?

That depended on how strongly she believed in Alana, didn't it? Maybe Leanne had been a daddy's girl from the moment Tug had come into their lives, during Leanne's first year, but Claire had always preferred Alana. She trusted her mother more than to accept, on circumstantial evidence alone, that Alana was an adulteress.

Breathing in through her nose and out through her mouth, Claire picked up the flashlight. "We'll show them, Mom," she promised. "We'll show them all."

Beneath the log, she ran across a list of typed "inconsistencies." These didn't appear to be written by David, but she was willing to bet he was the one who'd highlighted various passages. According to the date at the top, the list was Sheriff King's summary after taking over from Sheriff Meade.

> Tug said he was at work until he received Claire's call. Concerned that Alana's car was still in the drive and yet she was nowhere to be found, he left immediately.

> The next part was highlighted.

> Why would he be instantly worried? There's never been a kidnapping or a

murder in Pineview.

There'd been one murder since — Pat Stueben, the town Realtor — but that hadn't yet occurred when this was written.

Unless she kept it to herself, Alana had never been threatened and wasn't having problems with anyone. For all Tug knew, she'd walked down the block to talk to a neighbor and would be back any minute.

Was his reaction a bit too fast? There was always the threat of bears. They came around if people left out food. But no one in town, other than Isaac Morgan, who tracked and filmed wild animals for a living, had ever been attacked.

Claire's arms and legs tingled with apprehension. Tug was normally the last person to assume the worst. Why had he reacted so quickly?

She tried to remember every word of the conversation that had passed between them when she'd called that day.

What do you mean she's gone? she'd asked the minute she told him.

I've searched the whole house.

Did you check the bathrooms?

Of course.

She didn't leave a note?

Not that I can find. You haven't heard from her?

No. Stay there. I'm on my way.

At that point, it hadn't occurred to Claire that her mother could be in danger. She'd expected him to say something like, "Don't worry. I'm sure she'll be home soon." But he hadn't. And once he reached the house, he'd acted so tense, the same fear began to percolate through Claire. That was the first inkling she'd had that they were facing a major tragedy, and she'd taken her cue from her stepfather.

Had he already known what was wrong? Had he and Alana argued earlier, maybe when he came home for lunch? Possibly about Joe Kenyon? And had that argument gotten out of hand?

As much as she didn't want to believe it, she knew things like that happened. . . .

Chilled by the thought, she ran her free hand over the goose bumps on her arm. But it didn't help because she found Sheriff King's next point equally disturbing.

On the day Alana disappeared, she picked Leanne up at school at 11:15 a.m. for reason of "illness," but someone who didn't come to the office took her back shortly before two. The sign-in/sign-out log in the attendance office reflects this partial absence but Leanne has never mentioned that she was home for a portion of the day. And she has never said whether or not her mother was with her during that time.

"Impossible," Claire muttered. After all the years of searching and questioning, how was it that Leanne had never spoken of missing school? Why would she keep it to herself?

There had to be a reason. Hoping it might become apparent, Claire kept reading.

If she was sick, how did she recuperate so fast?

Exactly!

At 2:00 p.m. she brought a note to the office excusing her absence and signed herself in. The attendance lady didn't keep the note and doesn't remember who wrote it — mother or father — but she stands by her log. When asked if she could've gotten the date wrong, she insists it would be almost impossible. "If that's wrong, all the dates before it would have to be wrong, as well as the dates after."

Another highlighted part.

All the days are accounted for and run Monday through Friday, as they should.

Stunned, Claire sat staring at the yellow circle her flashlight created on the page. What did this mean? Why had the sheriff or his deputies even thought to check with the school? At sixteen, she could be considered a suspect. Everyone close to the missing person had to be ruled out. But *Leanne?* She hadn't yet had the sledding accident that broke her back, but she'd only been thirteen. What could she have done to Alana?

The discomfort of the hard floor and the scrabbling of some rodent in the corner began to bother Claire. It was too difficult to read for an extended period sitting in such an unfriendly spot, holding a heavy flashlight and trying to ignore the pack rats.

It was time to take the files home, where she could scour every interview, every note, at her leisure. No doubt David had been trying to find her mother for her. He was that kind of man. He probably hadn't told her in case he didn't come any closer than anyone else. He wouldn't want to raise her hopes, only to see them dashed. Probably a smart move. He certainly seemed to have run into more questions than answers. But she loved him for making the attempt.

Relieved to be going, she closed the files. But just as she slid them into the accordion folder, a noise from below brought her head up.

What was that?

Movement? If so, whoever or whatever made that noise was definitely bigger than a rat.

She'd thought she heard footsteps when she first arrived — and there'd been no one here.

Irritated that she kept spooking herself, she climbed down the ladder. She'd just set foot on the stairs heading to the ground floor when a draft of cool air, smelling distinctly of smoke from the fireworks, swept up to meet her.

Fresh air. From outside . . .

"Hello?" she called.

No answer. No corresponding rustle, either.

She angled her flashlight in every direction to illuminate the dark recesses below, but the beam would only reach so far. "Anybody there?"

Silence.

Her mind conjured up the gruesome images that sometimes came to her in nightmares, images of her mother being tortured and strangled by some crazed psychopath. Most people were killed by someone in their circle of family and friends. But not all. Murders committed by strangers were among the most difficult to solve.

Was that why no one could figure out what had happened? Was her mother's killer lurking in the shadows, waiting for her to move closer?

Half expecting the truth she'd been chasing for so long to become apparent in the most frightening way, she stood as if her feet were encased in concrete. The possibility of a violent ending didn't escape her.

But there were no footsteps, no madman rushing toward her, no more movement.

Had she imagined the change in temperature? The noise? In such an old structure, even a slight wind caused creaks and groans.

She wasn't convinced it was the wind, but she didn't see how staying on the landing, holding her breath, was going to help. She needed to get out.

Tightening her grip on the files, she crept

down the stairs, using her flashlight to scout for trouble — until she reached the living room. Then she aimed the beam straight ahead and ran for the door. But just as she reached it, she twisted around to look behind her.

And that was when she saw it.

A man's booted foot.

Someone was crouching behind her mother's old piano.

The scream curdled Isaac Morgan's blood. He'd seen headlights pass by his place, knew it was probably Claire. It'd been a while since she'd come to her mother's studio. He had a feeling his proximity served as a deterrent, especially since David's death. But even the chance of coming face-to-face with him in such a private setting didn't scare her away entirely.

He usually turned a blind eye to her visits and pretended not to notice. He understood what she'd been through, why she couldn't let go, and felt she deserved privacy to deal with her demons.

Lord knew he preferred privacy to deal with his.

It was the second set of headlights, appearing only a few minutes later, that had drawn him out of the house. He doubted she'd bring anyone up here; she tried too hard to act as if she was fine, as if the past didn't bother her, but it did. The amount of weight she'd lost was alarming.

Determined to investigate, he'd walked over. It was the Fourth of July, after all. The last thing he needed was a group of teenagers — teenagers who were even half as reckless as he'd been — coming up here and setting off fireworks. As dry as it'd been this summer, they could start a forest fire that would take every single cabin. But all he'd found was Claire's Camaro. He'd been skirting the property and using his flashlight to comb through the trees in search of the second car when that scream sliced through him.

Claire!

Forgetting everything except getting to the cabin, he took off at a full run, moving much faster than he should have amid so many rocks, logs, gopher holes, pinecones and trees. With his flashlight bouncing every time his foot landed on the forest floor, the ground blurred beneath him. But he didn't dare slow down — and that was why he never saw the tree branch that knocked him on his back.

The sudden impact left him breathless. Blinking up at the sky, he struggled to fill his lungs.

By the time he recovered and picked up his flashlight, which had gone flying, an engine roared to life on the far side of the property.

The other car. It'd gone beyond the cabin and circled behind, to an area he hadn't yet reached.

Isaac almost changed direction. He hated that someone might've hurt Claire and would get away with it if he didn't at least see the car. But if Claire was still alive and needed help, every second could matter.

The driver was tearing out of the forest as fast as possible, regardless of the damage such rough terrain might cause his vehicle. Isaac spotted a flash of taillights through the trees and wished he could see more, but he wasn't in the best condition to follow, even if whoever was behind the wheel had been moving more slowly. Blood soaked his shirt, causing the fabric to stick to him. That branch hadn't only knocked him down, it'd punched a hole in his chest.

But he might be in good shape compared to Claire. Afraid he was already too late, that she'd been killed as her mother had most likely been killed when they were in high school, he ignored the pain and hurried to the stoop, where he slowly pushed in the door. He wouldn't have been able to hear her scream so clearly if she hadn't been close. . . .

Sure enough, there was blood at the entrance. And the door would open only partway. . . .

Something, or someone, lay behind it.

When Claire came to, it was pitch-black and she was being carried. Where, she couldn't tell. A man's muscular chest provided a resting place for her head; one arm supported her back, the other her knees. She had no idea who she was with or where she was at, but she wasn't frightened because both her surroundings and this person smelled so familiar.

David's was the first name she thought of, but she disregarded that guess instantly. Her husband was dead. She'd had to remind herself of that every morning for the past thirteen months and had finally started to believe it, mostly because she felt so empty inside and she'd never felt empty when David was alive. Besides, David had sold insurance; he'd smelled like cologne, the occasional cigar and his briefcase. This man smelled like . . . soap and fir trees and wood smoke.

Where had she noticed that scent before?

With a groan, she lifted her head in an effort to see his face, but it was too dark. They were in the forest. The thick branches overhead blocked even the moon's glow, but the beam of the flashlight he held in one hand — the hand cradling her legs — showed the ground and confirmed her location. So did the pine needles that threatened to catch in her long, curly hair as they hurried through the trees.

Why was she in the forest? Who was she with? What had happened?

Then it came to her. She'd been attacked. At her mother's studio.

The man carrying her hadn't reacted when she first stirred. He was too focused on getting them wherever they were going. But when she screamed and tried to get down, he dropped the flashlight.

"Shh," he murmured. "I've got you."

That was the problem, wasn't it? "Who are you?"

"How quickly they forget."

The wry humor in his voice gave away his identity. This was Isaac Morgan. Of course. He lived closest. And it was no wonder she'd recognized his scent. During the two-year period when she and David had split up, when he'd attended Boise State and they'd both dated other people and been undecided about their future, she'd had sex with Isaac at least a hundred times. Maybe more. Often enough for her to have formed an addiction to his touch that hadn't been easy to break. Even after so long, she avoided him if possible; just the sight of him could send a powerful charge through her. The memories were *that* good.

She raised a hand to her aching head. "Why — why'd you hit me?"

With a groan, he squatted and managed to recover the flashlight. "I didn't hit you."

"Who did?"

The way he sucked air through his teeth as he lifted her again suggested he was struggling to bear her weight, but she couldn't figure out why. She weighed less now than ever, and he used to lift her up, hold her against the wall as long as he wanted while he —

Stop! She didn't want to remember, had trained herself *not* to remember.

"That's what I'd like to know," he said when they were moving again.

The image of a man's booted foot appeared in her mind. She'd seen that foot just before someone sprang at her and knocked the flashlight out of her hands.

Isaac probably had a similar pair of boots. Most men around here did. But she knew the person who'd shoved her after knocking her flashlight away hadn't been Isaac. Any confrontation with Isaac happened head-on. The few people in Pineview who'd experienced the brunt of his temper made sure they never tangled with him again. Cynical and remote, he was indifferent to her and, as much as she'd once wanted to believe otherwise, always had been. If she needed proof she only had to remember their last encounter. When she knew David was returning from school, she'd tried to talk with Isaac, to tell him she'd developed feelings for him. She and David hadn't promised each other anything, but they had a long history and he wasn't seeing anyone. She'd wanted to determine how she should respond if he called her, whether or not she and Isaac had a commitment — and Isaac had let her know she'd been mistaken in thinking sex equaled love.

That night when she left his house hurt and humiliated, she swore she'd never go back. And despite the terrible cravings he'd evoked over the years — dreams that were sometimes so vivid she woke gasping with the kind of pleasure he'd given her — she'd kept that promise so she could have a more meaningful relationship with David.

And it'd been worth it. Maybe sex with

David hadn't been as all-consuming, as *raw,* as it was with Isaac. Maybe she missed that bone-melting intensity. But David had made up for it by giving her so much more. Moody, unpredictable men were excellent bait, but the women who bit down on that hook were fools.

She couldn't believe she'd ever hoped for a commitment from Isaac. He wasn't the type to settle down. She'd known that from the beginning. Although they'd never been close friends, she and David had gone to school with him — they'd been in the same grade — so she'd seen firsthand how standoffish he could be. Ever since she could remember, he'd walked around with a camera, always on the other side of the lens, filming life but removed from it. And, if she'd forgotten how hard it was to connect with him, practically anyone in Pineview could remind her, including the women who'd tried to capture his heart and failed just as miserably.

"Where are . . . where are you taking me?" She had to make an effort to form coherent sentences. But if she was in Isaac's arms again, it was definitely time to speak up, to get away if she could.

"Hold still."

Great. He was being his typical accommodating self. But when he stopped to adjust his grip on her, she knew he'd spoken curtly from necessity. What was wrong with him? He'd never had any trouble carrying her before. Since their sexual heyday he'd become even more muscular, which should be making this easier. . . .

"Are you trying to . . . tell me you think I've gotten fat?"

"I'm trying to tell you that it hurts like hell every time you move."

Suddenly she realized she might not have been the only one who'd had a run-in with her attacker. "The man who hit me . . . he didn't . . . shoot you or . . . or anything, did he?"

Obviously intent on making progress, he didn't respond.

"Hello?" she said.

"Just take it easy." It came out as a command, which didn't surprise her. He was always in charge.

On second thought, she had to admit there'd been plenty of give-and-take in the bedroom. But she couldn't admire that without undermining her efforts to maintain some self-respect.

Fortunately — or unfortunately — there were plenty of other things to think about. Maybe he was struggling because the ground was so uneven. Or he'd been carrying her for too long.

Regardless, Claire knew she shouldn't let herself rely on him. He was dangerous for her, probably even more dangerous now that she had such a vacuum in her life. She missed David, but David was gone and Isaac was very much alive — as alive and capable as he'd ever been. Far too many times in the past six months her thoughts had gravitated to him and how quickly he could put an end to her lonely nights. Maybe he was a cheap substitute for David, but there were times when that seemed better than nothing.

"Put me down," she said.

He switched the flashlight to his other hand. "We're almost . . . there."

"I can walk." She wasn't really sure of that, but she pushed on his chest to convince him to let her go — and immediately regretted it. They both gasped as her hand touched a wet, sticky substance.

He was bleeding. She'd been right; he was hurt.

With a curse, he tightened his hold but didn't seem to be getting over what she'd done as quickly as she would've liked. "Shit, Claire, *will you hold still?*"

"Claire?" she echoed.

"Isn't that your name?"

It just sounded funny, coming from his lips after so long. Except for a few incidents when she'd found him staring at her at the tavern, or she'd glanced up while she was getting gas at the Fill 'n' Go to realize he was there, too, he'd made it look darn easy to forget her.

"Considering all the women you've been with, I figured you'd have a harder time keeping us straight, that's all." She was trying to hide how shaken she was to have his blood on her hand, not knowing how serious his wound was. He was always getting hurt; he'd often said he had nine lives. But she suspected he'd already used up that many.

Because of the pain in her head and her distress, she had to relax against his shoulder or risk throwing up. Closing her eyes, she shut out the shifting light, which only made her dizzier.

"How bad is it?" she mumbled when her concern for his well-being overcame her resistance to letting him know she cared.

"You're going to be fine."

"I was talking about *you*."

"We'll see."

Then the most terrible thing in the world happened — tears filled her eyes. She wasn't even sure why, except that she felt so helpless in the face of everything that had gone wrong. When would it end? First her mother's disappearance, then her sister's accident, then David's death, and now she'd been attacked. To top it all, she was being carried through the woods by the one person she'd do anything to hide her pain from — and couldn't because he was right there to witness it.

Damn it, she didn't want to be this transparent, didn't want Isaac to see her so near the breaking point.

Clenching her jaw, she blinked fast, but the tears came, anyway. So she began to pray he wouldn't notice — and knew that prayer hadn't been answered when he spoke to her in the same gentle tone she'd once heard him use with a lame horse.

"Shh, it's okay. Don't cry."

3

Although Isaac had called John Hunt, the only doctor in the area, and Sheriff King at the same time, Hunt arrived first. John, who lived nearby, worked in the emergency room in Libby, but kept his medical bag handy and helped out where he could. Emergencies were taken to the hospital by Life Flight, but once Isaac had had a chance to look at Claire and realized she had only one injury that didn't seem too bad, he'd been hesitant to call for the helicopter.

"How's she doing?" Hunt asked.

Isaac angled his head toward his bedroom, where he'd deposited Claire when he reached the cabin. "I'm pretty sure she's okay, that it's just your run-of-the-mill knock on the head, but . . ." He wanted to be positive. Head injuries could be tricky. "You can see for yourself."

Expecting him to walk past, Isaac waited so he could close the door, but the doctor didn't budge. Instead, he fixed his gaze on the bloody rag Isaac held to his bare chest, and his eyebrows rose. "You didn't mention you were hurt, too. But I guess you're due. You're my best customer. What happened this time?"

Once he'd cleaned the blood from Claire's head and made her as comfortable as he could, Isaac had removed his torn and bloodied shirt and attempted to clean his own injury, but it was too deep. He couldn't get the bleeding to stop. "Branch caught me as I was running through the woods. It's nothing serious."

But it *was* embarrassing. All the other injuries he'd sustained had been connected to his work and had an interesting story to go with them. The time he'd accidentally interrupted several wolves feeding on an elk, for instance. Or the confrontation he'd had with a mother bear. Folks around town asked him to tell and retell those stories, never seemed to grow tired of them. So he wasn't thrilled to admit he'd been injured by something that shouldn't have been a threat.

Hunt pulled the rag away so he could have a look. "Not serious, huh? It's serious enough to need quite a few stitches. Lie down on that couch. I'll get to you in a minute."

"I'm fine," Isaac insisted, and followed him into the bedroom.

Claire had fallen asleep. She lay in his bed — not unusual, at least in the past. That she was still wearing her clothes was a first, however. With her hair mussed and her mascara smeared, she wasn't at her best. But that made no difference. She was damned pretty. Isaac wished he didn't think so, but he did.

"Hey . . ." Hunt shook her arm. "Claire, can I have a minute?"

Her hand went to her head as if it hurt — and it probably did. Isaac hadn't offered her any painkillers. He'd wanted to wait until Hunt gave the all-clear.

When her fingers encountered the gauze he'd used to cover the wound, she frowned in confusion. "I'm wearing a headband?"

She didn't remember him putting that on? She'd seemed lucid at the time. . . .

"That's a bandage," Hunt explained. "Let's leave it alone for a few seconds, okay?" He guided her hand away. "Do you know who I am?"

"Of course. You're . . ." She struggled with the name and settled for "Lila's husband."

"That's right. Lila goes to your book group, doesn't she?"

This drew a faint smile. "Every Thursday night."

Isaac wondered what that smile meant. He got the impression she was making fun of herself and Lila, as if book group was the most exciting thing they ever did.

"Isaac says you have a bump above your ear. Would you mind letting me take a look?"

When she hesitated, he added, "Your other option would be to have us call the helicopter so you can be transported to the hospital."

"No, there's no need for that." She winced as she attempted to sit up, but he pressed her back.

"All you have to do is relax." Hunt unwound the gauze and gently prodded the area behind her left temple. Fresh blood gushed out of a small cut. "Scalps are notorious bleeders," he murmured. "This could use a couple stitches, but it isn't a concern. I'm more worried about the possibility of a concussion." He rested a hand on her arm to get her to focus on him, probably because her gaze kept straying to Isaac as if she thought he'd done this to her. "Can you tell me what happened?"

She seemed distracted by his presence so Isaac retreated a few steps and leaned against the wall, where he could observe from a distance.

"I was trying to get some . . . some paintings of my mother's."

Paintings? Unless whoever pushed her down had stolen them, she hadn't been carrying any paintings. Some file folders had spilled on the floor. That was what she'd had with her, but when Isaac opened his mouth to correct her, she shot him a look that shut him up.

"I didn't know I wasn't alone until I was leaving," she said.

"You went to get these paintings at night?" Dr. Hunt wasn't questioning her veracity, but he obviously thought there were better times for such an errand.

"I didn't care that it was dark. I had a flashlight." She sent another warning glance at Isaac, but he'd gotten the point. She didn't want the doctor to know what she'd been doing at the cabin. Why, Isaac couldn't even guess. But as far as he was concerned, it was no one's business but her own. He let it go.

Hunt passed her a clean bandage, which she held to her head. "And someone was waiting for you or . . . what?"

Seemingly relieved that Isaac was staying out of it, she finished in a rush. "I can't say for sure. All I know is that a man came at me, knocked my flashlight to the ground and shoved me so hard I fell."

"Any idea what you might've hit on the way down?"

"The corner of the table in the entryway, I guess. The entire bottom floor is filled with furniture." She cleared her throat. "Everyone feels it's the perfect place to store whatever they don't want anymore."

It wasn't the storage that bothered her; it was how easily others could deposit their cast-offs, forget the past and move on, because she couldn't do the same. Isaac understood. He'd known Claire since they were children and empathized with what she'd been through. He'd lost his mother, too. She might have driven off on purpose, but he'd had to face life without her. He'd been searching just like Claire — the biggest difference being that he hadn't had a stepfather to rely on. Fortunately in recent years he'd had the money to hire private investigators. Without so much as a birth certificate, it hadn't been easy to figure out where he came from.

Hunt checked for other injuries. "You know where you are now, don't you?"

A nostalgic expression appeared on her face. "This used to be my parents' bedroom," she said as if she was seeing it through much younger eyes. "My bedroom was across the hall. So was Leanne's. When we moved to town, we sold it to a family who later went to Spokane. You remember Rod Reynolds?"

"I do." Almost twenty years older than they were, Dr. Hunt had left for college about the time Isaac had been abandoned at Happy's Inn, just before first grade. But Hunt hadn't stayed away for much longer than it took to get his medical degree. He was familiar with most of the people in Pineview and their backgrounds.

Especially Isaac's. But then . . . everyone was familiar with the story of the little boy who'd been left, with nothing but the dollar he'd been given to buy candy, at a roadside café.

Distracted by a bowl of water on the nightstand, Hunt pointed to it. "This from you?" he asked Isaac.

The pink tinge to the water had no doubt prompted the question. " 'Fraid not. You're the one who said head wounds bleed a lot. Apparently, that's true." Isaac could've done a better job cleaning Claire up if he'd shaved her hair at the site of her wound, but he was pretty sure that would only make her hate him more.

Hunt frowned at the bloody rag Isaac held

to his injury. “Chest wounds can bleed a lot, too.”

Now that the doctor wasn’t so worried about Claire, he wanted to get started on Isaac. Isaac could tell.

Claire could tell, too. She began to insist he look after Isaac, but Isaac waved away her concern. “Finish here first.”

With a muttered curse at Isaac’s stubbornness, Hunt used a penlight to check Claire’s pupils. “What did you do earlier today, Claire?”

“What do you mean?” Like the doctor, she’d grown preoccupied with Isaac’s wound.

“I’m just asking about your day in general.”

“Oh.” Her forehead creased as if she didn’t see the point of further questioning, especially when someone else was bleeding, but Hunt was only being thorough. “I worked.”

Isaac wondered if she still regretted being unable to attend university. She’d talked about college just after high school, back when David was gone and they were seeing each other. During that time, she’d been treading water with a dead-end job managing Stuart’s Stop ’n’ Shop. But Leanne had been going through a series of operations, which her doctors hoped would restore some mobility, and Claire wouldn't leave her. "Can you remember who you saw?"

"Let's see . . . I did a cut and color for Joyce Sallow, a trim for Larry Morrill and a highlight for Alexis Rodgers."

"You were busy. Where's your sister tonight?"

"At the fireworks show. See? I'm fine. Just . . . shaken up. And my head's killing me but that's to be expected," she added. "Take care of Isaac."

"I will in a minute. And I'll give you something for the pain, too." Hunt recorded her blood pressure and heart rate. Then the doorbell rang and Isaac stepped out to answer. Sheriff King had arrived.

Not surprisingly, Myles's first thought was for Claire. But Isaac's injury didn't go unnoticed. "What happened to *you?*"

"Collateral damage," he replied. "She's in here."

Going along with the diversion, Myles followed Isaac into the bedroom. Claire was his wife's best friend; he was obviously more concerned about her. But Isaac had a feeling they'd return to the subject of his injury at some point, if only to see how it related to the attack at the cabin. King was nothing if not thorough. And Isaac wasn't the most trusted man in town.

"She'll be fine," Hunt said as they entered. "I'm going to sew up this cut. That'll take care of the bleeding. She should be watched, just in case she has a slight concussion. But this isn't serious."

"Good. Can the stitches wait until I have a word with her?" the sheriff wanted to know.

"Are you up to talking with Sheriff King for a few minutes?" Hunt asked Claire.

Claire continued to hold the bandage to her head. "Of course. Whatever will help. I want the person who did this caught."

When King asked for a few minutes alone with her, the doctor and Isaac left the room. Then Hunt insisted Isaac lie down so he could inspect the gash on his chest.

"Damn. This one's jagged and nasty," he said with a frown.

Isaac cocked an eyebrow at him. "Nice bedside manner. Aren't you supposed to tell me to relax, everything will be okay?"

Hunt grinned. "You can take it. You're the closest I've come to creating my own rag doll. You know the routine by now."

Thanks to several encounters with various wild animals, he did. Although he'd been out alone, filming wildlife since he was in junior high — camera equipment was all he'd ever asked for, and what Tippy, the man who'd raised him, had generously provided — it wasn't until he'd gotten older that he'd been harmed. He blamed himself for being careless or becoming too cavalier. But, his fault or not, that bear he'd tangled with four years ago had nearly cost him his left arm. And there might be more incidents in the future. That kind of danger went with his job. He had to get close enough to his subjects to capture good footage. That was what made his work better than most. Not only had he come within arm's distance of bears and wolves, he'd filmed cougars, moose, bison and elk. He'd flown to Florida to do a documentary on alligators, and the Amazon to do a show on spiders, and another on snakes for the Disney channel. In the past decade, he'd been all over the world — not bad for an abandoned kid who was almost entirely self-taught.

"How long's it been since you've had a tetanus shot?" The doctor spoke as he numbed the area.

"When I was attacked by that bear."

"Are you sure it wasn't the time before that — with the wolves?"

"No, it was the bear." It'd been almost seven years since the incident with the wolves. He'd had a gun with him on that occasion. Firing a shot into the sky had mitigated the damage. He wasn't sure how he'd survived mama bear. From what he remembered, she simply got distracted and galloped off.

"I'm glad one of us can keep it straight," Hunt grumbled.

He was in the middle of stitching Isaac up when the sheriff came out of the bedroom.

"Any idea who attacked Claire?" he asked Isaac.

A local anesthetic had put Isaac out of pain. "No."

"You didn't see *anything?*"

"Headlights."

"How'd you know she was hurt?"

"I heard her scream." The memory of it still raised the hair on his arms.

"From way over here?"

"From the edge of the clearing." Isaac explained everything that had happened in as much detail as he could, including his run-in with the unyielding tree.

When he'd finished, the sheriff put his notepad in his pocket, checked Isaac's wound to make sure it was consistent with his story, then scratched his neck. "So . . . it could be anyone with a car that has headlights and taillights. That narrows it down."

Isaac wished the doctor would hurry up

and finish. Pain or no pain, he didn't like needles. "It's someone who knows the area."

"Why do you say that?"

"He was familiar with the back way. He followed her in, so I expected to find his vehicle close to hers. But he took the alternate route just after my place, the long way, and went up and around. That's why I didn't spot his car until he was driving off."

Myles rested his hands on his utility belt. "That doesn't narrow it down too much, either. What do you think he wanted?"

Isaac shook his head. The culprit hadn't attempted to rape her. He hadn't really tried to hurt her, either. She might've ended up unharmed had she not fallen.

Still, it was chilling to think that someone had followed her and crept into the house while she was there alone at night. "No clue."

"Thanks for helping her out." King shifted his attention to John Hunt. "Is it okay to move her? Can I take her home?"

When Hunt hesitated midstitch, Isaac tried to ignore the doctor's gloved hand, covered with blood, holding that needle.

"Not if she's going to be there alone."

"Her sister lives next door," Myles said. "Leanne will look after her."

"Fine with me. As long as Leanne's willing and up to it."

Isaac would've offered to let her stay, to watch over her through the night and give her a ride in the morning, but he knew she wouldn't want that.

As the sheriff went to get her, Isaac closed his eyes. Although he experienced no pain, he felt a tugging sensation with each stitch.

The sound of movement made him glance up. Claire was walking under her own power but King had a tight grip on her upper arm, as if he didn't quite trust that she wouldn't fall.

Isaac thought she'd leave with just a perfunctory thank-you. He knew she probably wasn't pleased they'd met up again after so long. But she turned back at the last moment, eyebrows gathered as she studied his wound.

"I'm really sorry you got dragged into this," she said.

Dragged . . . He managed a bitter smile as the door closed behind them and wondered what she'd think if she knew how panicked he'd been, how hard he'd pushed himself to reach her.

He had a hole in his chest to prove it. But she'd be surprised to learn there'd been any kind of personal involvement in what he'd done — so surprised she'd never believe it.

Neither would she believe how completely she held his attention whenever she was in the same vicinity.

Or how many times he thought of her even when she wasn't.

Jeremy was shaking when he got home. After parking in the garage next to his father's old Jeep, he hurried into the house and charged down the stairs to his room, where he closed and locked the door.

"Hey, the village idiot's back! Where've you been?" His father had heard him come in; the noise had brought him to the top of the stairs. Rarely did he venture any closer these days. Jeremy had gotten too big. But that hadn't always been true. He used to show up all the time, usually with his belt off and at the ready.

"Watching the fireworks."

"I didn't see you at the show."

Trying to shut out the memory of how easily Claire had fallen when he pushed her, he sat on his unmade bed and dropped his head in his hands. "I was there," he said through his fingers. "Where else would I go?"

"That's what I'd like to know."

"I was there," he said again. Then he waited to see if his father would come down and bang on the door, because if that happened, he'd cry, and crying would only make his dad yell and say bad words. *You're a fucking giant! Quit acting like a little girl!*

Maybe he did act like a girl sometimes, but he couldn't help it. Had he hurt Claire? And who'd been holding the flashlight in the forest when he came running out of the studio? *Someone* had been there. Had he been seen?

He supposed he'd find out soon enough if someone from the sheriff's department showed up.

The creak of footsteps overhead told him his father had left the opening to the basement and was going about his business. Hopefully, he'd get into bed soon. Don liked to ramble around and watch TV for most of the night. Since he'd gone on disability, it wasn't as if he had to get up for work. But Jeremy liked it better when the house was quiet. . . .

The clock ticked loudly on his desk. Jeremy counted those ticks until he thought he'd go mad. He kept wondering if he'd hear a knock at the door. But no one came.

Slowly his heart rate returned to normal. Everything would be okay. He hadn't meant to do any harm. It wasn't his fault that she was so small and he was so strong.

When he was fairly confident his father wouldn't bother him again, he lay back and started rattling off all the numbers in his head. He was good with numbers. They calmed him. He could remember any number anyone ever told him. It made his father proud, and made him feel smart.

But that was the only time he ever felt smart.

382-24-6832 . . . 406-385-9472 . . . 406-269-2698 . . . 12/24/89 . . .

Why had Claire lied when she'd been asked why she'd gone to the cabin?

Now that Isaac was all stitched up and everyone was gone, he couldn't help being curious. Those files had to be important or she wouldn't have been so evasive. Neither would she have driven out to the cabin at night, in the middle of the Fourth of July celebration, knowing she'd have only the benefit of a flashlight to retrieve them.

Whatever the reason, it wouldn't remain a secret for long. Surely she had to realize that. As soon as the sheriff left her in her sister's care, he'd head over to the studio to see what he could find. What did she think — that he'd wait until morning? That she'd have an opportunity to recover those documents herself?

Knowing Myles King, Isaac doubted he'd hold off. Given what'd happened to Claire's mother, the sheriff would dust for prints, check for tire tracks, do all he could to figure out who'd followed her to the studio, and why. And he'd do it as soon as possible, hoping that his efforts might also shed light on Alana's disappearance — or at least convince everyone there was no connection between the two incidents.

Gingerly pulling on a clean T-shirt, Isaac decided to go back and get the files Claire had dropped. If he hurried, he should be able to get in and out without anyone being the wiser. What with the twenty-minute drive each way, helping Claire into the house and explaining to Leanne, it would take Myles at least an hour to get back. Isaac just had to dodge the deputies Myles had promised to send for her car.

Maybe she wouldn't thank him for helping her, but he felt he owed her for letting her down all those years ago. He'd been an ass. Even he had to admit it. But there was something about her that brought out the worst in him.

Of course, she'd had her revenge. He'd had a long time to regret what he'd done, a long time to miss her. Although he'd made love with plenty of other women since, including several from around here, it had never been the same. And then there was the torture of one particular memory that didn't go quite that far back. . . .

He'd been tracking a moose in the Cabinet Mountains southwest of Libby, hoping to get a few good shots for a magazine called *Montana Wilds,* when he came across Claire and David camping out in the woods. They were newlyweds at the time and probably too poor to do any more than borrow Claire's stepfather's Winnebago to get away, so he wasn't surprised that they hadn't gone farther from home.

He was surprised, however, that of all the campers in the Chain of Lakes area he had to stumble on *them.* What seeing them together had done to him came as an even greater shock. They hadn't heard him — they were far too engrossed in each other. He'd stood right where he'd emerged from the woods, only partially concealed by the trees, and watched David kiss and fondle his new bride as they made breakfast.

The sight had made him sick. And when he'd finally managed to clear his throat so they'd know they weren't alone — he refused to slink off as if he'd been spying on them — Claire had angled her head to see around her husband's shoulder. Embarrassment had registered on her face, but something else, as well. The look in her eyes told him she recognized the envy he was feeling.

Even worse, she'd derived a certain amount of satisfaction from it.

He hated that memory. Sometimes he hated Claire, too, for having such a strong hold on him despite his efforts to escape it. He was pretty sure she returned the sentiment. She wouldn't even speak to him. If she saw him coming, she'd whip around and walk the other way. His career had taken off after a documentary he'd made on the impact of endangered status on the wolf population came to the attention of the editor at *National Geographic* a year or so after they'd quit seeing each other. That was when he'd started to travel. But Pineview was too small not to bump into her whenever he returned.

So, if he preferred to stay out of her life, why was he heading back to Alana's studio to rescue whatever Claire didn't want the sheriff to see?

He had no explanation for that. There was just something about her that made him do stupid things. Like sleeping with her for six months and not expecting to form an attachment. Like not turning away when she was being lovey-dovey with her husband so he wouldn't have to carry that lasting and painful memory around with him. Like running hell-bent through the forest in an effort to reach her when she screamed — and just about puncturing his lung on a tree.

When he entered the studio's clearing for the second time that evening, he found the place quiet and dark. The door stood open, exactly as he'd left it — a sign that no one had been there since.

He'd arrived in time. The files lay scattered on the floor.

Aiming his flashlight at the documents that had spilled out, he glanced over them and soon determined that they were case files — part of the investigation into Claire's mother's disappearance. He wasn't sure why this was a secret. The sheriff must have a copy. That had to be where Claire had gotten this stuff in the first place.

He was sure of it until he read a report that talked about "inconsistencies" and realized that certain aspects of the case hadn't been reported to the public. That meant Claire probably wasn't supposed to know about them, suggesting she'd come by these through unofficial means.

Isaac raked a hand through his hair. "So that's it."

Careful not to pull on his stitches — Lord

knew he'd bled enough for one night — he took all the papers and left the door halfway open, just as it had been before.

A car approached as he neared his own place. Using the darkness and the trees for cover, he crept close enough to the pitted dirt road to see who it was, and easily recognized the squad car. The deputies had arrived. Would they look around while they had the chance? Maybe . . .

Briefly, Isaac considered stopping whoever it was so he could hand over what he'd taken. Maybe there was something in these documents that would tell the sheriff why Claire had been attacked.

But he knew she didn't want to give them up or she wouldn't have lied, so Isaac figured he'd return them to her when he had the chance to do it discreetly.

He felt good about that decision — until he got home. After two hours spent reading through the various reports and interviews, he began to get a terrible feeling.

Something peculiar stood out. . . .

He had to be wrong. Surely someone else would've noticed what he was seeing and brought it up if it was even a possibility.

Rubbing his eyes, which were bleary with fatigue, he wanted to let it go at that. He could be wrong. What was going through his mind wasn't directly related to individual facts. It was more of a gut feeling about what all this information meant.

But it wouldn't leave him alone. . . .

"Shit," he said when he set the files aside. If what he suspected was true, Claire was about to face another nasty shock.

And the sheriff was going to face his next big case.

4

Leanne wasn't happy but that didn't come as a surprise. To Claire's dismay, her sister *never* seemed happy.

She watched Leanne maneuver her wheelchair to reach the nightstand, where she set the glass of water and the pain pills she'd brought in case Claire needed them later. The disgruntled frown that tugged at her lips bothered Claire, but not as much as the low-cut pink nightgown her sister was wearing. Held up by two black ribbons tied in bows, one over each shoulder, it went to her ankles — but it was too low-cut to be worn in front of a man other than an intimate boyfriend or husband.

And this was how she'd answered the door when Myles brought Claire home.

Unable to bite her tongue any longer, Claire broke the tense silence that'd fallen between them as soon as the sheriff left. She knew Leanne had plenty to say about what'd happened at the studio tonight — plenty about how she shouldn't have been there in the first place — and thought she might as well air her own grievances before Leanne could get started. "You didn't mind letting Myles see you like that?"

Her sister's chin jutted out. "Like what?"

"Wearing sexy lingerie?" With no effort at all, Claire could make out the tattoo of a mermaid on her sister's right breast. When Leanne bent forward, she could see clear to her navel — but glanced away. Leanne's lack of modesty embarrassed her now as much as it had a few minutes earlier. What had gotten into her lately? Why was she acting like this?

Claire knew she struggled to feel attractive despite her handicap. It was heartbreaking to watch and the primary reason Claire had agreed with Leanne's decision to get breast implants. She'd even helped pay for the operation. But Leanne had changed so drastically since the surgery, had become so blatantly sexual. Was she trying to prove that she was just as attractive and capable of pleasing a man as anyone who could walk?

It felt that way. But passing herself around to every guy who showed interest wouldn't solve her self-esteem problem. And it wouldn't do her reputation any favors, either, especially in such a small community.

"What are you talking about?" Leanne asked. "It's not like this is transparent or anything."

It didn't need to be transparent to be inappropriate. Claire made an effort to hold on to her temper. She knew how easily this could blow up into a major argument and didn't relish the idea of any more trouble with her sister. They always seemed to be at each other's throats these days. "But you hate gossip. Why make yourself the focus of it?"

Leanne shrugged. "Folks around here are going to stare and talk no matter what. I have this wheelchair to thank for that. And Mom didn't do us any favors when she ran off."

Claire couldn't stop herself from bristling. Leanne had just thrown her first jab, no doubt one of many. "You don't know she ran off, Lee."

"I know that's the most likely answer — and I'm tough enough to accept it."

Unlike her. The implication was too obvious to ignore. "Don't start."

Her sister's blue eyes, a shade lighter than her own, flashed with the anger she'd kept concealed while Myles was in the house. "You need to hear it. You think finding out the truth will somehow make things better? That you'll be able to prove she loved you? That's pathetic. Dad and I have asked you and asked you to leave the past alone, but you won't. You just have to convince yourself that no one would ever willingly abandon *you.*"

She meant Tug when she said Dad. They called Tug and Roni Dad and Mom, even though their real dad was alive and in Wyoming with his other family. He was such an angry individual, so difficult to deal with, that Alana had preferred to let him go on his way unfettered — and he'd had no argument with that plan because he'd signed the adoption papers the moment she sent them. He was probably glad to escape legal responsibility for the children he'd left behind so he could pretend he'd never been married the first time. "I've accepted that our real dad didn't love us enough to hang on, haven't I?"

"That was easier. He took off when you were three and I was a baby. Tug's the one who's loved us and looked after us but you don't care about what's best for him." She motioned to the bump on Claire's head. "And this is what you get."

Claire shoved herself into a sitting position. "Are you saying I *deserved* this?"

"I'm saying it could've been avoided if you weren't so damn selfish."

The barb stung, especially because Claire couldn't be sure it wasn't true. "Selfish, Lee? Really? This isn't about me. There's more to what happened when Mom disappeared than you think. And I feel a certain . . . obligation to get to the bottom of it. What I can't understand is why you don't feel the same. She was your mother, too!"

"*I* have some loyalty to the parent who *did* stick around. Why aren't you more grateful to Dad?"

Claire remembered what she'd read in the files at the cabin. She almost asked Leanne why she'd never told anyone she'd been out of school for three hours on the day their mother went missing. Where had she gone? And why? Was she being loyal to their father when it came to *that* information, too?

Claire was dying to know — but she wasn't willing to reveal what she'd learned. Not yet. She hadn't even read everything in those files. But she hoped to. As soon as Leanne went to bed, Claire planned to return to the cabin and collect what she'd dropped — if it was still there. Chances were good that Myles would beat her to it. As they were pulling away from Isaac's place, he'd radioed for a couple of deputies to get her car, told them to leave her keys under the mat by Leanne's front door. They might pick up those files, too. Or the sheriff himself could return to the cabin tonight instead of waiting until morning.

"I *am* grateful to Dad," she said. "I just don't see why I can't be loyal to both."

"Maybe Dad and I don't want to accept that she didn't love us enough to stay. Have you ever thought of that?"

"Of course, but . . . she did love you. She loved all of us. I prefer to have faith."

"Faith?" Leanne scoffed. "Maybe I'm crippled, but you're blind."

When would the meds the doctor gave her kick in? Claire's head felt as if it was about to explode. Forcing herself to lie down, she sighed in frustration. "I don't want to talk about it anymore. I had the sheriff call off the investigation for your sake and Dad's. That's something."

"It'd be something if *you* could finally let it go, too. Let us live in peace, instead of just . . . placating us."

"Fine, I'll let it go if you'll develop a little self-respect and restraint." The words rushed out before Claire could stop them.

Leanne had started to wheel herself to the door, but at this she paused. *"What?"*

Already regretting the statement — it was nothing if not an invitation to fight — Claire pulled the covers up to her neck. She wanted to crawl into a hole until she felt well enough to deal with her sister. "You're not even wearing a bra, Lee. When you bend over you can see everything."

"The sheriff wasn't here long enough for me to bend over," she said with a grimace. "Anyway, I have the right to wear pretty things. Why can't I enjoy sexy lingerie as much as the next woman?"

They were back to her handicap. It was the quickest way to disarm Claire, and Leanne didn't hesitate to wield the power it gave her.

Claire felt so bad about what her sister had suffered, and continued to suffer, that she was willing to put up with almost anything. But Leanne had gone too far with Sheriff King tonight. Claire would never forget the stunned look on his face. She *had* to make her point, before Leanne's behavior got any worse.

"I don't have a problem with you enjoying sexy lingerie," she said.

"You're the one who brought it up."

Claire lifted her head — and paid the price when it felt as if someone had just taken a swing at her with a baseball bat.

"Because —" she waited until the pounding began to diminish "— you came to the door in a nightgown that barely covers your nipples. Myles is a married man. Not only that, but he's with my best friend, and they have three children."

"His and hers," she said flippantly.

"So? What difference does that make?"

Leanne gestured in a dismissive fashion. "You're blowing this all out of proportion. He's married to a beautiful woman. Why would he want a cripple when he has Laurel?"

Claire massaged her temples. Thankfully, the painkiller was starting to take the edge off her pain. "Stop defining yourself exclusively by your condition! That's not the issue."

Leanne's voice climbed an octave. "Then what is? You've been telling me what to do since we were kids, but I'm an adult now, and I'll live my own life! You're freaking out over nothing. He didn't even notice me."

But she'd been *hoping* he'd notice, hoping he wouldn't be able to resist admiring her new double Ds *in spite* of his pretty wife.

"Of course he noticed," Claire said. "Anyone would. The whole encounter made him uncomfortable — and embarrassed me."

"Oh, and I would never want to embarrass *you!* God, all you care about is yourself!"

Sometimes Claire just wanted to put some space between her and Leanne. But she couldn't. She felt too much obligation to every member of her family, even her missing mother — *especially* her missing mother.

"All I'm saying is that you should've covered up when he came to the door. That's it. Quit trying to twist this into something it isn't."

"It was late and I was in bed. You know how much harder it is for me to change clothes than it would be for you or anyone else."

That was an excuse. The sheriff had called dispatch so Nadine Archer could tell Leanne what had happened. Leanne had had some warning, could've slipped on a robe. She'd *wanted* him to see her in that nightie, wanted to find out if she could turn his head.

"I'm trying to tell you that you're acting strange these days, and it's becoming apparent to others."

Her sister rolled her eyes. "Quit with the scare tactics."

"I can hear the cars that come over here late at night. I live next door, remember?"

"Oh, so now you want to know who I see? You think I should get your permission before I have sex? You may have decided never to make love again, but that doesn't mean I'm going to be celibate, too. Why shouldn't I take what pleasure I can while I'm young? It's not as if my life will ever get any better. What man's going to want to marry *me?*"

Claire's breath caught in her throat. It would be terrible to think she'd lost her chance at love just because of a sledding accident. "That's not true! You have so much to offer —"

"Oh, stop it." Leanne pressed the button that powered her wheelchair and headed for the hall. "Don't try to tell me what I should or shouldn't do. I'll make those decisions. How I entertain myself, day or night, is none of your business. It's nobody's business. I don't care what other people think."

"I'm telling you this for your own good," Claire called after her. "I only want you to be happy."

She swung around in the doorway. "You want me to be happy?"

Claire hadn't expected a response. Taken off guard, she blinked. "Of course."

"Then stop digging around in the past. Can you do that much?"

If only she could promise she would, but she couldn't. And it was time — past time

— to admit it. "I'm sorry. I can't," she said. "I *have* to know what happened, have to make sure Mom gets justice."

"Justice." Leanne laughed bitterly. "What if justice isn't what you think?"

"You've lost me."

"Maybe you can understand this — she's gone, Claire. That's all that matters."

Leanne's words seemed to echo off the walls long after she'd left. *All that matters . . . All that matters . . .*

Was it?

Not to Claire.

"Sometimes I hate you," she whispered. But she loved her sister, too, and she knew her mixed feelings weren't likely to change. Leanne had always been difficult to deal with, even before the accident. She'd never made life any easier on herself — or anyone else.

Unwilling to let the evening end so negatively, Claire got out of bed and went to find her. She wanted to put their argument behind them, wanted to give her sister whatever she'd like. But Leanne's demand that she forget the past warred with what Claire needed most and, selfish or not, she couldn't help it.

The painkiller was finally doing its job. For the first time since she'd hit her head,

Claire could walk without staggering or using the walls to prop herself up. But as she approached the kitchen, she heard Leanne getting a bottle from the liquor cabinet and stopped.

On top of everything else, Leanne was drinking too much. Claire had suspected it for a while. That was probably part of the reason Leanne had changed so much in the past year. But Claire couldn't do any more about her sister's drinking than her behavior with men. Claire definitely knew better than to call her on it tonight. They'd only get into a bigger fight if she did.

Quietly returning to her room, she waited until she heard a car outside. Then she got dressed, slipped out while Leanne was still in the kitchen and retrieved her car keys from under the mat.

The files were gone. There wasn't a single one left.

"Damn it." Claire slumped against the door frame, aiming the flashlight she'd brought from home at the bare floor.

A twig or tree branch snapped in the forest. Straightening, she jerked her flashlight in that direction. It could be a rodent, a bear or even the man who'd attacked her before, but she wasn't seriously concerned. The pain meds had hit her full force. She wasn't feeling any anxiety. Maybe she was even too high to drive. . . .

What now? she asked herself. There were more boxes in the attic she could tote home. She'd come all this way, felt she should make the trip as productive as possible. But she couldn't bring herself to visit the attic. Not with the memory of being attacked so fresh in her mind.

She stood on the front stoop, wondering about whether Sheriff King would call to ask where she'd gotten those files. Should she go on the offensive and demand to know everything they contained if he did? And . . . how was she going to get back home, since she probably shouldn't drive?

The memory of Isaac Morgan carrying her through the forest intruded. He lived within walking distance. Maybe it was self-destructive but there wasn't another living soul she'd rather see.

That was usually the case when it got this late, wasn't it?

She couldn't deny her desire for him. The temptation he posed tugged at her more powerfully the longer she lived without David. But she'd promised herself that she wouldn't go to his house, wouldn't get involved with him again. They'd only end up in bed.

But . . . why would that be so bad? If David wasn't around to care, to be with her, why hold back?

Suddenly she couldn't think of a single thing it would hurt. She'd slept with Isaac before. Lots of times. One last hurrah wouldn't make any difference.

A little voice in her head protested as she trudged off. But the fireworks were over. The whole town was asleep. Unlike her previous trip, she felt completely alone and capable of doing whatever she wanted without anyone's knowing, and that left her vulnerable to her weaker self, especially now, when she was depressed about the way things had gone with Leanne and the fact that the sheriff had taken the files.

Isaac's house was completely dark. Even the porch light had been turned off. He was obviously in bed. She felt guilty for disturbing him. Like her, he'd been injured tonight — probably more seriously than she had. But she was standing outside at nearly three in the morning with nothing except a flashlight and didn't know where else to go. Returning to her car and attempting to drive home didn't seem feasible when she was so light-headed. She couldn't even remember what she'd done with her car keys. . . .

Would he get angry if she woke him up?

Maybe he would if she expected him to drive her home. But she didn't. She only wanted more of what he used to give her — a night of the most exciting sex imaginable. The Isaac she knew wouldn't object to putting his talents to work, injured or no. After she'd stopped frequenting his place but before she married David, he'd called her many times, always in the middle of the night — just to get her attention, to remind her that he was waiting, willing and hoping she'd come back.

It'd taken her ten years. But here she was.

5

She got him to come to the door. He was groggy and half-asleep, but that was okay. She preferred him to be half-asleep. Had he been any more alert, he might've questioned her, made her grovel, maybe even refused her to pay her back for ignoring the attempts he'd made to reach out to her. She'd never forget how upset he'd looked when he chanced upon her and David in the forest shortly after they were married. Isaac didn't care about her, but he was possessive enough that seeing her with another man bothered him, probably more than he wanted to admit. He'd never reacted with jealousy any other time.

As it was, he seemed a little startled when she pushed him back into the house the moment he opened the door. He asked what was going on, but when she switched off the light he'd just turned on and reached for him, he figured it out fast enough.

Becoming instantly alert, and hard just as quickly, he welcomed her into his arms. Then his breath shortened and his hands grew very purposeful as they made their way beneath her clothes.

"That's it," she murmured, but she was thinking, *At last,* when her T-shirt hit the floor and his mouth, with its perfect lips, found her breast.

Allowing her eyes to close, she surrendered completely. She could no longer recall why she'd been denying herself. There were reasons, of course. Just none she was willing to list right now.

When her hands clenched in his thick black hair and she began to gasp, he groaned in appreciation of her eagerness and picked her up in his arms.

Briefly, she thought of his stitches, wanted to caution him not to do anything that could rip them out, but he didn't seem to be worried or in any more pain than she was. Maybe they were both high on meds. She would've laughed that something as unforeseen as an attack could bring them together after the protracted battle she'd fought to stay away. But she knew in her heart that it wasn't a laughing matter. She'd be sorry tomorrow.

When he placed her on the bed, she

expected him to back off long enough to remove the jeans he'd put on to answer the door, expected him to get right down to business. He'd won, hadn't he? Surely he'd want her to know it, to prove it to her in no uncertain terms. This wasn't a sweet and gentle lovemaking session likely to progress slowly. She hadn't meant it to be. Sweet and gentle was David's territory. When she had sex with Isaac, the need to get closer and closer consumed her. He made her buck and moan.

But he didn't seem willing to leave her yet, not even for the few seconds taking off his pants would require. He pinned her beneath him, hands above her head, and kissed her in a way that left her in no doubt that he craved what she'd denied him for the past decade.

Soon Claire was so sensitive to his touch she could hardly contain the building excitement. No wonder she thought of Isaac so often, had to fight the desire to visit him on a nightly basis. It'd only been a year since she'd slept with her husband, but it'd been a decade since she'd slept with Isaac. She wasn't sure how she could feel so strongly about him when she loved David as much as she did, but it was true.

Letting go of her wrists, he covered her

breasts with his palms. She could feel his hard length pressing into her stomach as he gently tweaked her nipples. Then *she* was trying to remove his pants because she couldn't wait a second longer.

"God, I've missed you," he murmured as he helped rid them both of what remained of their clothes.

She didn't believe him. How could he miss her if he'd never cared about her to begin with? He missed the sexual release she could provide. Somehow, whatever magic he held for her, she seemed to hold for him, too. They were both cursed.

Or she was projecting. Maybe it wasn't that way for him at all, just male pride or the refusal to believe he could lose her to someone else. Otherwise, he wouldn't care that she'd moved on.

Too bad the past went much deeper than merely a release for her. She'd been in love with him. Maybe she still was — a little, anyway. That was the part that frightened her, that made her fear it'd been a mistake to come here. She wasn't sure how she'd ever find the strength to let go of him again. Not without David to make the difference.

But that was something she'd have to deal with later. For right now, for this moment, she was going to take everything Isaac could give her, grab it all before she had time to rethink her actions or regret them or even acknowledge that this was how it should've been with David.

"No one can make love like you," she whispered.

He froze above her, as if she'd slapped him instead of complimenting him. "That's what brought you back?"

Did it matter? He had what he wanted. "Yeah. It . . . it hasn't been easy for me after David. But this is better than being alone. And since you seem to be free for the night, you don't have anything to lose, either."

Silence. Then, "He made you happy."

"Yes." And yet she was glad it was Isaac touching her now. But she didn't add that, because it made no sense.

Isaac shifted so he could rest part of his weight on the bed. "Then . . . this means nothing to you."

His voice sounded slightly strangled. She thought it was odd that he'd even ask. He'd certainly never asked before. But they'd been young. And they'd ended badly. She rushed to reassure him that he didn't have to worry about her acting like a lovesick fool this time around. "No, I'm still totally in love with David. You don't have to worry."

"Worry?"

"That I'll want anything more from you."

"I see." She felt his chest rise, heard him take a quick breath.

His reaction confused her. "You're relieved, right?"

"Of course. David was a . . . a great guy, a perfect husband."

"He was everything to me." Just saying it brought tears to her eyes. David was generous, kind, consistent, transparent. Yet here she was, asking for more of the one thing Isaac could give her, and that was ecstasy.

Still supporting himself on his elbow, Isaac wiped away her tears. "Well, we wouldn't want you to be lonely. . . ."

Was he being sarcastic? His touch was so . . . gentle. Damn him. Why did he have to complicate everything?

She tried harder to clarify what she meant. Didn't he believe her? Was he remembering the last time, how sickeningly she'd clung to him? "We won't have to acknowledge it ever happened."

"Maybe you can pretend I'm him."

That was impossible, but she wasn't about to explain that no one could compare to Isaac, not even David. "Sure. Maybe. Or it can be like . . . like it was for you before," she reminded him. "Just . . . physical. We don't have to tell anybody."

She thought he'd be happy that she'd made it so easy for him. He was the one who didn't do well with commitments. When she'd told him she loved him the last night they were together, he'd panicked, said he wasn't the marrying type, that she should find someone who'd make a better husband. He'd even said she was stupid to think he could ever fall for her. So she'd moved on. She'd gotten back together with David, but David had been taken away from her, and now she had nothing.

Except this highly erotic, clandestine meeting with her former lover.

"It'll be our little secret," he said.

She breathed a sigh of relief. "Yes." She didn't want to start any rumors, didn't want to answer any questions about him. And she certainly didn't want to explain to her sister why she'd gotten involved with Isaac Morgan again — not after she'd just warned Leanne to be careful about who *she* spent time with. "That'd probably be best."

When there was no response on his part, no movement, either, she began to feel uncertain. "What's wrong?"

"Nothing," he replied. But something told her that wasn't quite true. The way he touched her, the way he made love from that moment on, was different. It almost seemed as if his stitches were hurting him. She asked if he'd changed his mind, but he didn't answer. He gave her what she wanted, at least on a physical level, but only with his mouth. He refused to fully make love.

She wasn't sure if he was out of condoms, or he was trying to withhold the one thing she wanted more than any other — to feel him inside her again after so long. Maybe it was neither. Maybe he'd lost his desire for her and she'd only imagined the unbridled excitement she'd sensed at the beginning, because he wouldn't even let her satisfy him in return.

He finished as if he was merely servicing her, then rolled over to go to sleep, and she lay awake, feeling like an idiot. Why was she asking for more of the same mixed signals, the same confusion, she'd endured ten years ago?

The smell of her was everywhere. On his pillow. On his sheets. On his *skin.*

But she was gone.

Thank God. It was too hard to have her lying next to him, knowing her presence in his bed didn't mean he had the second chance he'd been hoping for. When she'd walked through his front door and let him know she wanted him, he'd thought they could go back to the way it used to be, that he'd have the opportunity to start over with her.

But that was crazy. She was still in love with David; she'd said as much. And he couldn't possibly compete with a guy like that. David had been Pineview's golden boy. He'd had no rough edges, no unsavory past. To make matters worse, now that David was gone, he'd practically been canonized. Saint David.

Trying to minimize the strength of the scent that lingered, Isaac shoved the blankets off him. Maybe David was now a saint, but Isaac was still human and would never be able to outdistance his past. He'd been kicked out of school so often he couldn't remember the number of times. He'd dropped out before he could graduate. He'd been thrown out of the Kicking Horse Saloon for fighting on several different occasions and had spent a few nights in jail as a result. He'd once been chased off with a shotgun when he'd dared to date a girl whose father felt she was too good for him. And, as his crowning achievement, he'd stolen a car on a dare just before he turned eighteen and served a few months in juvie.

What he'd created with his career had come as a surprise to everyone. He made more money than most people around here. The residents of Pineview didn't know the half of it. But no one considered him to be safe or reliable. They admired him, were attracted to the celebrity he'd gained, but they were afraid to really embrace him. In short, it was generally understood that he wasn't a good bet.

He squinted against the light streaming into his bedroom, then rolled away from the window. He hadn't hung any blinds. No one lived close enough to see into his house, and he didn't mind the sun. He typically woke early, just as he had today. He liked to get moving, had more energy than he knew what to do with.

But he wasn't ready to get out of bed *this* morning. He felt like he'd been run over by a logging truck, and he was pretty sure he couldn't blame that sensation entirely on his latest wound.

Reminded of his injury, he removed the bandage and bent his head to see the neat row of stitches.

"Great. I'm looking more like Frankenstein's monster every day," he said through a yawn. He'd probably have another scar — this one right over his heart. That seemed fitting. As far as he was concerned, he deserved whatever he got when it came to

Claire. She'd offered him her love, and he'd rejected it. He'd told her he didn't care about her, even though everything she'd said was exactly what he'd longed to hear. He'd spoken the truth with his body — many times — and would've done so again last night if she hadn't told him he no longer mattered to her. But he couldn't verbalize his feelings. It had been too hard for him to believe her love wouldn't wane the minute he began to return it, to count on it. His past was too much of a hurdle. His own mother had left him standing in front of Happy's Inn when he was five years old, had driven off into the sunset and never come back. He'd waited in that spot every day for two months before he'd gotten the point that she'd *meant* to leave him behind when she let him out to go to the restroom and buy a candy bar.

He still wasn't sure what he would've done if Old Man Tippy hadn't taken him in. No doubt he would've been sent to an orphanage somewhere. But when Tippy volunteered, the law sort of looked the other way so he could have a new home without all the red tape — and it was a good home, for the most part. Tippy had been kind. He'd put a roof over Isaac's head, provided the basics and taught him everything he knew about photography, which he'd spent a lifetime studying. But he hadn't lived long. At sixteen, Isaac had inherited all of Tippy's video and photography equipment, along with the little shack they'd shared on Crystal Lake. He'd upgraded the equipment more than once, but he still owned the shack, and went there on occasion. He'd been alone ever since Tippy's death and that was how he felt safest. If he was alone he didn't have to worry about being left.

Refastening the bandage over the stitching that held his skin together, he sat up. It was after Tippy died that he'd really begun to act out. He'd been so angry and self-destructive, so unable to control his own emotions, that Pineview hadn't known how to handle him. The more others tried to control him, the harder he fought. He was twenty-one when he'd had his first sexual encounter with Claire. He'd been with other girls but no one like her and he wasn't ready for the way she affected him. Maybe if they'd gotten together later, after he'd learned to channel his excess energy into his work, they would've had a chance. Instead of acknowledging how much he cared, he'd denied his feelings for her, even to himself, did everything he could to prove that she was just a piece of ass.

So she'd given up on him and gone back to David, where she belonged. David knew how to treat her; he was the only person Isaac had ever secretly envied. David had graduated with honors and gone to college. He had more friends and family than he'd known what to do with. Isaac couldn't name a single person who hadn't liked the guy.

And yet there had to be *one,* didn't there? If what Isaac had come to suspect after reading the files on Alana was correct, the hunting accident that had taken David's life was no accident at all.

He glanced at the phone. He hadn't told Claire what he believed, hadn't even mentioned that he had her files. Seeing her like that had caused such a torrent of emotion, his thoughts had headed down a completely different path. And by the time he could think straight, he'd begun to question his own conclusions. He had nothing to back up his suspicions, except that David had been pursuing his own investigation into Alana's disappearance, and just as he seemed to be making headway, he was killed.

Coincidence? Or murder?

Getting shot by another hunter was so rare. . . .

His stitches pulled when he got to his feet.

He needed another couple of aspirin.

He felt marginally better once he'd given himself a few minutes to acclimate to a vertical position. Then he made his way into the kitchen, where he skipped the aspirin in favor of finding the phone book.

Two other hunters had gone into the forest with David the day he was shot, both of them friends of his from high school. Rusty Clegg, a deputy sheriff, was one of them. Leland Faust, who owned a farm near Big Fork since he'd married Bella Wagoner, was the other. Isaac didn't particularly care for Rusty. They'd had a couple of run-ins at the Kicking Horse Saloon. He got the impression that Rusty liked the power he wielded just a little too much, and that grated on Isaac. So he looked up Leland's number instead.

Just as he expected, Leland was listed.

Grabbing his phone, Isaac slumped into a chair at the kitchen table.

Leland's wife answered. She told him her husband was already out on the farm but supplied his cell phone number.

Isaac had a cell phone, too. He used it when he traveled, but there wasn't any service in Pineview so it was useless here. Only Kalispell, Big Fork and some of the larger cities had reception. Apparently,

Leland lived close enough to Big Fork to be able to use his.

" 'Lo?"

A gruff voice came through above the hum of a large motor — a tractor, maybe?

"Leland, it's Isaac Morgan."

The engine died. "Who?"

"Isaac Morgan." Isaac had never called him before. They'd never had any trouble, but they weren't exactly friends.

"That's what I thought you said. What can I do for you?"

"I was wondering if you could answer a few questions."

"About . . ."

"David O'Toole."

This met with a protracted silence. "Why would you want to know anything about David?"

"Let's call it general curiosity, for now."

"I'm not sure that's enough reason to get me to talk about him."

Isaac understood. Those memories had to be difficult. "Then I'll be more specific. I'm afraid the accident that took his life *wasn't* an accident." He waited for an exclamation of shock or surprise, but didn't receive one. The pause felt charged with some strong emotion, but because Leland hadn't spoken, Isaac couldn't tell which emotion or why.

"You still there?" he prompted.

"Yeah, I'm here. What makes you say that?"

This was the question Isaac had assumed would come immediately after his earlier statement. Why had it been delayed? What was going on in Leland's head? Was he remembering? Wondering if what Isaac had just said could be true? Or was he thinking that he'd suspected the same thing?

"I'd rather not explain at the moment," Isaac replied. "But . . . maybe you can convince me otherwise."

"And if I can't?"

Isaac felt his eyebrows shoot up. "What does that mean?"

"It means nothing. Never mind. I don't want to talk about this," he said, and the phone went dead.

6

When Claire opened her eyes and saw the sun creeping around the corners of her blinds, she pulled her extra pillow over her head. It couldn't be morning. Not yet.

"Claire? You going to answer or not?"

Claire wished she could ignore the voice at her front door. Once she got up, she'd have to come to full awareness, and with full awareness she'd be faced with the memory of what she'd done last night. After ten years, she'd gone back to Isaac's house, and his bed. But instead of being fulfilled, instead of feeling as satisfied as she once had, she battled regret — just as she'd expected. Served her right.

Why had she given in after so long? She'd known he wasn't what she wanted, that he could never be the kind of companion David had been.

Shit . . .

Bang. Bang. Bang.

There went the door again. She had to deal with her sister whether she felt like it or not. Leanne knew she was home.

"What do you want?" Claire remained where she was and, for a change, didn't bother to soften her voice.

"It'd be nice to know you survived the night, for one thing," her sister yelled back. "I was supposed to check on you every few hours, remember?"

Had she even tried? Or had she gotten drunk and passed out?

Claire was willing to bet Leanne hadn't thought of her until this morning.

Her sister's negligence might've hurt, except that Claire was used to it. All the care and attention between the two of them went in the other direction — from her to Leanne. As the baby of the family, Leanne was used to being coddled, and the sledding accident had only exacerbated that, all but cementing Claire as the one who would forever compromise, give, tolerate, cajole.

"I'm alive," Claire responded. "You can go home. You're off the hook."

"That's it?" Leanne's surprise almost made Claire chuckle. "You're not coming to the door?"

"I have a head injury, remember?"

"Does that mean you're not working today?"

Scooting closer to the nightstand, she checked the alarm clock. Eight-thirty. Her first appointment was at ten, and then she was booked solid until six, with a half-hour lunch break.

Considering the size of her headache, she couldn't stand on her feet all day. She didn't want to field the questions she'd be asked, either. No doubt word of the incident had spread. Maybe it'd even been reported in the paper, like every other call to the sheriff's department, including the minor ones. "I'll have to cancel."

"Okay, well . . ." Leanne didn't seem to know what to do with herself. It wasn't enough of an excuse that Claire was hurt; Leanne was used to Claire being at her beck and call, whether it was convenient or not.

Remembering Isaac's mouth on her breast — and elsewhere — Claire barely stifled a groan. She was an idiot. But sleeping with her ex-lover wasn't her only problem. What about the man who'd attacked her at the cabin? She had no idea who he was or what he'd wanted.

The lost files and the information she'd picked up from what she'd managed to read complicated things further. . . .

The warning from her subconscious had been correct. This wasn't a good morning. But she might as well confront it head-on.

"Wait a second," she called out.

"I'm still here," Leanne said.

Frowning because of everything that'd passed between them last night, Claire got out of bed and, supporting herself against the walls, made her way to the living room, where she opened the door.

"Wow, you look like hell," Leanne muttered.

"I feel like hell. But thanks for making my morning that much more enjoyable. I can always count on you."

Leanne gave her an odd glance. "Just thought you'd want to know."

"Not necessarily." Had she looked okay when she'd appeared at Isaac's cabin? She couldn't imagine she had, but it made her mad that she'd even care. Anyway, Leanne didn't look much better. She'd put on a robe, but she was still in that nightgown she'd been wearing the night before — not a positive association as far as Claire was concerned.

Fortunately, they didn't have any neighbors. They lived at the end of a rutted dirt road next to the old park, which wasn't used anymore. This area, called River Dell, was considered the poor side of town, but Claire liked the privacy of having their own cul de sac. They both worked out of their homes, which had been purchased with the trust money their grandparents had left them, although that was gone now. Leanne made stained-glass windows and lamps, which she sold online and by referral. Her shop, like Claire's salon, was attached to her house.

They weren't getting rich, but they were self-employed and self-sufficient. That freedom meant a lot to Claire.

Suddenly, Leanne leaned close. "Is that a hickey on your neck?"

Isaac had wanted to leave a mark; he'd done it on purpose to spite her. "Of course not. I . . . I hit something when I fell. It's just a red mark."

Leanne didn't seem completely convinced, but she let it go. "So . . . do you need me to make you some breakfast?"

An offer like that meant she was feeling contrite. But the emotion wouldn't last. She wasn't that big on taking responsibility for her actions. "No, I'm fine." Claire hesitated, fought with herself and eventually came to a decision. "I have a question for you, though."

Her sister's expression turned stony. "If it's about my personal life, I don't want to discuss it."

"It's about the day Mom went missing."

Leanne started to roll away. "That's even worse."

The same unease Claire had experienced at the studio snaked through her. After their argument last night, she didn't want to pursue the question that kept surfacing in her mind, but couldn't hold back any longer. "Where did you go when she took you out of school?"

The whine of the wheelchair motor fell silent as Leanne stopped. "I don't know what you're talking about."

"You don't? The school attendance records show you went home sick."

Claire felt the weight of her sister's stare.

"Who says?" Leanne finally responded. "Dad picked me up after school, just like he picked you up. You know that. We waited for him together."

"You were gone for three hours. Someone brought you back at two. Who was it?"

"No one. I don't know where you heard that, but it's wrong. I never went home, sick or otherwise," she said, and continued on her way.

Tug woke Claire from a deep sleep two hours after she'd canceled her appointments. When she raised her head and saw his name on caller ID, she didn't want to answer. She wasn't up to talking to anyone else today, even her stepfather. But she knew he was probably worried. If she didn't answer, he and Roni might drive over.

That was more than she could handle right now.

Taking most of the bedding with her, she rolled toward the phone but dropped the handset. "Hello?" she said once she'd picked it up.

"You okay?"

Making an effort to shake the exhaustion that dragged at her as if she was under ten feet of water, she rubbed her face. He was worried, as she'd thought. She could hear it in his voice. "Fine. Who told you about the attack?"

"Leanne."

"It's not in the paper?"

"Might be. Haven't checked."

Everyone would hear about it, anyway, and they'd be talking. "Are you upset with me?" Claire knew he couldn't be pleased. He was as adamant as Leanne that she leave the past alone.

"Not at all," he replied. "I'm glad you're okay."

At last, a ray of sunshine for her soul.

"Really?" She was almost afraid to believe it.

"Of course. I understand the . . . loss of your mother has been hard on you. I just . . . I wish you could let it go so you could be happy. That's all."

Why was she the only one who couldn't? That drove her almost as crazy as everything else about her mother's disappearance. "Don't *you* want to know what happened? Where she went? Don't you ever wonder?"

He seemed to be choosing his words carefully. "Of course I do. I wouldn't be human if I didn't. You know I hired a private eye right after she went missing, even offered a sizable reward, but it was all for nothing. We can't let tragedy destroy our lives. Sometimes these things happen and there are no answers. At some point, you have to cut away the bad and focus on the good, forget the past and move toward the future."

He'd done that. So had Leanne. She was the only one clinging to Alana's memory. Was she being loyal? Or was she ruining her life?

"But what if there *are* answers out there?" she asked. "What if we could find them if we pursued them hard enough?"

"We could put all our time, energy and resources into this and still come up empty-handed and brokenhearted."

He had Roni to help him look toward the future. Her stepfather was happy in his marriage, maybe even happier than he'd been with her mother. How much did that figure into his attitude?

Would she be so set on pursuing this if David hadn't died?

Probably not. She'd felt less driven when she'd had him as an incentive to live and love again, to forget.

But he was gone, and the burning passion was back. It'd been building recently, returning to levels she hadn't experienced since the years right after it happened. Which was why she had to ask Tug what she'd asked Leanne. "Do you know about Leanne coming home sick from school the day Mom went missing, Dad?"

She sensed surprise, but when he answered, he spoke in an even, measured tone. "No. Who told you she came home sick?"

"It's in the school's attendance log."

A brief pause suggested he was scrambling for what to say next, and that upset her. She wanted to trust him. She *did* trust him. So why did she get the impression that he was trying to dodge this question?

"Wow, you really are chasing this thing again, aren't you," he finally said.

Draping her arm over her eyes, she sank back onto her pillow. "I have to, Dad. For whatever reason — for a lot of reasons — I can't let it go."

He didn't respond right away, but when he did she could tell that something had changed. "Fine. You do what you have to, honey. And I'll support you in it."

Claire threw the covers aside and swung her feet over the edge of the bed. "You mean that?"

"Of course I do."

Those four simple words subdued the sinking feeling that had settled in when she woke up. He wouldn't relent if he'd killed Alana. He'd keep fighting to stop her. His past reluctance had troubled her all these years, so being able to move forward with his blessing meant a lot. "Why the change of heart?"

"What happened last night scares me. I lost your mother. I don't want to lose you."

When Claire's chest constricted, she knew his feelings toward the investigation had been a bigger problem for her than she'd ever wanted to admit. "Leanne said it was my fault for going there in the first place."

"You should be able to go to your mother's studio without feeling you might get hurt. Maybe it was a freak encounter, or an attempted robbery. I got off the phone with the sheriff a second ago. He said there's nothing to indicate it's more than that, since whoever it was just shoved you and ran off. But . . . the fact that it occurred at Alana's studio has him worried, and me, too."

"You think it might be related to the past?"

"Everyone does, although there's no proof. You didn't get a look at the guy?"

"No."

"Concentrate, honey. Can you remember *anything* about him? His height? His weight? Maybe some detail about his clothes or his smell?"

She wished she could, but it'd happened too fast. "No, nothing."

"What about his car?"

"I didn't realize he had a car, Dad. I didn't see anyone behind me on the road, didn't hear a vehicle approach. He must've followed at a distance and parked too far away."

"The sheriff said Isaac Morgan came to your rescue."

Again, Isaac's passionate kiss, his hands on her body and his erection pressing against her legs flashed through her mind. Just when the memories of their nights together had grown tired and dim, she'd gone and created a fresh one. "Yes."

"How do you know he didn't shove you to begin with?"

"Because he'd have no reason to do that. And it's not who he is."

"He never liked that you ended up with David."

He could've stopped it if he'd cared enough. "Believe me, that was no skin off his nose."

"But he watches you. I've seen him do it."

Her father had never mentioned this before. "What are you talking about? When does Isaac *watch* me?"

"Whenever. He can't keep his eyes off you. At the bar. At the café. At the grocery store. Anywhere you both happen to be."

That was because of their history. She watched him, too. She could feel his presence before she even saw him. "Trust me on this. It wasn't Isaac. What we had didn't mean anything to him. You know how he is with women. Anyway, the attack on me might've turned into more than just a shove if he hadn't come running." How else would he have gotten that terrible gash in his chest?

"Maybe, maybe not. But it's awfully convenient that he was right there."

"He lives close by."

"Not close enough to hear anything. And . . . Claire?"

"Yes?"

He seemed to be struggling with what he wanted to say next.

"Dad?"

He sighed. "It's so hard to know what to reveal and what not to reveal."

Claire gripped the phone tighter. "There's something you haven't told me?"

"It's not directly connected to Alana going missing. I'm sure of that. But . . . I've often debated whether it would make things easier on you to know. And now that you've asked . . . I don't want this eating away at you, sending you down the wrong path."

"Tell me."

"You asked about Leanne being out of school for three hours on the day your mother went missing."

A hard knot formed in Claire's stomach. His manner worried her. "Yes?"

"That did happen."

Leanne had just denied it. Initially, he'd denied it, too. "Then why'd you say —"

"The question took me off guard," he broke in. "I'm so used to protecting her, so used to minimizing the damage caused by that day, it's become instinctive to lie about it."

Claire swallowed hard. "I don't understand. There must be a reason you'd say she was out of school and keep saying it."

"Yes. And if you're going to pursue this, you need to know what it is."

Whatever "it" was sounded pretty ominous. She took a shaky breath. "I'm listening."

"It wasn't your mother who was . . . involved in some way with Joe Kenyon."

"Who was it?" Claire could barely make herself heard, but she must've spoken loudly enough because he responded with the name she'd suddenly guessed he was going to say.

"Leanne."

"That *can't* be true," she said. "Leanne was only thirteen at the time. If . . . if Joe was molesting her, he should've been punished. Why would you lie to keep what he did a secret?"

"Because he *didn't* molest her. What happened wasn't his fault."

Claire stared at the carpet, studying the large flowers as if tracing them on paper. "That doesn't make sense. He was at least seventeen to eighteen years older than she was."

"But she had a thing for him. You remember Katie, don't you?"

How could she forget Katie? Her sister's best friend had been almost as hard to put up with as Leanne. "Of course. She lived next door to Joe until her family moved during her and Leanne's junior year."

"That's right. I guess —" his words fell off but he seemed to marshal the resolve to continue "— I guess Leanne was coming on to him."

Sickened, Claire covered her mouth and spoke through her fingers. "How does a thirteen-year-old girl come on to a thirty-something man?"

"I can't talk about it. I . . . won't talk about it. It's too upsetting to me, and I'd rather keep the unflattering details private, for your sister's sake. To be fair to her, that was a long time ago, and . . . and sometimes girls get themselves mixed up in stuff like that when they're discovering their sexuality. Or so I'm told," he added in a mumble.

Claire had never even been tempted to come on to a man nearly two decades older, but . . . she decided to give her sister the benefit of the doubt.

"Just know that she was young and confused and tried to . . . *entice* him," he went on.

"And you're sure he —" Her throat closed up. After swallowing, she began again. "Did he act on what she offered him?"

"No."

"He might have done more than you think. Maybe that's what instigated . . . her interest."

"He had proof when he called us, Claire."

Claire couldn't help thinking of Leanne in that nightgown. She'd assumed her sister's promiscuity stemmed from the accident, but this made her wonder if it'd started at a much earlier age. "What kind of proof?"

"A video she made for him."

Gross . . . Claire couldn't bear to think about it. But she still needed the answers she'd been searching for from the beginning. "So . . . what does Leanne's being out of school on the day Mom went missing have to do with any of this?"

"It was that morning Joe contacted us with the . . . news. Your mother was so upset when she heard it, she called me in tears. I'd dropped her off after having a cup of coffee and a doughnut with her, had just arrived at the gun shop, so I asked her to wait until I could get off work, told her we'd deal with it then. I couldn't leave. I had nobody to watch the store. Walt was out of town and depending on me, and Don Salter, who could've replaced me, wouldn't answer his phone." He took a moment to gather his thoughts or his emotions or both before continuing. "But apparently she couldn't wait. She marched down and signed Leanne out of school so she could talk to her before you were home."

"And what did Leanne have to say?"

"She denied the whole thing. So Alana took her over to Joe's, and he showed them the tape."

That was why Leanne had never mentioned being out of school. She didn't want to admit she'd made a pornographic video at thirteen, which she used to solicit a married man. Claire also understood why Tug had kept quiet all these years. But how had Joe and that tape and Leanne's behavior affected the investigation into Alana's disappearance? It must have hampered the sheriff's ability to do a thorough job with everyone being careful not to say too much about the day in question.

"Why hasn't Joe told anyone?" Claire asked. "Like one of the investigators you hired?"

"Because he's a good man."

If what she was hearing was true, Claire had to agree. He'd tolerated a lot of talk, been convicted of committing adultery with her mother in the court of public opinion, and yet he'd never stepped forward to point a finger at Leanne. That certainly changed how she thought of him.

Now she could explain some of those "inconsistencies" listed in that file. But what did that have to do with her mother's disappearance? Or were the incident with Joe and the kidnapping two separate items?

"So . . . Mom took her back to school?" Claire remembered there being some confusion about that in what she'd read.

"No. She was crying too hard. She'd had a terrible fight with Leanne. You can imagine what it must've been like after they left Joe's. So I closed up and took Leanne back to school for her. I thought it might help your mother to have some time alone."

"When was that?"

"I can't remember exactly. About one o'clock, I think."

But the log said Leanne hadn't signed in until *two.* "And Mom was . . ."

"At the house. That's where I left her."

"And she was fine?"

"As fine as could be expected, under the circumstances."

That meant Alana had gone missing between one and three-thirty, when she and Leanne got home. "That's why you were so worried when I called that day."

"Yes. I was worried *before* you called."

This made sense, but what about the previous sightings of her car at Joe's house

— if those reports were true? "Thanks for telling me."

He lowered his voice. "What are you going to do with the information? Roni, even Joe's wife — they don't know, Claire. I don't want it coming out. It would really hurt Leanne and could cause problems for Joe."

Obviously, he felt that being honest with her had betrayed her sister. They'd always been close. "Nothing. For now," she told him.

"Leanne's your sister." The caution in his tone suggested she should protect the secret as well as he had. But if everyone was protecting this secret or that secret, how would the sheriff's department ever get to the bottom of what had gone wrong?

Claire felt she owed Leanne a lot. They were sisters, as her stepfather had just pointed out. She understood how the slightest upset could throw Leanne into a tailspin, especially since the accident. But did those considerations outweigh the hope that full disclosure and absolute honesty might bring Alana back — or catch the man who killed her?

7

Working for himself made it possible for Isaac to accept only jobs that excited him. It also enabled him to do a lot of projects on spec. He often edited his own footage and created pilots and trailers, which his agent submitted to various film and television producers. For the print photography side of his business, he had a different agent who sent his pictures to various magazines internationally, as well as book publishers. He'd recently sold a coffee-table book, which would be a collection of some of his finest photographs.

He loved what he did. He could get lost in editing and refining his films and photographs for hours. After Claire had married David, his work gave him something he could devote himself to full-time so he wouldn't have to dwell on his personal life — what he'd thrown away when he rejected Claire. His career also meant he was gone a lot, so he didn't have to be constantly reminded. . . .

But somewhere along the line, all the flights and airport transfers and taxis and hotels had begun to wear on him. Traveling so much started feeling more like drudgery, like running away, than career advancement. Which was why he'd decided to take an extended break. It wasn't as if he *had* to go anywhere. He was in the middle of several projects he could finish right here, like the Alaskan sled dog series he was working on. He had plenty of footage from last winter when he'd gone to live with a family of Eskimos in northern Alaska. He was pretty sure he'd be able to sell it to his friend at *Nat Geo.* Michael had bought a lot of pictures from him in the past, had been a fan since his first spread in *National Geographic,* back when Michael had worked for the magazine, before he joined the TV network.

But today Isaac wasn't making much progress. He couldn't concentrate. He kept glancing over at the files he'd brought from Alana's studio, wondering who had attacked Claire and why, whether David had been killed in an accident or on purpose, and if he should air his suspicions or keep his mouth shut. He'd hoped Leland would be able to convince him he was way off base, but Leland's response to his call had only left Isaac more unsettled.

He drummed his fingers on the desk while staring at a frozen image of Kitbohn, the leader of the pack of dogs he'd become so close to last winter, on his computer screen. Something about the accident that had killed David wasn't as it seemed. Leland obviously believed it, too, and yet he hadn't sounded the alarm.

Why? Surely, he was in a better position than Isaac to do so.

He was probably holding off for the same reason Isaac was: no proof. Isaac didn't want to stir up any drama, or hurt Claire by dragging her through more of the same crap she'd already been through. He'd caused her enough pain when she'd told him she loved him and he couldn't reciprocate.

David's death, even Alana's disappearance, wasn't any of his business. He prided himself on staying out of matters that didn't concern him. He had enough to deal with in his own life.

So why was he tempted to jump into this?

Because he couldn't get Claire out of his mind. He knew how much finding her mother meant to her, how much she loved David and would want to see his killer punished — if he'd been purposely shot. It was a testament to Isaac's fascination with her that he was so willing to give her what she wanted, even when it came to the man who'd replaced him.

Or was it his way of making up for his own shortcomings?

Should he call and ask her to pick up the files?

He wasn't sure if she was on her feet. He also wasn't sure he wanted her in his house again. Touching her last night had convinced him that the past ten years had changed nothing. Not for him.

With a sigh, he watched the clock tick away. Ten, twelve, fifteen minutes. Frustrated at the waste of time, he tried to focus on the computer, but it was no use. He wasn't worth a damn today.

Cursing his own stubborn heart, he retrieved the accordion folder he'd stashed under his bed. Then he got his keys. He'd pay Claire a visit, just to drop these off, and keep his suspicions to himself. Maybe then he could return to his normal routine. He'd thought about her before last night, especially when he was in town, because there was always the possibility of bumping into her, but his emotions hadn't seemed *quite* so intense. Today, every time he heard her voice in his head, saying, "It hasn't been easy for me after David. But this is better than being alone," he felt as if she'd rammed a knife in his gut.

He hadn't gotten over her.

But he would. Just as soon as he got her files out of his house, he'd wash his hands of her for good.

Claire wasn't sleeping, but she was in bed where she'd spent the whole day, tightly curled up, thinking about David. How could she miss him so much, love him so much, when Isaac affected her as strongly as he did? What did that say about her? Had she been as faithful to David in her heart as she'd believed?

She'd never cheated on him, even though there were moments when the look on Isaac's face told her he probably wouldn't turn her away if she decided to pay him a visit. He'd never called her after she'd said "I do," and she respected him for that, especially since the desire was still there, for both of them. She'd never been able to completely eradicate it, and he had no reason to bother trying. Maybe he didn't love her, maybe he never had, but he certainly liked getting in her pants. Focusing on what she felt for David and her duty as a wife was the only thing that'd made it possible to stay away from him.

But David was gone.

The doorbell rang. She waited, expecting it to be Leanne again, but no one called out.

Maybe it was a client who wanted a haircut. She took walk-ins on the days she worked, and Tuesday was definitely one of those days.

She hoped whoever it was would go away when she didn't respond, but that wasn't the case. The doorbell rang three more times.

"I should've put up a sign," she grumbled, and got out of bed.

The mirror showed her a sleepy face. Red, puffy eyes revealed that she'd been crying. She'd cried so much in the past year she rarely wore makeup anymore. And with her hair falling around her shoulders in a tangled mass of curls, she looked as unkempt as Leanne had said earlier.

The image staring back at her hardly made her eager for company. But who did she have to impress? She wasn't dating anyone, had no hope of finding romance in Pineview. A few guys asked her out. Rusty Clegg, the sheriff's deputy who'd probably helped David get hold of her mother's files, was one who wouldn't give up. He called incessantly. But he and all the others had been good friends with her and David. She liked them, but there wasn't any . . . chemistry.

Shoving her hair out of her face, she grabbed an old woolen robe as whoever was at her door knocked again. July was too hot for such a heavy garment, but Leanne's reaction to the mark on her neck told her she needed a high collar.

When she noted the size of the blurry image on the other side of the glass, she hesitated. She'd been right. This wasn't Leanne. And there wasn't any point in hiding the hickey. It was the man who'd given it to her.

"Come on, Claire. Open up!"

Damn! This would be her third encounter with him in less than twenty-four hours. Once or twice a month was hard enough.

Tightening the belt on her robe, she told herself she didn't care that he was about to see her at her worst and opened the door.

Wearing a simple T-shirt and a pair of faded jeans that rested low on his hips, he loomed over her by almost a foot. Generally speaking, she didn't mind being short. But she always longed for a little more height when dealing with him. . . .

"What can I do for you?" She blocked the

entrance and kept one hand on the knob. But then she spotted the accordion file beneath his arm and understood why he'd come.

Quickly checking to make sure Leanne wasn't out — she didn't want to be grilled about the reason Isaac Morgan had shown up at her house — she flung the door wide and waved him in.

His sardonic smile told her he knew it wasn't *him* she was so excited to see. But he was wrong. To her own chagrin, seeing him always excited her.

"Nice place."

He'd never been inside her house. She'd been living in a small apartment above Stuart's Stop 'n' Shop when they were "together." Once David returned from college and accepted a job in Kalispell, she'd moved there, too, to attend beauty school. After she graduated, David opened his State Farm office and they both came back to Pineview, where they'd lived on David's parents' property until Tug finished building her house. Once it was done, they'd married and moved in.

"It's small but comfortable." She wasn't sure if his compliment had been sincere, and she didn't really care. She'd lost interest in so many things since David had died, not the least of which were cooking and cleaning. "Where did you get that?" She motioned to the file she'd attempted to remove from her mother's studio.

He turned to face her. "Where do you think?"

"You went to the studio? Before the sheriff could get there?"

"I did. I could tell you wanted this."

"That can't be the only reason." Such generosity wasn't like him.

His expression hardened. "Why not?"

"It was late, you were injured and this is *my* problem."

"Right. Why would I care? I'd never do anything just because it's important to you. Only David would do that."

She didn't know how to respond. She wasn't up to an argument today, and he seemed even more defensive than usual. "Regardless of your reasons, I'm grateful." She tried to take it from him so he'd leave. Now that she'd canceled all her appointments, she'd have the privacy and time to go through all the reports without being interrupted. But he held them beyond her reach.

"Why didn't you want the sheriff to get hold of this?" he asked. "It came from his office in the first place, didn't it? Which means you could always get another copy."

She didn't want to focus on his eyes with their golden-brown irises, but neither did she want to focus on the long, tanned fingers that could work such magic on whatever they touched. Clearing her throat, she kept her own eyes on those files. "Not necessarily. That folder contains much more than he'd release to me."

His dark eyebrows gathered. "And he doesn't know you have it?"

"*I* didn't even know until yesterday. I found it in the attic of the studio. David must've gotten it for me . . . somehow."

"Ah, David again." His mouth twisted into a sneer. "Your knight in shining armor."

She raised her chin. "Yes. Always." She'd sensed long ago that Isaac had never liked David. David had certainly never liked Isaac, and it wasn't exclusively due to jealousy. He hated Isaac because of the way Isaac had used her. He'd often told her she should hate him, too, and she'd pretended, but it was hard to blame Isaac when she was a willing participant in the whirlwind of desire that had brought them crashing together. He'd never forced her to visit his cabin. She'd been so eager for his touch she could scarcely wait from one encounter till the next.

He lowered his voice. "What did he know about us?"

She didn't want to talk about this. It was too . . . . intimate. She nearly told him so, but she feared that would only confirm how sensitive an issue he'd been between her and David. She decided it might be less revealing to simply answer. "He knew we slept together. I don't — *didn't* — keep anything from him." Other than the depth of her feelings for Isaac, and the fact that those feelings never seemed to change or go away.

His voice dropped even further, and this time a pained expression accompanied his words. "Is he the reason you've been crying?"

"I haven't been crying." She wasn't sure why she was attempting to lie. The truth was all too apparent. But she hated the idea of Isaac knowing she was in such a bad state. It was stupid and weak that she couldn't seem to get back on her feet.

She aimed to be just as tough, just as indifferent, as he was. Maybe someday she'd actually accomplish it.

"Right." He rolled his eyes.

Ignoring his reaction, she drew a deep breath. "So are you going to give me the files?"

He pursed his lips. "I'm thinking about it."

"I don't understand why you'd even hesitate."

"Have you eaten today?"

She gaped at him. "Have I . . . *eaten?* What difference does that make?" Especially to him?

"It's a simple enough question," he said with a shrug.

"It's nearly dinnertime. Of course I've eaten." Another lie. She'd lost too much weight in the past year. Everyone was nagging her about it, especially her best friend, Laurel, and her stepfather.

"What did you have?"

Letting go of the collar of her robe, which she'd been holding closed, she fiddled with the belt — as if it was the way she'd tied it that made her look so thin. "Again, I don't see why that matters."

"Then it should be easy to tell me."

She glanced toward the kitchen. She wasn't hungry, even now. She'd lost her appetite when David died. "Breakfast. I had breakfast."

"Which consisted of . . ."

"Eggs. Oatmeal. Cereal." She rubbed her hands over her face. "I don't know." It all sounded terrible to her.

A frown tugged at the corners of his mouth. "You haven't eaten a damn thing."

"So?" she challenged.

"So where's your sister?"

"I guess she's at home. Or working in her shop."

"She should be here, taking care of you."

"I can take care of myself."

"You're not doing a very good job of it."

"All I need is what you've got right there." Again, she motioned to the files.

He glared down at her. "Why do you think Saint David had so much information about your mother?"

"Saint David?"

"Just to let you know I'm clear about his status."

"You — Never mind." She curled her fingernails into her palms. "I'm guessing he was investigating her disappearance. I'm sure you've looked through those reports. Isn't that what you'd guess?"

"You didn't know he was doing it?"

"No. He never said a word about it."

A funny look came over Isaac's face, a look that made her believe he was tempted to say more.

"What is it?" she asked.

"Nothing." He blew out a sigh and held

up the files. “How badly do you want this stuff?”

Feeling even more leery, she narrowed her eyes. “How badly do you think?”

“Badly enough to compensate me for the time and effort I put into saving it for you?”

She could feel her heartbeat pulsing in her fingertips, her throat. He was taking a new direction, had made some kind of decision. “What is it you want?”

When he reached for her robe, she thought she already knew. Uncertain as to whether she could let him touch her in David’s house, she stiffened. But he didn’t make any sexual advances. He merely examined the mark he’d left on her neck. “I want the opportunity to redo last night.”

“Why? What’s changed?”

“I’ve had a chance to think about it.”

“And?”

“That’s it.”

What was going on? Was he upset that she’d been able to walk away from him the last time they were together? That she’d been able to replace him with someone who treated her so much better? Or was he determined to prove he could get her back?

If that was the case, she was just as determined to prove he couldn’t.

“Not a good idea.”

"Because . . ."

Because being with him again would only remove another brick from the wall she'd built to keep him out. If she wasn't careful, she'd fall right back into the routine she'd had such trouble breaking the last time — only there'd be no David to rescue her and make her feel valued and loved.

"I have enough going on in my life right now. I don't think we should see each other a second time." She didn't have the energy to pit herself against him. She knew he'd win. Again. She always led with her heart, which made it hard to deal with a man who didn't have one.

He chuckled when his gaze lowered to the opening of her robe and she hurried to pull it closed. "Last night you said you were still in love with David, that what you wanted from me was purely physical."

"So?"

He studied her. "Is that true?"

She'd die before she'd admit it wasn't. "Of course."

"Then what do you have to lose?"

Herself, like she had before. Without her husband, who had also been her best friend, she was already lost. What good would it do to fall into the same mess she'd made before?

And yet Pineview had nothing better to offer. Even gravity seemed to be working against her, seemed to be pulling her into Isaac's arms.

"I'll make us dinner," he said.

"Don't bother. I'm not coming."

"I hope you do. *Someone* should start making you eat," he said, and left.

8

The files contained one significant piece of information Claire hadn't known before: Joe Kenyon didn't have a solid alibi for the hours during which Alana went missing. Claire had always been told that Peter, his brother, had confirmed that Joe was on a job site all afternoon. According to his account *and* Joe's, Joe went home for lunch at noon — Claire guessed this was when Alana and Leanne visited his house and viewed the tape — but supposedly returned to work shortly after one and stayed until five.

In a second interview, however, done years later when Sheriff King briefly pursued the case, Joe's brother admitted he'd only seen Joe return to work before driving over to Marion to give someone an estimate.

Since Marion was a twenty-minute drive, Peter would've been gone close to an hour, especially if the estimate was at all complicated. During that hour, Joe was supposed to be stacking a cord of wood in Patty Chicawa's backyard, but she worked at the bank until five and couldn't say if he'd been there the whole time or not.

Even more compelling was that Patty's house was less than five minutes away from where Alana and Tug had been living.

Could Joe have been angry about what had happened over lunch? Could he have feared that Alana might get him into trouble with his wife and maybe the authorities? He could've shown up, hoping to convince himself he'd done the right thing in giving her the tape, and considering the emotions of the moment, maybe they'd fought and he'd lost his temper. . . .

A plausible scenario, but it was difficult to say whether or not Joe was capable of *murder.* Claire assumed anyone could be, given the right incentive. Still, he was a hard man to read. Was he as honorable as Tug believed? Or had he been having an affair with Alana and, in an attempt to salvage their relationship, gone over to convince her that he hadn't acted inappropriately with her daughter?

Whatever the answers to the questions raised by Peter's revelation, it bothered Claire that his story had changed. According to the notes she'd read, it had bothered

David, too. He'd thought Peter knew more than he was saying.

But Peter could've done what so many other family members do in similar situations. Maybe he'd panicked and, fearing his brother would become a suspect, provided an alibi. After several years had passed, and the threat didn't seem so real, he might have relaxed enough to reveal the truth.

An hour wasn't very long in which to kill someone and dispose of a body, but Joe had privacy. That meant it didn't need to happen all at once. His wife's mother had been ill for years. She spent a lot of time in Idaho, helping take care of her, and had been gone that entire week, along with the kids. Joe could've killed Alana and put her in her own suitcase to transport her to his home. That suitcase could've been in his garage the whole time the sheriff and his deputies were searching for her. It wasn't as if they had probable cause to go into his house.

Or maybe everyone else was right. Maybe Alana had simply had it with Pineview and run away.

Cursing, Claire shoved the files to one side of her kitchen table and got up to stretch her legs. She'd been sitting for four hours, poring through every page in an attempt to puzzle out the mystery. But there wasn't enough information to solve it.

She needed to get out, do something different, give herself a break.

She immediately recalled Isaac's dinner invitation. Once she'd read through the case files and learned all they had to tell her, she'd been surreptitiously watching the clock as she went over them again. She'd even looked up his number, thinking she might call to see if he was still expecting her. But she didn't call and she didn't plan to go. Last night had left her wary of even his ability to bring her physical fulfillment. Another night with him wouldn't make her life better. He'd withhold *something* and she'd feel even worse. Why give him that power?

Because it was an escape and, after a whole day in the house, she needed that. She couldn't turn to her sister. She hadn't seen Leanne since that earlier visit. Leanne was probably in a huff about what Claire had implied by asking why she'd been out of school the day their mother went missing. Either that or she didn't want to talk about it, since she'd denied a fact Claire could prove. Considering what Tug had told her, Claire didn't want to talk about it, either.

Anxious and unsettled, she stood at the

window, brooding as she stared across the courtyard. Was Leanne staying in drinking again? She told herself she should go over and check. Maybe bringing up the past had pushed Leanne into another depression. Claire didn't want that, but neither did she want to let her sister punish her for asking the wrong question. Leanne could be so dark.

But Claire had her own issues. And because of those issues, she had to leave the house, or she'd weaken and head over to Isaac's cabin. He'd never offered to make her dinner before. She was curious as to how that would play out, but not curious enough to let it override her better judgment. Regardless of how the night started, by morning she'd crave more of Isaac Morgan than she could get, emotionally if not physically. That was the story of their whole relationship.

To protect against that, she called Deputy Clegg — Rusty — and asked if he'd like to go out tonight.

He was so eager, he told her he'd be right over and showed up at her house while she was still scrambling to get ready. It wasn't easy to find a top that covered Isaac's hickey. She finally settled on a sleeveless turtleneck sweater that was part of an ensemble she normally wore in winter.

They had dinner at Seritella's, an Italian restaurant, where she picked at a salad while he put down most of a large pizza. From there, they went dancing at the Kicking Horse Saloon. She thought the crowd and the music might keep her from dwelling on Isaac or the disconcerting details she'd discovered in her mother's case files. But nothing really helped — the time dragged on and on. It didn't take her long to figure out that she was even less interested in Rusty than she'd thought when she'd turned down all his previous invitations.

At eleven o'clock he suggested going to her place to watch a movie. She'd just told him it was too late for that when Joe Kenyon showed up.

Claire had always been a little afraid of Joe. After what she'd read in the case files, she was even more so. If he'd killed her mother, and then David for resuming the investigation, he could come after her someday. He was so . . . laconic. So hard to know.

But considering the lurid details her stepfather had shared, she'd realized he was either far more evil than she'd ever dreamed — or downright saintly.

As soon as Rusty went to get another beer,

she slid onto the empty stool next to Joe's. "Hey."

He nearly fell off his chair when he turned to see who'd addressed him. The last time she'd confronted him was during Sheriff Meade's investigation. When he wouldn't come to the door, she'd lost her temper and stood on his front stoop, yelling that he was a cold-blooded killer. It wasn't her finest moment, and she could see how that might make him reluctant to talk to her.

His lips formed the word *hi,* but the way he pulled the bowl of peanuts closer and slumped over his drink communicated, *Get lost.*

She was bothering him and he didn't like it, but she wasn't willing to give up that easily. "You don't come here very often," she said, but for all she knew he appeared nightly. She was the one who didn't come here often.

Right or wrong, he didn't correct her. He popped nuts into his mouth and hunched down even farther.

"How's the family?"

He blinked at her and broke down enough to respond. "Fine."

"Your wife out of town again?"

"Yep. Mother's had a setback."

"Then you're home alone?"

Nothing. He pretended to be preoccupied.

"I said, 'You're home alone?' " she persisted.

He shot her an exasperated look. "If they're gone, I'm home alone, yeah."

"So the kids went with her?"

"It's summer. They like to see their grandparents."

"How long will they be gone?"

His scowl darkened. "Do you want something?"

"I was just making small talk."

"They'll be gone the rest of the month, maybe longer. Like I said, it's summer. Are we done yet?"

Claire drew a deep breath. "I bet it gets lonely when they're away."

Shoving the nuts aside, he got up and grabbed his drink, but she caught his arm before he could leave.

"Can't we have a conversation, Joe? Please, sit down and . . . and talk to me for a minute."

His eyes darted toward the door. "I'd rather not."

"But I want to tell you I'm sorry about before. The way things have gone . . . it's not fair to you. I realize that now I know . . . about Leanne."

His beer sloshed onto the bar as he

slammed down his mug. He hadn't had a chance to drink much of it, so she thought he'd relent, but he shook his head. "As far as I'm concerned, that's ancient history. I've said all I'm going to say." Then he walked out.

Claire propped her chin on her fist. So much for making friends with Joe Kenyon. He wanted nothing to do with her. That sentiment probably extended to her whole family, except Tug, who gave him quite a bit of tree work.

Rusty weaved through the small group of patrons still there, coming toward her with his drink. She wanted to tell him she was ready to go, but when he reached her, he set his beer down and pulled her onto the dance floor. "I like this song!" he yelled over the music.

From eight to midnight, four nights a week, five homegrown boys took the stage at the Kicking Horse Saloon. They weren't fantastic musicians, but they weren't bad, either, considering that their music was only a sideline to the farming and ranching they did during the day. As part of their final set for the evening, they were playing a slow song, which gave Rusty the perfect excuse to hold her tight.

The beer he'd drunk smelled sour on his

breath. Trying to avoid his mouth, Claire turned her head in the other direction, which he took as an invitation to skim his lips over the inch of skin above her turtleneck. She shivered, but not because she'd enjoyed it. The exact opposite was true. She didn't want to be this close to him, didn't want him to touch her at all.

Afraid someone would see them dancing so intimately and assume they were now an item, she tried to put more space between them, but he tightened his grip and rubbed his pelvis against her as if he thought he was turning her on.

It was all Claire could do not to embarrass him by wrenching free and stalking off the floor. She might've done it, except that she blamed herself as much as him for her current predicament. She didn't really return his interest; she shouldn't have called him. But she'd never dreamed he'd move so fast.

"I — I'm not over David," she murmured, ducking her head to avoid his mouth when he tried to kiss her.

He tensed but didn't release her. "Ah, come on, Claire. I've known you all your life, waited forever for this date. I hate what happened to David. You know I cared about him, too. But he's been gone for over a year.

How long are you going to hold on?"

His response irritated her. "It's not like I can give you a specific day, Rusty. I'm not missing him to be difficult. That's just the way it is for me. He was my *husband.*"

"And he was one of my best friends!"

Rusty had been with David at the end. He didn't like to talk about it, which told her as much as anything what a horrible experience it had been. "Then you, of all people, should understand."

"I guess guys are just more practical, you know? It was a tragedy, for sure, but you didn't die when he did. He wouldn't want you to be unhappy. So why are you hiding out in that house of yours, wasting away?"

"I can't simply forget I loved him and transfer my affections to the next person in line." The tension of holding him so rigidly made her shoulders ache. It was stupid that she couldn't relax, but she felt . . . nothing. No, worse than nothing, she was repulsed.

She might as well have gone to Isaac's. Avoiding him hadn't improved her situation. "I just . . . need you to be my friend."

"I've been your friend for years. I'm ready for more. I won't lie . . . I've always admired you, even when you were married to David. I thought he was the luckiest guy in the world."

"I appreciate that, but —"

"Your sister's come on to me before. You know that, right?"

Claire felt a blush rise to her cheeks. This wasn't welcome news but she wasn't all that surprised. "What you and Leanne do is none of my business."

"But that's just it. I shut her down. I want you, not her."

If he thought that was going to make any difference, he was wrong. "I'm not ready," she said again.

"Fine. Then we're wasting our time here."

"Another practical response?" she snapped.

"The truth. Let's go."

He headed for the door, but she didn't follow. She couldn't bring herself to spend another second in his company. This date had been a disaster.

"You comin' or not?" he called, holding his keys.

She felt like telling him to grow up and quit pouting, but she knew that would only make matters worse. She shook her head.

A pained expression created deep grooves on either side of his mouth. "I drove. How will you get home?"

She met him at the edge of the dance floor so she wouldn't have to raise her voice. "My dad will give me a ride."

"You really want to call him at this hour?"

"Yeah. I do."

He threw up his hands. "Suit yourself," he said.

The minute he left, Claire went to the pay phone in the alcove where the restrooms were, but she had no intention of waking Tug. She dialed Isaac's number instead.

"Hello?"

She closed her eyes. Just hearing his voice made her want him as much as she ever had.

"Hello?" he said again. But she couldn't bring herself to respond. Instead, she hung up and started the long walk home.

Jeremy drove past Claire twice. She was on the side of the road, and he was trying to get a good look at her face. Was she crying?

Hard to tell. Maybe. He liked to imagine himself comforting her, holding her in his arms and gently wiping away her tears. He was glad she was okay after what had happened last night, but he wasn't pleased to see that she was out alone, especially so late. She wasn't paying attention to what was going on around her. She never did. And that was dangerous. She felt safe, but anything could happen to her out here.

He considered warning her. Only he

didn't think she'd listen. She seemed too sad to care.

Maybe he should ask if she needed a ride home.

Did he dare? What would his father say?

Don Salter would say no. But he wasn't here. And Jeremy was fairly confident she'd get in the car with him. Why wouldn't she? He'd always been very careful around her, never said anything that made her look at him the way his father did — as if he was stupid. He never frightened her or tried to touch her. She liked him. When she cut his hair every month she treated him just as nicely as she treated everyone else.

Of course he should stop to help.

As soon as he made that decision, his pulse leaped. The idea of having Claire O'Toole in his car, so *close,* made him warm and jittery inside. His father wouldn't like it; he'd been warned, plenty of times, to keep his distance. But . . . oh, how he'd dreamed of being close to her. And thanks to his boss at the burger stand, he had a car. Hank had given him the old Impala a year ago so he wouldn't have to walk like Claire was walking now. A lot of people, including his father, thought he shouldn't drive. Someone who'd been in special ed shouldn't be allowed to operate a vehicle, they said. But he'd shown them he could do it. He was a good driver.

Easing off the gas, he proved that he was a good driver by making a U-turn only where it was legal to do so. He remembered where he could and where he couldn't because he didn't like getting pulled over, answering all those questions. Cops were far too nosy. Even his father agreed with him on that.

After he'd turned the car around, he saw Claire up ahead, but before he could reach her, the big white truck in front of him pulled alongside her.

No! Someone else had gotten to her first. It was Isaac Morgan. Jeremy would know Isaac's truck anywhere.

She stood on the passenger side, talking through the window when Jeremy passed. He would've turned around again, just to see what happened, but he was afraid she'd notice. And if she didn't, Isaac might. Isaac made him nervous. He didn't want anything to do with him. Isaac could fight a bear and live to tell about it. How many times had he heard that story?

Isaac would bring her home.

Deciding to go to his favorite spot near her house instead, Jeremy gave the Impala some gas. If he beat them, he'd just get out of the car and wait. After Isaac dropped her off, maybe Claire would watch TV like she usually did, and Jeremy could pretend she'd invited him in so they could watch together.

But once he reached River Dell, he waited and waited and waited — and it was all for nothing because she didn't come home and watch TV.

She didn't come home at all.

9

Claire frowned at the steak on the plate in front of her. "I told you. I already had dinner."

Isaac folded his arms and leaned against the counter. The plastic containers he'd taken from the refrigerator were still strewn across the counter as if he thought she might want seconds. But as good as the food looked — there were sweet potatoes and asparagus to go with the steak — she couldn't possibly eat more than he'd served her.

"You're the reason I cooked extra," he said with a wink.

She arched her eyebrows at him. "Don't act like I stood you up. I *told* you I wasn't coming."

"You're here now."

Because it hadn't occurred to her that caller ID would identify the pay phone at the Kicking Horse Saloon. Or that he'd get out of bed to look for her in the middle of the night. "I don't understand why it matters to you whether I eat."

"You mean I'm such a hard-hearted bastard I don't mind watching you waste away?"

"I'm not wasting away."

"You won't if you eat." He motioned to her plate. "Dig in."

"Fine." Too tired to argue, Claire shoveled a bite of sweet potato into her mouth. She should've stayed home tonight. She hadn't expected her date with Rusty to be exciting, but neither had she expected it to fail quite as badly as it did. "It feels weird to be sitting in the kitchen where I lived as a child," she said.

He poured a glass of cranberry juice and put it on the table beside her. "Oh, yeah? Do you like what I've done with the place?"

Obviously, he was joking. It was well-maintained, but he hadn't changed a single thing since he moved in three years ago and neither had the people who'd owned it before him. "I wouldn't plan on hiring out as a decorator if I were you."

He shrugged. "Maybe someday I'll remodel."

He'd done a lot with the shack he'd inherited from Tippy. It was small but well-kept and in such a beautiful setting he'd stayed there much longer than anyone had expected. That was where she'd always visited him before, where she'd always pictured him even after he bought this place.

"What made you give up Tippy's house on the lake?" she asked.

"Mostly the size. I needed more room and this gave me a different view and even more privacy."

"The pictures you've hung make it a nice bachelor's pad." Mostly wildlife photos he'd taken himself, they added a masculine touch. "It's easy to tell you like what you do." Her gaze lingered on a framed print of a hippopotamus submerged in a swampy river with just his eyes, ears and nostrils showing. "I think it's great how much you love your work. You're the perfect kind of guy for it."

He poured himself some juice. "What kind of guy does it take?"

"Someone who likes to ramble, who feels most at home when he's on the road. Or in the wilderness, as the case may be." She wished he'd start putting the rest of the food away and stop watching her. His presence was forcing her to eat more than she wanted. "Have you had any close encounters since that bear attack — other than with the tree that nearly wiped you out last night?"

He finished his juice and rinsed the glass. "I got a strange spider bite in Kenya a few months ago." He spoke over his shoulder. "Made my hand swell up to three times its size." He showed her the scar.

"Do you know the kind of spider it was?"

"No. It didn't happen while I was shooting. It happened while I was sleeping."

"Were you someplace you could get medical help?"

"Not really. One of the guys I was traveling with lanced it and sucked out the poison."

"That must've been fun." She nibbled on her asparagus. "What's your favorite place you've ever been?"

He leaned against the counter. "You mean besides here?"

"You *like* Pineview?"

"Don't you?"

"It's okay." She drank a sip of her own juice. "But I'm leaving here someday."

"When?"

"As soon as I figure out what happened to my mom and feel Leanne will be fine on her own."

He crossed his feet. "Where do you want to go?"

She thought of all the exotic places he'd

been and felt like a country bumpkin by comparison. She'd never left Montana. "I don't know. Someplace far away and metropolitan. Maybe Los Angeles or New York."

"You've lived in a small town all your life. You don't think that'd be lonely?"

She was already lonely. She doubted it could get much worse. At least she'd have the promise of something new and different around the next corner. "It'd be nice to have a change of pace, a chance to meet new people."

"You seemed to like it here when David was alive."

"It felt different then."

"In what way?"

"Lots of ways."

"Such as?"

"I assumed we'd have a family. This would be a great place to raise kids, but if I'm going to be single I'd rather be somewhere with more . . . possibility."

He shoved his hands in his pockets. "There's no one in Pineview you'd like to date?"

"No."

His lips pursed. "It's getting easier and easier to see why you came here last night."

She owed him an apology for that. He hadn't invited her. And he'd hurt himself trying to help her. "I'm sorry," she said. "I shouldn't have kept you up."

His voice held a wry note when he responded. "I didn't mind."

"I'm glad." But if that was true, why had he stopped short of making love to her? She wanted to ask but knew it was territory they'd be wise to avoid. "Thanks for dinner, but . . . I'd better get going."

Although he took her plate, he didn't turn toward the sink. "You're not staying?"

A tremor of desire passed through her, as strong as ever. But she knew she'd be a fool to continue what she'd started last night. She was only making it harder to fall in love with someone else, someone who might actually be right for her. "No, um, not tonight." She got up and edged toward the door. "But I appreciate dinner."

He set her plate on the counter. "You didn't eat much."

"But it was good." At least, she assumed it was. Everything tasted like cardboard these days.

When he came over to her, she forced herself not to back away. She wouldn't look up, had no idea what he was thinking, but it was impossible not to shiver when he slid his hand down her arm.

"You didn't enjoy yourself last night?" he

murmured.

Her eyes lifted, seemingly of their own volition, and locked with his. He was so close. All she had to do was rise on tiptoe, and he'd kiss her.

She almost did it. But fulfilling her desire wasn't worth the regret she'd struggle with tomorrow — she knew because of what she'd dealt with today.

"It was fine, er, generous of you to, ah, accommodate me, since you weren't interested yourself. It's just . . . I'm a little lost right now. I think I need to figure out who I am without David, and where I'm going with my life, before I start sleeping around *too* much." She gave him a wry smile to indicate that she was joking about the sleeping-around part. "But if I ever decide to play fast and loose again, you'll be the first person I call."

"No one can make love like I can." He wore an inscrutable expression when he repeated her words from their night together, but she'd made the right decision this time. She had to heal, become whole, before she could manage any kind of relationship, particularly with someone who could wield as much power over her as Isaac Morgan.

"True." She clicked her tongue. "Just one

of the many reasons all the ladies line up at your door."

"What's another?"

Reaching for the unobtainable came to mind, but she didn't say that. "You know how to grill a steak."

"You ate two bites of it."

"That doesn't mean it wasn't good."

"Now that you're impervious to my appeal *and* my cooking, you might as well stay over," he said. "I don't have an extra bedroom. One's my office and the other's a darkroom. But the couch is free. At least you won't be alone."

It was an appealing offer. One she wanted to accept, especially when she thought of returning home and facing the pictures of her and David on the walls. Or Leanne and the growing concern that she was drinking too much. Or the mystery shrouding her mother's disappearance.

Her problems seemed insurmountable.

Because she was too tired, she told herself. Why not check out of regular life for a little while?

"That sounds good." She briefly touched his chest in thanks. "Maybe we'll be better friends than we were lovers, huh?"

She could tell she'd surprised him. He'd probably never had a woman over who'd opted to sleep alone.

"That's what you want? To be friends?"

She thought about it for a second, then nodded. "Yeah. I could use a friend right now."

He lowered his eyes. She suspected he was looking at the monkey bite he'd given her, which burned as if his mouth was still latched onto her skin. "I'll get you some bedding."

Generous of you to accommodate me, since you weren't interested yourself.

Isaac almost laughed aloud when he remembered that line. Maybe he'd lost interest in other women — for months, he hadn't paid any attention to who or what was available — but he definitely hadn't lost interest in Claire.

She had no clue what she did to him, but he wasn't about to let on. She was right when she said she was a little lost. The weight loss told him that much. If he really cared about her, he'd be the friend she needed and leave it at that. He had far less chance of letting her down as a friend than he did as a lover. There were still times when he felt he had to head out into the wilderness, to be alone for extended periods. He couldn't imagine how that would go over if he ever entered a committed relationship. He just wasn't cut out to be the kind of steady, reliable man David was.

Claire needed another David. She didn't need him.

But it wasn't easy to have her so close and not take her to bed. He should've made love to her last night while he had the chance. Then maybe he wouldn't be staring at the ceiling now. He'd wanted to, but he'd been too stung, too disappointed that she hadn't come for the reasons he'd wished. . . .

The shower went on, which only made matters worse. He'd given her a towel, told her she could make herself at home, but picturing the water rolling over her naked body was driving him crazy. The shower used to be one of their favorite places to make love.

Actually, he couldn't remember a place they *hadn't* liked.

The phone rang. Surprised that he'd be getting a call so late, he checked the clock — 1:20 — as he reached for the handset. Was it someone looking for Claire?

Caller ID read Restricted.

"Hello?"

"What the hell do you think you're doing blindsiding Leland with that bullshit about David's death not being an accident?"

His caller hadn't bothered to identify himself, but Isaac recognized the voice. Rusty Clegg.

"What business of it is yours whether or not I call Leland about anything?" he responded. "It's not as if I have anything to say to you."

"It's my business if it concerns David. You hardly even knew him."

"I knew him well enough. Anyway, what does that have to do with whether or not his death was an accident?"

"It makes me wonder why you're even getting involved."

"And that makes *me* wonder why you're so upset that I raised the question. Did I hit too close to the truth, Rusty? Do you know something you should've told the sheriff?"

"I work for the sheriff, damn it. And if there'd been the slightest chance that David's death was anything but an accident, I would've jumped all over it."

"Then you know he was investigating Alana O'Toole's disappearance."

There was a moment of silence. "That's bullshit. David wasn't doing any such thing."

"You sure about that?"

"If he was, he would've mentioned it to me — not only because we were friends but because I was already working for the sheriff's department. I'm the person he would've gone to for help."

"Maybe he didn't trust you."

"What the hell are you talking about?"

Adrenaline had vanquished any sleepiness Isaac had begun to feel. He got out of bed to pace. "Either that, or he didn't have a lot of confidence in your ability, because he *was* investigating. And that's a fact."

"I don't see how you could know anything about it. You weren't even in town when he died."

But he'd heard the news and flown back to attend the funeral. The whole town had turned out on that rainy day. Isaac would never forget hovering at the edge of the cemetery, wanting to comfort Claire as she stood crying under that umbrella long after everyone had left. He hadn't let himself go anywhere close. Since he still cared about her it'd seemed too self-serving to sidle up to the grieving widow. But he hadn't been able to leave until she did. "I didn't realize you kept such close track of my whereabouts, Rusty."

"I notice you."

"Because . . ."

"Because I've never liked you much, okay? And neither did David. He knew you wanted his wife. Don't think he didn't."

Isaac could've had his wife before she married David. He was pretty sure he could have Claire now. She'd been in his bed last night, hadn't she? *Getting* her wasn't the problem; doing right by her was. There was a magnetism between them that had been there for a long time.

Maybe others could feel that chemistry, too. Maybe that was the real problem. "Is there a reason my call to Leland upset you, Rusty?"

"It's just not the kind of message I want on my answering machine when I get home after a long day. If David was murdered, I would've done something about it."

"So you've at least considered the possibility."

"No! Why would I? It was an accident, pure and simple. I was there that day, in case you've forgotten."

"And there's no way you could've gotten it wrong."

"Absolutely not! The hunter who hit him felt terrible. Can you imagine what that would be like?"

He could imagine it. Lord knew he'd made enough of his own mistakes to understand the pain of regret. But he could also imagine a scenario where someone used the cover of hunting season to commit the perfect murder. "Did anyone check the caliber of the bullet? Trace it back to that hunter's rifle?"

"Of course. We did our homework."

"What was the hunter's name? Where was he from?"

"I'm not giving you that information. He was just some guy from out of state who thought he was shooting at a bear, okay? Don't start anything and get Claire all upset. She's still recovering from David's death."

Isaac tensed as he remembered finding Claire walking along the side of the road. "If you care so much about her, why'd you leave her stranded at the Kicking Horse tonight?"

Isaac had told himself he wouldn't mention it. It was better if he and Claire kept what they felt for each other on the down low. They'd have more privacy that way. But he was angry at Rusty for being stupid enough to let her walk alone so late at night, especially after the incident at Alana's studio. Rusty was a sheriff's deputy, for Christ's sake. He, of all people, should have been more cautious.

There was another long silence. "I went back, looking for her. Spent over an hour driving up and down every street between the Kicking Horse and her place, but I couldn't find her. What, did she call you for a ride? Is that how you know?"

She *had* called him. She hadn't said anything, but he'd known it was her, even though he'd had other women contact him from the same pay phone. Hayley Peters was one of them. She called whenever she got enough alcohol in her to lower her inhibitions. But he'd been expecting to hear from Claire all evening. So he'd taken the chance it was her and not Hayley, and he'd been right. "I happened to be driving by, but I sure as hell wasn't going to leave her stranded."

Rusty cursed, sighed and cursed again. "That was a mistake. I was . . . upset. Was she okay when you found her?"

"She was fine, no thanks to you."

"I've tried to call and apologize. She won't pick up."

"I'm sure she's asleep by now." He wished that was the case. Then he could quit obsessing about her having a shower in his bathroom.

"I shouldn't have reacted like I did. Of course she wants to take things slow."

"You think she's interested in *you?*"

"Why not? I care about her."

"You have a funny way of showing it."

He bristled again. "What happened tonight is none of your business. And neither is whatever happened to David."

Isaac wasn't willing to accept that. He had confidence in Myles King; Myles was a damn good sheriff. But as far as Isaac was concerned, Rusty wasn't much of a deputy, and it was Rusty who'd been with David, not Myles. "Did you check to see if the hunter had any ties to anyone here in Pineview?"

"Why would I do that? It was an accident! Besides, who in Pineview had anything against David? And how would anyone here find, let alone hire, someone to kill for them?"

It was called the internet. Or friends of friends of friends. Montana had more than its share of gun lovers. And gun lovers had contacts regular people did not. Maybe killing for hire didn't happen often, but that didn't mean it *couldn't* happen. If someone didn't want David delving into Alana's disappearance, the chances of taking a bullet from a hired assassin were as high as getting shot by a random hunter. Rusty was letting his familiarity with this place and its people influence him too much. If whoever killed Alana — supposing she *was* killed —

felt they were about to be exposed, they could easily decide to act again.

But confronting Rusty wasn't working. Isaac decided it might be smarter to pretend he was backing off. Perhaps then Rusty would relax and lower his defenses. "Yeah, you're right. That'd be a stretch. Forget I said anything."

He hesitated. "That's it?"

"That's it. Except . . ."

"What?" He sounded leery.

"How did you know which hunter shot David? Did he come forward on his own?"

"No. He couldn't find a downed bear, thought he'd missed his shot and was leaving the area. We tracked him ourselves." Rusty was as defensive as ever, but at least he was answering a few questions — probably because he felt that being able to identify the shooter proved he was as competent at his job as he wanted to appear.

"And what'd the guy say when you found him?"

"He was shocked, said he was sorry. He'd just killed one of my best friends. What do you think he'd say?"

"Did he attend the funeral?"

"No, he felt that might be too upsetting to the community. But he sent Claire some flowers along with a hefty check to pay for

David's funeral. Said it was the least he could do."

That meant Claire knew who he was. Maybe she had his contact information. "That *is* the least he could do." And it would make his remorse seem all the more sincere.

"Now I have a question for you," Rusty said.

Isaac tensed.

"Why are you bringing this up now? I mean, it's been over a year since David died. If you thought he was investigating Alana's disappearance and that's what got him killed, why'd you wait so long to mention it?"

"I think you already know the answer to that."

"You just found out."

Isaac didn't confirm it. The truth was obvious enough.

"Does this have anything to do with what happened to Claire last night at the studio?" he asked.

"You're the sheriff's deputy. You tell me."

Isaac was done with Rusty. He wasn't going to learn any more from him, so he disconnected.

When he pivoted to return the phone to its base, he saw Claire standing in his doorway wearing one towel wrapped around her head and another around her body.

"What was that all about?" she asked, but judging by the stark expression on her face, she knew. He'd become so involved in the conversation he wasn't sure exactly when the shower had gone off or how long she'd been listening, but she'd heard enough.

Isaac shoved a hand through his hair. He should've talked to her about this when he went to her house with those files. Or gone to greater lengths to keep his suspicions a secret. This wasn't how he'd wanted the question to be raised. But now that she knew what he believed . . . there wasn't any way to take it back. "Surely you've asked yourself whether or not David's death was the accident you've been told it was."

Her knuckles whitened as she clung to the towel she held closed at her bustline. "You think Les Weaver killed him *on purpose?*"

"That was the hunter's name?" It was silly, even childish, for Rusty to refuse to answer; of course there'd be others who would know. It would've been in the papers, had Isaac been around to read them. He'd probably heard the name, just couldn't remember. At that time, he'd been trying his best to ignore the whole situation, to ignore the fact that Claire was suddenly available again.

"Yes."

"You read those files you found at the studio. Do *you* think it's possible?"

Her teeth sank into her lower lip. "I don't know. I had a plausible explanation for his death, so I focused on what those files might tell me about my *mother.* I could totally see David trying to uncover the truth for me. He was that kind of guy, so nice I can't believe anyone would want to harm him."

Isaac was feeling worse by the minute. What if he was wrong about David? He had no proof; he was the first to acknowledge that. And now, because of him, Claire had to deal with a very painful possibility, maybe for no reason at all. "I'm guessing it had nothing to do with *want.* Maybe he was getting close to information that was threatening someone. Maybe whoever it was felt forced."

"But Les was from out of town."

"A hired gun?"

She sagged against the door frame. "But . . . Weaver sent me money for the funeral expenses."

"He'd be stupid not to make it look good."

"Wouldn't the sheriff's department have checked him out?"

"They did, a little. They just didn't dig deep. Think about it. Until last summer, when we had our first murder, nothing that violent had ever happened here. Other than your mother's disappearance, which was an old mystery by the time Myles became sheriff, he hadn't dealt with any crime more serious than a speeding ticket since he took over for Sheriff Meade. On top of that, he'd lost his wife to a protracted battle with cancer, was raising his daughter on his own and adjusting to being a single father. My guess? He was taking everything at face value, expecting this place to be as safe and uncomplicated as he'd been told. Plus, David was shot so long after Alana's disappearance Myles might not have realized there could be a connection. For one thing, he doesn't seem to be aware that David was looking into her case."

"What makes you say that?"

"Rusty wasn't even aware of it."

She frowned. "Then who gave David a copy of those files?"

"I have no idea."

Fresh resolve seemed to stiffen her spine. "If someone killed David, it has to be the same someone who kidnapped my mother."

"*If* is the key word here. I could be way off base. That's why I didn't mention it to you before. Judging by what I got from those files, David wasn't only determined to get to the truth, he was pressing people for answers, revealing inconsistencies in various interviews that suggested Alana didn't leave on her own. Then everything came to a very convenient stop with his death. It seems too . . . coincidental, given his progress. But that's all I've got to go on. You understand this is merely conjecture on my part, right?"

"*Something* connects the two. I —"

His phone interrupted her, and he leaned over to check caller ID. Restricted. "It's Rusty again." What were the chances it'd be anyone else?

She leaned against the wall as he answered.

"She's there with you, isn't she," Rusty snapped.

He'd obviously been to Claire's place — and concluded that she wasn't home sleeping.

"She who?"

"Quit playing games. You know who I mean. Are you filling her head with that bullshit about David being killed just so you can get close enough to get inside her pants?"

"I think you need to hang up, Rusty. What you're asking doesn't concern you."

"David was one of my closest friends."

"And that gives you first dibs on his widow?"

"He'd rather it was me than you!"

"How do you know? Did he come to you in a dream?"

"You bastard!"

"I've never liked you much, either," he said and hung up.

Claire watched him set down the phone. "What was that all about?"

"You have a not-so-secret admirer."

"Rusty knows I'm here?"

"I think he's been over to your place a number of times tonight and realized you're not there."

She covered her face with the hand that wasn't clutching the towel.

"Would you like me to take you home?" he asked.

"No, definitely not." Dropping her hand, she looked up at him. "Especially if he's going to be hanging around my house to see if and when I return."

"I could tell him to leave you alone."

"But I wouldn't want to see what you might have to do to enforce it. And he'll have to leave me alone if I stay here. So will Leanne. I just . . . I need some sleep."

"Dry your hair," he said. "You can have

the bed."

When she came back into the room she was wearing the T-shirt he'd given her when he provided the towels. He had no idea what she had on underneath, but he spent the next two hours on the couch wondering about it.

10

Claire woke to the smell of bacon and knew that Isaac was planning to force-feed her another meal. "Don't make any for me," she yelled. "I'm not hungry!"

He opened the door and stood there, freshly showered and holding a spatula. "In case you haven't heard, breakfast is the most important meal of the day."

He was being a smart-ass. She covered a yawn. "It hasn't been that long since you fed me a steak."

One dark eyebrow arched. "Don't be rude to your host."

"I have hair clients. I have to go."

"The food will be done by the time you finish getting ready."

"I don't have anything to get ready with. I'm just going to pull on my clothes."

"And then you'll eat."

"No, then I'll leave." She gave a cocky laugh as if she'd do exactly as she pleased and started to get out of bed, but she'd underestimated his determination. Hauling her over one shoulder, he carried her out of the bedroom.

"So you *are* wearing panties," he muttered when the T-shirt floated up and he inadvertently touched her bottom.

"What does that have to do with anything?" she gasped.

"Everything."

He was flirting with her, which was something she needed to ignore. He deposited her on a chair at the kitchen table. Then he pointed his spatula at her and ordered her to remain where she was.

"Here you go," he said, delivering her plate.

She glared at the eggs, bacon and toast. "I should've gone home last night."

"You had a choice."

"I didn't know giving me a place to hide came with mandatory calorie consumption."

"I'm looking out for you. We're friends now, remember?"

She rolled her eyes. "I liked you better as a lover."

"That's not what you said before." His grin grew more meaningful. "But I sort of liked that program myself. Let me know if you ever want to go back to it."

She felt she'd probably have more of him this way. If they were merely friends he'd have no reason to throw up his defenses or block her out. If they were merely friends she wouldn't expect more of him than he was willing to give. She'd solved their dilemma . . . at last. All — friends *and* lovers — was more than he could handle. None was less than she wanted. So they were meeting in the middle. Perfect. Except for the physical craving that seemed to grow sharper with each passing moment.

She lowered her eyes before he could read what she was feeling. "I'm not *that* stupid."

"Then you can be strong for both of us," he said, and cracked another egg into his frying pan.

"Do you always cook a big breakfast — one with so much . . . animal fat?"

"Only when I have someone I need to fatten up."

She crossed her legs as she toyed with her fork. "And how often is that?"

"Actually, this a first for me."

"And if I eat like a good little girl?" she quipped.

"I'll give you a ride home so you don't miss all your appointments."

"Generous of you," she said sarcastically.

"Do I have something else you want?"

He had a lot to offer a woman, but marriage and family wasn't on the list, and she wanted both. After David, she'd never be satisfied with a casual relationship. "I'd like a copy of that hippo picture." She indicated the photograph she admired.

His eyes moved to it. "I could arrange that. Since we're friends and all." He brought his own plate to the table. "But there is one catch."

"What's that?"

"I need something from you in return."

"And that is . . ."

She was expecting him to tease her some more, but he sobered. "Les Weaver's contact information."

Nearly dropping her fork, she cleared her throat. "You're going to call him?"

"I have some questions for him, yes."

Could the man who'd sent her that money have shot David *on purpose?* "The only thing I remember is that he's from Coeur d'Alene."

"Do you have his phone number?"

"At home somewhere. I kept a copy of the check he sent just in case I ever get audited by the IRS."

"Great."

She managed to choke down a few bites

of scrambled egg while he made quick work of his own breakfast. "Isaac?"

His mouth was full so he didn't answer, but he raised his head to let her know he was listening.

"Why are you doing this?"

"Doing what?" he said after he swallowed.

"Helping me."

His eyes met hers. "Maybe I don't want you to think I'm *all* bad."

"You're joking, aren't you?" she said uncertainly. He didn't care what she or anyone else thought, and he'd done his best — for years — to make sure everyone knew it.

Taking his plate, he went to rinse it in the sink. "Yeah, I'm joking."

It was eight o'clock, early enough that Claire hoped she'd be able to slip into her house without being seen by her sister. Leanne wasn't an early riser, particularly if she'd been drinking the night before. But she was up and around today, and must've been watching through the window, because she came rolling toward Claire the minute Claire got out of Isaac's truck.

"Where've you been?" she demanded as he drove off.

Claire smoothed her clothes. She didn't

want her sister to jump to any conclusions — as unavoidable as that seemed after having been out all night. "I ran into a bit of trouble."

Eyes narrowed with suspicion and curiosity, her sister stared after Isaac's truck. Claire hoped Leanne wouldn't recognize it, but that wasn't likely. Everyone knew Isaac. Thanks to the success of his work and his reputation for being enigmatic, he was a local celebrity. And since he took his vehicle off-road so often in order to reach the remote places where he filmed, it had a lift kit, a row bar with floodlights and a giant locking tool chest that made it distinctive.

"Trouble?" Leanne echoed. "What kind of trouble? Don't tell me you've gone back to your old flame. Especially after what you said to *me* about stirring up gossip."

Ducking her head, Claire searched her purse for her house key. "No, he just . . . put me up for the night."

Leanne followed her to the door. "You're telling me you stayed with Isaac Morgan but didn't have sex with him, even for old times' sake?"

Claire wished she'd never told Leanne about Isaac, but she had. Her whole family knew he'd broken her heart and the news had traveled from there.

"I didn't sleep with him. Really." *For once . . .* Her denial would be more convincing if she reminded her sister that she was still grieving over David, that she hadn't even been willing to *date* anyone. But she'd been intimate with Isaac just the night before and felt too slimy using her love for her dead husband to support what was essentially a lie.

"That makes no sense."

"What are you talking about?"

Claire stepped back and Leanne maneuvered herself into the living room, where she wheeled around to confront Claire. "What else would he want with you?"

"Maybe he likes me, Leanne," she said evenly as she closed the door behind them. "Maybe he was being a nice, compassionate member of the community."

"Right!" Leanne added a dramatic roll of her eyes. "If I remember correctly, he was never that compassionate to you before. You haven't said much about him since you married David, but I've always gotten the impression that you don't like him . . . after what happened."

"It's not like we're enemies." She explained about going out with Rusty and how she'd been walking on the side of the road when Isaac picked her up.

"So why didn't he bring you here?"

"He said I needed to eat, but nothing was open."

"You're telling me Isaac wanted to make you *dinner?*"

It was true; he'd been set on it. But Claire wasn't sure she'd believe it if she were Leanne. "He says I'm too thin."

"Why does he care?"

Claire didn't have an answer for that. If she had to guess, she'd say he felt guilty for the way their relationship had ended. But there was no telling what Isaac thought. For one thing, it could change from day to day depending on his mood. "Who knows?"

"What about after dinner?"

Grateful for the chance to turn her back, Claire put her purse on the kitchen counter. "I dozed off on the couch while he was cleaning up, so he threw a blanket over me and let me sleep."

"That's so unlike anything I've ever heard about him," Leanne marveled. "He thinks he's too good for the rest of us. He doesn't mind using locals to get off — *you* learned that the hard way — but he'd never take anyone in Pineview seriously. We're all hicks to the *famous photographer.*"

"Thanks for the reminder, but he loves this place." He'd just told her so.

"He likes living in a remote location. That doesn't mean he likes the people here."

Claire had heard others charge Isaac with the same thing. He *could* seem arrogant. But some of that was simply a product of being so appealing. His good looks, his talent and keen mind intimidated people, made them search for some flaw in order to prove he wasn't as perfect as he seemed. And he was more than willing to expose every weakness, just to show that he didn't need their approval. "Let's . . . give him the benefit of the doubt, okay?"

"He does you one kindness after how he treated you before and now you're sticking up for him?"

Again she regretted ever letting her sister know how she'd felt about him. "I'm not sticking up for him. I'm trying to look at the whole picture. We were together a long time ago, and people change. He's . . . guarded, but don't forget he was abandoned as a little boy, then raised by Old Man Tippy, who scarcely said a word that wasn't about his beloved photography. You remember how Tippy was. It's understandable that Isaac might be unwilling — or *unable* — to get close to people."

Leanne maneuvered her chair past the couch. "Oh, come on. He gets close to people all the time. He was close to you once. And there've certainly been others who've visited his place after dark and gone home so well-ridden they can hardly walk."

The crudeness of that statement made Claire cringe. She didn't like the image it created, or how foolish it implied she'd been. But Leanne wasn't feeling the contempt she pretended to feel, at least not exclusively. Claire sensed envy, too — and the last thing she needed was for Leanne to come on to Isaac.

"He's made some mistakes, but I don't think he's as . . . bad as he once was." After she'd stopped sleeping with him, Isaac had gone from one girl to the next. Word of his "sexcapades" had spread all over town. There'd even been rumors that he was having an affair with Claudia Hampton, a rich older woman whose husband, the CEO of a Fortune 500 company, stayed in Houston most of the time she'd lived in Pineview and rarely bothered to visit.

"You're convinced he isn't a womanizer anymore? Just because he made you dinner without taking you to bed?"

Leanne didn't believe a man like Isaac was likely to change, and she was probably right. But Claire refused to concede the point.

"I'm saying we don't really know, so why judge?"

"He makes his true self impossible to miss!"

"Maybe he uses his hard-ass image to hide who he really is."

"And why would he do that?"

"It's a defense mechanism. If everyone thinks the worst of him he has no expectations to meet and no disappointment to face."

"Where did you learn that psychobabble bullshit?" she said with a laugh.

It was just something she'd been thinking about now that she was older and could look at the situation from a perspective less affected by her own unfulfilled desires. But even if she was right, understanding the reason for his sharp angles didn't make them any less capable of cutting anyone who ventured too close, and she wasn't about to forget that. "Could you lay off? What he does isn't any of our business."

"Whatever you say, as long as you realize that it doesn't matter whether or not he helped you out last night. Isaac Morgan hasn't changed as much as you want to believe. He's done everything he can to earn his reputation."

And Leanne was earning hers, which

made it ironic that she was the one pointing a finger. But Claire wasn't going to make an issue of it. Her sister had reasons for her behavior, too. "I've got to shower. My first appointment will be here in forty minutes."

"Wait a second. I came over because . . . I want to explain something before you . . . jump to the wrong conclusion."

Her halting words alerted Claire that Isaac was no longer the subject of their conversation. "I'm listening."

"What you asked me yesterday about . . . about being out of school on the day Mom went missing."

Claire stiffened. Thanks to what Tug had told her, she didn't want to discuss this. She was surprised Leanne had even brought it up. "Yes?"

"I know you've been told."

Their stepfather must've felt too guilty to keep his indiscretion to himself. Claire kneaded her forehead so she wouldn't have to look at her sister. "Is it true?"

"I had a crush on Joe, thought I was in love with him."

"That's a yes."

Silence.

Claire *had* to look at Leanne now. "He was married. And two and a half times your age. What were you thinking?"

"I wasn't thinking. I was *thirteen,* okay?"

"But . . . how did you even get hold of a video camera?"

"I borrowed Mom's. Dad had just given it to her for Christmas, remember, and I was using it for a school project at the time. I'm embarrassed, and I have been for years, but . . . there's more to what happened than my stupid mistake. That's the part you need to hear if you want to find Mom."

A chill ran up Claire's spine. "Tell me."

"Mom *was* having an affair with Joe."

Claire curved her fingernails into her palms. "No."

"Yes!"

"What makes you so sure?"

"That's why she freaked out. She considered him *her* man, her guilty pleasure, and was afraid he'd been messing around with *both* of us. So the confrontation at his place involved as much accusation as anything else. That's why he showed her the tape. So he could blame it all on me."

Claire grappled to understand how such a situation might have played out. "She thought he acted on your . . . overtures?"

"Worse. He exposed himself to me first."

Remembering how charitable she'd been feeling toward Joe at the bar, Claire stepped back. "You've got to be kidding me."

"No. We'd been flirting for weeks. A thirteen-year-old girl doesn't do something that bold out of the blue, without some expectation that it'll be welcomed."

That made sense, but . . . "Mom wouldn't believe it?"

"Of course not. Not after that tape."

Claire shook her head. "I can't believe what you're saying, either."

Leanne's jaw dropped. "What part of it?"

"All of it. That he came on to you. That you and he had a relationship. That Mom was jealous instead of hurt and sickened by what you'd done."

"You don't trust me? Just because I didn't want to tell you I masturbated on video for a man I thought I loved?"

Squeezing her eyes shut, Claire pressed cold hands to her hot face. "I'm saying you've been keeping secrets about that day for a long time. How do I know even *this* is the full truth?"

"Because I don't have anything to hide anymore! I've told you the worst of it!"

But she wasn't as embarrassed as she should've been. She was almost . . . defiant or . . . or proud in some perverse way. As if she thought it was some kind of feather in her cap that she could interest a married man at such a young age — or compete with her own mother. "You're reacting to the rumors, that's all. Maybe you're projecting. It's easy to tell yourself you have no reason to feel bad for what you've done when someone else has misbehaved, too."

At that, Leanne started to laugh. "I saw the way they were together that day, the way his eyes followed her around the room, the way he tried to touch her. It wasn't how you'd expect an acquaintance to behave."

"She was probably heartbroken to think her young daughter would make a pornographic video, and he was trying to comfort her."

Leanne threw up her hands. "This is a waste of time. You see Mom through rose-colored glasses and no amount of reality will change your mind."

"Where is the video?" Maybe there was something on that, something Leanne had said or done to preface her actions that would clarify the situation. It wasn't what Claire *wanted* to view and yet she couldn't judge what Leanne was thinking back then without seeing at least the beginning.

"Mom destroyed it. She ripped out the tape, then set fire to it in our fireplace."

Claire was down to twenty minutes before her first haircut showed up, but she couldn't pull herself away. "Why are you telling me now?"

"Because you need to understand that Mom *left.* Remember when they searched the house and discovered a suitcase was missing? Where do you suppose it went?"

Who could say? Claire had always feared it'd been used to dispose of her mother's body. Alana hadn't taken a damn thing. She hadn't even packed. None of her clothes were missing, none of her toiletries. And her car had been sitting in the drive, the engine cold. "If she'd been carrying a suitcase, someone would've noticed her walking down the street. A woman toting luggage isn't a sight you see every day, especially in a community as small as this one."

"She could've had a friend pick her up at the house."

"What friend, Leanne? If she was having an affair with Joe, why would she leave with someone else?"

"Because he wouldn't sacrifice his marriage for their love — or whatever it was. Mom was as upset about that as she was about the video."

The person Leanne described wasn't the person Claire had known as her mother. "So how would she have met this other . . .

friend?"

"Maybe it was an old boyfriend, a high school sweetheart from California."

Where she was born and raised until her parents moved to Pineview her senior year to enjoy their retirement. "And how would they have kept in touch, become close enough to decide they'd run away together?"

"By email. How else?"

Claire shook her head. "No, not by email. The police checked our computer. Mom had written to some old friends, but there was nothing questionable in that correspondence."

"Our sheriff's department isn't the most sophisticated in the world, in case you haven't noticed. And that was fourteen years ago, before forensic science was as advanced as it is today. Who knows what they might've missed?"

"Still, she would've mentioned *someone,* and she didn't."

"We were kids! Do you think she'd tell us?"

Was that what she thought? Human beings were complex, often reacting differently depending on circumstances. And Claire was only sixteen at the time, caught up in all the typical teenage drama. Was it feasible that her mother had been far less happy than she'd assumed? Had Alana grown disenchanted with her marriage and begun to cast around for something more fulfilling? Did she get involved with Joe Kenyon and then realize, when everything came to a head because of Leanne's shocking video, that she had no hope for happiness there, either? Had she kept in touch with someone from her past and thrown away everything she'd established in Montana to return to California?

Claire knew Alana had missed her home state. She'd liked to visit there, especially after her parents, tired of the cold winters, moved back, but . . .

"Dad would've known if there was someone else," she said. "And he would've told the police. He never accused her. It was other people, with no proof. Some of them didn't even know her well."

"Maybe he didn't reveal everything he could because he didn't want to hurt us by tarnishing her memory."

The way Leanne was doing now. "That would hardly help bring her back."

"Maybe he didn't want her to be found. Maybe he was relieved she left."

That statement hit Claire like a splash of cold water in the face. She'd considered the possibility that her stepfather might not have been as upset as he'd seemed. She couldn't question whether he might be culpable of Alana's murder and not examine the likelihood of insincerity. But even if he wasn't the person who'd harmed Alana, had he been glad to have her gone?

Tug had acted distraught, but Roni moved in with them less than six months later. And by then he and Roni were so far along in their relationship Claire sometimes wondered if they might've been involved before — not that she'd ever let herself fully embrace that suspicion.

"With Mom gone, he didn't have to worry about losing us," Leanne said.

"So now you're blaming Dad? Are you suggesting he killed her?"

"Of course not!"

"But why would he want *us?* We aren't even his children."

It was Leanne's turn to be shocked. "You know how much he loves us. He's always loved us. We were part of the reason he wanted to marry Mom. He tells that to everyone. And it wasn't as if he had any competition from our real dad, who didn't even put up a fight when he adopted us."

Was it all about love? Or was it more about making do because he couldn't have children of his own? Claire wasn't positive he was infertile. He'd never spoken of it. But he'd never fathered a child, either, even with his first wife. And Claire was pretty sure her mother had once mentioned, on the phone with Grandma Pierce, that she thought he was sterile. Claire had walked in on the middle of the conversation and been curious about it, but her mother had changed the subject and shushed her when she tried to confirm what she'd heard.

"Mom was gone, so not only could he keep us, he was free to be with whoever he wanted without a nasty divorce," Leanne said. "And he'd inherit everything Mom had just received from Grandma and Grandpa Pierce. It was the perfect setup for a man who loved us but no longer loved her."

Leanne had never approached the subject from this angle before. Claire had no idea why she was doing it now. Was it revenge for what Tug had finally revealed about that tape? "We can't know how Dad feels. Only he knows that. But we can look at the facts. A suitcase was missing but nothing else. Where would Mom go with an empty suitcase?"

"She could've filled it with brand-new clothes for her brand-new life."

"She didn't use her debit card, or any

credit cards, after she went missing."

"Of course not. They'd be too easy to trace. But she might've had cash. She and her sister had just split four and a half million dollars. Who knows how much she hid away?"

The money had changed a lot of things in their lives — or promised to. They didn't have it for very long before Alana went missing. For nearly twenty years, Tug had worked at Walt Goodman's gun store and Alana had clerked part-time at the Stop 'n' Shop. She sold some of her artwork, which helped, too, but not for much money. She hadn't yet fulfilled her dream of making her mark on the art world. They'd lived hand to mouth — until Grandma and Grandpa Pierce died.

Maybe some of what Leanne said was plausible, but Claire couldn't accept that Alana had left them. She couldn't accept that Alana had left her only sister, either. Claire would never forget standing at the grave of her cousin, Aunt Jodi's son, who'd drowned while surfing off the coast of Maui. She'd repeatedly scanned the cemetery for anyone who might look like her mother. That was the day she'd known without a doubt that Alana hadn't left voluntarily. She wouldn't have missed Chris's funeral.

"What do you have to hide, Lee?" Claire whispered. "There's more than you're saying, despite everything you've told me about that pornographic video. I can't figure out what it is, but . . . it's not that Mom was having an affair with the married man you were trying to tempt. There's something else."

The blood drained from her sister's face. "You're crazy. I'm not hiding anything. I just don't want you to accuse someone and realize later that you were wrong."

"Why? Because you think I might accuse *you?* Is that where you're afraid my search will lead me?"

"No!" she cried, but she'd already turned to the door. "I was thirteen, Claire. I don't know how you can even ask me that."

Neither did Claire. But she'd never guessed her younger sister would set her sights on a married man while she was still in junior high. Or be aggressive enough to make a sex tape for him. Or entertain all the eligible men in town now that she was an adult. Was the one person she believed she knew best actually someone she didn't know at all?

"Did you hurt her, Lee?" she called.

Did she even want an answer? What if Leanne said yes? Wasn't a life spent in a wheelchair punishment enough for anything? If it was Leanne who'd hurt Alana, she must've acted in anger, and Tug must've helped hide the evidence. Claire couldn't imagine any other interpretation. Leanne wouldn't, couldn't, harm those who were closest to her in a *calculated* way. She wasn't like the psychopaths Claire had studied in her quest for answers, wasn't so narcissistic as to be completely indifferent to the pain of others.

Or was she? She was certainly smart enough to mimic true emotion. Was there a killer behind the mask of her pretty face?

The very idea made Claire shudder. No. That would mean she'd faked other things, as well — such as the love she professed to feel for Tug, Roni, even Claire.

Leanne stopped when she reached the porch. "Quit being ridiculous," she said, and it was a comfort to hear her state it so emphatically. "I should've known you wouldn't be able to see the truth. It doesn't matter how much time goes by, you're as stubbornly ignorant as ever."

Stubbornly ignorant, or doggedly determined to reveal facts Leanne desperately wanted to keep hidden? "I'm going to find out, Lee," Claire said softly. "Whatever it is, I'm going to find out."

The slam of the screen door was her only answer.

11

Claire had called Isaac with the address on Les Weaver's check not long after he'd returned home from dropping her off. But it was only a P.O. box. Isaac had to use Weaver's phone number and a reverse directory to come up with a physical address.

Now he wondered if he had the right place. The man who answered his knock lived in a rambling Mediterranean-style home located in an exclusive community, and he wore a tailored suit, which was a far cry from what Isaac had expected him to be wearing. Hunters could be all sorts of people — professionals in their day jobs — but this guy didn't have the ruddy countenance or work-roughened hands Isaac usually saw on experienced outdoorsmen. Lean and angular, with dark hair gelled off his face, he looked about forty years old and seemed far too sophisticated to have made such a terrible mistake.

"Mr. Weaver?"

He held a set of keys in his left hand, which also sported a wedding band with a large diamond. Isaac guessed he'd caught Weaver just as he was about to leave. "Yes?"

"*Les* Weaver?"

His knuckles whitened on the door as if he was tempted to slam it. "Yes. Who are you?"

"Isaac Morgan. From Montana." He thrust out his hand, but Weaver didn't shake it.

"You're a long way from home, Mr. Morgan. What can I do for you?"

Isaac thought the mere mention of his home state might cause a visible reaction, considering Weaver had killed a man there, but other than a subtle tightening in the muscles of his face and his refusal to shake, he didn't let on that he had any bad memories of the place.

Dropping his hand, Isaac stepped back and gazed around. "Nice house."

"Thanks. I think. You still haven't told me what you want."

"I was wondering if I could speak to you about what happened in the Cabinet Mountains a year ago."

Weaver studied Isaac without any visible change in expression. "Are you with the sheriff's office?"

"No, I'm a P.I. hired by Mr. O'Toole's wife."

His eyes slid to Isaac's truck, which didn't make Isaac look any more like a private investigator than this man's suit made him look like a hunter. "Do you have a card?"

Isaac wished he'd thought to create some sort of proof to substantiate the lie. But he hadn't planned that far ahead. As soon as he had an address, he'd taken off. It wasn't until he saw who he'd be dealing with that he realized he needed to approach Weaver in a professional capacity if he expected this to go anywhere. Weaver was the kind of man who'd respect nothing less. "Not on me. But I'm sure there's one in the truck. I'll go —"

"I'm in a bit of a hurry." He glanced over his shoulder as though he was afraid someone might overhear. "Just tell me why you're here. Why would Mrs. O'Toole hire a private investigator?"

"Some evidence that's recently come to light suggests her husband's death wasn't so much an accident as murder."

He paled. "What evidence?"

He was growing agitated beneath that calm exterior, but even a man who'd shot someone by accident wouldn't be happy to hear this. "I'm not at liberty to say."

"That death couldn't have been a murder."

"Why not?"

"Because I shot him myself, and it was definitely an accident. The police know all this. I've already spoken to them."

"Les? Is it for me?" a female voice called.

"No, I've got it, honey," he called back.

Isaac went on as if they hadn't been interrupted. "They're considering reopening the case, so you'll probably be hearing from them."

"Oh, God." He raked a hand through his hair, messing up that perfect lift at his forehead. "I don't know what more I can say. I saw movement. I thought it was the bear I'd been tracking, and I took a shot. That was the worst decision of my life."

His remorse sounded sincere enough that Isaac felt a little foolish for doubting him. If Weaver was as innocent as he claimed, Isaac had no desire to make his life more difficult. This man's education, manner of dress and home lent him credibility. He wasn't some thug, as Isaac had imagined.

Isaac almost apologized and left. But he figured he might as well finish the interview. "You were alone when it happened, is that correct?"

"Yes. The sheriff who questioned me knows I was."

"Do you often go hunting alone?"

"I used to. That was how I cleared my head."

"What made you choose the Cabinet Mountains?"

"They're relatively close, and I'd heard they have a lot of game."

"You don't have friends in Pineview?"

"No."

"Do you know anyone in the area?"

"Not a soul. That was the first time I'd ever been to that part of Montana, and I haven't been back since."

"But you still hunt?"

He stretched his neck. "No. Are you kidding? I'm done with it. I'm sure you can understand why. Shortly after that . . . unfortunate event, I got rid of all my guns. I don't even want to see one, let alone fire it." He added a rueful laugh that sounded as believable as the rest of his admission.

"I'm guessing guns don't play much of a role in your day job." Isaac indicated his attire.

A wry smile curved his lips as he brushed some lint from his suit. "No. That last incident didn't have anything to do with me. Not directly."

Isaac had all but decided he'd made a wasted trip. Until now. "That *last* incident?"

He grimaced. "I'm a bankruptcy attorney. Not long ago I had a client shoot himself in my office. It's tough to lose everything, you know? BK really hits some people hard." He looked confused. "I assumed that's what started this up again. His wife refuses to believe he was suicidal, so she's been digging around in my past, trying to cause me trouble. But I couldn't have saved her husband. It happened too fast." Bowing his head, he muttered, "It was terrible."

"I can only imagine."

"Now you know why I don't want to see this old . . . hunting nightmare crop up again," he said as he straightened. "David O'Toole's death was my fault, but I didn't mean to kill him. I swear it."

"Les, you ready?" the same female voice called out.

Isaac caught a glimpse of a woman through the railing of a winding staircase.

"I've already got the keys," he told her. Then he lowered his voice. "We've got a luncheon today. We raise money for autistic kids and we're going to meet with the board of our charity. So if you have any other questions, maybe you can visit me at my office? I really don't want to upset my wife.

Both tragedies have affected her as deeply as they have me."

"Of course." Isaac took the business card Weaver presented him and stepped away. *Les S. Weaver, Attorney at Law,* he read as the door closed.

Isaac was still sitting in his truck with the engine idling, staring at the embossed lettering and thinking about a guy who raised money for autistic kids but was also, in one way or another, involved in two highly unlikely deaths, when the garage door opened. Weaver and an attractive blonde rolled down the driveway in a black Mercedes. Isaac watched to see if he'd look up or wave, but he acted as if Isaac wasn't sitting at the curb and drove off.

With a frown, Isaac put the transmission in gear and gave the truck some gas, but then he circled back. It couldn't hurt to have a quick look around while the Weavers were gone, just to make sure Les was as honest as he sounded.

It didn't take much effort. What he could see through the back window convinced him he hadn't been wrong to drive down here, after all.

Claire's stepfather came in to get his hair cut as she was finishing up for the day.

Considering how rocky things were between her and Leanne, she wasn't sure if he really needed his hair trimmed — he was a bit obsessive about his appearance, but it hadn't been that long since she'd done it — or he wanted to talk. She couldn't remember a time when her stepfather hadn't tried to smooth over any problem Leanne had. He'd always championed the baby of the family, even before the accident.

Usually Claire didn't mind. Today, however, the idea that he might try to squeeze an apology out of her got on her nerves. No one felt worse about her sister's loss of mobility than Claire. But Leanne had to be held accountable for her actions, just like anybody else. They were doing her no favors by making excuses for her every time she acted out.

"Is something wrong?" she asked as she used her spray bottle.

Pensive, he watched her in the mirror, and she realized how quickly he seemed to be aging these days. He'd been three years younger than her mother when they married, but at fifty-six, the lines around his eyes and mouth were more pronounced. "Just wanted to let you know I told Leanne about our last conversation."

"You mean the one where you explained

the tape."

Wanda Fitzgerald, Claire's last client, sat under the hair dryer, reading a magazine. Tug glanced over at her as if he feared she might be listening, saw that she was preoccupied and murmured, "Yes."

Because of what Leanne had said earlier, Claire already knew he'd confessed to revealing her indiscretion as a thirteen-year-old. "Is that the reason you're here?"

"That and a haircut."

Or he didn't want to address what was on his mind while others were present. Claire didn't want to address what was on hers, either. Since her conversation with Isaac, she couldn't stop thinking about the possibility that David had been murdered.

She rinsed and styled Wanda's hair as her father swept up his own trimmings.

"Have you ever confronted Joe about Mom?" she asked once they were alone.

With what sounded like a heartfelt sigh, Tug leaned on the broom while she put the checks she'd received into a deposit bag.

"Yes."

Again, Claire sensed a certain amount of resignation, which was a change from before. "And?"

"He claims they weren't intimate."

"But?"

"I think they were."

No longer interested in the mundane details of finishing up work, Claire dropped the deposit bag onto her desk. "You told me yourself that wasn't the case. You said, 'It wasn't your mother who was involved with Joe.' Now you're saying the opposite? That you believe Mom was cheating on you?"

He nodded.

"Why? And why didn't you say so before?"

"I didn't want to acknowledge that she might not have been as happy with me as I hoped she was."

Several heartbeats passed before Claire could speak again. "But you and Joe are friends. He does the tree work on every property you own."

"He lost someone he loved, too. And he's always protected her memory. I respect that. I respect that he's kept his mouth shut about what Leanne did, too."

"So what makes you think they were . . . involved?"

"A lot of . . . little things, really."

"Like . . ."

"She was very quiet, even secretive, in the months leading up to her disappearance."

Claire couldn't remember any of that. According to the police report, Alana and Tug had gone out for doughnuts and coffee the morning of the day in question. That certainly sounded amiable. "Are you sure this is something you noticed *before* she went missing and not a way to make losing her easier?"

Considering everything that had been said about Alana's visits to Joe's house, Claire could understand how Tug might struggle to maintain faith in Alana's fidelity. Claire thought maybe his opinion had changed over the years, fallen more in line with what others believed in order to alleviate his guilt for moving on so quickly and completely.

"I'm sure. There were . . . other signs, too. She'd been taking birth control pills, something we never bothered with, since we wanted another child. I found the package in the false bottom of her jewelry box a week before she disappeared."

"Where is it now?"

"Gone. I was so angry, I threw it away the day I confronted her about it."

Given what Claire had heard her mother say about Tug's inability to father a child, this made no sense. He'd obviously been hoping lightning would strike, because he certainly didn't admit — or perhaps accept — his inability to father a child. She was tempted to mention overhearing that conversation, but she feared Tug would take it as further proof that Alana had been cheating. If she really believed he *couldn't* impregnate her, why would she need birth control?

"You were forty-one when you married Roni. She was thirty-seven. Why didn't you have a baby with her?" As far as Claire knew, they hadn't even tried. They definitely hadn't visited a fertility specialist. That would've required trips to Libby, Kalispell or somewhere else that had a specialist.

He still didn't admit it. "Roni had already raised four children for her ex-husband, three of whom have never treated her very well. They couldn't get over the fact that she'd replaced their mother and blamed her for the divorce."

They also accused her of being too controlling, too strict. The three Tug referred to wouldn't even speak to her, including the one living in Pineview who was close to Claire's age. Fortunately, Roni had softened by the time she'd become her and Leanne's stepmother.

"She wasn't ready to start over with a new baby," her father was saying. "Not only that, but your mother had recently gone missing. You two were so hurt and confused. It didn't seem like the best time to bring another child into the family."

Claire tucked her hair behind her ears. It was only five o'clock, but it'd been a long day. "I don't understand. First you tell me about the video, a secret you've kept hidden for fifteen years —"

"I kept it hidden because it has no bearing on the case and — and I didn't want to make your sister look bad."

"How do you know it has no bearing on the case? It could make a huge difference in how the police interpret certain events. Then you come here to admit you think Mom was unfaithful?"

He hung his head. "I know how unreliable I must seem. Roni has always said you and Leanne need me to be consistent more than you need to hear my doubts. So I've stuck to my story. To be honest, I haven't wanted to face the possibilities that come up when I veer away from it. But that incident at the cabin, when you could've been hurt much worse than you were, is making me rethink my approach. If there's someone out there who hurt your mother, we need to know why and whether that person poses a risk to you and Leanne." He put the broom in the closet. "Some days I'm convinced Alana loved me. Others, I'm convinced she didn't."

The buzzer sounded. "You couldn't have

left me a note?" Roni said to her husband as she walked in. "I've been searching all over town for you."

Tug cleared his throat and gave Claire a look that said the conversation was over. "Sorry, I didn't expect you back until later."

The only stepdaughter from her previous marriage still on speaking terms with Roni was divorced with a child of her own. Roni visited them on occasion in Kalispell. Usually Tug went with her because she didn't like the drive. Claire wasn't sure why he hadn't gone this time.

"Little Ashley had ballet lessons, so I didn't stay long."

Suddenly eager to go, Tug dropped a kiss on Claire's forehead and started toward the door. "Did Liz say how her siblings are doing?" he asked Roni.

"I didn't ask," Roni replied. "You know those kids aren't worth a damn. They don't deserve our concern."

An awkward silence followed this harsh declaration, but Claire wasn't surprised by what Roni had said. She'd heard her stepmother make statements like that before. Roni didn't seem to care that it made her look as bad as them. "You must be feeling better," she said, sizing up her husband.

Tug nodded. "Yeah, I am."

Claire caught him before he could open the door. "You've been sick?"

He wouldn't meet her eyes. "Woke up a bit off, that's all."

She'd just been thinking about how quickly he was aging. Could there be something more serious going on? "I'm sorry. I hope . . . I hope it doesn't have any connection with what I'm doing."

"No."

"You're sure?" She gave him a hug. She loved Roni, respected her for being consistent and responsible and, on the whole, a kind enough stepmother. But she'd always been somewhat perfunctory. It was Claire's stepfather who held the biggest piece of her heart, and she knew Leanne felt the same.

"Don't worry about me."

It wasn't until she stepped back that she noticed the strange expression on Roni's face.

"What is it?" her stepmother demanded, glancing between them. "What's going on?"

She didn't know? Claire would've explained, but she had the feeling her father might be in trouble for not mentioning it himself. Roni could be authoritative and opinionated, and upsetting her was never a pleasant experience.

Claire hesitated, letting Tug respond.

"Nothing new." He reached for the door handle, but Roni stopped him.

"What is it?" she repeated. "What aren't you telling me?"

Tug's lips thinned. It was the first time Claire had ever seen him show displeasure at Roni's behavior. Normally he took whatever she said with a patient and loving smile. Was there some friction in their marriage after all? "Claire's researching her mother's disappearance again."

Roni turned to confront Claire. "Is this true?"

"I've never really quit looking," Claire said. "Sometimes I get discouraged and tread water for a while. And with David's death I've been pretty preoccupied. But . . . the need to find out what happened never leaves me. It's as strong now as ever."

"What more can you do?" she asked. "Even the sheriff's given up."

"He and his deputies don't have the same level of personal interest I do."

Lines, deeper than she'd seen before, appeared on Roni's forehead, showing how much she'd aged, too. "What about Leanne?"

Was she about to hear all the reasons she should, once again, put her sister's needs and desires first? "What about her?"

Roni looked at Tug. When he didn't speak, she continued herself. "This can't be good for her. She's dealing with enough anger and . . . and other emotional challenges without dredging up the second-most hurtful experience of her life."

"Her handicap has nothing to do with this."

"It's something you should take into account. We don't live in a vacuum. She's drinking now. You know that, don't you?"

"She's been drinking for a while. And she should want the truth as badly as I do. Maybe once she has some answers, she can let go of her anger. Our mom didn't leave us."

"That's just as possible as any other scenario," Roni said. "But more to the point — when will enough be enough? When will you accept what is and move on with your life?"

Claire thought of the files she'd found and what they could signify about David's death. She knew she shouldn't say anything about that. Not yet. She needed to substantiate her suspicions first. But her stepmother was accusing her of making their lives miserable without having even the remotest chance of learning anything new. "When I'm satisfied that I've done all I can."

"I think you've reached that place."

"No." Claire shook her head. "David found more. If he can do it, so can I."

Roni's purse slid down to her hand. "What are you talking about?"

"David picked up where the police left off. He was doing his own investigation when he was killed. I'm wondering if there's a connection between that and his death."

Tug blinked at her in surprise. "You can't mean —"

"Yes, I can. I'm saying maybe his death wasn't an accident."

"But . . . but that's crazy!" Roni sputtered. "It *was* an accident. Everyone knows that."

"*I* don't," she said. "Not anymore."

"Then you're kidding yourself. You're looking for someone to blame and sometimes there is no one. Think about Leanne's accident. You'd both been down that mountain before. But on *this* occasion, she was going too fast when she hit the bottom. No one was responsible. It just . . . happened."

Why was Roni bringing up the sledding accident? Just to make the sharp edge of guilt cut a little deeper? Claire had been there that day. Why wasn't she the one thrown from a sled? "Someone doesn't simply disappear."

"No, but they can walk off without an

explanation. And hunting accidents aren't completely unheard of."

Her mother hadn't walked off. And David hadn't been killed by a hunter who mistook him for a bear. The more she thought about the possibilities, the more Claire believed the two incidents were related. It made a dark sort of sense. Especially because she wasn't the only one to see a connection. Isaac had raised the possibility first. Not that she planned to mention that.

"Who'd want to harm David?" her father asked, his voice hoarse with shock and concern.

Claire never took her eyes off Roni. "The same person who killed my mother, chopped her up and put her in her own suitcase."

"That's sick." Tug looked green, but Roni didn't. Face red, eyes shiny, she stuck a finger in Claire's chest.

"You're just trying to upset us. You're trying to upset everyone. Why would you paint such a morbid picture for your father? You're talking about a woman who was once his wife."

"You're worried about *me* upsetting *him?* My mother's been missing for fifteen years. I'm sure he's imagined just about every scenario by now, including that one."

"Maybe *she's* not what's in that case!"

"Then what is?"

Roni was blinking and breathing faster than normal. "Listen, Claire. You need to stop. We're happy the way we are. We don't want you messing that up."

Claire's blood seemed to roar through her ears. "I'm ruining your happiness because I want to find my mother? Because I won't forget about her like you want me to? Because I won't pretend you were with us all along instead of her?"

"Claire, please, this isn't helping." Tug tried to put a hand on her shoulder but she moved out of reach.

"It's too late," Roni went on. "What don't you understand? She's gone, and there's nothing you can do about that. God, you're as bad as my other stepkids!"

A warning flashed in Claire's mind, but she was too frazzled and angry to heed it. Over the years, she'd had very few serious arguments with her stepmother. It was easier to tolerate the minor irritations that cropped up than to deal with the aftermath of an argument. Roni was basically a good woman. And Claire cared enough about her father to bite her tongue before offending his wife. But she couldn't seem to manage that today. "Because I'm not giving in to what you want? Because I'm insisting on the truth even though you wish I wouldn't?"

"Because you don't know when you're crossing the line!"

"Were you seeing my father before my mother disappeared?" Claire screamed.

Roni's jaw dropped. *"What?"*

Claire covered her mouth. She was screwing up all over the place, accusing everyone. She'd be friendless before this was over, but she couldn't seem to hold in her doubts and questions anymore. "You two were together within six months of my mother's disappearance."

"So? What does that tell you? Now you think *I* killed her? Do you trust *anyone?*"

"No," Claire said softly, "I don't." And there it was. What she'd hidden for as many years as her mother had been missing. She harbored some suspicion toward her stepfather *and* his wife. And since she'd learned about Leanne's being out of school on the day Alana went missing, she even wondered about her sister.

12

The call came in just after dark.

Jeremy stood at the bottom of the stairs, listening to his father talk. He eavesdropped a lot; sometimes it was his only way of knowing what was going to happen before it did.

He didn't care much about this conversation, though. It was just about someone showing up unexpectedly, some private investigator. But no private investigator had shown up here, and that was what mattered.

Yawning, he nearly walked back into his room to listen to his music. When the iPod he'd saved up for was playing in his ears, his father ceased to exist. But before he could turn away, he heard anger in his father's voice — and the name Les. Then he froze. He knew who Les was. His father had found Les through a cousin who lived in Wyoming. Cousin Blake got himself in trouble a lot. He'd even been in prison —

twice. He'd said Les was a person who could "take care of anything." Jeremy had heard his father use those exact words when he arranged for Les to "take care" of David. And then David died and everyone started calling it an accident. That was how good Les was. His father even said he was good, said it out loud as if he'd included Jeremy in his plans from the beginning. His father was like that sometimes.

Claire's name came up next. He'd been right to be so worried these past few days. She was getting herself in trouble, just like he'd feared when he followed her to the cabin. If Les was coming back to Pineview, that was bad. His father had once said to Les, "How many people have you . . . helped the way you're helping me?" And the answer must've been big because his father had whistled.

Jeremy wanted to warn her, but he couldn't. She'd ask how he knew, and that was something he couldn't ever reveal.

His father slammed down the phone. The floor creaked, keys jingled, the garage door opened and the Jeep engine roared to life.

Where was his father going? Not to hurt Claire . . .

Wringing his hands, Jeremy paced in the laundry area for several minutes while images — terrible images — crowded his head. His father wouldn't act right away, would he? Someone might see or tell. He'd wait for Les, and Les lived someplace called Idaho that sounded far away.

Again, Jeremy wanted to go to Claire. Instead, he grabbed his flashlight and hurried to the crawl space under the stairs. He hadn't been in there for years, not since he'd attached six padlocks to be sure nothing could get in or out. The dank smell and spiderwebs alone were enough to keep him from wanting to return. But maybe it was time to check on the situation under there. He'd known he would probably need to make changes at some point. That was what kept him up so often at night.

He never forgot a number, so he had no problem with the combinations for the locks. But the five-foot space was far too short for him, and it grew more cramped as he neared the outer edges. Where the dirt had been thrown up against the foundation, he had to crawl.

The scent of the moist earth filled his nostrils. He imagined another smell, one that made him gag, but he kept going and before long, he sat on his haunches, aiming his flashlight at the dusty suitcase he'd hidden there fifteen years earlier. It was worn on one side, completely scraped from when he'd had to drag it up the driveway. It'd been a cheap case to begin with, one without wheels, which had made his job harder. He could really have used some wheels. . . .

His heart slammed against his rib cage — *ba-bump . . . ba-bump* — which happened whenever he thought of the crawl space because then he remembered the night it all happened. How weak he'd felt when he brought that suitcase here. How badly he'd been shaking and sweating. He'd vomited after he got to his room. The *contents* of the suitcase — he couldn't bear to think of what was inside in any other way — had been so much heavier than he'd expected. Then there was the disgusting liquid that'd begun to leak out. He'd thought the trail it left behind would lead anyone who chose to look right to him.

But the storm had washed it away. Big fat raindrops had started to fall just when he was certain he'd be caught. The wind had even concealed his grunts and labored breathing. It was almost as if he'd been invisible — not that anyone would be able to overhear him, anyway. He and his father lived in the woods.

Absently, Jeremy rubbed his stomach, which was cramping as if this night was that night, and studied what was left of the case. If he had to move it, he supposed it wouldn't be heavy anymore. Things changed with time. He'd seen proof on TV.

It'd been a decade and a half — he heard that often, whenever anyone spoke of Alana. What would he find if he unzipped the lid?

Don't think about that! You'll be sick again.

Maybe he should get a shovel. He hadn't before because he'd wanted that suitcase to be easy to reach if he ever had to retrieve it. Besides, any sign of freshly disturbed dirt could give away its location if the police ever came to call. They looked for that type of thing. One program he'd watched showed them using a ground sensor to locate a dead body that'd been buried for several years.

The idea of the police coming into the crawl space, with or without such a device, made it difficult to breathe. He didn't want to go to prison. His father had told him what would happen if he ended up there.

There are hundreds of men ready to rape you in the ass, little buddy. And that's after they knock your stupid block off.

Jeremy covered his ears, but the words were still there, humming in his brain. He couldn't avoid them. Probably because, with Claire causing trouble the way David had caused trouble, he had to do *something.* If the sheriff came to their door, he had to be ready. . . .

The taste of blood made him realize he was biting his lip. *Too hard. Ease up.* He'd think of something. His father wouldn't be happy to learn the suitcase was on the property. But Jeremy hadn't been able to abandon it in the woods as he'd been told. A bear might get to it.

If he buried it, he'd bury it here, where no one would stumble on it. Then it would be safe but gone.

Unless the police brought in a ground sensor . . .

Jeremy began to rock back and forth. What to do? What to do? It was always so hard to decide. . . .

Dropping his head, he rubbed his eyes. His cheeks were wet. When had he started crying? Grown men didn't cry. Nothing made his father angrier.

What a pussy! What'd I ever do to deserve a son like you?

"Shut up, Dad!" His voice was vehement, but only because his father wasn't around. He'd never dare say that to his face. The hitting would start if he did.

Maybe the suitcase should continue to wait right where it was. Knowing his father, there might soon be *another* thing to hide.

Jeremy grimaced. If only he could stop that . . .

But he couldn't. Not unless he wanted those men in prison to knock his block off.

The phone rang and rang, but Claire wouldn't answer. She couldn't trust herself to speak to anybody tonight. There was no predicting what she might say. She'd already argued with her sister, her stepmother and her stepfather. She didn't want to alienate anyone else.

But it wasn't her family who kept calling. They were so angry she wasn't convinced they'd ever bother with her again. It was Isaac. She could see his name lit up by caller ID, and couldn't bring herself to answer. Why was she letting their paths cross again? *He* was the one she couldn't trust, wasn't he?

"Go away." She threw her extra pillow at the phone, knocking it off the hook. She could hear him saying, "Claire? Claire, are you there?"

No, she wasn't. Not completely. Or she wouldn't be going around hurting everyone close to her.

Now you think I *killed her? Do you trust* anyone?

No, I don't . . .

Those ungrateful words plagued her long after Isaac's voice went silent. The beeping that started after he hung up finally ended, too. Then there was nothing except blessed silence. . . .

The whine of a chain saw intruded, blasting her eardrums. Claire couldn't hear her own voice above the noise, but that didn't stop her from screaming as blood spurted onto her face, making it impossible to draw breath.

Her mother's suitcase lay open on the ground nearby with a severed arm and a leg inside. As she watched, Alana's head fell, creating a splash in the growing pool of blood as Claire fought with the person doing the cutting, whose identity switched among Leanne, who could miraculously walk, Roni and Tug.

"No! Stop pleeeeease!" she cried, but the words were drowned out by the *rrrr . . . rrrrrrr . . . rr . . . rrrr.*

Claire was trying to keep Leanne from turning the chain saw on *her* when a knock at the door startled her awake.

Drenched in sweat and gasping for breath, she lay staring at the ceiling until she realized she was safe in bed and had all her body parts. Based on the amount of time that had passed since she'd last looked, she hadn't been sleeping long. The clock showed barely thirty minutes.

Still, she was glad to be disturbed, glad to be released from the clutches of that terrible nightmare. She'd been sobbing and thrashing about while struggling to stop the chain saw.

"Congratulations. You escaped," she muttered. But her mother hadn't. Alana was as gone as ever.

Wiping away the tears that'd rolled into her hair, Claire told herself to calm down. She'd had this dream before. It'd just never been as vivid. And she'd never been able to identify the person wielding the saw.

"Claire?"

Isaac called to her from the front stoop. But she didn't want him to know she was so . . . down. That was part of the reason she hadn't answered when he'd tried to call earlier. She needed to be strong when she dealt with him so she could maintain some emotional distance.

What now? It wasn't as if he'd just walk away. What she'd done with the phone must have spooked him. She should've answered.

Determined to regain her composure, she got up, pulled on a pair of sweat bottoms and padded through the living room.

Answering the door in what she'd worn to

bed — David's T-shirt — she tried to forget that last night it'd been Isaac's T-shirt. "It's late," she said. "Is something wrong?"

She hadn't turned on the porch light. She hadn't turned on *any* lights. Thanks to an almost full moon, however, it wasn't difficult to see.

His gaze lowered to the O'Toole Insurance logo on her chest before sweeping over the rest of her. But he was frowning when he raised his eyes to her face. "You okay?"

The air smelled like rain, which made Claire wonder if they were in for a summer shower. "I'm fine."

"Really? You look wiped."

She was damp enough that what would otherwise be a mild night felt chilly. "I was . . . having a bad dream." *Another* bad dream, only much worse.

"Is that why you didn't pick up earlier? You were already asleep? You scared the shit out of me."

She'd scared him in a manner of speaking. She needed to qualify what he said. That kind of statement didn't mean he really cared, as it would with David. Isaac had said things like that when they were together before.

"I'm . . . sorry. I must've thought the phone was in my dream and knocked it off the hook." It was *still* off the hook. She'd purposely left it that way. There wasn't anyone she wanted to hear from. Except David, which was impossible. Or her mother, which was probably just as impossible.

A slight wind ruffled Isaac's hair. Besides his amber-flecked eyes and artist's mouth, his hair was one of his best features. He wore it on the long side but it had enough natural curl to give it body.

"We need to talk," he said when she made no move to let him in.

The gravity in his voice caused her stomach muscles to tighten. "About . . ."

"Les Weaver."

The man who'd shot David. She straightened. "You called him already?"

"I paid him a visit."

"You drove all the way to Coeur D'Alene?"

"Got back an hour ago."

"Why didn't you *call* him?"

"I wanted to see his face and check out his situation."

What did he find? She doubted he'd show up at her door wearing such a serious expression if he'd come to report that David had been killed accidentally, as everyone believed. "I'm not . . . doing so well right now," she admitted. "Maybe I could get back to you in the morning after I've . . . I've had some sleep." *And a chance to prepare myself for what you might say. . . .* Somehow the idea had been less upsetting when it was all conjecture.

He wiped the sweat beading on her upper lip with his thumb. It was an intimate gesture; she would even call it tender, if she'd thought he meant it that way. "Because of the dream?"

"Because of . . . everything."

"What have you eaten?"

The panic crushing her chest seemed to ease a little. "Why do you think food solves everything?"

"You can't cope if you don't take care of yourself. And you're looking more fragile as the days go by."

"I'm coping." She lifted her hand to wave him off, but that only enabled him to push the door wide enough to squeeze past her. "Where are you going?"

She didn't need an answer. She could see that he was heading straight to the kitchen.

"Get in here," he said when she didn't follow.

With a sigh, she went as far as the entrance. "What are you doing?"

Cupboards slammed as he rummaged

through them. "Do you have any tea?"

"To the right of the sink. But . . . I hope it's not for me. I don't like tea."

"Then why do you have it?"

"For Leanne."

"Depending on what kind you've got, it might help you sleep." He found the box she'd directed him to. "Chamomile," he said, showing it to her. "This should do the trick."

"Ugh!" She grimaced. "Right now, all I need is a sleeping pill."

He filled a mug with water and put it in the microwave. "Sorry, you're not getting started on pills."

She blinked at his response. "You're joking, right?"

"Not in the least. Maybe if you didn't look so depressed I'd consider it, but —"

"You have no say in what I do!"

"You need to address the problem, not mask it," he said.

She was sure he meant well, but his response irritated her. "And how am I supposed to address the fact that I have to watch someone cut my mother into pieces with a chain saw whenever I close my eyes?"

He hesitated. He must have heard the bite in her voice, but he didn't react to it. She detected a hint of empathy in his face as he added the tea bag to the water and set it in front of her. "Let's try this first."

Convinced she wouldn't get him out of her kitchen until she'd drunk the darn tea *and* listened to what he'd found, she sank into the closest chair. "Tell me."

He didn't ask her to clarify. He knew what she was talking about. "In the morning."

"Now."

"It'll only upset you when I'm trying to help you relax."

"The truth has to be better than what I'm imagining."

"Not necessarily," he said, but he must've understood that she needed to assert her will on *something.*

Taking the seat across from her, he spoke in a somber voice. "Les is an oily bastard. An attorney."

Claire couldn't remember Mr. Weaver ever telling her what he did for a living. But he'd handed over quite a chunk of money — five thousand dollars — so she assumed he wasn't hard-pressed. "And that makes him untrustworthy from the get-go?" she said with a weak chuckle.

"It was more the look of him. He just . . . didn't fit the stereotype."

She grimaced at the taste of the tea, but he leaned forward and stirred in a spoonful of sugar. Then it wasn't too bad. "Not every hunter does."

"Exactly. So I ignored what my instincts were telling me and asked him a few questions."

"Like . . ."

"Had he been in the area before? Did he still hunt? That sort of thing."

The hot liquid soothed her despite the suspense. "And?"

"He didn't talk like a hunter, either. I asked him about previous hunts, but he wouldn't elaborate. Every hunter I've ever met can give you a list of where he's been and what he's bagged."

"Maybe killing David soured him on the whole experience."

"That's what he wanted me to believe. He even told me that after David died he got rid of every gun he owned. Said he can't bear to even *look* at a firearm."

"I can understand why."

"Me, too. Except . . ."

She shifted, trying to brace for what he had coming. "Except . . ."

"He's still got a whole gun cabinet filled with them. That's hardly getting rid of all his guns."

Cradling the mug, Claire concentrated on the smooth ceramic and the way it transferred warmth to her cold hands. "How do you know he has that many if he told you —"

"I saw them through the back window. They were right there in the living room, next to the couch."

"Shit . . . Why would Weaver lie?"

Isaac rubbed his chin as he answered. "He wasn't expecting me to check."

"But he volunteered that information, correct?"

"I believe he wants to appear more contrite than he feels —"

"Prick!"

"— so that no one looks any closer."

She studied Isaac from beneath her lashes. "He killed David on purpose."

"That's my guess."

"This changes everything."

"It could."

Or it could lead nowhere. She'd learned, long ago, not to get her hopes up. "We'd have to prove it, find someone in Pineview who has some connection to him. And that might be easier said than done."

"Not if we get the sheriff involved again," he said. "Someone needs to take a look at his phone records, and that requires a subpoena."

"Do you think one lie over whether or not

he still owns guns will be enough to get a judge to sign off? It's such an invasion of privacy. He's an attorney. That'll make everyone cautious."

"I'm going to do some more research first, see if I can come up with more on him."

With a nod, she forced herself to finish her tea. But when she stood to carry her cup to the sink, he took it from her and rinsed it himself.

"Feeling better?"

"A little." It was true. But she was pretty sure his presence and his support had more to do with it than anything else.

13

Claire woke up smashed against something wonderful. Warm. Solid. Comfortable. Whatever it was smelled good, too. Like deodorant, soap and warm male —

She'd been burrowing closer but the moment she recognized those scents, she lifted her head and squinted in the light filtering through the blinds. Sure enough, she was in bed with Isaac. They both had clothes on — that was a good sign — but her sister, if she'd already spotted his truck out front, wouldn't know that. When Claire had gotten out of the shower last night after that terrible dream and he said he was going to lie down with her, that he'd be right next to her in case she had another nightmare, she hadn't argued. After what he'd told her about Les Weaver, she'd been even more unsettled, afraid she might dream about that, making the comfort and security Isaac offered too tempting to refuse.

But he hadn't gotten up and left as she'd expected. He'd fallen asleep along with her.

Why was he still here? He couldn't have hung around because he expected to get laid. She'd made the parameters of their new relationship perfectly clear.

The doorbell rang, and her heart skipped a beat. Who could that be so early?

She craned her neck to see the clock on the nightstand and experienced a jolt of panic. It wasn't early at all. It was five after nine!

"Oh, no." Her first appointment, who just happened to be Laurel King, her best friend, had arrived. Laurel would definitely notice Isaac's truck. And — Claire consulted the mirror above the dresser — as tousled as she looked, it wouldn't be hard to guess she'd come straight from bed.

Could she get away with not answering?

"Your heart's racing a mile a minute." Isaac was half-asleep but sounded concerned. "What's wrong? Don't tell me you had another nightmare."

"No. I overslept. My appointments are arriving."

The emergency in her voice brought him awake. But being able to determine she was okay also relieved him. "Is that all?" he muttered, hiding a yawn.

"Is that *all?*" she repeated.

He punched his pillow. "So you slept in. You got to bed late."

"Lack of sleep isn't a viable excuse. Some of us have to work whether we want to or not, and that means we have to get up early and be prepared."

"Sucks for you, doesn't it?" he teased, and closed his eyes as if sinking back into sleep.

She had to tell him he couldn't stay. She didn't want any more of her clients thinking they were seeing each other.

But he'd been nice enough to drive three hours to Coeur d'Alene on her behalf, and he'd offered her comfort through a difficult night. She couldn't be so rude as to kick him out.

Bang, bang, bang. "Claire? You in there? It's Laurel."

She *knew* it was Laurel. That was part of the problem. What was she going to do?

"Why aren't you getting the door?" Isaac looked at her again, this time with a hint of the shrewdness he usually exhibited.

"I'm debating whether to pretend I'm not home."

"With my truck at the curb? If you don't answer, whoever it is will think they caught us in the middle of something."

But if she *did* answer, she'd have to explain

about her visitor and she wasn't quite sure how to do that.

"Claire?" he prompted.

"You're right." Not responding wasn't an option. She realized it now that he'd put the alternative in perspective.

Scrambling off the bed, she ran her fingers through her hair, but there was no way to get it to lie properly without wetting it down. "This won't look good," she grumbled.

He met her eyes in the mirror. "You're stressing over nothing."

"I am? My best friend will think we've been . . . together." And she'd never even mentioned him. Well, not recently. And not in any kind of positive light. Laurel would be offended if she thought Claire had a secret lover.

The bed squeaked as he shifted. "We *have* been together."

"Not for years."

"Unless you count three nights ago."

"We're *not* counting three nights ago. I — I'd just been conked on the head. Obviously, I wasn't thinking straight."

"You seemed to know what you wanted."

She ignored that. "And we didn't really make love," she added.

Resting his weight on his elbows, he

cocked an eyebrow at her. "You were faking that orgasm?"

She whirled around to face him. "Stop it! Quit teasing me, especially because that —" her face flushed hot "— momentary lapse in judgment doesn't count."

His eyes narrowed. She should've taken that as a warning, but she was too frantic to heed it. "Those moans sounded pretty convincing to me."

"Claire?" Laurel called. "Why aren't you answering?"

"In the bathroom. Coming!" she yelled back. Then she gestured for him to get up. "Can you at least vacate my bed?"

He did as she asked but his dark scowl let her know he wasn't happy about the way she was acting. "I don't get why this is such an emergency. So she thinks we're seeing each other. What difference does it make? We're both single."

"My husband just died."

"A year ago! Does that mean you're expected to be celibate for the rest of your life?"

"Not necessarily. But I'd rather not have everyone in town thinking I'm idiot enough to let you use me again."

A muscle jumped in his cheek. "Because, of course, that's all I'm capable of."

"Everyone knows you're a player. You've made sure they know it." She had to expose her underwear in order to pull on her jeans, but she was too nervous to wait for him to leave the room. It also seemed rather pointless after everything he'd already seen, and touched, over the years.

Her jeans were baggier than ever but she hoped he wouldn't notice. She didn't want him going on about the weight she'd lost. She'd heard enough about that already. "No need to have everyone trying to caution me against getting involved with you again."

As she turned away to put on her bra and swap David's T-shirt for a blouse of her own, she glanced over her shoulder to see that his eyes had gone flat. "You're that convinced I'm a bad bet? That they know me better than you do? That I haven't grown up in ten years?"

She wasn't willing to take the chance. To her mind, his inadequacies had more to do with the type of person he was rather than his level of maturity. He'd been an adult since he was sixteen; that meant he'd grown up fast. But there was no time to argue. "Maybe if you hurry out to the salon, she'll assume you're here for a haircut."

She'd never cut his hair before. She'd often wondered where he had it done. If the men in town didn't come to her, they typically went to a barber in Libby, but Isaac's hair looked too styled for a ten-dollar buzz-and-go.

"I'll just head out the back."

"No! You can't slink away. Now that she's seen your truck, she has to see *you,* too, and we have to act as if you're no different from any other client."

"I see." That muscle twitched in his cheek again, but he strode into the hall that connected her house and salon without another word.

"You could've at least tried to make it look as though you hadn't just rolled out of bed," she muttered when he was gone, but she pasted a smile on her face and went to answer the door.

"What took you so long?" Laurel stood with her arms folded, keys in hand, suggesting she'd nearly given up.

"I'm sorry. Somehow I didn't get your appointment in my day planner and double-booked myself." Her laugh sounded awkward, even to her, but she hoped Laurel wouldn't notice. "I was in the salon."

Laurel seemed confused. "But I went to the salon. It was dark."

"Oh, you must've arrived earlier than I thought. I offered Isaac a cup of coffee. We were probably in the kitchen."

She chewed on her bottom lip as if she wasn't quite mollified. "I saw his truck, of course, but . . ."

Claire put some extra wattage into her smile. "But?"

"I couldn't figure out why he'd be here. I didn't know he was a client. I've always gotten the impression you don't like him."

"I don't have strong feelings for him one way or the other."

The sound of a door closing made Claire's heart skip a beat. It'd been soft, barely discernible. She was sure Laurel hadn't heard. But she cringed to think Isaac might've picked up on what she'd just said. She was fighting her attraction to him; she wasn't out to mistreat him. Especially after he'd been so nice to her these past few days.

"Do you want me to come back later?" Laurel asked. "If you're too busy . . ."

Claire realized she hadn't stepped aside and invited her friend in. "Of course not. You know I work fast. I can cut you both. Come on, we'll go through the house."

Isaac sat completely still while Claire trimmed his hair. She liked running her fingers through his curls but, considering the situation, she couldn't enjoy it as much as she wanted. Had she severed their tenuous friendship?

She got that feeling. Guilt dragged at her like hundred-pound weights tied to each limb, but she couldn't apologize with Laurel looking on.

When Laurel answered a call on her cell, Claire took the opportunity to squeeze Isaac's shoulder as a sort of silent apology, but the look he gave her in the mirror made her drop her hand. He was angry. And no one was more formidable when angry.

"Will you, um, tilt your head a little more . . . ? That's it," she murmured.

He allowed her to manipulate his head and sat through the cut, but the steeliness of his eyes stabbed at her the whole time. She wanted to do a good job on the trim, at least, but with so much dark emotion rolling off him, and Laurel watching curiously, she was in too much of a hurry.

What if her best friend could see everything she was trying to hide? What if Laurel could tell that just being near Isaac made her heart race? That he was the only one who could ease the pain of losing David?

If Laurel saw the truth, then she'd have to face it herself. And she couldn't do that. Not right now.

In case she was more transparent than she

wanted to be, she refused to meet his gaze again. She snipped and snipped, then used her blow dryer to get rid of the hair that had fallen on his neck. After that she offered him a fake smile and pulled off the drape she'd fastened on him when he sat down. "There you go. Thanks for coming in."

She couldn't get him out of there fast enough. . . .

"How much do I owe you?" he said dryly.

For a haircut he hadn't even wanted. She hesitated to charge him, but that would make her deception a bit too obvious. "Twenty bucks ought to do it."

He leaned closer. "What'd you say?"

She'd spoken too quietly. Clearing her throat, she tried again. "Twenty dollars."

He tossed some money onto the shelf of her station and walked out.

A lump grew in her throat as the door shut. She'd ruined whatever trust had begun to emerge between them. But she didn't have time to mope over it. She'd known all along that she was better off without Isaac Morgan in her life.

Trying to force a smile, she turned to Laurel. "Sorry you had to wait."

"No problem. I didn't mind. But . . . is he always surly like that?" She gestured to indicate Isaac, and together they watched through the window as he started his truck.

No, he could be as kind, sexy, gentle and funny as he could be fierce or indifferent. He'd stayed with her all night because he knew she was scared to be alone. But she didn't want to think about that. It made the whole mess worse.

"I guess." She shrugged. "I don't really know him that well."

"Neither do I," Laurel mused. "But he's a heck of a photographer."

"So I've heard."

"You haven't seen his work?"

That was going too far. Of course she'd seen it. Everyone had, especially around here. "Some pieces. The Amish store on the way to Libby sells a few of them."

"The Kicking Horse Saloon has some, too. Only they're not for sale."

"It's great that he can make a living doing what he loves."

Those words were filler, something she could say without revealing the poignancy of her feelings, but Laurel gave her a funny look all the same. "You're not impressed with his work?"

"Of course. I just haven't paid much attention to his photographs, that's all."

"Wait — he's the one who helped you

when you hit your head the other night, isn't he? Myles told me."

Claire had been so busy building the perception of distance between her and Isaac, she'd forgotten about that. Her eyes cut to the twenty dollars he'd tossed on her shelf. She could've said she'd given him a gift certificate as a thank-you. That would've saved her from adding insult to injury by charging him. Too bad she hadn't thought of it earlier.

"Yes."

Laurel sat in the chair near the sink so Claire could wash her hair. "We haven't even had a chance to talk about that. I've called a couple of times, but . . ."

Claire hadn't called her back. She felt terrible about that, in addition to everything else, but Laurel wasn't the only friend she'd neglected. She'd been dodging all her calls. "I was down for a whole day because of that bump on my head, and the time I lost really put me behind."

"But you're okay?"

The water wasn't getting hot fast enough. "Of course," she said briskly. "I'm fine."

Laurel resisted when Claire tried to recline the chair. "Are you sure? I've been worried about you. You're losing so much weight. . . ."

"I seem to be hearing that from all sides lately."

"It's true. I've been afraid to say anything for fear it'll upset you, but . . . I think it's time we acknowledged there might be a problem. You're not recovering like you should."

Claire's defenses slammed into place despite the little voice inside her head that warned her not to offend Laurel. "You're saying you could get over Myles's death in a year?"

"That's too horrible to even contemplate," she said. "I'm not faulting you, or saying I could do any better. I just . . . I want you to be happy. That's all. And if it takes admitting that you need help —"

"I don't need help!"

Once again, Laurel resisted when Claire tried to wash her hair. "Fine. Then will you do me one favor?"

"I'm not seeing a shrink, if that's where you're going."

"It's not. What I want is free and easy for you to give."

"And that means . . ."

"I'd like you to go out with that guy I've been trying to set you up with."

Claire rolled her eyes. "Not this again."

"Come on! He's *so* nice. Handsome, too."

Laurel had been badgering her about this for weeks. "I'm not ready."

"How do you know unless you try?"

"I *did* try," she replied. "With Rusty, the other night."

Laurel clutched the arms of the chair. "You went out with Rusty? Myles's deputy?"

"One and the same."

"That's great! He's wanted to take you out since forever! He's made no secret of that."

"I know."

"And?"

She grimaced. "It sucked. We got into an argument because he was coming on too strong and I ended up walking home." She left out the part about Isaac picking her up and letting her hide at his place for the rest of the night.

"That's too bad," Laurel said. "But this'll be different. Myles and I will be with you. The four of us will go out to dinner. We'll have a great time, no pressure at all. I promise."

Claire blew out a sigh. Why not? She couldn't do any worse than she'd done with Rusty. And maybe this blind date would get her mind off Isaac. "Why do you think he's so perfect for me?"

"He's very stable, for one."

"You did say he's an *accountant.*"

"Don't say it so deadpan. He's an *interesting* accountant."

"Who's not married because . . ."

"He hasn't found the right girl."

"Or he picks his nose in public or eats gum that's already been chewed or has some other revolting idiosyncrasy!"

Laurel looked hurt. "That's what you think of my taste in men? My, aren't you positive today!"

With a laugh, Claire shook her head. "Myles is wonderful, and you know it. I'm sorry." She thought of telling Laurel why she was having such a hard time. Her friend would sympathize with her, maybe even have some advice on how to repair the damage Claire had inflicted on her family relationships.

But she wasn't ready to smooth things over with Tug, Roni or Leanne. For some reason, she'd reached a threshold where the truth mattered more than anything else, and playing nice was a handicap in that regard.

"Claire? You okay?"

She'd been staring off into space. Refocusing, she infused her smile with a fresh dose of determination. "How do you know him . . . this interesting accountant?"

At last, Laurel allowed Claire to recline

the chair. "Most everyone who works for the sheriff's department uses him to prepare their taxes."

"So worst-case scenario —" she squirted shampoo into her palm "— I've found a new tax consultant."

Laurel applauded her improved attitude. "That's the spirit."

"When do you want to go?"

"I'll have Myles see when he's available and get back to you."

That sounded loose enough. Hoping she'd be able to put the date off indefinitely, Claire agreed and hurried to finish. She was eager for Laurel to leave so she could call Isaac and apologize. But hurrying didn't do any good. After Laurel had left and she was free to call, Isaac didn't answer. Even worse, Laurel contacted her only an hour later to say that accountant, "Owen Rodriguez," happened to be free Saturday night.

"Sounds like his social calendar is as full as mine," Claire murmured.

Laurel sighed. "Drop the sarcasm, okay? Don't start being negative again."

"Okay, okay. I'll be ready at seven."

"What will you wear?"

Claire didn't feel passionate enough about the event to plan that far ahead. "I'll find something."

■ ■ ■ ■

Twenty-four hours later, Claire still had Isaac's twenty bucks in her pocket. She hadn't been able to give it back because she couldn't get him to answer his darn phone or return one of her many messages, which upset her for two reasons. Not only did she want to apologize, she wanted to tell him that a stranger had called her last night, just before bed — a man — to ask if she'd hired a private investigator. When he wouldn't identify himself, she refused to answer, and he'd hung up. That was the extent of their exchange. She'd tried using star sixty-nine but he must've called from a blocked number because it didn't work. The whole thing made her uneasy. She guessed it was Les Weaver, trying to determine if what Isaac had told him was true.

She wished she could discuss it with Isaac. He'd mentioned that he was going to do some more research. After what had happened yesterday, she was pretty sure he'd dumped that idea, along with their "friendship," but she needed to put right what she'd destroyed. So, after holding out until late afternoon, hoping she'd hear from him, she paid him a visit, which didn't help, either. He wasn't home.

She frowned at his empty driveway as she plodded back to her Camaro. Where had he gone? Had he left town on another extended trip? He'd said that he was taking some time off from all the travel. She'd thought that meant he'd be sticking around Pineview for a while. . . .

Maybe he got an offer he couldn't refuse.

"Damn." If only she could talk to him. He hadn't been happy when he threw that twenty on her station, but he couldn't be *that* mad, could he? So what if she didn't want her best friend or anyone else to assume they were in a romantic relationship? What difference would it make to him? His list of conquests was impressive enough; it wasn't as if he needed the ego boost of making their relationship public.

So what was going on? Was he out of town? Or was he purposely avoiding her?

Irritated that he wouldn't give her the opportunity to apologize and return his money, she sat in her car with the engine idling, hoping he was merely out running errands and would return shortly.

After twenty minutes and still no sign of him, the wait began to feel futile.

"Fine," she grumbled. "Have it your way." She stuffed the money in an envelope she'd brought with her, wrote a quick note on the outside and left it under his mat. Then she drove back to town and, once again, told herself to forget him.

Which worked about as well as it had the other three thousand times.

"I told you not to get involved. I told you this would happen. You can't even be friends or he takes over every waking moment."

But the question was why? *Why* did he have such a big impact on her?

As obvious as the answer was, she didn't want to accept it. Disappearing completely from her life after being with her so much lately had left her with a fresh void to fill. Suddenly, she missed David even more poignantly. She was also tempted to visit her stepfather and stepmother to see if she could make peace with Roni.

In other words, she was going right back to the life she'd always had.

Or maybe not.

She stomped on the brake as she spotted April, the youngest of Roni's stepchildren from her former marriage, coming out of the store where she worked — Merkley's Mercantile. Although they were only two years apart and had gone to school together, they generally averted their eyes and passed each other without speaking. Loyalty demanded that Claire side with her family, and Roni was part of that. But the confrontation she'd had with her stepmother yesterday made her more curious than she'd ever been. If she was hoping to reconcile with Tug and Roni after only twenty-four hours, how could April hold a grudge for years and years? Even April's ex-husband hated Roni. What could she have done that was so bad April would prefer to have *no* mother? Roni had been difficult in some respects, but there'd also been times, a lot of them, when Claire felt quite close to her.

As she parked, April's eyes flicked toward her, but obviously assuming it was one of those accidental encounters they muddled through by ignoring each other, she lifted her chin and marched on.

Claire wasn't sure she could get April to stop, let alone speak to her, but she decided to give it a try. She would've approached her long ago if she hadn't been so worried about what April might say. April believed Roni was the reason her father had committed suicide. Claire already knew that. But she wasn't convinced it was true, and she didn't want to risk letting April change her opinion. She also had to worry about what Roni might do if she found out Claire had gone behind her back. If she wound up estranged from her stepmother, she'd be estranged from her stepfather, too. They came as a package.

But the way Roni had acted yesterday . . . It made Claire fear she'd remained blind for too long. If she wanted the truth, she had to look under every rock, even the ones that might be hiding something unpleasant.

She parked and climbed out, but by then April was halfway down the block.

When she realized who was coming up behind her, April veered toward the curb, planning to cross to the other side, just as Claire had seen her do to avoid Roni.

Throat so dry she could hardly speak, Claire swallowed hard and called out, "Wait!"

April glanced over her shoulder. She'd heard. Twelve-year-old Johnny Goodman was the only other person nearby, and he was practicing skateboard tricks. Clearly Claire was speaking to her, but April didn't stop walking.

"April! I want to talk to you."

This time she paused, but her rigid posture telegraphed her displeasure at being hailed. "That doesn't mean I want to talk to you," she said. "I have to get my kids from day care."

"Can't you . . . wait a second?"

"Why?" she said with exasperation. "What do you want?"

Claire let out her breath in a rush. "I was hoping . . . I was hoping we could . . . have a discussion."

Her brown eyes narrowed. "About what?"

Suddenly even more afraid that Roni or Tug or even Leanne would see them, she licked her lips. "About Roni, of course. What else?"

"I don't have anything to say about her."

She checked for traffic, but Claire caught her arm before she could step off the curb. "Please? Will you sit down with me for five minutes? Can your kids wait that long?"

Her gaze riveted on Claire's hand long enough that Claire, embarrassed at touching her, released her grip. Then April scanned the shops closest to them as if she expected Roni to step out from one of the doorways. "It's just you? For real?"

"It's just me."

"Why? What could you possibly want to hear me say?"

Would someone tell Roni? Should she drop this? Walk off? Part of her wanted to, but the other part demanded she stay. "I'd like to know what you have against her, why you —" she hesitated to bring up the death of her father "— hate her so much."

"That's personal." She hurried into the street and Claire supposed that would be the end of it, but April slowed before reaching the other side and turned.

They stared at each other for several seconds — until a car honked at April. She jumped out of the way so it could pass, then walked back.

When she was close enough to speak in a normal tone, she said, "Where do you want to go?"

Claire hadn't thought that through. She pivoted to see what restaurant might be closest, but April shook her head when Claire indicated Big Sky Diner at the end of the block. "If you don't want to be seen with me, why would we go to a public place?"

Apparently, Claire's concern about maintaining some privacy was more visible than she'd realized. "Do you have a better idea?"

"I'll put off getting the kids for a half hour. Meet me at my house. Do you know where that is?"

Scarcely able to believe she was going to the home of her stepmother's nemesis, a place she'd always ignored as completely as she usually ignored its occupant, she nodded.

"See you there," April said, and hurried off.

14

Dust motes swirled in the late-afternoon sunlight pouring through the window. Claire watched them shimmy above the table as she sat in April's kitchen, awaiting the glass of iced tea April had offered her. Far too warm, even in her skirt, sandals and lightweight top, she shifted uncomfortably. If April had air-conditioning, she wasn't using it. She'd turned on a fan when they walked through the living room, but it wasn't enough.

There were other signs of cost-cutting. Drab, well-worn furniture. Sheets in place of blinds. Tattered rugs covering the wooden floor. The house itself was so old it still had a cast-iron stove in the corner. But it was clean and well-maintained and smelled like fresh paint. And it was only a block off Main Street. Grandma Bigelow, who'd taught piano lessons most of her life, had owned it for sixty years before she passed away. Now

April rented it from Roger Bigelow and his son Clyde, who also owned a big cattle ranch outside town.

"I can't believe it's taken you so long to come to me."

It was April who'd broken the silence, but this wasn't even close to what Claire had imagined she'd say. "Excuse me?"

Ice clinked against glass as April put her drink down. "After what I told the police years ago, I expected to hear from you sooner."

Claire wasn't sure how to respond to this. "I'm sorry, there's nothing in the case files about you or anything you said."

April's expression bordered on belligerent. "My statement has to be there. I signed it and everything."

"I'm telling you, there's nothing from or about you." At least not in the accordion file Claire had found at the studio. She'd read everything twice.

She blinked. "How do you know? The police might not be telling you everything."

"I've seen the files."

"All of them?"

"I think so. What I read seemed pretty exhaustive." When she explained about what she'd discovered at her mother's studio, disgust curled April's lip.

"Why should I be surprised my statement went missing?" she said.

"What does that mean?" Claire asked.

"We live in a small town where everyone knows everyone else."

"You're saying you think someone deep-sixed it? *On purpose?*"

"As a favor to a friend, namely your father. He's an important figure around here these days."

Since the inheritance. He hadn't been important before he became wealthy. He'd worked by the hour in a gun shop. But Claire didn't like the tone of April's voice; it made her defensive even though April was right — Tug had more power now than he'd ever possessed. "What did it say, your statement?"

She pursed her lips, studied Claire, then smiled. "You can't guess?"

"That Roni was responsible for my mother's disappearance?" Maybe the police hadn't bothered to keep her statement since it was so obviously sour grapes.

She chuckled as she took the seat opposite Claire. "Bingo. But you're wrong about everything else."

"What do you mean?"

"You think I said it just because I hate her and would love to get her in trouble."

Claire sipped her iced tea. "There's never been any love lost between you." Especially after April's father hanged himself in Copper Grady's old barn.

"No kidding. Don't know how *you've* been able to stomach her."

Roni had her moments, but she could be sweet and surprisingly generous, and she'd been consistently supportive. Even when she was difficult, Claire muddled through for the sake of keeping peace in the family. What good would it do to reject her stepmother? Did she want to end up like April? Bitter and lonely and estranged? "Leanne and I have both gotten along with her."

She shrugged. "No accounting for taste, I suppose. Still, I expected you to have more sense than your silly sister seems to —"

Claire stood. "I didn't come here so you could bash my sister."

April's palm smacked the table. "You didn't come here for the truth, either. Your mind's already made up, so why'd you want to talk to me?"

Because she was trying to expand her search in hopes of actually learning something that would make a difference.

Curling her fingers around the edge of the table, Claire took a deep breath. "Do you have any facts on which you're basing such an accusation against Roni?"

"You mean other than believing she's capable of it?"

Claire shoved a hand through her hair. "How can you say that?"

"I saw what she did to my father."

"Your father had a hard life. I — I'm sorry about what happened. But depression did him in, not Roni."

"*Desperation* did him in. The head games she played did him in. And that started when he met her."

They could argue about this all day, but what was the point? Claire wasn't close enough to that situation to know what was true and what wasn't. "Tell me why you think she killed my mother."

"She wanted her out of the way."

Claire sank back into her seat. "Why?"

"Roni hated your mother. She was jealous of her years before she acted on that jealousy."

Shoving the tea aside, Claire leaned forward. "Don't state it as a known fact because —"

"I'll state it any way I like," she interrupted. "And if you really want to do right by your mom, you'll listen."

Claire almost stood again, but she figured she'd come this far, she might as well hear the rest. Then it would all be out, and there'd be one less rock to look under. Clenching her jaw, she said, "Tell me what you have to say."

"They were having an affair. That wasn't conjecture on my part. I heard all the shit she said."

"But Tug and Roni weren't even particularly good friends."

"That's where you're wrong." April touched the condensation on her glass. "They worked at the gun shop together."

This was it? What she was basing everything on? "Of course I know that, but —"

"They fell in love, Claire."

"According to you. I'm not sure I believe it."

"Trust me. Roni wanted him. But there was one problem. Tug already had a wife."

"And Roni already had a husband."

"She wasn't worried about that. She'd toyed with his heart until she had him so beaten down he wasn't the same man he'd been when I was young. Why he loved her so much, I can't even guess, but part of his anguish came from knowing he had no chance of keeping her. My dad, God rest his soul, didn't have the same . . . *prospects* as Tug."

The fan in the other room stirred Claire's

hair as it moved from side to side but did little to cool the kitchen. "You're talking about the money my parents had just inherited."

"Yes."

Claire had expected to hear something like this and yet it grated on her. "Do you have proof?"

"Once I began to suspect, I wanted to know for sure. So I hacked into her email account and read their messages. They were pretty hot."

"But no one's ever accused *him* of cheating." Except her. Hadn't she just asked him and Roni at the salon?

"They hid it well. It's too bad your mother didn't do the same."

The burning in her throat threatened to choke Claire. "You're saying you think my mom was having an affair, too."

"Of course. Don't you? Why would so many people point a finger at her if it wasn't true?"

"Because they're searching for answers they don't have, so they come up with the only explanation they can."

She drummed her fingers on the table. "If that's what you want to believe."

"Why *shouldn't* I? You didn't hack into *her* email account, did you?"

April didn't respond immediately. When she did, her voice was softer. "No. That part is pure conjecture."

Claire wished she'd never instigated this conversation. "So, according to you, Tug and Roni were having an affair and so was my mother. But if they'd both found happiness with someone else, why didn't they simply divorce? How does that situation develop into murder?"

"Far too easily, I'm afraid. Roni was making Tug feel like a desirable man, the only man for her, and you and I both know how susceptible he is to that."

Claire gave no indication whether she agreed with this or not. Being attractive to the opposite sex had always been important to him. The way he dressed, far younger than his age, said as much. But April didn't know Tug, not really.

"As long as he could provide the lifestyle she craved — the lifestyle *my* father failed to provide — he'd be her heartthrob."

Even though she wished she could prevent it, the mansion Roni lived in courtesy of her mother's inheritance popped into Claire's mind. She and Leanne had each received ninety thousand, which they'd spent on their houses and on school, but Tug had kept the bulk of Alana's inheritance. "So you think it was all about money."

"That, and he didn't want to lose you and Leanne."

Leanne's words during their last argument came back to Claire. Her sister had stopped short of accusing Tug of murder, but she'd also said he wasn't sad about losing Alana because it meant he wouldn't have to worry about being separated from her children. Did a consensus make that true?

No. She was allowing this to go too far. April hated Roni and Tug. She had a vested interest in describing them in the worst possible light. And Claire was letting her. "You don't know how he felt about us so don't pretend you do —"

"You're wrong there, too. He wrote what I just said in one of those emails." April picked up her glass, stared at it in the light of the sun and took a swallow before setting it back down. "He really cares about you, if that makes you feel any better."

It didn't. Claire was sick inside. "Most stepparents don't go to such lengths to keep their stepchildren."

"But he wasn't going to get any more. Roni had herself fixed when she married my father. He already had the four of us. She didn't want a fifth mouth to feed. And Tug couldn't have any of his own."

Claire nearly dropped her glass. "What did you say?"

April watched her more closely. "You mean the part about Tug being infertile? You didn't know?"

He wouldn't admit it. She suspected the reason for that was his ego. He didn't want to be perceived as damaged goods or less capable, less attactive to women. But she *did* know. That was the problem. She'd overheard her own mother say it, and that lent April's whole terrible story more credibility than she wanted it to have. "Who told you?"

"It was in one of the emails. I'm guessing he sent it before she told him she couldn't conceive, because he was trying to reassure her that she didn't have to worry about getting pregnant." She tore at some loose skin on her lips with her teeth, apparently struggling to recall the specifics. "If I remember right, he said something like, 'All I ever dream about is making a baby with you. But even with Alana out of the way, you need to know it wouldn't be possible.' Then he went on to say that when his first wife couldn't get pregnant, she dragged him to the doctor and they learned he had a low sperm count. He claimed that's why she divorced him."

When Claire merely stared, slack-jawed, April grimaced. "I really didn't expect this to shock you quite so badly. You have to believe *someone* killed your mother. Who else could it be?"

Anyone. Joe. His brother. His wife. A . . . a stranger. A psychopath.

"Just be glad you weren't the one to read those sickly sweet emails," April told her. "I get a cavity just remembering them. But it was the sexual ones that really grossed me out."

Claire lifted a hand to stop her. "Spare me the details, please."

"No problem. I've already blocked them from memory."

It seemed a bit convenient that she could remember so much about the other ones, especially after fifteen years. "Do you have copies of those emails?"

"No. I was afraid my father would see them, and —" her voice wavered "— I didn't want him to be hurt."

April had lost a parent, too. Claire sympathized. But that didn't mean it was right for April to blame Roni. "So she never figured out that you knew?"

"She didn't have to figure it out. Several months later, I accused her of it."

Claire folded her arms. "If she's so diabolical, weren't you afraid of what she might do to shut you up?"

"She hadn't killed anyone at that point. I knew she was a selfish bitch, but I never dreamed she'd go quite so far — until it happened. That convinced me pretty fast." She pushed her lip to one side so she could reach a different spot with her teeth. "I'll never forget where I was when I heard the news that your mother was missing. I was sitting in my father's trailer, crying. He was drunk, passed out yet again, but the TV was blaring in the background, showing the police going in and out of your house."

"You immediately knew Roni was responsible?"

"Of course. That's why I went to the police."

But there was no record of her contact with the sheriff's department. Claire would have to ask Myles if he knew anything about it. "If you weren't scared before, you should've been then."

"I was. But I was married at the time and didn't feel so vulnerable. As the days, months and years passed, and she got everything she wanted, I realized I wasn't at risk. She doesn't consider me a threat. If what I knew could hurt her, she would've been in prison long ago."

"I still can't believe you've stayed here."

"Where would I go?"

"You have siblings elsewhere in Montana."

"But this place is all I know. And my children's father works for the fire department. Scott wouldn't let me take them away even if I wanted to move."

Claire counted the rotations of the fan. The steady *swoop* sounded like a propeller circling in her head. "So you're telling me she doesn't have to worry because you have no proof those emails ever existed."

April sat as straight as the chair. "The police should've confiscated her computer. But they didn't."

"No copies, like I said."

Her gaze fell to the table. "No copies. Just what I can remember, what I told you." Her eyes lifted to meet Claire's. "You don't believe me, do you?"

"No, I don't," Claire said, and fled the house before the tears welling in her eyes could roll down her cheeks.

But she couldn't lie to herself quite so easily. Maybe she didn't *want* to believe April had hacked into Roni's computer and read such damning correspondence. But if what she said *wasn't* true, how did she know Tug was sterile?

■ ■ ■ ■

This time he was going to turn her away. No matter what.

Yesterday when he left her salon, Isaac had made the decision not to have any more contact with Claire. Her problems weren't his problems. He wasn't even sure why he'd been getting so involved. After a random two-day photo shoot in the mountains, he'd come home determined to avoid the emotions she evoked in him, which he could only do by avoiding *her.*

But an hour after he walked through the door, she stood on his stoop with tears streaking her face, looking as if her world had just come to an end. He wanted to ask what was wrong, what had happened. He could tell it was something significant. But he couldn't allow himself to be drawn in again. He was done hanging on, regretting, hoping, craving.

"I found the money under the mat. There was no need to return it. I got the haircut. But thank you," he said, and closed the door.

He hadn't given her the chance to say a word. Part of him hoped he'd made her mad enough to knock again. Shouting at each other would be better than this oppressive silence. He felt as if he couldn't breathe. But she didn't make a second attempt. He heard nothing until her car started. Then a new wave of regret washed over him, and it was all he could do not to fly out of the cabin and flag her down.

He would have, if he'd thought it would help either one of them.

But it wouldn't. He had to be more realistic about his own shortcomings. If sex was all there was to a relationship, he could give her that. He'd done it before. But not love. He didn't know how to give love, or be loved. His own mother hadn't even been able to love him.

He let his breath seep out as the sound of her engine dimmed. The temptation was over. She was gone.

But no sooner had that thought crossed his mind than he grabbed his keys and went after her.

As much as he'd tried to ignore it, tried to tell himself he didn't care, he did. He had to know why she'd been crying.

15

Isaac came racing up from behind, honking his horn, but Claire was too angry to pull over. She shouldn't have gone to him for comfort. What had she been thinking?

She *hadn't* been thinking. She'd been so upset she'd kept driving, and the next thing she knew, she was sitting in front of his cabin, wanting his arms around her more than ever before.

And what did *he* do when she showed up, so vulnerable and heartbroken? He'd looked down his nose at her, muttered a few words and slammed the door in her face.

She'd been stupid to set herself up. She'd known he was angry with her. He had good reason to be. She'd mishandled the situation at her salon. But for ten years she'd had good reason to be angry with *him* and she'd let it go.

A pothole jerked the Camaro to one side, causing her to veer dangerously close to a tree, but she managed to bring the car under control. A check in her rearview mirror told her that Isaac was right on her bumper. Why was he coming after her? Why couldn't he just leave her alone?

Because that would be too simple, and nothing involving Isaac was simple. That was why she had to stay away from him. The past few days he'd made her feel as if he was the only person who understood what she was going through, the only person who gave a damn about it. And she'd bought in to that, assumed they'd have a *real* friendship.

Or maybe *she* was the one complicating the situation. Maybe she couldn't handle having him back in her life because she had so many other things going on — so many painful things.

Had her stepfather and stepmother schemed to kill Alana as April claimed? Had they purposely taken Alana out of the picture so they could have what they wanted?

If what Isaac believed was true, the same trusted loved ones hired Les Weaver to kill David in order to cover up what they'd already done.

She couldn't fathom that Tug or Roni would ever go *that* far. It would make a lie of everything she'd always thought they felt for her, but all the evidence seemed to point in their direction.

Isaac's big tires sprayed dirt against the side of her car as he drew even with her. He honked and swerved toward her, trying to force her to pull over, but she refused to do that. In most places, the road wasn't wide enough for two cars. She could hear tree branches scraping her passenger door. But she gave her car more gas instead of less, assuming he'd fall back when he realized she wouldn't stop.

He didn't. He continued to honk his horn.

When she looked over, she saw that he'd lowered his window and was yelling for her to stop. She knew she was being reckless. But so was he. And the anger behind her actions numbed the pain she'd been feeling a few minutes earlier. That alone caused her to embrace it.

She tried to cut him off, get *him* to stop, without success. He was too damn stubborn, and too confident in his driving ability to worry about his own safety —

The tree root seemed to come out of nowhere. When she hit it, the car jerked to the left. Then she overcorrected and had to slam on her brakes before smashing into a tamarack.

That gave him his chance. He whipped around her and came to a skidding stop, blocking her in so she couldn't move forward.

They both got out at the same time.

"What the *hell* were you trying to prove just now?" he shouted as he stalked through the swirling dust. "Were you trying to get yourself killed?"

That was an exaggeration. She doubted she would've died. She could've been injured, though. Her heart pounded from the near miss, but she liked the adrenaline rush. It made her feel invincible for a change. "You're the one who nearly caused an accident. You had no right to come up beside me on this road!"

"I was just trying to make you pull over!"

"Why? *What do you want from me?*"

He stared at her for several seconds, then the hard edge of his anger crumbled and he looked lost, as if he had no more idea than she did. "I don't know," he admitted. "I just . . . I can't help what you do to me."

"I hate you," she whispered, but there was no fire behind those words, and a mutinous tear ran down her cheek as she said them — because she couldn't help what he did to her, either.

"Then I guess this won't make things any

worse." He moved closer, challenging her to push him away. She got the impression he halfway wanted her to do just that. But she couldn't. She was back to craving his arms around her, the desire suddenly so strong it felt like emotional whiplash. So when he lowered his head and gently pressed his lips against hers, she simply closed her eyes and let herself enjoy his touch.

"You want this, right?" He tilted her head so she had to look up at him.

She considered lying, but was afraid he might take her at her word and leave her standing in the road. Instead, she allowed the explosive energy of their clashing wills to carry her to a new level of desire and clenched her hands in his hair as she kissed him much harder. "What do you think?"

"God, you make me feel so helpless." The tone of his voice had changed. He sounded more weary than angry; that was a small victory. But he didn't *act* weary. His arms tightened around her as if that kiss had snapped all restraint.

She arched her neck as his mouth moved over her, licking, sucking, devouring. He'd left a love bite on her neck three nights ago. Dimly, she realized he might do it again. He was suddenly wild, out of control — they both were. But she had no intention of holding back. This was what she wanted, what she'd wanted for a long, long time — Isaac unleashed.

He raised her skirt. The cool night air swirled across the bare skin he'd exposed before he pushed her up against the warm metal of the car. Pinning her in place with his hips, he slid his fingers beneath her panties.

She jumped as he touched her.

"How much do you hate me?" he murmured.

"A lot," she said.

He suckled her breast as another finger joined the first and slid inside her. "And how much do you want me?"

"A lot," she said again as she undid his belt and shoved down his jeans. Both answers were true; she hated him because she couldn't stop loving him.

"I feel the same," he said, and lifted her onto his erection.

Isaac's muscles quivered at the building pleasure. They'd established a frantic yet perfect rhythm, one that made him want to throw his head back and howl like the wolves. With his heart pounding as fast as it was, he almost felt as if he might have a heart attack before they were through, but he couldn't think of a better way to go.

"Hey." He was so short of breath he could barely speak.

Her eyes opened and locked with his. She looked high on his touch, completely in the moment, and that turned him on even more.

"For what it's worth, I've never wanted another woman like I want you."

This seemed to make her more aware of the practicalities. "Why aren't you . . . getting out . . . a condom?"

He wasn't getting one out because he didn't have one. "I don't . . . carry them on me. I . . . haven't had occasion to use one . . . in months." The cheap flings that had kept him occupied for several years after they'd broken up felt so empty these days that he no longer bothered. He dated once in a while, had women over but rarely slept with anyone. He suspected most people in Pineview would be surprised to learn that. They seemed to think he was as wild now as he ever was. But he hadn't been able to replace Claire. So he'd slowly lost interest, even quit buying condoms.

He certainly hadn't expected to have *this* opportunity. Not fifteen minutes earlier, he'd been telling himself he couldn't see her again.

She seemed to be struggling to think amid

the delicious friction, but those hands, guiding him with the pressure they exerted on his back, urged him not to stop. "You've always been . . . prepared in the past —"

"I'll pull out," he promised. Although that was no guarantee, it was the only method available to them. But that meant he needed to withdraw *now,* at the most critical moment for her, and she tightened her legs to hold him in place for just a second too long. She probably had no idea he was so close to going over the edge. He should've warned her, but when she reached climax so did he. It happened so fast he didn't even realize he was in trouble until that initial surge of ecstasy ripped through him.

By then it was too late.

Isaac couldn't remember the last time he'd done anything so irresponsible. He'd been reckless as a kid, but never reckless with sex. Not after being an unwanted child himself.

Somehow he was never in control with Claire. He did everything wrong when it came to her.

"You didn't pull out!" Her eyes widened.

That was obvious. "I was too late."

"What if . . . what if I get pregnant?" she gasped.

He eased some of her weight onto the car.

"You know I'll help." At least he was older and financially capable of caring for a child if they had one, but he doubted she'd find that any consolation. "Not that you . . . should worry. It's only . . . one time," he said, trying to catch his breath. "Chances are you won't get pregnant. If we're lucky . . ."

One time was all it took. But what else could he say? While the idea of having a baby didn't sound half-bad to him, she was still in love with David. And she didn't admire him a whole lot. He guessed she'd feel just the opposite.

"You okay?" he murmured when she didn't respond. He was braced for the worst, for more tears. But she didn't cry. She didn't answer, either. She pulled his head down to hers and kissed him again, hard.

She was more demanding than he remembered her being, but he liked it. It made him want to make love to her again. They'd held back the tide of their desire for so long there wasn't any way to shore it up now that the barriers had come down. . . .

"Let's go back to your place," she breathed against his lips.

He didn't argue. As far as he was concerned, they were just getting started. But first he was going to buy some condoms.

Claire hadn't made love so many times in one night since her honeymoon. But they were making up for lost time. They began as soon as they stepped through the front door, right in the living room. After that, it was the bedroom, then the shower. By the time they were too exhausted to move, they were lying in bed with the sun coming up.

"Seriously?" Claire scowled at the intruding light as she rested her chin on his chest. "Where are your blinds?"

He pushed her hair away from her face. "What?"

"You have nothing covering the windows."

"We could put up some sheets. If we had the energy," he added with a chuckle.

"That light is really annoying." Trying to shut it out, she buried her face between his arm and chest. "How's a girl supposed to sleep? I have to work in two hours."

She wasn't sure he'd understand her muffled words, but he must've been able to make them out because he answered. "Oddly enough, the light's never bothered me before."

She raised her head. "Haven't any of your bed partners complained?"

"What bed partners?" he said on a yawn.

"Yeah, right."

He didn't respond, and she was sort of glad. She didn't want to hear about his other lovers.

"This has been incredible," he said after several seconds of silence.

That statement sounded like a serious one but, afraid she might read too much into it, she laid her head on his chest and tried to laugh it off. "You haven't lost a thing. Is that what you want me to say?"

His eyes drifted closed. "Only if you feel so compelled."

"I'll leave that to the others." She regretted mentioning his love life for a second time, but she needed to keep his casual attitude toward sex in mind. Maybe caution would help her retain some perspective so she wouldn't get emotionally entangled. Loving him was one thing; knowing he didn't or couldn't love her back the way she wanted, the way she needed, was another.

Fortunately, he didn't complain or accuse her of the jealousy that lurked beneath her reference. "What about *your* other lovers?"

She rubbed a hand over the contours of his taut stomach. "You know I don't have any. Not anymore."

His lips brushed her forehead with a quick kiss. "How do *I* know that?"

"Because my husband is dead and there's never been anyone besides the two of you."

The tone of her voice probably told him he'd struck a nerve. She felt his chest lift as he drew a deep breath. "So this was your first time since David."

"You thought otherwise?"

"I know you're still in love with him. But a year's a long time to sleep alone when you're used to having someone in your bed. And I've been gone so much. For all I know, there could've been some other man."

"There's been no one else," she insisted.

He played with her hair. He'd always said how much he liked it. "Are you actually going to your salon after being up all night?"

"I have to."

"What would happen if you didn't? Can't you cancel?"

"No, I've already missed one day this week. And it's Saturday, my busiest day." She refused to give anyone a reason to question why she had to cancel, or to delve into where she'd been. The attack at her mother's studio had been sensational enough. If she was going to screw up her life, she'd rather do it privately. "Fortunately, I have tomorrow and Monday off. I can recover then."

"We'll get into bed early tonight."

She almost said yes, then remembered she had a commitment. "I can't see you this evening."

"Why not?"

"I have a date."

There was another silence. She was hoping he'd leave it at that, but he didn't. "Who with?"

"Some guy Laurel's been wanting to introduce me to. I haven't met him yet."

"What's his name?"

"Owen Rodriguez. He's from Libby."

"What's he do?"

Did it matter? She covered a yawn. "He's an accountant."

"Sounds steady."

She couldn't tell if he was bothered by the fact that she'd be seeing someone else. She couldn't imagine he was. "He's supposed to be a real stand-up guy."

"Just your type."

"Yeah." It beat having her heart torn to shreds. . . .

"So why were you crying last night?" Although his voice was gentle and his hand slid reassuringly back and forth on her shoulder, she couldn't talk about her meeting with April. What she'd learned formed a morass of dark emotion swirling somewhere in her brain, but that morass didn't have a hold on her at this particular moment. Being in Isaac's arms somehow protected her — as long as they didn't venture too close to the subjects she needed to avoid, at least for now. "I don't want to go into it."

"Why not?"

"I can't face it."

"But you'll have to face it sometime."

"Morning will be soon enough."

He moved the hand that had been rubbing her back to gesture at the light pouring into the room. "Didn't you just point out that it *is* morning?"

"After I sleep for a bit."

"Okay. I guess you'll tell me when you're ready." They shifted until she was on her side and he was spooning her. "But will you do me a favor?"

Had she dreamed that he'd just asked for a favor? It was becoming difficult to talk. She was too languid, too warm, too comfortable and content, if not actually safe. She clung to that sense of peace, couldn't give it up quite yet. "Hmm?"

"Promise me you'll eat better."

"I thought we hated each other," she mumbled.

He nipped at her shoulder. "Nah, we're friends, remember?"

Friends with benefits. She'd done it. She'd

put herself right back where she'd been ten years ago. But she couldn't think about that, either, or all the rest — what April had said and what it meant — would come back, too. It was all part of the same reality.

After Claire left, Isaac pulled on a pair of sweatpants and wandered into his office. There, he unlocked the safe in which he stored the flash drives that contained originals of all his work and took a manila folder from the bottom shelf. Inside were two pages — all the private investigators had been able to dig up on his mother.

She wasn't bad-looking, he thought as he stared down at her mug shot. She might even have been pretty, before her drug habit. By the time this picture was taken, two years before her accidental overdose, she'd been living on the streets and selling her body to survive. If she hadn't been arrested for prostitution, he wouldn't have a single photograph of her.

What he'd found when he'd gone looking for the person who'd abandoned him hadn't been anything like he'd hoped — but he'd found answers. The mystery that had plagued him for so long, that had kept him restless day and night, had been solved when he'd finally come to terms with the fact that he had to know and had stopped lying to himself, stopped saying that it didn't matter. His mother had driven off in her rattletrap car and left him in the bathroom at a roadside convenience store/café, and she'd done it because she loved crack more than she loved him.

Bailey Rawlings. That was the name she was using at the time of her arrest. He wasn't sure if that had always been her name. For all he knew, she could've made it up so she wouldn't embarrass her family, or in case they ever wanted to find her. At five, she'd merely been Mommy to him. The P.I. had dug up Isaac's birth certificate, which had the name Morgan on it but no father.

When the P.I. managed to track down Bailey's parents, whose surname was Morgan, Isaac had gone to see them in South Carolina. They hadn't known whether she'd ever married; if the name *Rawlings* meant she had, they'd never been told. They hadn't known she had a child either, so it'd been awkward. As soon as he learned they couldn't tell him anything about his dad, he'd said goodbye and they hadn't been in touch since, except for the Christmas card he'd received last December. He hadn't bothered searching for his father beyond that. It was enough to know what had happened to his mother. Considering her lifestyle, he could guess that his father was probably some john who wouldn't be too interested in discovering he'd had a baby with a prostitute.

Sketchy though the details were, the information in this folder had turned him around. Made him grateful for what he had. Made him realize he was almost certainly better off than he would've been if she'd kept him. He'd been raised in a good place by people with the best of intentions who'd tolerated him despite the trouble he gave them. He wished he'd treated Old Man Tippy with more respect when he'd had the chance.

He had his answers, so he could bind up that festering wound. But Claire was where he'd been two years ago and could not. Before she left, she'd told him what April had said. He could tell she was more conflicted than ever. She had to know whom to trust. The questions were eating her up inside, and it was killing him to watch, because he *understood.*

Maybe that was why they were drawn to each other, why everything between them was always so intense.

I hate you. . . . If that was true, she had a funny way of showing it. What she hated was herself, because she couldn't seem to alleviate the pain and fulfill her obligations as a good sister and daughter at the same time.

She needed to hire a quality P.I. like he had, someone better than the ones Tug had used, to finally get to the bottom of what had happened fifteen years ago. It was the only way to find peace. But she didn't have the money. And Tug had long since given up. *That's why I'm going to step in.* Maybe she was still in love with David. And maybe he'd never be able to compare to such a good man. But, as imperfect as Isaac knew he was, he was all Claire had.

Removing the business card that'd been clipped to the manila folder, he picked up the phone.

16

"Where were you Thursday night?"

Claire was cutting Carrie Oldman, one of the eight women in her book group. She'd already received a message from Carrie, as well as Laurel and one other friend, wondering why she didn't show, but she'd been too caught up in everything else to respond. "Um, I was . . . not feeling well," she finished lamely. Even if she was sick, it would be unusual for her not to call. Rarely did anyone miss their meetings. But that was the best answer she could conjure up on the spot.

Carrie frowned into the mirror. "Are you better now?"

"I'm not contagious, if that's what you mean. Why?"

"You seem . . . a little out of it."

Claire kept her attention on the short bob she was creating out of Carrie's long, straight hair. With all the thinning and breaking as Carrie aged, she definitely needed a change. But it'd taken a year to talk her into this new style. And she'd chosen today of all days to go for it.

"I haven't been getting much sleep," Claire said. But that wasn't everything. It was what April had said during their discussion yesterday that weighed so heavily on her: *You mean the part about Tug being infertile? You didn't know?*

The drape rustled as Carrie brought her hand out to scratch her nose. "I'm really worried about you. We all are. You know that, don't you? Once it was obvious that you weren't going to come, Laurel hardly said a word the rest of the night."

Claire would be able to reassure Laurel tonight. They had that date, which she didn't want to go on. "I'm fine. Really. You guys need to quit worrying."

Carrie's hand came out again, this time to loosen the fastening of the drape. "You were just a little sick? That's all it was?"

"That's right."

She looked slightly hurt. "But we called, and when you didn't answer, a couple of us came by. You weren't home."

Claire hurried to shore up the lie. "I must've walked over to Leanne's."

"Your car was gone, so we knocked at Leanne's door. She said she hadn't seen you."

"I guess I saw her later, after I got back." Claire gave a laugh she hoped didn't sound as nervous as she felt. She really didn't want her association with Isaac to get out. She had to come to terms with too many other things first. "I drove over to my parents'. You know how it is when you feel sick. Sometimes you want someone else to take care of you."

Uncertainty flickered in Carrie's eyes. "Oh, you were at Tug and Roni's."

She hoped they hadn't checked there, too. Claire wouldn't put it past them. She loved every member, but a few of them didn't know how to mind their own business. Of course, the same could be said about most people in Pineview. "For a while."

"So what happened yesterday?"

"Yesterday? Nothing. Why?"

"Ellie saw your car at April's house."

Her heart began to thump but Claire kept cutting.

"We didn't think you and April were friends," Carrie added. She had a sweet way about her, but she was better at wheedling information out of a person than almost anyone else in town.

"We've never had a disagreement," Claire said.

"So . . . you *were* there? You went to *April's?*"

Shit . . . Sometimes her hometown drove her crazy. "Roni had a photo of April's nephew she wanted me to drop off." Maybe if Carrie thought Roni already knew about the visit, had even requested it, there'd be nothing scandalous to report. Claire preferred to keep that visit, and what she'd learned, to herself until she figured out who and what to believe.

Seemingly satisfied, Carrie's piqued expression cleared. "I get it. Of course she wouldn't want to deliver it herself. They're still not speaking."

"I'm not sure they ever will." Considering what April thought, Claire doubted it. . . .

Carrie lowered her voice. "April thinks Roni caused her father's death. Divorces are difficult, but suicide . . . that's an individual choice."

Perhaps. But Roni could be more culpable than she let on — for April's father's suicide *and* Alana's disappearance, not that Claire wanted to accept that. She had too many positive memories of her stepmother taking her back-to-school shopping or planning her birthday parties or snapping pictures of her in her prom dress.

Instead of answering, Claire pretended

complete absorption while measuring the hair on either side of Carrie's face. "Looks straight," she murmured, and backed away. "How do you like it?"

Carrie's smile was more hesitant than Claire would've liked. "It's . . . going to take some getting used to."

She looked darling, much better than when she'd walked in, but familiarity counted for a lot. Claire just hoped Carrie did get used to the change, and that her ultraconservative husband would react favorably. She couldn't deal with a disgruntled client today, not one who was disgruntled over an *improvement.* "I think the new look takes five years off your age."

She perked up. "Really?"

"Definitely."

The bell jingled over the door. As Claire removed Carrie's drape, she turned to welcome her next client, but it was her sister.

"Where'd you go last night?" Leanne demanded without the courtesy of a greeting. Obviously, she was still angry.

A trickle of unease went through Claire. She didn't want another confrontation with her sister, especially with Carrie listening in. If her parents or David's parents learned she was seeing Isaac, they wouldn't be happy. They'd remind her of what happened last time and she'd probably end up in another argument with them. "Funny you should ask. Give me a minute so we don't hold Carrie up," she said, and turned back to her client. "That's twenty-five dollars, as always."

Leanne's displeasure hung over the room like an overcast sky. No doubt Carrie could sense it. She kept glancing at Lee as she wrote her check. "Here you go." She seemed about to linger, no doubt hoping to hear their conversation. But Claire walked her to the door.

"It was great to see you, Car. Sorry I missed book group but I'll be there next week."

Carrie's eyes darted back to Leanne. "You should come, too, Lee. This week we're reading *Room* by Emma Donoghue. It's a really intriguing story."

"I have no interest in books." Leanne said it as if she had no interest in the group, either, which she didn't. Claire had invited her before. She said she'd have plenty of time for book groups when she was old and couldn't do anything more "fun."

Perhaps some of the members weren't the most interesting people in town — a few were downright stuffy — but reading helped

Claire keep her mind off David, and knowing she had a deadline made her more focused on getting through each book. Without that, she'd lie in front of the TV every night missing her husband, something she did far too often as it was.

"Thanks again." Claire held the door.

Since she was cornered into leaving, Carrie finally nodded. "See you Thursday."

Claire breathed a sigh of relief as the door swung shut. "I'm expecting another client," she said. "So if you've come to start an argument, I'd appreciate it if you waited until I'm off. You might get your workshop all to yourself every day, but I have to maintain a professional atmosphere."

Leanne maneuvered the chair to face her. "Quit trying to delay this. No one's here now, and it won't take you more than a second to explain why you never came home last night — again."

"If what you do is none of my business, then what I do is none of yours, right?"

This wasn't the answer she'd been expecting. Her mouth opened and closed twice before she found words. "That's it? That's all you've got to say?"

"That's all." If she didn't offer a lie, Leanne couldn't catch her in it later.

Her sister's eyes narrowed. "Are you seeing someone, Claire?"

"No. Stop it."

"You are, aren't you? It's Isaac Morgan! You've gone back to him."

Claire wasn't surprised she'd guessed, not when she'd seen his truck in front of her place twice — and it had stayed there all night one of those times. But it was important to downplay her and Isaac's relationship, or the whole town would start buzzing with the news that David's widow was having sex with her former lover.

"He's a friend. That's all."

"A friend who spends the night with you?"

Denying it wasn't going to work. Even if she could convince Leanne, Leanne wasn't the only one who knew they'd been together. Rusty did, too. And other people might have seen her get into Isaac's truck when he picked her up on the street. Isaac wasn't the boy next door; he had a reputation. No one would believe they were hanging out together as mere friends.

Which left Claire one option — to confront all questions with absolute transparency. If she admitted to a romantic involvement, there'd be less for the curious to ferret out and, she hoped, the scandal would blow over more quickly.

"Yes, actually. Friends with benefits," she

said. "You've heard of that, right?" Of course she had, but Claire didn't want her to think she was trying to get away with less than the truth.

"Everyone's heard of that, except maybe the ladies you see on Thursday nights. Some of them grew up in the Big Band Era. So you're not really . . . *dating.*"

"Nope. Just sleeping together." And their encounters generally included some force-feeding, but no one would care about that. It wasn't sensational enough. "Does that answer your question?"

Leanne gaped at her. "Do you realize who he is, Claire?"

"I know he's amazing in bed. That's all that matters at the moment."

"But just a couple nights ago you were warning *me* not to ruin my reputation. Now you're going to sew a giant *F* on your chest? Be the talk of the town? Even when Isaac tries to be discreet, people pay too much attention to him. He's a celebrity around here, for crying out loud."

Claire angled her chin in a belligerent fashion. "You said you don't mind gossip. Maybe I decided to take a page from *your* book."

They glared at each other — until Leanne broke the silence.

"Claire, listen. I — I'm sorry. I didn't realize you were so close to the edge. I know what happened with Mom really did a number on you, but you've always been strong. I guess . . . I guess I figured you could move on if I could. Losing her wasn't easy on me, either. But . . . I feel responsible for this, as if I pushed you into his arms. We haven't been getting along and that hasn't left you with anyone you can really talk to. But I don't want to see you hurt again."

Claire didn't want to hear this. She bent over her desk to count the number of clients remaining on the schedule. Already dead on her feet, she wished she could just crawl into bed.

Fortunately, her workday ended at four, only two hours away. Maybe she'd have time for a nap before the big date. "Come on, you're overreacting. What do you think he's going to do to me?"

What he'd done to her before, of course. At least Leanne wasn't asking about April. The book group ladies must not have mentioned seeing her car there when they went to Leanne's house. It could get back to her eventually, but it wasn't now and that was a small blessing. Maybe with such big news as her involvement with Isaac hitting the gossip scene, that tidbit would fall by the wayside completely.

One could hope. She'd didn't want to hurt Roni.

"You're kidding!" Leanne said. "Isaac Morgan's a bona fide heartbreaker, and no one knows that better than you. And now you're on the rebound. He'll chew you up and spit you out."

God, even her hard-drinking sister could plainly see what was in store. Still, Claire wouldn't acknowledge the danger. If she did pay a price for her actions, she'd suffer without letting anyone know, unless, of course, that price included pregnancy. But she'd deal with that if she had to. "I won't get hurt. He's just a friend, a way to break up the monotony."

Leanne slid her tongue over her teeth. "He's got to be more fun than that geriatric book group you've got going."

"Those ladies aren't geriatric."

"Half of them are over seventy."

"So? They're nice."

"I'm not talking about *nice.* I'm saying they can't give you the same kind of thrill."

"No woman can."

"Not very many men, either," she said with a conspirator's laugh.

Claire didn't find that comment funny. The appreciation in her sister's voice jammed a shard of fear into her chest. "Wait a second. *You've* never been with him, have you?" The question alone made it difficult to breathe. *Say no. Please say no, or I'm going to be sick right here. . . .* She'd heard the vehicles that sometimes came and went in the night, but she usually didn't get up to see who was driving. She didn't want to know. Not knowing made it easier to pretend Leanne didn't entertain as often as she did.

Her sister winked at her. "I'm not the type to kiss and tell."

There was no time to push for more. Selina Spangler had walked in for her cut and color.

Myles King got up and closed the door to his office almost as soon as Isaac arrived. "I'm glad you came by. Rusty Clegg asked me to have a word with you."

Isaac removed his sunglasses. The drive to Libby took thirty minutes, and the sun seemed especially bright today. "Rusty already told me to back off, if that's what you're intending to do."

"Rusty was upset by your conversation, which is why he asked me to intervene. David meant a lot to him."

"David meant a lot to many people. That's

one of the reasons I believe you owe it to Pineview to confirm that he died the way we think he did."

Myles didn't take even a second to respond. "I'm not sure I'll like what you have to say any more than Rusty did."

Great, not only had he been tipped off, he'd been prejudiced. Refusing to let that upset him, Isaac took the seat across from Myles. If he was going to get anywhere with Les Weaver, he needed the sheriff's help. "I don't blame you," he said. "Murder one is a serious accusation."

"Not only that but I don't want to get the whole community up in arms until I have proof. David's parents have been through enough, losing him the way they did, and at such a young age. Claire has been through enough, too. She still hasn't recovered. All you have to do is look at her to know that."

Which was why Isaac thought it was time to intervene. "You don't think I've considered what you're saying?"

The sheriff's chair squealed as he pulled it away from the desk so he could sit. "I guess where I get confused is this — what's your interest in the situation, Isaac? Why are you getting involved?"

His interest was Claire. Now that she was back in his life, he wanted to be sure she achieved the resolution she needed. But he also knew how quickly everyone would doubt him if he said he was trying to do a good deed. No one would believe it was that simple. Although he hadn't landed himself in trouble in years, they'd treat him like he was the big bad wolf coming to blow down the poor widow's house.

The people of Pineview had tolerated — more kindly than some towns would have — an abandoned child in their midst, but they possessed very long memories. They would never let him live down his past. "Someone's got to make sure it is what it appears to be. Might as well be me."

"That's it? That's all there is to it?"

"That's it."

Myles swiveled back and forth as he mulled over Isaac's response. "But I'm not convinced there's any connection between David's death and Alana's disappearance," he finally said.

"I think you're wrong."

"Do you have any evidence to support your opinion?"

Clasping his hands loosely between his legs, Isaac leaned forward. "No evidence. Yet. But I've come across some interesting coincidences."

Myles opened a notebook. "I'm all ears."

"First of all, David was researching Alana's death and was raising enough questions to negate the argument that she ran off. What he was doing would eventually lead to police involvement, which made someone very nervous."

"I'm supposed to take what you say David was doing on faith?"

"You don't have to. It's all in the files."

"What files?"

"The case files."

Now Myles was *really* skeptical. No longer the open-minded listener, he leaned forward. "And how would *you* know anything about the case files?"

"Somehow, David got a copy of them before he died. They had to have come from your office so I initially thought Rusty must've provided them. But when I spoke to him, he denied it and seemed completely unaware that David was even pursuing the mystery."

Someone knocked on the door, a deputy, but Myles hollered that he'd be out in a few minutes. Then his eyes shifted back to Isaac. "You haven't mentioned how you know he had any files."

"Claire found them at the studio the night she was pushed down by that unknown assailant. They had his writing all over them."

The sheriff dropped his pen. He was beginning to catch on. "Why weren't they there when I searched?"

"Because I'd already taken them. She was afraid she'd lose them otherwise. They contained information she hadn't been privy to before. Some progress David had made, like I said. And some conflicting testimony and facts that didn't quite jive with what she'd been told. Things law enforcement kept from her and the press."

"Like . . ."

Was this a test? "Leanne's absence from school on the day in question."

His mouth flattened into a thin line. If it had been a test, he'd just passed. "Then you're right. That had to come from my office. But I have no idea how."

Isaac couldn't help him there. "All I know is what I saw."

The chair creaked as he rocked back. "David having copies of what's in our files doesn't mean he was killed because of it."

"That's not all I've got to tell you."

"Go on."

"I went to see the man who shot him."

At this Myles straightened. "In Idaho?"

"That's right."

"You're damn serious about all of this."

"I am."

"And what did you learn?"

Isaac pictured the polished, wealthy lawyer. "He's a far cry from any hunter I've ever met. And he's not exactly a stand-up guy."

"You gathered that from one meeting? How long were you there?"

"Not long. He brushed me off as soon as he could, but not before he gave me some song and dance about how devastated he was by what he'd done."

"Which you didn't believe."

Isaac stretched out his legs and crossed them at the ankles. "I did at first. He told me he was so traumatized he couldn't hunt anymore, that he'd got rid of every gun he owned because he can't bear the sight of them."

Myles steepled his fingers. "Any man would feel that way."

"But it was a lie. He still has a whole cabinet full of guns. I could see them from his backyard."

"They could belong to a friend or family member."

"They were inside *his* house. And there was something else that struck me as odd."

"What's that?"

"He's a bankruptcy attorney."

"That makes him a bloodsucker, not a

murderer," Myles joked.

"But how many bankruptcy attorneys do you know who've witnessed a client shoot himself to death?"

Myles got to his feet. "This happened to him?"

"He said it did — right in his office."

"Why would he tell you that?"

"He thought it's what motivated my visit."

"Shit." Turning, he stared through the slats of the blind.

Isaac stood, too. "So now you have someone who's accidentally shot a man while hunting and who's also been involved in another unusual death."

"Suicide isn't murder," he argued, but he didn't sound nearly as unfriendly or unconvinced as he had when Isaac first arrived.

"Maybe it wasn't suicide," Isaac suggested.

Myles blew out a sigh. "I admit these coincidences are odd, but . . . the suicide must've checked out."

"If the police did their homework, it shouldn't be too difficult to get a look at their findings. The details might shed some more light on Les Weaver."

No response.

"Come on, all I'm asking is that you poke around a bit. Learn how and why someone died in his office and figure out whether or not he had any connection to Pineview. He claims he came here alone, for the first time, without knowing a soul. A check of his phone records for the months leading up to David's death would tell us if he was having regular conversations with anyone in this area. And if he was . . ."

"We could have a killer on the loose," Myles finished.

17

Claire wasted her opportunity to nap by going to a clothing shop in town. She wouldn't have been able to sleep, anyway. Not after her sister had planted the terrible thought that maybe she and Isaac had been together.

Had he used them both?

She didn't want to face it if he had. She was tired of her own pressing concerns. She was also tired of feeling dowdy. If she was going on a date, she wanted to look and feel as attractive as possible. So she distracted herself from her troubles by buying some tight jeans, a silky gold sheath top that brought out the highlights in her hair and a pair of high-heeled sandals. She even splurged on dangly earrings that swung when she moved her head and lotion that made her skin feel satiny soft.

By the time Myles and Laurel arrived to pick her up, she was actually looking forward to acting like a normal person for a change, someone who could go out to eat and chat with friends. Someone who wasn't constantly obsessing about her dead husband or missing mother — or even the scandal that waited for her as word spread that she'd become Isaac's latest conquest. With any luck, that news wouldn't take center stage until tomorrow. She figured she might as well enjoy her last night of being pitied simply for the unfortunate incidents that had affected her life so far. Soon she'd be pitied *and* taken for a fool.

If he'd slept with Leanne — even if he'd done it only once — she *was* a fool and would never forgive herself for her stupidity.

Owen Rodriguez met them at Harry Dog's Steakhouse. Dressed in loafers, a pair of dark jeans and a white golf shirt that contrasted nicely with his café au lait skin, he had close-cropped hair, dark, intelligent eyes and a broad, friendly smile. Only his glasses made him look remotely like the stereotypical accountant, but they were far more stylish than nerdy. She liked him immediately.

"So what do you think?" Laurel whispered as he stopped to speak to a gentleman he happened to know while they were making their way to the table.

Claire squeezed her hand. "He's cute."

Myles seemed distracted throughout dinner. Every time his eyes landed on Claire they slipped away again, and he didn't say much. Claire wondered if he'd heard that she and Isaac were romantically involved. If so, she knew he wouldn't like it. He was almost as protective of her as Laurel was.

Other than his general preoccupation, he didn't indicate what he might have learned, so she had no way of knowing, but dinner went smoothly in spite of that. Owen was easy to talk to. He kept the conversation going and had them laughing for much of the meal.

The fatigue Claire had been feeling earlier began to drag at her as they left the restaurant, but everyone else wanted to go dancing, so she figured she'd have to catch up on her sleep tomorrow. She had Sunday and Monday off, thank goodness. But she would never have agreed to go to the Kicking Horse if she'd known Isaac was going to be there.

She spotted him almost as soon as she came through the door. Judging by the expression on his face, he hadn't expected to see her, either. He sat up as they walked in, his gaze immediately lowering to Owen's hand on her waist.

"Would you like a drink?"

Claire blinked and focused on her date. "Um, yeah, that'd be great. Thank you."

"A glass of wine or —"

"Wine's good. Any kind."

She didn't care what he brought her as long as he gave her a few minutes alone. It was difficult to smile or act normal when her thoughts had suddenly stalled. This was such an awkward situation. And it didn't make any sense. As nice as Owen Rodriguez was, she didn't want to be here with him. She wanted Isaac.

Some things never change. . . .

Forcing herself to break eye contact, she turned to Laurel. "How do you like your hair? Did I do okay this time?"

Laurel wasn't deceived by Claire's attempt to distract her. She'd seen Isaac, too, and noticed the lingering glance between them. "What's going on with you two?" she whispered.

Fortunately, Myles had accompanied Owen to the bar. Even so, Claire preferred not to admit the truth, especially with Isaac sitting only fifteen or twenty feet away. But she knew Laurel would find out in a matter of days that they'd been together and would be hurt if she was the last to know. "What I said earlier about . . . Isaac coming to get his hair cut?"

Laurel's eyebrows shot up. "Y-e-s . . ."

"That wasn't true. He'd just spent the night."

Stunned silence, then, "You're kidding me."

"No. We didn't have sex that night . . . but we have been together."

Laurel grabbed her arm. "What about David?"

She couldn't explain that she loved David in a different way. She doubted anyone else would understand exactly what loving both of them had been like. She'd given her marriage everything she had control over, would never have hurt David and still missed him terribly. But . . . what was she supposed to do without him? "He's not here anymore."

"But you know Isaac will never do right by you! You were with him before."

Closing her eyes, Claire rubbed her forehead. She wished she had the energy to put on the same it's-merely-casual-and-I'm-okay-with-it show she'd managed for Leanne, but she couldn't. She was too exhausted. "I know."

"Owen is a great guy, Claire," Laurel said. "Don't let Isaac get in the way. You won't, will you? Please give Owen a chance."

"I'm trying."

Laurel tightened the hold she had on Claire's arm. "God, I can't *believe* Isaac's here. Why does he have to be here?"

That was Claire's question. Tonight had been the first time she'd felt some hope of finding a legitimate romantic interest since David.

Now she just wanted to go home. But she felt obligated, to Laurel for setting this up and to Owen for allowing Laurel to do it, and that kept her from walking out. The least she could do was try to have fun.

Isaac had to get out of the bar. If he didn't, he'd wind up in a fight before the night was over, after which he'd probably spend some time in the county jail. It wouldn't go over well if he broke the jaw of the sheriff's buddy.

But he couldn't make himself stand and walk to the exit. He remained in the booth, brooding over his beer and watching Claire dance with her date while remembering how hard seeing her with David had been all those years.

He didn't want to go through the same thing again. But if he really cared about her he'd let it be. She needed another man just like the one she'd had — and Glasses certainly looked the part. His smile stretched from ear to ear as they danced, and he kept bending his head to say something that made her laugh.

Still, if his hands moved any closer to her ass —

"You okay?"

Isaac glanced up to see Myles towering over him. He'd been so mired in jealousy he hadn't even noticed the sheriff weaving through the crowd toward him. "Fine. Why? I don't look fine to you?"

"You look like a tightly coiled snake. One that's ready to strike. I don't think that's a good sign with a man like you."

Isaac twirled his mug in the condensation on the table. "And what kind of man am I, Sheriff?"

"One with a huge chip on his shoulder."

"Oh, yeah? Well, who gives a shit what you think? I haven't done anything wrong. You have no right to bother me." They'd been friends, more or less, in Myles's office this morning. But that was then. The sheriff was obviously throwing his support behind Glasses, which put them on opposite sides of this issue. Myles had probably chosen the better man, but it didn't feel particularly good.

"I'll pretend you didn't say that. I know you're not really yourself at the moment.

And I'll offer you an incentive to make sure you don't ruin the evening."

What was this shit about an incentive? Since when did the sheriff have anything Isaac wanted?

Shifting his gaze from Claire's tight jeans to the sheriff's face, he drained his mug. "What are you talking about?"

"I've subpoenaed Les Weaver's telephone records. You leave now, I'll call you when they come in and we'll go over them together. Fair enough?"

It was only a date, a blind date. Claire had mentioned it to him. Isaac had just never dreamed he'd have a front-row seat as they got to know each other, or that it'd be so difficult to watch — not this soon. Maybe it was because Glasses reminded him so much of David, in manner if not in appearance.

"I'm not about to start anything, Sheriff," he grumbled. Then he threw some money on the table and left.

Jeremy rambled around the empty house. He usually liked being home by himself. Then he could watch a little TV or make himself a bite to eat without worrying about his father getting mad at him for some stupid mistake. But he didn't like being the only one home tonight. The way his father was acting these days, the calls that'd come in with the whispering and the cursing and the reassuring, made him nervous. What was going on?

His father wouldn't tell him who was on the other end of the line — he'd yelled at him just for asking — but Jeremy guessed it had to do with Claire's mother. He was pretty sure Don had been talking to Les Weaver. He'd heard him that one time. And he knew who Les Weaver was, and what he did for a living. Once, when Don was drunk, he said Les killed people for money, that he might kill Jeremy someday if he caused any trouble.

Jeremy didn't want to cause trouble. He just wanted to go to Claire's. He needed to make sure she was okay. But he couldn't. His father had told him not to leave the house. He'd also taken Jeremy's Impala, the car that Hank, his boss, had given him because the Jeep wouldn't start. If Jeremy wanted to go anywhere, he'd have to walk. It was dangerous to walk on the highway, but his father didn't care about that. He didn't care that the Impala didn't belong to him, either. He took it whenever he wanted.

The moon glimmered on the lake outside. The mountains Jeremy loved so much rose just beyond it. He considered leaving the house despite being told to stay. Maybe he'd camp out until he was scheduled to work on Monday. That would show his father that he couldn't boss him around anymore, wouldn't it? If he didn't come home tonight? His old man laughed whenever he talked about heading into the wild, said he wouldn't last a day, but his father didn't know anything. The mountains were going to be his safe place. Even Les couldn't find him there. And he had all the gear, had been collecting it for years.

He hadn't yet braved an all-nighter, but he camped out in the yard sometimes.

His stomach growled as he went into the kitchen and opened the fridge.

Nothing but a few bottles of beer, a jar of olives and some condiments. His father was drinking away more and more of his disability money. He'd already spent Jeremy's paycheck, too, or so he'd said this morning when Jeremy asked if they could go to the grocery store.

The thought of being so broke made Jeremy feel that panicky feeling he hated. He didn't want the power company coming to turn off the electricity again. It was scary enough in the basement with his bedroom so close to the crawl space. He wondered if there really was such a thing as zombies, and if they ate people like they did on TV.

Better not to think about that . . .

He closed the fridge. If he wanted to eat, he'd have to go to Hank's. He'd worked at the burger joint for almost fifteen years, flipping meat patties, making fries and shakes, sweeping floors and taking out the trash. He did whatever Hank asked, even if he was just stopping in to say hi, and Hank appreciated it. Hank had recently said, "Jeremy, you do a darn good job, son. I don't know where I'd be without you." And then he promised Jeremy he could eat at the restaurant whenever he pleased. "You'll never go hungry long as I'm alive. You remember that, okay? There's food here for you. There will always be food here."

"Thank you, Hank," he'd murmured, because there wasn't much food at home these days.

Intent on getting a burger, Jeremy headed for the door, but there was one problem. His father would get mad if he left. Actually, there were two problems. How would he get to the diner even if he had the nerve to disobey? He wouldn't walk there anymore. Not past the cemetery. The idea of so many dead people buried in the earth upset him, and ever since his father had pretended he was going to run him down, Jeremy was afraid to be out on the highway. He believed Don might really do it someday.

If he could just make it to the other end of town, he could eat *and* visit Claire's. He liked watching over her. It made him feel so much better about Alana. He'd promised Alana long ago that he'd look after Claire. He would've done the same for Leanne, but Leanne wasn't a very nice person. She snapped at him every time he came close. He didn't really like her.

The phone rang. Was it his father, checking in to be sure he hadn't left?

Maybe. They didn't have caller ID; caller ID cost money.

Drawing a deep breath because he never knew what kind of mood his father might be in, Jeremy picked up the handset. "Good evening. Salter residence." He always answered the phone that way. The people who called said it was very polite.

"Jeremy?"

"Yes?" It wasn't his father. It was Tug. But even after he recognized the voice, Jeremy couldn't relax. Tug had already called and he sounded upset. He definitely wasn't his normal friendly self today. Jeremy should know. Tug used to be his dad's best friend when they both worked at Walt's gun store.

"Is Don around?"

"No, sir. He's not home."

"Do you have any idea where he's at?"

"No."

"Are you sure? I really need to talk to him."

Why? Tug and his father didn't even like each other anymore. His father said Tug thought he was too good for everyone now that he had money. He also said it wasn't fair for Tug to have so much while they had so little. He would never explain why, but sometimes, when he was drunk and Jeremy was pulling off his shoes to put him to bed, he mumbled about Tug having "blood money."

Jeremy had never heard of blood money, but he didn't like the sound of it. "He said he'd skin me alive if I left, and then he took my car."

Tug didn't seem pleased. "I see he's as kind to you as ever."

Jeremy didn't know how to respond to this. What Tug said was nice to him but not nice to his father.

"Okay, don't worry about it." Tug filled the silence.

"He might be at the Kicking Horse having a drink." Jeremy thought that was pretty obvious, but he wanted to be helpful.

"I can't go looking for him tonight. I've

got too much going on." He seemed distracted when he added, "I'll be right there, honey."

"Excuse me?" Jeremy said.

His voice grew stronger. "Honey" had been someone else. "If he comes back in the next hour or so, have him give me a call, will you? If not, I'll track him down in the morning."

After Jeremy hung up, he stared at the phone. *Was* his father at the bar? If so, maybe he'd be getting a call from the bartender. Sammy usually asked Jeremy to pick Don up when he spent this much time there.

Maybe Jeremy could call to check. If his father was at the Kicking Horse, he could probably stop worrying about Claire.

Feeling instantly better, he dragged out the phone book and found the number. But Sammy said he hadn't seen Don at all tonight.

Where else could he have gone? His father didn't have that many friends left. . . .

"Please, not Claire's. Just leave her alone," Jeremy whispered, but he had no faith his father would actually do that. Not if he felt she was a threat to him. He'd kill her while it was dark, then he'd hide her body in the woods. Or maybe he'd bring it home for

Jeremy to hide. He felt Jeremy should do anything he asked, no matter what it was.

Jeremy eyed the door. He had to walk to Claire's, along the highway, past the cemetery. That was the only way he'd be sure.

But then he remembered Isaac. She'd been with Isaac so much the past week, just like she'd been with him after high school. She was probably with him now. Which meant she'd be okay. No one wanted to mess with Isaac. Even his truck looked mean.

Ignoring his hunger pangs, Jeremy plopped down in front of the TV to wait for his father. But when Don still wasn't home four hours later, Jeremy grew so frantic he decided he *had* to leave. As frightening as it was to walk, he had to reach a pay phone. He needed to warn Isaac to look after Claire, and he couldn't use the house phone or Isaac would know who it was. He'd learned that the hard way, when he'd gotten in trouble for calling Claire too many times.

"Go . . . go!" he told himself. He could do it. But then he glanced at the clock and felt even more worried. Maybe his father had already gotten to her. Maybe it was already too late.

Claire stared into the mirror hanging on

her closet. She looked good. But that was about all she could say for her night.

With a discouraged sigh, she tossed her purse on her bed and kicked off her high heels. After Isaac had left the bar, she'd had to stay another two hours, which had felt more like two days, and now she was so tired she could hardly remain on her feet.

Bed. She needed to sleep. But her mind kept churning up snatches of conversation that made her emotions swing in all directions. With April: "You didn't know he was infertile?" With Leanne: "I don't kiss and tell." With Owen: "I'd like to take you out again."

She'd given Owen her number but felt no enthusiasm for a second date. He seemed like a great guy — he certainly appealed to her a lot more than Rusty did — but there wasn't any spark. What little flicker she'd felt in the beginning had been doused the minute she walked into the Kicking Horse, spotted Isaac and realized she wasn't ready to give him up, not after ten years of missing him despite her love for David.

The light blinked on her answering machine.

She eyed it warily. Did she dare listen? According to the display, she'd missed five calls. They could all be hair clients, hoping to get an appointment; if so, she could handle that tomorrow. Or maybe one of the calls was from Isaac, although she wasn't sure why he'd bother. He hadn't been too happy when he left the bar. After what they'd shared last night she could understand why. It felt disloyal of her to be with another man. But he'd said they were only friends, and friends didn't expect — or require — exclusivity.

Unable to resist, she pushed the play button.

"Claire? Please tell me you're not stupid enough to get involved with Isaac Morgan again." Roni. Word had reached her. "What's going on with you? You've changed. None of us knows what to do about it, but you're going to get hurt if you're not careful."

It didn't take a genius to figure that out. Claire skipped the rest of her message.

Carrie came on next. "Isaac? Really? I could tell you were holding back but I never suspected an affair with Isaac Morgan. I don't blame you. I'd like to have an affair with him myself," she said with a laugh. "Be careful, though. He's as wild as the animals he photographs —"

"And just as dangerous," Claire added, and hit Skip.

Besides those two messages, there were three hang-up calls. One had come in as late as twelve-thirty. Could that have been Isaac? Should she call him back?

No. She should shut out everything that was confusing her and try to sleep.

"Why do I have to love *you?*" she muttered, and curled up on the bed without even taking off her clothes.

If David were here, none of this would be happening, she thought. But it wasn't David she dreamed about when she drifted off to sleep.

18

When Claire opened her eyes, she could tell she hadn't been sleeping long, and the clock confirmed it. 1:58 a.m. Why was she awake? She wanted to sink back into the nothingness she'd just left — and would have if not for the odd noise that nudged her toward consciousness.

It sounded like someone was at the back door.

Was it Leanne? She couldn't think of anyone besides her sister who'd come over so late. . . .

In the next instant, she sat bolt upright. Leanne wouldn't be at her back door in the middle of the night. Someone was trying to get in. She could hear the *click, click* of the knob as it turned back and forth.

Who was it? And why was that person here?

Wondering if maybe those noises hadn't been as distinctive as she'd first imagined, if maybe it was just some animal rustling around, she got out of bed and tiptoed into the living room, where she could peer around the corner and through the moonlit kitchen.

She hadn't been imagining anything. The dark shadow of a man stood on the other side of the glass.

Her heart jumped into her throat. As she watched, too panic-stricken to move, he left the door and went around to press his face to the window over her sink.

Claire screamed before she realized it was Isaac. Then her chest heaved as she tried to recover from the fright he'd given her. Why was he prowling around her yard?

He'd heard her. She saw his head turn in her direction. He probably couldn't see her, since she was hidden behind the wall and it was darker inside than out, but he jogged to the front, where she met him as he stepped onto the porch.

"What are you doing here?" she cried. "You scared the shit out of me!"

He didn't seem chastised; he seemed concerned. His eyes ran over her from head to foot. "You're okay?"

Why wouldn't she be okay? Before he'd disturbed her, she'd been getting some much-needed rest. "I'm fine, why?"

"Someone called me from a pay phone. I'm pretty sure it was a man, but even that was hard to tell. He had the mouthpiece covered and was talking so low I could barely hear. He said, 'Claire's in trouble.' "

"Are you serious?"

His hair stood up on one side as if he'd just rolled out of bed himself. "Do I look like I'm doing this for kicks?"

"No, but . . ." Her heart rate still hadn't returned to normal. "That's so strange. You don't have any idea who it was?"

"None."

"When was this?"

He rubbed a hand over the razor stubble on his chin. "Twenty minutes ago. Just long enough for me to drive over here. Everything looked so peaceful when I arrived, I thought it had to be somebody's idea of a joke to scare me like that. So I was checking things out, trying to see if there was any reason to worry."

Claire had been so exhausted she hadn't even taken off her makeup, but she was too uneasy to be sleepy now. "Why would anyone crank-call you about *me?*"

He shrugged. "Who knows? It could've been someone who heard about what happened at your mother's studio and thought it would be funny to send me on a fool's errand."

Or someone who'd heard they were seeing each other and wanted to determine whether he cared enough to come to her rescue. She wouldn't put that past a couple of the women who talked about him incessantly.

That was the extent of it, she told herself, but then she remembered the call *she'd* received from the person who'd asked if she'd hired a P.I. She'd forgotten to tell Isaac about that. Life had been such a whirlwind since then she'd scarcely thought of it herself.

"That call must have come from Les," Isaac agreed when Claire had described the brief conversation. "Besides you and me, no one else knows I told him I was a P.I."

Had he called Isaac, too?

Either way, the idea of a raspy-voiced caller foretelling her doom sent chills down her spine, especially after that incident on the Fourth of July. "Sorry someone put you to so much trouble," she said. "That's a long drive in the middle of the night, especially for nothing."

"That's okay. I'm *glad* it was for nothing." Shoving his hands in the pockets of his jeans, he leaned against the door frame.

"So . . . did you have fun with your date tonight?"

She hadn't expected him to confront her about Owen. She'd thought the fact that she was dating other men would be one of those things they wouldn't talk about, even if they did continue to see each other. He didn't want to commit to a relationship, but he didn't want to lose her, either. That pretty much left ignoring the other men in her life as his only option. "It was okay."

His gaze shifted toward her bedroom. "Is he gone?"

"What difference would it make to you even if he wasn't?" she countered.

He studied her carefully. "I'm not very good at sharing."

"We're just friends, remember?"

"I remember, but that doesn't seem to help."

"Fine, he's gone."

"Good." He stepped inside and shut the door behind him. "So what happened after I left?"

"We danced." She shrugged. "That's it."

He scowled as if he didn't want to ask his next question but couldn't resist. "Did he kiss you?"

Scowling right back at him, she said, "Don't ask if you don't want to know."

One eyebrow shot up. "A simple 'no' would be nice. Then maybe I could stop the damn reel of the two of you together that keeps playing in my head."

She put her hands on her hips. "Okay, if you want to talk about bad images — have you ever been with my sister?"

Even without the lights on, she could see the curl of his lip. *"What?"*

The answer he had yet to give frightened her so much she had to take a deep breath. "Leanne. Have you ever slept with her?"

"Hell, no! I've never even *looked* at her. God, what do you think I am?"

"I think that's clear."

"No, it's not. You don't know me if you believe I'd sleep with your sister. Why would you even ask me that?"

Relief finally eased the fear that'd kept her on edge ever since Leanne had shown up in her salon, pretending to have more intimate knowledge of Isaac than she did. "For the same reason you asked me about Owen."

He glared at her. "You're jealous."

"Of course I'm jealous! I've loved you for ten years!" The words tumbled out before she could stop them. She hadn't even realized she was going to say them.

Her confession hung in the air like the scent of gunpowder. She'd probably just shot to hell any chance she had of being with him. She'd gone so far she couldn't even salvage her pride. This was how she'd ruined their relationship the last time — by letting him mean too much.

Maybe it was for the best. Maybe this would put a decisive end to whatever was starting between them again. He'd make sure of it. Then she wouldn't have to fight her natural inclinations any longer.

She held her breath, expecting him to walk out without another word, or to explain, as he'd explained before, that he didn't reciprocate those feelings.

Instead, he stepped close and lifted her chin with one finger. "I thought you were still in love with David."

Of course he'd call her on that. But there was no gloating in his voice. It was an earnest question. "I am," she whispered. "Don't listen to me."

When he tilted his head to study her, she knew she'd given herself away. "I mean nothing to you?" he asked.

"You're good in bed. That's all. Now get out of here." She tried to shove him toward the door, but he resisted.

"You could be pregnant with my baby." Considering the time of the month, it wasn't likely, but it was possible. They hadn't used any birth control that first time. She'd thought of the chance she might be carrying his child often throughout the day, let her heart curl around it almost as a secret wish. But his remark came out of nowhere, as if it had escaped from him just like what *she'd* said a moment earlier.

Her hand automatically went to her stomach. "Does that scare the hell out of you or what?" She gave an awkward laugh. In one way, being a single mother frightened her. She knew it wouldn't be easy, that it would only complicate and strengthen what she felt for Isaac. But she was ready for the next stage of life, ready to love and cherish again, and nothing was more lovable than a baby. Especially Isaac's baby. Somehow it seemed . . . right.

He stared down at her. "I've been thinking about it."

She braced herself in case he mentioned abortion. She wouldn't do it. She'd take the baby and run away if she had to, but she wouldn't terminate the pregnancy. "And . . ."

"It scares the hell out of me."

"No surprise there."

Lowering his head, he kissed her tenderly. "But I kind of like the idea."

A languid, warm feeling began to overcome the butterflies in her stomach as she melted into him. "You're saying you want a baby?"

Raising his head, he cupped her face. "I'm saying I want *you.* Do you think we could make it — be happy together — if we tried?"

It wasn't "I love you," but it was close. In any event, *he* was the one who had to believe they could survive the demons of his past; *he* was the one who had to make the commitment to conquer those doubts and fears. "Maybe we should just take it one day at a time," she said.

"That sounds good. But I don't want you seeing anyone else."

She arched her eyebrows. "Then you can't see anyone else, either."

"As long as you give me what I want whenever I want it, I won't have to," he teased, and swept her into his arms.

He was about to carry her to the bedroom, but she stopped him. "Let's go to your place."

He hesitated. "Any particular reason?"

"The phone call you got would be one. If there's any danger here, we wouldn't be in harm's way. Leanne living so close would be another. And I have two days off. . . ."

"I like the third reason." He reversed direction. But there was one thing Claire had left out. This was still David's house. There was no question that she loved Isaac — as she'd never loved anyone else — but she'd loved David in a unique way, too. And Isaac hadn't proven he could take the place of her husband. Not quite yet.

Isaac was cooking breakfast again. Claire could smell it.

"You're not going to feed me every time I stay over, are you?" she called out, but she wasn't serious. Oddly enough, she was hungry — perhaps because it was past noon.

"That's the price of my stud services," he called back.

"So now you think you're good enough to charge?"

"I didn't hear any complaints last night."

Smiling at the thought that only a crazy woman would complain about the kind of pleasure he'd given her, she buried her face in his pillow.

"Ready for breakfast?" he called a moment later.

Claire was so hopeful and happy she could hardly stand it. And that frightened her. Could she count on Isaac, when the entire town would tell her no? When he had such scars from his childhood? When he'd hurt her once already?

It could be that she was setting herself up for another fall.

"Yeah, just a sec." She crawled out of bed and pulled on the T-shirt he'd taken off last night. Before she could reach the kitchen, however, the phone rang, and Isaac answered. He sounded congenial at first, but then his voice went hard.

"Who is it?" she asked, coming up behind him.

He glanced over his shoulder. "Your sister."

Anxiety bit deep. Was it all going bad so soon? "Why is she calling?"

"We'll be right there," he said into the phone, and hung up.

"Isaac?"

When he turned to face her, he put his hands on her shoulders as if what he had to say wouldn't be easy to hear. "Someone broke into your house last night, Claire."

"What?" She couldn't even imagine such a thing. She'd been in her bedroom as late as two — Isaac had been with her the last few minutes — which meant it could have happened shortly after they left. Once the sun came up would be far riskier and therefore unlikely.

"They kicked in the back door and tossed the place."

Claire had experienced a little foreboding but only because she felt guilty for finding happiness in Isaac's arms. She'd never expected *this.* "Leanne found it that way, or someone called her or —"

"She said she went over to see how you were doing. When she couldn't rouse you at the front door, she went around to the back and saw the damage."

Claire made a mental list of the kinds of possessions typically stolen from residences. She had a computer, a flat-screen TV and one painting of her mother's that she wouldn't want to lose, but other than her furniture, there wasn't much someone would want. She certainly didn't have any drugs or cash or jewelry. "What'd they take?"

He set the pans he'd been using to one side and turned off the stove. "That's what we're going over to find out."

When Isaac parked in Claire's drive, he glanced over at her, saw how rigidly she was sitting and wished he could take the blow for her. But there was nothing he could do. She got out of the car before he could even say anything.

Sheriff King had beaten them to the house and, apparently, already viewed the damage. He was standing on the porch, using his radio. His nostrils flared when he saw them together. No doubt he'd have a word with Claire later, warning her about the company she was keeping, but he was too preoccupied, and too sensitive to what Claire was about to see, to make a fuss at this point. He greeted her with a hug but ignored Isaac.

"If you want to wait a minute, I'll walk through it with you," Myles told her, but the person he was talking to had just come back on the radio, and she motioned for him to go ahead.

Isaac followed her inside — and instantly wanted to find the man who'd done this and teach him a lesson. There was so much damage. Whoever it was hadn't stolen her TV, they'd busted it, along with her computer and almost everything else she owned, whether it had value or not. The mirrors were cracked, her bedding and much of her clothing had been slashed, the pictures torn from the walls. Even her wedding album and her mother's painting had been destroyed. Whoever had done this had paid special attention to the things that would matter most to her.

Why? The destruction was such a senseless waste. Isaac couldn't understand risking prison for the sake of vandalism. As he peered into room after room, he also wondered how she'd replace all this stuff on a hairdresser's salary. He hoped she had insurance because he knew the money she'd inherited from her grandparents had all been spent on cosmetology school, building her house and starting her own business.

Some of the things she'd lost *couldn't* be replaced. She mumbled that Tug and Roni and David's parents had some of her wedding pictures, but there were many they wouldn't have, that no one would have, and that had to hurt.

He watched her dash a hand across her cheeks when she spotted several photographs floating in the tub. That someone had wanted to hurt her to this degree, for no apparent reason, created such rage he could hardly stay inside, looking at it all.

Other than wiping away silent tears, she didn't react. She seemed stunned as she went from one wrecked item to the next.

Leanne watched the proceedings from her wheelchair in the living room. She couldn't follow. Too much broken glass, electronic components, picture frames and other decorations littered the floor.

"Who would do something like this?" Claire asked as they left her bedroom and went back to the living room.

Isaac didn't have an answer. As far as he knew, no one disliked her or had any reason to be angry with her, except maybe Rusty. Rusty wasn't happy she'd spurned him. But would he go this far? Would he take that kind of risk?

In the background, Isaac could hear Myles's clipped voice as he spoke with some forensic techs. He wanted them to come over and help out with fingerprinting. He sounded almost as upset as Isaac was.

Leanne had murmured a few words of sympathy when they first walked in. "I'm so sorry, Claire. . . . I can't believe this. . . . I'm just glad you weren't here and that you're okay." But she'd been silent ever since. When Isaac glanced over at her, their eyes met and for the briefest second, he saw a strange look on her face.

It was gone as quickly as it had appeared — so fast he wasn't sure he'd seen it at all. But he got the uncomfortable impression she was taking some sort of pleasure in her sister's pain, and that made him even angrier.

He'd known from when he and Claire were together years before that Leanne had problems. Claire always made excuses for her, tried to keep the peace and help her be happy, but Leanne wasn't easy to get along with. In Isaac's mind there was no question that jealousy played a part in their relationship. He wondered just how big a part.

Was Leanne jealous enough to do this?

He hoped not. He didn't want that nasty surprise waiting for Claire when they reached the truth — because they *would* reach the truth. Whoever did this would be exposed and punished if Isaac had to spend every dime he owned to see it happen.

"I mean . . . this is so . . . *destructive.*" Claire's voice cracked as she spoke but, for the most part, she retained a tight hold on her emotions. "Whoever did this has to *hate* me."

Not necessarily. Was something else at play? Something that had been at play for fifteen years but only cropped up whenever a certain person felt threatened? "Where'd you put the files?" he asked.

She'd been so shocked by this seemingly random attack, she hadn't connected it to her mother's case files. When she did, her eyes widened. "You don't think —"

"The timing is certainly suspect," he said.

"Of course. Oh, God . . ." She hurried to the kitchen and gestured at the kitchen table, which was lying on its side. "They were here."

And now they were gone. Every last interview, every last sheet of paper. "Someone doesn't like the fact that you're looking into your mother's disappearance."

"But I've already read everything. What could this person — or persons — hope to gain by taking the files now?"

"Maybe they didn't know where they were before or they would've taken them sooner. They're not worth as much anymore, but at least they know what you know, whether or not you're a threat."

"What are you saying?" Leanne had managed to roll over various objects in order to reach the kitchen. "You think this has something to do with our mother?"

Isaac turned to face her. "Don't you?"

That strange look entered her eyes again. "Not really. Why does everything have to relate to that? She went missing fifteen years ago, for crying out loud. For all we know, this could've been done by one of your many lovers. Or some other woman who's had her eye on you for a long time and is envious that you're sleeping with my sister."

"You mean someone who calls me night and day even though I don't respond?" he retorted.

Claire whirled around to see what was going on between them, but his words had already had the intended effect. Leanne seemed to think better of whatever attack she'd been planning to launch. Clamping her mouth shut, she rolled out of the house.

A moment later, they could see her through the kitchen window crossing the road.

"What happened?" Claire asked, her normally smooth forehead furrowed.

Since Leanne had seen him bringing Claire home on Wednesday morning, she'd called him probably ten times. Over the years, she'd made other overtures. But Isaac didn't want to tell Claire, not after she'd asked him earlier whether or not he'd ever been with her sister.

"She's conflicted when it comes to you. You're aware of that, aren't you?"

He could tell Claire didn't want to think about it. "She's her own worst enemy, but . . . she's not as bad as she seems."

Could they be sure about that? No. Especially now. "Just know that you can't trust her," he said, and left it at that because Myles had come into the house.

"Do you have any idea who might've done this?" he asked.

Claire shook her head. "None."

"Is anything missing?"

"Doesn't look like it." She rubbed her eyes

as if she was merely tired, but Isaac knew she was fighting back tears. "Just my mother's case files."

Myles turned to him. "The ones you mentioned in my office. I've been checking into those."

"And?"

"Leland Faust told me what happened. He and David showed up at the station to visit Rusty late one night when we had only a skeleton crew. While Leland distracted Rusty, David got what he wanted."

But visitors had to be buzzed in. With the jail on the other side of the building, there were video cameras in the lobby, and the dispatch operator sat right inside the front door behind bulletproof glass. "How?"

"Easy. No one had opened those files since Claire called off the investigation last time. They'd been gathering dust in Jared's cubicle. David simply stuck them under his winter coat and walked out."

"How'd he get the originals back in?" Claire wanted to know.

"Same way. Except Leland did it for him."

That explained why Leland had acted so funny on the phone with Isaac. He knew David had been investigating Alana's murder and probably wondered if there was any connection between that and his death.

"Claire, if I didn't tell you some detail about your mother's case, it was because I had no proof and no answers," Myles was explaining. "Investigations are works in progress. We can't reveal every question, every inconsistency, or it's that much easier for whoever we're chasing to stay one step ahead of us. You understand that, don't you?"

"I do. But you have to see the situation from my side, too, Myles. I want to know. It's been fifteen years. I'm tired of waiting for answers."

He nodded. "I understand. And there's some good news in all of this."

"There is?" she said wryly.

"Maybe whoever did this left something of himself behind, a latent print or other forensic evidence we can use to track him down. Although this is painful, maybe it'll end up being what cracks the case. You have homeowner's insurance, right?"

"I do, but . . . it won't replace the stuff that really mattered."

"I know. And I don't think you're going to find any prints," Isaac said. "This guy spent some time here, which tells me he was experienced enough to wear gloves."

Myles didn't like that comment, and his expression showed it, but Isaac saw no point in giving Claire false hope. False hope would only serve up more disappointment later.

"We're going to check, just in case. We're going to do all we can," he promised. His radio crackled again, and he started to leave the room but Claire stopped him.

"Myles?"

Letting the radio summons wait, he shifted his attention to her.

"Have you ever come across anything concerning April Cox while pursuing this investigation?"

His eyebrows came together. "Like what?"

"She claims she found some emails on Roni's computer that prove Roni was having an affair with Tug before my mother went missing."

"I've never seen or heard anything like that."

"So her interview or testimony or whatever wasn't in your copy of the case files, either."

"No. But I can call Sheriff Meade to see if he remembers her being involved. Far as I know, he's still alive and enjoying his retirement in Big Fork."

"But if he purposely dropped that information from the file as a favor to my parents, he probably wouldn't admit it," she said.

Myles ran a hand through his hair. "You think Tug or Roni might be behind this?"

"Can you rule them out?"

"No," he said. "I can't."

19

Claire had never dreamed she'd be moving in with Isaac. They'd gone from not speaking to renewing their torrid affair to living together in only a week's time. She was bowled over by this sudden reversal and wondered if he felt the same. If so, he didn't show it. He was the one who'd insisted she pack some of the clothes that hadn't been destroyed and stay with him. He didn't think she'd be safe anywhere else.

Myles had overheard them discussing her temporary relocation and interrupted to say that his home was available to her, too. Claire knew he wasn't pleased about her relationship with a known heartbreaker. No doubt he thought Laurel would be upset about it. But Myles and Laurel had each other and a family to care for. She couldn't see herself crowding in with them, interrupting their lives. She'd tried to argue that she could stay right where she was, or with

Leanne, but Isaac wouldn't hear of it. Leanne hadn't returned, which hardly made her seem sympathetic.

After putting her bags in the back of his truck, they'd spent several hours cleaning up the mess, which included wiping away the fingerprint dust the police had used in hopes of figuring out who might've broken in. They'd lifted so many prints, most of which probably belonged to her or Leanne or maybe even Isaac, it was going to take a couple of weeks to sort through them all.

"You okay?"

Claire glanced up to see Isaac watching her from across the table at Hank's Burger Joint. They'd spent so much time trying to put her house back together and make a list for the insurance company that it was now late afternoon.

"You haven't said a word since we got here."

She stared at her plate as she sighed. "It wasn't easy seeing things I've worked hard to accumulate swept into a dustpan and thrown in the trash, but . . . I'm okay." For the most part. Her life with David was slowly being dismantled and carted off; even the memories were beginning to feel distant. Coping with that, and the disloyalty she felt, complicated an already complicated situation. So did how much she cared about Isaac, because she worried that allowing herself to depend on him would turn out to be her biggest mistake yet.

On the other hand, she had things to be grateful for. She had insurance, which would cover some of it. And she could've been home, and hurt, when whoever it was broke in and trashed her place.

"You're not eating much. Again," he said. "You're just picking at that burger."

His pointed frown encouraged her to take another big bite. "I'm making progress."

Rocking back, he rested his elbows on top of the booth. "Hard to believe Leanne didn't see or hear anything last night, don't you think? She lives so close."

Two teenage girls came in, spotted Isaac and began to whisper and giggle. As a local celebrity, he drew stares wherever he went. She wondered if he hated that as much as she thought he would but she was too dejected to bring it up. He seemed to ignore the attention.

"It probably happened while she was asleep," she said. "And once she's asleep . . . I don't think anything disturbs her. There's a strong possibility that she was drunk."

"Your sister drinks that much?"

She squirted ketchup on her fries. "I don't

know if she passes out. I'm just saying she's been drinking more than I want to admit."

"Why is she so opposed to reopening your mother's case?"

Claire knew where he was going with this. He didn't care for Leanne. That had become apparent at the house. He guessed she had a secret to hide, and he was right. Loyalty made it impossible for Claire to reveal exactly what that fifteen-year-old secret was. She wasn't willing to talk about a pornographic video starring her baby sister. But she had to give him *some* reason his instincts were on alert, so he'd know that she understood why Leanne was acting so strange about the past.

"She did something she regrets, but it's got nothing to do with my mother's disappearance." Here she was, echoing her father's opinion — ironic, since she'd blasted him for saying the same thing.

But she didn't know how else to approach this and still be loyal to her sister.

"Something she regrets . . ." he repeated.

"Yes."

"You're not going to tell me what?"

She couldn't get any more food down. Pushing her plate away, she reached for her water instead. "I can't. It's . . . very personal and embarrassing. Nothing I'd ever want to become public."

"I wouldn't tell anyone. I hope you realize that."

"I do." She knew he could be discreet. It was more than that. "She wouldn't want you to hear about this. But you're right in believing she's withholding some information, because she is."

"What's the nature of this information?"

"I can't even tell you that much. Really. I'd be mortified if I'd done what she did."

"It doesn't have to do with your mother?"

"Not . . . directly," she hedged.

"Is it something you wouldn't want a private investigator digging up?"

"Excuse me?"

Leaning forward again, he helped himself to her fries. "I've hired someone, Claire."

She blinked at him. "For what?"

"To pursue your mother's case."

"But . . . When did you do that? I've been with you all day."

"I made the decision yesterday."

Before her house was trashed? "But . . . I can't let you do that. Private investigators are expensive. And we tried that route."

"Some are better than others. And you don't have to pay."

"I don't even know when I'd be able to reimburse you."

"That's not a problem. I'm only telling you because she's going to be digging to find everything she can. If your sister has a deep dark secret, it might not be a secret much longer. Will that be a problem?"

Claire squirmed at the thought of Leanne's indiscretion going public, which would happen if the P.I. found something, or there'd be no point in having her search in the first place. She'd have to report any evidence to the police. Could she allow such a no-holds-barred investigation? If she did, Leanne might not be the only casualty. What if it came out that her mother was on birth control without Tug's knowledge? Or that Tug and Roni were indeed having an affair?

What if Isaac's P.I. learned just enough to make everyone look terrible but came up with nothing more?

She'd drag her whole family through the mud for nothing. . . .

"How good is she?" she asked.

"The best. She found my mother. And she had almost nothing to go on."

This was a revelation Claire had never expected Isaac to share with her. His background was pretty much off-limits and always had been. He certainly never spoke of the woman who'd abandoned him.

Distracted from her own misery, she

watched him carefully. "Where is she?"

"Dead."

He showed no emotion, but he had to feel *something.* She wanted to know what had happened, why his mother had done what she'd done. But asking just to appease her curiosity would be far too intrusive. "I'm sorry."

A muscle flexed in his cheek. "Your mother's dead, too. I'm convinced of it. But she deserves justice. And you deserve answers."

"I want answers, but . . . I have to ask myself — at what price?"

"That's for you to decide. I'll pay for the P.I. as long as you can live with what she finds. Could you tolerate seeing your sister or your stepfather or someone else you love going to prison?"

"You think the person who killed her is that close to me?"

"After what April told you? In my mind, there's no question."

Jeremy Salter cleared his throat. He was standing at their table. Claire had been so engrossed in the conversation she hadn't paid any attention to his approach, but she shouldn't have been surprised. Jeremy had had a crush on her since they were children. He always gravitated toward her, no matter where they were. "Can I get you any more ketchup or . . . or a refill of your soda, Claire?" he asked.

She managed a smile. "No, thanks."

He put some extra napkins at her elbow. "I — I'm sorry to hear about the, um, fall you took at the studio. I'm really sorry. *Very* sorry."

Claire fingered the stitches above her ear. She needed to see Dr. Hunt to have them removed. "Thanks, Jeremy. I appreciate that."

Isaac had been hurt, too, but Jeremy hadn't heard about that, or he didn't care. Unlike the teenage girls now sitting at a booth across the restaurant, who kept glancing over at Isaac, Jeremy hardly seemed to notice that he was there. But he didn't think like other people, had always been "different." Although, as far as Claire knew, his parents had never sought an official diagnosis, he had some undeniable mental and emotional problems, but he meant well. She thought he was sweet.

"Will you have time to give me a haircut this week?" he asked.

She cleared her throat. She'd endured his obsession for years, but every once in a while his devotion made her uneasy. "Isn't your appointment already scheduled?"

"I don't remember."

He should have a card on which she'd written his next appointment. She always sent him home with one. He wasn't a client she was dying to keep — she cut his hair for whatever change he had in his pocket — but she figured it was the least she could do for someone who'd been as teased, shunned and mistreated as he had. It was no secret that his father would never win any parenting awards; he had too many problems of his own. Don Salter had managed Walt's gun shop for years after Tug quit, until Walt accused him of stealing. Don's complicity in the theft was never proven, but the suspicion was enough to cost him his job.

After that, he worked in various capacities, eventually becoming a roofer. Then he fell off a house and hurt his back and hadn't held a job since. She bumped into him every now and then. If he wasn't inebriated he was hungover, but that wasn't why she didn't like him. Some people claimed he was merely neglectful to Jeremy; she feared he was borderline abusive. She or someone else in town might've tried to get some government agency to intercede, except that Jeremy would probably be institutionalized if he was taken from his father. It wasn't as if he had a loving mother. His mother moved to Oregon when he was just a kid, and refused to take him with her.

"I'm sure it's on the books," she said. "I don't have my schedule with me, but I'll check and give you a call."

"That'd be nice, Claire. That'd be real nice."

She stirred the ice in her drink. "If it's this week, we might need to reschedule, though," she added. "I'm taking some time off."

"You are? Why? Are you going out of town?"

He seemed almost panic-stricken, but Claire had known him long enough to understand that anything beyond his normal routines upset him. "I've got some . . . problems to take care of. But we'll get you in soon. Don't worry."

"I am worried," he said. "I'm really worried."

He looked it. She reached out to squeeze his arm. "It's going to be okay. I promise."

"You're a nice person, Claire. You — you don't deserve what's happening."

She supposed he meant the bump on her head. She doubted he'd heard about her house yet, but in this town she could never be sure. At any rate, Jeremy frequently said odd things. "Thanks again. Tell Hank the burger was delicious."

"Can I get you a shake?" he asked. "I can make it really thick. For free. To make up for your fall."

"I appreciate the offer, but I'm stuffed."

"Okay."

"Maybe you could get *me* a shake," Isaac said.

Jeremy looked startled, as if he'd forgotten Isaac was sitting there. "Um, yeah, sure. I guess I could. What kind would you like?"

Isaac's lips curved into a smile. "Actually, I'm stuffed, too. But thanks."

"If you say so." Jeremy's eyes darted back to Claire. "I'm glad you came in. It's always good to see you, Claire."

After several more rounds of thanks and compliments, Jeremy finally went back to work. Claire wanted to return to the conversation they'd been having before he'd interrupted, but Isaac's wry smile stopped her.

"Looks like I have some competition."

"Jeremy's harmless. You remember him from high school, don't you? He was —" And then it hit her where Isaac had gotten at least some of his reputation as a fighter. "Wait! Of course you remember him. You beat up every kid who looked at him crosswise."

"I can tell he's grateful," he said with a chuckle as he gathered up his wrappers.

"Apparently, my paltry friendship can't compare to your pretty face. But I'm not surprised. He's had a thing for you since I can remember."

She was sliding out of the booth when the bell jingled over the door and her stepmother walked in. Roni didn't usually eat red meat, so Claire was surprised to see her here — until she made it clear she hadn't come to order dinner. When she hurried over, Claire realized she'd only stopped because she'd spotted Isaac's truck.

"Is it true?" she demanded.

Claire hesitated. "Is what true?"

"Did you go to April's house?"

Word was getting out. She'd feared as much. "We — we had a short chat, but —"

"But I'm not supposed to be offended, is that it? It's not as if you were there discussing *me.*"

Claire didn't respond.

"Of course you were discussing me. What else would you have to say to each other? What's wrong with you? What have we done to make you turn on us?"

"You've done nothing. It's just that . . . I have to look everywhere, hear it all."

Her lip quivered. "I can't believe you suspect us. After everything we've done for you."

"I don't know who to suspect, Mom. I'm merely searching for answers."

"And meanwhile, you're moving in with a man who'll dump you as soon as the mood strikes him. Just like before."

Isaac tensed. Claire could sense it. "Mom, please. Leave my personal life out of this."

"How am I supposed to do that?" she retorted. "I raised you!"

Not really. But Claire let that slide. "And I'm grateful —"

"You have a funny way of showing it." She paused. "Leanne says you two are moving in together."

Claire began to wonder if everyone else was right and she was wrong. . . . "For a short while, yes. Until I get my house fixed up. If you've talked to Leanne you must've heard what happened."

"Of course we've heard. I'm meeting your father there now, but I saw Isaac's truck and realized we'd missed you."

"Yet you come in here upset that I spoke with April. Don't you care about my house and everything else that's going on?"

"I can help you fix up your house. You don't have to go to Isaac's. You can stay with us. Or Leanne."

She had no desire to go either place. "I've already decided. As I said, it's not for long."

"It's long enough to ask for trouble. What if he gets you pregnant? What then?"

Claire knew that could already be true but she refused to let on.

"He'll never treat you the way David did," Roni was saying. "He'll walk away as soon as you have a baby in your belly."

Isaac didn't defend himself, but his eyes took on that hard, glittery look, warning that he might retaliate with words equally biting and unkind.

"Let me worry about my reputation, okay?" She hoped to get him out of the burger joint before he got involved. The rift between her and her stepmother was complicated enough. She wasn't sure how or when they'd be able to move beyond it.

"You think he'll be better to you than we've been?" Roni asked. "You think he'll look out for your interests?"

Claire didn't want to have this discussion, not in public and not in front of Isaac. He'd already exhibited more control than she'd ever expected. Had Roni been a man, that might not have been the case. "We'll talk about it later," she insisted, but Roni was too upset to relent.

"Leanne told me how you've been acting lately."

"She . . . *what?*" Claire said. "I don't even

know what that means. I'm doing whatever I can to get by. If you guys can't understand —"

"What we understand," she interrupted, "is that you're trying to blame what happened to your mother on us. And we don't like it."

"I'm not *trying* to blame anyone. I want the truth. At last. Is that too much to ask?"

"Is that why you stabbed me in the back by going to April? To gather dirt on me?"

Claire wasn't sure she could claim that *wasn't* why she'd gone. She'd known what to expect. "Roni —"

"So I'm Roni now?" Her voice went shrill. "I'm not your mother, who's been good to you for fifteen years?"

"Of course you are!"

"Then why didn't you call me when your house was broken into this morning? And why haven't you apologized for your behavior at the salon?"

Forever conscious of creating a scene, Claire made an effort to keep her voice down. Everyone was staring. "Please, stop. You're blowing this out of proportion."

"Leave her alone!" Jeremy yelled.

Claire motioned for her ardent admirer to calm down. "I'm fine, Jeremy. Don't worry about me."

Roni wagged a finger at him. "You stay out of it, Jeremy Salter, or I'll go to your dad and you know what he'll do."

Claire stepped between them to divert Roni's attention. "Please don't threaten him. It's me you're upset with. I haven't called because I've been . . . busy."

"Getting laid?" she snapped.

Isaac's growl told Claire he'd reached the end of his patience. He took her hand, obviously intending to lead her out whether her stepmother liked it or not, but Claire sent him a look pleading for a few more seconds. "That was uncalled for. You — you have no right to judge Isaac or me or anyone else."

"I don't care what she thinks of me," Isaac said.

Claire ignored him. "Just go home," she said to Roni, "and . . . and let me have some space, okay? I'll be in touch when I get my life figured out."

With that, she and Isaac left. They had to end the confrontation before it grew any worse. But Roni wasn't about to give her the last word.

"Don't think you can come crawling back to us when he breaks your heart," she called.

Claire couldn't believe her ears. That sounded so permanent. Would she regret this? Until two days ago, she'd never had a major disagreement with her stepmother; now she'd had two. It upset her to think they were at odds, that maybe she was letting her doubts and fears get the best of her.

Her world was as upside down as her house had been this morning. But Isaac was walking briskly, and he had a firm hold on her hand. Before she knew it they were in his truck and she was watching Hank's Burger Joint grow smaller and smaller through the back window.

20

Claire stared at her reflection through the steam covering Isaac's bathroom mirror. She hadn't really needed a shower. She just hadn't known what else to do with herself. Disappearing into the bathroom was the only thing she could think of that would give her a few minutes to be alone and regroup.

"Are you crazy for being here?" she whispered to herself.

"Certifiable," came her own answer. And yet what could she have done differently? She felt as if she was being carried along on a giant wave that'd come crashing out of her past to bring her to some new place — but whether that place would be better or worse remained to be seen. In any case, she couldn't pinpoint where she was to blame for what was happening. It wasn't her fault that she felt compelled to find her mother. It wasn't her fault that someone might've hired Les Weaver to shoot her husband. And it wasn't her fault that certain people didn't have an alibi, or that rumors abounded — rumors of marriage infidelity and jealousy and greed. She was only trying to sort it all out.

The phone rang. Isaac's voice, when he answered it, came through the door as a low rumble, too low for her to hear what he said. She wondered if that call could be for her, but he didn't knock at the door, and she wasn't about to act at home enough to yell, "Who is it?"

What if it was another woman? Hayley Peters, who worked at the boutique where Claire had bought her new clothes, was a beautiful woman with a *huge* crush on Isaac. She talked about him nonstop whenever Claire went into the shop because she knew they'd once been together and openly envied her. If Hayley called him or dropped in while Claire was here, it could be awkward, especially if Hayley and Isaac had been intimate in recent months.

Claire didn't know how she could stay with Isaac for any length of time without getting in his way. He said he didn't want her to see other men, and he acted as if he didn't plan to see anyone else, either, but that would necessitate a pretty big change of behavior, and she had no confidence he could pull it off long-term. In a day or two, maybe even tomorrow, she could be packing her bags and dragging them somewhere else, humiliated because the whole town would then be privy to their breakup. She'd placed her pride — as well as almost all her other relationships — on the line.

A soft knock interrupted. "You going to be in there all night?"

Claire wished she could stay in the bathroom. It felt safer than anywhere else at the moment. "I'm coming."

"That was your friend on the phone," he volunteered.

She put on a pair of panties and a T-shirt, one of her own. She couldn't wear David's when she was with Isaac. But she craved the comfort and familiarity of it. She craved David's blessing on what she was doing, too. He'd always been a stabilizing influence in her life. "Laurel?"

"Yeah."

"Is she waiting to speak to me?"

"No. I said you were in the shower."

"What did she want?"

"To pick you up."

David, should I go to Laurel's?

There was no point in asking — she received no answer. She hadn't felt her husband's presence in a long time. Had he left her for good?

"What did you tell her?"

"That you're fine here."

Was she?

"Isn't that true?" he asked when she didn't respond.

"Of course. I — I appreciate your hospitality. But I can't imagine I'll need to inconvenience you for long."

There was a significant pause before he spoke again. "Is that what you're doing? Inconveniencing me?"

She was coming across as too stilted, but she didn't know how to act anymore. She'd become estranged from the people who were normally close to her, and grown close to the one person from whom she was normally estranged. "I don't know," she said. "It's been a rough day. Do we have to define . . . anything?"

His tone softened. "No. I think we're both too tired for that."

"Thanks."

"Does that mean you'll open the door and come to bed?"

The number of beds in his house hadn't changed. Unless she opted for the couch, they'd be sleeping together.

Tonight she probably would've chosen the

couch, except she didn't feel that would seem very grateful after all he'd done for her. "Sure, I'll be right there."

Hoping he'd be asleep when she slipped into the room, she turned on the sink faucet as if she still had to brush her teeth. She'd already done it, twice, but she didn't want to talk. She didn't even want the lights on. She hoped to crawl in beside him and escape consciousness until she could rebound, at least a little.

But when she came out, he was leaning against the wall with his arms folded, waiting for her. "You okay?"

He'd asked her this at the diner. She was tempted to give the same meaningless and automatic answer — to conceal the morass of emotion inside her. Except that she wasn't "fine." Not at all. "I don't want to lose my family," she admitted.

"Are you saying you'd like me to fire the P.I.? That you'd like to let the past stand as it is? That's an option, you know."

It *wasn't* an option. Not anymore. It was too late. "This has gone too far. If I turn back now I'll always doubt them."

"If they hurt your mother, they should be held accountable."

Part of her agreed with that. The other part felt it would be another catastrophe, another loss. “I know.”

“You can handle whatever happens.”

Right or wrong, his words were reassuring. With a crooked grin that seemed to echo his confidence in her, he led her into his room. She thought maybe he’d waited for her to come out of the bathroom because he wanted to make love, but she didn’t have it in her, and he seemed to understand. He peeled off his jeans and tossed them on a chair, but he didn’t remove his T-shirt and boxers or try to convince her to disrobe. He simply pulled her into bed with him and held her until she felt so warm and secure the tension drained away.

She could get used to sleeping with him, she thought. Even with the disaster her life seemed to be at the moment, resting her head on his shoulder made her happy. But that was exactly what scared her.

Sleep weighed down her eyelids, but she forced them open so she could see his profile in the dark. “Isaac?”

“Hmm?” He sounded half-asleep himself.

“It could’ve been Les Weaver who trashed my house.”

He shifted, ran a hand through her hair. “What makes you think that?”

“The call he made to me. He might’ve been the one who called you, too.”

His arm curled, bringing her even closer. "Thinking it was Les is easier than thinking it was your sister."

"That's not the only reason. My sister would never hurt me like that."

He changed the subject, which led her to believe he didn't agree. "I'll call Myles first thing in the morning. I'm not sure he'll be happy to hear from me, but I want to see if he ever came up with those phone records."

Myles hadn't treated Isaac all that well at her house today. They'd exchanged a few terse words, but for the most part Myles had addressed her as if Isaac wasn't there. "My friends are just trying to look out for me. You understand that, don't you?" she murmured.

"I understand."

Sliding her hand up under his shirt, she lightly fingered his stitches to reassure herself that his wound was healing. Then she placed her palm on his pectoral muscle, taking solace in the steady thump of his heart. She hadn't wanted to be with him when she got here tonight, hadn't known how to react to all the changes, but she felt calmer now, and grateful for his support.

"Isaac?"

"What?"

"You feel good," she said.

"Even though I'm not David?"
"Even though you're not David."
His lips brushed her temple. "You're safe here, Claire. Get some sleep."

21

It was midmorning by the time Isaac woke, easily ten or eleven o'clock. Even then it wasn't the brightness of the sun or the late hour that brought him to consciousness; it was Claire. She was stirring — no, more than stirring. She'd taken off her clothes and was trying to remove his.

He shifted so she could pull off his T-shirt. His boxers went next. Then they were completely naked. They'd been this way before, many times, especially ten years ago, and yet *something* was different.

"You sleep okay?" He tried to draw her out, to account for the change, but the fact that she didn't answer, didn't seem to want to talk, told him what he needed to know. She was somber, subdued, absolutely intent — on him.

Isaac had never experienced such a deep level of intimacy with anyone else. He knew that would be impossible, because no other woman had ever meant what she meant to him. Every touch felt like truth in motion. Even as the pleasure mounted, the physical sensation was only one element of the whole, and not the most critical. She was lowering her guard, offering herself without begrudging the fact that she wanted to.

This was a second chance.

They made love slowly, silently, eyes open and locked for much of the time. When her lips parted and her breathing grew short, he rolled over and pulled her on top of him so he could watch her. Her wild hair tumbled around her face and shoulders as her eyelids closed, but she didn't speed up the rhythm. The build was so slow, so exquisite, he knew, even if everything fell apart after this, he'd never forget this moment.

Their union was heaven — and it was hell. That she could evoke such a powerful response in him was terrifying. He hadn't allowed himself to become so emotionally attached to anyone since his mother, had been absolutely vigilant in avoiding entanglements. After what he'd been through, he felt less threatened by neglect, abuse, derision, indifference.

Love made him vulnerable, and vulnerability made him want to run.

Fortunately, he *couldn't* run, because

Claire needed him too badly. He'd never let anyone else hurt her.

But he wasn't sure how long he'd be able to save her from himself.

"I'm going to visit Myles," Isaac announced at breakfast. "He must have Les Weaver's phone records by now. And if he doesn't, I want to light a fire under his ass to get it done. What happened to your house should've convinced him that he has to act and act quickly. Whatever's going on is definitely linked to the past."

Claire agreed, but she didn't have much to contribute to his comments. She'd already let her body do all the talking she wanted to this morning. She felt so strongly about Isaac that she hadn't been able to hide it, and now she was drained, emotionally and physically.

"You're quiet today," he said.

"I'm just trying to think it all through." It was a lot to process, especially with her feelings for him added into the mix. She couldn't help acknowledging that some of what her stepmother had screamed at her in Hank's Burger Joint could be true, or come to pass later. But Isaac cared about her. He wouldn't be paying for a private investigator or protecting her like he was if he didn't. She supposed, in some way, she'd always known he *cared.* His jealousy of David and the crackling connection she'd felt whenever she ran into him confirmed it. But she still had a hard time believing he could sustain a relationship. She was pretty sure he worried about that, too. He certainly hadn't made any commitments, no more than a good friend would make.

"I'm glad you were able to eat, at least," he said as he collected the dishes from their oatmeal, toast and juice.

She hadn't realized she'd finished what was in her bowl. She'd been too preoccupied. Now that they'd climbed out of bed and returned to the "real" world, she had to pick up her burdens again. Her mother's disappearance was the same problem that had been waiting for her every day for the past fifteen years, and now she had David's alleged murder to add to that load. "It was good."

"I'd ask you to come with me," he went on, reverting to what he'd been saying earlier, "but I think I'll be able to lean on Myles a little harder if you're not there."

In other words, he preferred she not hear their exchange, which was fine with her. She had other plans. She'd let Joe Kenyon stonewall her too long already. She was going to pay him a visit. Thanks to the pornographic tape her sister had created, and the fact that Claire couldn't let anyone know about it, even Isaac, this was something she had to do on her own.

"No problem."

"Any chance I can talk you into staying here and getting some more rest?" he asked.

"No. I need to take advantage of having the day off work. Just drop me at my place, okay? I'll do some more cleaning."

He frowned as if he might argue.

"It's broad daylight and my sister lives next door. I'll be perfectly safe," she told him.

He didn't say it — he took her home as she wished — but she knew what he was thinking: *it was broad daylight when your mother went missing.*

Joe and his brother were still partners in the tree business. Claire guessed they'd be working together — trimming trees, hauling debris and selling wood — for the rest of their lives. To quote one of the older ladies in her book group, they were "thick as thieves," which was why she doubted what Peter had to say about Joe's whereabouts on the day her mother disappeared. Their close relationship also made her wonder why, if Joe denied having an affair with her mother, Peter had offered information that seemed to contradict his brother's statement.

A curious breach of loyalty . . . Had it caused problems between them? That certainly didn't appear to be the case. But it must have angered Joe that his twin hadn't acted to protect his marriage. Joe's wife, Lilly, had stuck by him despite the rumors, but Peter had no way of knowing that when he spouted off about that supposedly "odd" phone call.

Maybe Peter didn't like Lilly. He was divorced. Maybe he wanted to get rid of her. Then he and his brother would be similarly unfettered and have even more time to build their business, go hunting, fishing or hang out at the bar.

Claire planned to ask Joe, again, why his brother had said what he did — if she ever got the opportunity to talk to him. His truck sat in the driveway, but he wasn't answering his door.

Lifting her hand, she pounded on the panel for a second time. "Joe? I'm not leaving. You might as well open up."

Nothing.

"Joe? Come on. I really need to talk to you."

She heard her name. But it wasn't Joe who said it. This voice came from across the street.

When Claire turned she saw Carly Ortega, the woman who claimed to have seen Alana's car at Joe's house on more than one occasion, once late at night. Claire had spoken to her a couple of times over the years. She stood by her original testimony. "Did you just call me?" she asked.

Carly stepped out of the shade and into the sun. Ill more often than not with a variety of maladies, some more than likely psychosomatic, Carly was wearing a robe. "I'm just trying to tell you it won't do any good to keep knocking. He's not home."

Because she rarely left the house, Carly probably experienced more than her share of boredom. But did she have to be quite as nosy as she was? "You're sure?" Claire yelled back. "His truck's here."

"I saw him leave with Donald Salter an hour ago."

What would he want with Jeremy's father? Claire hadn't thought they knew each other all that well.

She crossed the street so she could talk to Carly without raising her voice. "I didn't realize he and Don were friends."

"Neither did I. Don doesn't come around

here very often."

"Any idea where they might have gone?" It was none of her business, of course, but Claire figured she might as well learn as much as Carly would tell her. Carly didn't care if she was inserting herself in matters that didn't concern her; maybe she had information that would indicate when Joe might return.

"No clue. Joe keeps to himself. You know that."

Probably better than anyone. How frustrating for a gossipmonger like Carly. "Right. Well —" she glanced at Joe's closed-up house "— thanks for letting me know."

"Want me to tell him you stopped by?"

It didn't matter what Claire said; Carly would do it, anyway. No doubt she'd march over with the news as soon as he got home. "If you want."

Claire started for her car, but Carly surprised her by speaking again.

"You hold it against me, don't you?"

She pivoted. "Excuse me?"

"What I told the police about your mom."

"That she and Joe were having an affair? I don't hold it against you. I just don't believe it's true."

"I didn't say they were having an affair."

She went to the hose faucet, turned it on and began watering her roses. "I said she came over here. I saw her. I wasn't lying about that."

"So you've told me before."

"But —" She hesitated.

"But?"

"Falling in love with someone other than her husband wouldn't mean she's a bad person."

"Marital infidelity is hardly honorable."

"Still, Joe's been miserable with Lilly from the beginning. Maybe your mother was just as unhappy with Tug."

"She could've divorced him."

"She'd already failed at her first marriage. And he was a good father to you and your sister, so she probably felt guilty for not wanting him. Maybe she couldn't face another divorce and got caught up in something that was bigger than she was."

"That's a very romantic view. Anyway, what makes you think Joe and Lilly are unhappy?"

"You don't go to Idaho as often as she does unless you want to."

"Her mother's sick."

"She has a sister who helps out a lot."

Claire nibbled on her bottom lip. She didn't feel good about looking for secrets and lies in other people's lives. And yet . . . she needed to pull at any loose threads — the details that might lead to more.

"Does *Lilly* believe her husband was cheating on her?" Claire had tried talking to Lilly, but she was even more closed than Joe. No matter what Claire asked, she'd reply, "I have nothing to say."

"I believe she wouldn't put it past him. She's hanging on for the sake of their kids. Just between us, she's said as much to me. Once they're grown-up, in another four years or so, I see her moving to Idaho."

Claire stared down the street, wondering at her mother's feelings when she drove Leanne here the day she'd learned about the tape. She must have felt shock and horror. But what other emotions? Jealousy? Anger? Fear? Embarrassment? "Do you remember the Fishman family?" she asked.

"Of course." Carly pointed at the house next to Joe's.

Unfortunately, the Welches lived there these days and hadn't taken care of the place, but it'd been a nice home once upon a time, certainly better than the smattering of old trailers that were so prevalent in the Thompson Chain of Lakes area.

"They lived right there for ten years," she said.

"Leanne used to be good friends with Katie."

"I remember that, too. She was over all the time. They used to take turns babysitting for Joe and Lilly."

Which meant Joe had certainly had occasion to expose himself to Leanne, just as she'd had occasion to develop inappropriate fantasies, at least one of which she'd acted out.

"Yes, they'd just had Chantelle, their oldest. Hard to fathom it's been that long."

"Where do the Fishmans live now?" Claire asked. "Do you know?"

Other than a standard interview performed a couple of weeks after Alana's disappearance, in which the Fishmans said they hadn't noticed whether or not Alana's car was ever parked at Joe's house, they'd never been questioned. But that pornographic video changed Claire's level of interest in what they might have to say. Surely if Joe had made inappropriate advances toward Leanne, Leanne would've told Katie about it.

"They're in Salt Lake," Carly said. "I got a card from them last Christmas."

"Katie's there, too?"

"I'm not sure. She got married several years ago."

Did she and Leanne still keep in touch? If so, Leanne hadn't mentioned her for years. "Would you mind giving me their address?" Knowing she had to come up with a plausible reason, one that wouldn't arouse Carly's curiosity, she added, "I'd like to surprise Leanne with it."

"That's a great idea! I bet Katie would love to hear from her. Just a sec." After handing Claire the hose, she went inside the house.

Before she could return, a car careered around the corner and sped down the street. It was Don, with Joe in the passenger seat. Claire doubted she would've recognized Jeremy's father if he hadn't been driving Jeremy's car, a rattletrap Impala that was pretty unmistakable.

A moment later, Don whipped into Joe's driveway and Joe got out. He glanced over, but then ducked his head and headed to the front door as if he couldn't get in fast enough. Obviously, he'd recognized her and was running for cover.

Claire was about to drop the hose and hurry after him. She didn't want to miss her chance to speak to him; she doubted he'd come to the door if she knocked. But Don had backed out of the drive and was sitting in the street between them, staring at her through the open window. He'd aged twenty years, it seemed, since she'd seen him last.

"Is something wrong?" she asked.

He shook his head. "No. Nothing." His tires squealed as he drove off, but their brief interaction had made Joe pause, too. He looked after Don, an enigmatic expression on his face, as Carly came out.

"Here you go. You should be able to reach Katie through her parents, even if she's not in Salt Lake."

Claire relinquished the garden hose and accepted the paper. "Thanks, Carly. I appreciate it." She thought she'd have to hurry over, that Joe would try to avoid her as he had in the past, but he didn't. This time, he waited.

"Are you ready to talk to me?" she asked as she walked up his drive.

His gaze fell to the paper in her hand. She doubted he could read it. She crumpled it, just in case, but she knew he'd seen Carly give it to her, so maybe that was the reason for his interest. "I don't have a choice. You won't quit."

Claire's mouth went dry. "Is that a yes?"

Shading his eyes from the sun, he looked across at his neighbor. "What'd Carly have to say?"

"I'll tell you if you invite me in."

His forehead creased as he cursed. "No. I don't want her or anyone else to see us talking. Meet me at my brother's place in fifteen minutes."

"I don't know where he lives."

After some quick directions, he went inside and slammed the door, but she didn't care. He'd finally agreed to talk to her — after fifteen years.

Hope made her steps light as she returned to her car and started the engine. She was so sure that having Joe's cooperation would make a difference, she even managed a smile and a wave for Carly.

But once she got to Peter's house, she realized just how remote it was and began to grow uneasy. She'd kept on driving, hoping he lived in a cluster of houses as was so often the case in Pineview, but the house she came upon was the only one in the area.

Joe hadn't invited her to the back of beyond as some kind of a trap, had he?

She pulled in behind Peter's truck, which was parked in the drive. He was home, but that didn't make her feel a whole lot better. Not long ago she'd seen a horrifying forensics program about *four* brothers who'd beaten a man to death and supposedly fed his body to their hogs. . . .

Thick as thieves . . . The words her friends had used to describe Joe and Peter ran through her mind as she gazed out at Peter's small cabin. Could both brothers have been party to whatever happened to her mother?

Claire couldn't believe that. Peter wouldn't have said he thought Joe was having an affair with Alana if he'd helped murder her. Maybe he'd made a mistake. Maybe he'd opened his mouth before learning that his brother was responsible.

She was letting her imagination run away with her. But she didn't have a cell phone since there was no service. And now that she'd seen this isolated setting, showing up here seemed an unnecessary risk. No one even knew where she was.

Planning to leave while she still could, she put the transmission in Reverse, but she had nowhere to go. Joe had arrived and parked behind her, effectively trapping her car. She saw his grille in her rearview mirror just as she was about to back out and had to stomp on the brake.

"Shit!" she breathed, her mind racing as he got out.

He came toward her wearing a dark scowl and paused near her door with his hands on his hips as if he expected her to get out and go inside with him.

Eyes gravitating to his work boots — they looked just like the pair she'd seen on the man who'd followed her to the cabin — her pulse leaped.

What was she going to do?

Peter came out, distracting them both. He exchanged a few words with Joe that culminated in angry voices and plenty of cursing, which got louder, making it easy to hear what they were saying.

"It's your fault," Joe responded. "You're the one who told everyone Alana and I were having an affair."

"That's before I knew it could get you —" Peter glanced in her direction and stopped. "Shit, Joe. This is screwed up, man. I don't want to be dragged into this. I'm the one who told you to stay away from Alana in the first place. What if the cops —"

Claire screamed as Joe slammed a fist down on the hood of her car. "I don't care. This won't go away! Let's take her inside and get it over with. Otherwise, she'll head back to town and go straight to the sheriff."

Get *what* over with? Claire had heard enough. She put her car in Drive but there was no more room to go forward than there was to go back. She could only remain in her locked car.

But that was hardly safe. If they really

wanted to get to her, all they had to do was break a window.

Joe was already knocking on the glass. Peter had walked across the lawn and was on the passenger side. Their vehicles penned her in front and back, and the two men penned her in on the left and right.

Leaning on the roof of her car with both hands, Peter shook his head as Joe yelled for her to get out.

"No!" she called back. "Let me go!"

"You can't let her drive away now," Peter warned. "Man, this was such a mistake! What were you thinking, bringing her up here?"

"Shut up!" Joe knocked harder. "Claire, get out. I'm not going to hurt you, I swear."

"What is it you want?"

"I have something to show you. It might tell you what happened to your mother."

Or he was lying, the information he claimed to possess simply an incentive to lure her inside.

"What did you do to her?" she yelled. "*Why* did you do it?"

"I didn't do anything! Would you quit freaking out? I'm trying to help you!"

"Then why did you follow me to her studio?"

"That wasn't me!"

"Did you trash my house?"

"No!"

"How'd you hear about it?"

"You're kidding, right? There are no secrets in Pineview."

Except the one she'd been chasing for fifteen years.

"Just get out and come inside with us, and I'll tell you what I know. That way, maybe we can put a stop to what's going on."

She didn't trust him. She started her car, determined to crash into both vehicles if necessary in order to create enough space to get her Camaro out from between them, but she didn't have the chance.

Peter picked up a rock and bashed in the passenger's-side window just as her car jumped forward and struck his bumper. The impact threw her back against the seat, but she reached for the gearshift, planning to reverse and punch the gas again when Peter climbed in through the passenger side and held her hand in place so she couldn't.

A second later, Joe dragged her from the car.

22

When Isaac went by Claire's house, her car wasn't there and the place was locked. No one responded to his knock.

He jimmied open the back door — it still had to be fixed from before — but couldn't see that she'd made any progress on the cleanup. Everything looked exactly as they'd left it, giving him the distinct impression that she hadn't even been at the house.

He'd dropped her there four hours ago. She must've taken off immediately after.

He wished he could contact her by cell phone, but that wasn't possible in Pineview. No one had reception. Usually, Isaac didn't have a problem with that. He liked the community's laid-back lifestyle enough to sacrifice this modern convenience, but being unable to communicate with Claire meant that all he could do was perform a very random search.

The thought that something terrible had

happened, or might happen if he didn't find her *fast,* took center stage in his mind. Someone had most likely kidnapped and killed her mother. Someone had followed her to the studio several days ago. Someone had broken into her house only the night before last.

God, he should never have let her come here. Why had he? He hadn't liked the idea from the beginning. . . .

But maybe he was jumping to conclusions. Since her car was gone, chances were she'd simply changed plans and driven over to make peace with her family. Or she'd gone to Laurel's. Laurel had asked her to come over last night, hadn't she?

Telling himself not to panic too soon, he strode next door to see if her sister had heard from her.

"Leanne?" he called as he knocked. After yesterday's confrontation, he hoped she wouldn't ignore him. "It's Isaac."

To his relief, she opened the door almost immediately. She'd probably heard his truck when he drove up and was already aware of his presence. "You want *me?*" she said with false sweetness.

Too concerned about Claire to bother with niceties, he scowled. "Cut the bullshit. Where is she?"

She jerked up her chin. "Where is *who?*"

Was she joking? "Your sister, of course. Who else?"

"How would I know?" She spread her hands wide. "She's not talking to me at the moment, remember? She basically flipped off her whole family when she went home with you."

Was Leanne holding back? What if *no one* knew where Claire was? "That wasn't what she intended, so don't take it that way. Why not cut her some slack?"

"Cut *her* some slack? What about *me?*"

"She's going through a hard time."

"Maybe we all are."

He caught hold of the door as she attempted to close it. "Claire was supposed to be at the house, cleaning up. You must've seen her."

"I don't notice everything that happens, or I'd know who broke in."

"That was at night. When I brought her here this morning it was daylight, and you seem to notice most of what happens during the day."

She blew out a sigh. "Fine. You want to hear what I know? As soon as you drove away, she got in her car and left. That's it."

Why hadn't she mentioned that she was going somewhere else? "Where could she have gone?"

"Your guess is as good as mine. Probably better. You're her new confidant."

He ignored this latest jab. "Call your parents. Call Laurel. Call anyone you think might've seen her. And call my house to see if she went back there for some reason."

"She's not at my parents'. I spoke to them only two hours —"

"Just make the calls!" he broke in.

"Why should I do anything to help *you?*"

"You're not helping *me!*"

"Fine!" Her grimace let him know she resented his demands, but she left the door open and rolled into the kitchen.

Although he couldn't make out what she said — by design or she would've used the phone in the living room — he could hear the drone of her voice while he paced on the stoop. He was still fighting his gut reaction, telling himself there had to be some innocuous explanation for Claire's absence, when Leanne came back, but before she even opened her mouth, the look on her face kicked his stomach into his throat. Genuine concern had replaced her snide expression.

"No one's seen her," she said. "And there's no answer at your place." Her throat worked as she swallowed. "You don't think —"

He didn't wait for her to finish. "Call 9-1-1 and get the sheriff involved," he said as he jogged to his truck. Maybe, just maybe, she'd returned to his house and fallen asleep. Or she'd gone back to her mother's studio. . . .

He hoped that was it. But in his heart, Isaac didn't believe the problem was that simple. She was somewhere she wasn't supposed to be.

"What did you do with her?" Mouth dry, heart pounding, Jeremy nearly wet his pants as his father lifted his head. Confronting him like this was asking for trouble — asking to have his father knock his block off like the men in prison would do if he was ever sent there. Especially because his father had been drinking. He reeked of alcohol, still held a bottle loosely in one hand.

But Jeremy had to ask, had to know. Claire meant everything to him and always had.

"What did you say?" His father's words came out a disbelieving whisper.

Jeremy swallowed hard. "Claire. She's m-missing. I — I heard about it at Hank's. Everyone's looking for her."

His father glared at him, forever it seemed

— until Jeremy waved a hand in front of his face with a tentative "Hello?"

The life was back in his eyes. "Just stay out of it, you hear?" He took a long swig of the scotch he liked so well. "That's all you've got to do — stay the hell out of it and keep your damn mouth shut."

Jeremy knew he'd pushed his luck as far it would go. His father remained on the couch, looking whipped and eager to finish what was in his bottle, but he could change in a split second. Jeremy needed to get out of the house before the alcohol made Don any meaner than he already was.

He started to go. He wanted to run away, like he'd planned for so long. But he didn't have any of his gear. He didn't even have his car keys. They were on the side table next to his father. He was afraid to get them for fear his father would grab his hand.

He needed those keys. Didn't want to walk. Couldn't walk. The cemetery lay between him and anywhere he'd want to go, except the bait-and-tackle shop where he'd used the pay phone to warn Isaac that Claire might not be safe. Why hadn't Isaac looked out for her?

Someone had broken into her house. He'd heard about that, too. And now she was gone. . . .

The hatred he felt toward his father distilled into a hard ball in the pit of his stomach. If she was hurt, Don was to blame. Don had too many secrets to let her keep digging up the past. He said that over and over. Or maybe he'd hired Les Weaver. Like before. Les had killed David. Jeremy would never forget the call his father had received the day David was shot. "It's done," he'd heard when he accidentally picked up the extension at the same time his father answered.

Gathering his courage, Jeremy turned around to confront Don again. "She's dead, like her mother. Isn't she?"

Eyebrows jerking together like furry caterpillars, his father started to laugh.

Jeremy couldn't figure out how to react to that. His father never laughed anymore. He was acting strange. "What's so funny?"

With a pained sigh, he leaned back. "You don't want to know."

"I do. I want to know what's going on. Is it Tug? You saw him again. You were with Joe, too. I heard you talking to them on the phone before you left."

"You think I should explain?" He didn't wait for a response. "Fine. This is what's going on. I'm sitting here wondering what I ever did to deserve you. How is it that *I* married a no-good woman who bears a retarded son, then divorces me and refuses to take responsibility for the kid we created? How is it that *I* get falsely accused at the gun shop and lose my job? That I hurt my back? It's funny, isn't it? Here I am, with nothing, nothing but you — the one thing I don't want."

Jeremy felt his lip come out. "That's not nice. I'm not . . . *retarded.* That's a bad word. You're not supposed to say it."

"I'll say it if I want to!" His face beamed scarlet as he jumped to his feet. "You're not right in the head. I should've done what George did to Lennie. Lord knows I've thought about it often enough."

Who was this George and Lennie his father kept talking about? George and Lennie and sometimes Curly's wife. *You have to shoot your own dog,* he'd mutter, mostly when he was drunk.

But they didn't have a dog. Neither did they know a George, or a Lennie, or even a Curly. Jeremy hated hearing about those people. If they were friends of his father's, Jeremy had never seen them, but whoever they were, they were always on his father's side.

"I don't want to hear about Lennie anymore." The words weren't very loud. They sort of squeaked out, but Jeremy was proud of himself for speaking at all. He'd never stood up to his father before. "No more about shooting dogs, either. *You're* the one who's not right in the head."

Look what he'd done to Alana. . . . Jeremy had proof in the crawl space, didn't he? How would his father like it if he pulled that suitcase out?

He didn't have a chance to ask. His father lunged forward, baring his yellow teeth. "Maybe it's not too late. No, it's not too late. Why not do it now?" Steadying himself with one hand on the wall, he gestured toward the kitchen. "Get my gun."

Jeremy leaped back, out of the way, and nearly peed his pants again. What did his father want with a gun? He shouldn't have a gun. Not when he was drinking. Even a car was dangerous. Drunk Driving Kills. Jeremy had seen those bumper stickers. But he wasn't sure he'd be able to talk his father out of what he had planned. Don suddenly looked like someone who was a stranger to him, probably because he seemed almost sober. That scared Jeremy more than knowing he was saying those things when he wasn't thinking straight.

"I won't." Jeremy refused to go anywhere near him, not even to scoot past and reach the kitchen, and the gun, before him. "It — it's not safe."

"That's the point, isn't it? It's time to shoot my own damn dog." Letting go of the wall, he staggered into the other room. "Everyone feels so sorry for you," he ranted as he went. "Everyone thinks I'm such an ogre, that I should be nicer to poor Jeremy. But what would they do if they were me? I don't see anyone stepping up to help. You're *my* responsibility. Mine alone."

Jeremy's hands curled into fists as he found his voice and set it free. "Why would they?" he yelled. The anger had broken through, seemed to be filling his whole body, and he doubted he'd ever be able to put it back. This was the end of one or both of them. He and his father couldn't live in the same house anymore. "They're my friends but . . . they're not *family.* They're not *blood.*"

"How much is a father expected to do?"

Since this came from the kitchen, Jeremy could barely hear it. His father wasn't yelling anymore. He wasn't asking as if he expected an answer. Jeremy could tell by his tone that his eyes had returned to the blank stare that had felt so strange a moment earlier. Don had slipped inside himself and was seeing only he knew what — maybe his imaginary friends — Curly's wife or . . . or Lennie.

"I've done my best to look after you," he continued to mumble, "but I can't do it anymore. I can't even take care of myself these days. It's better if you go this way."

Jeremy heard a cupboard open and close, knew which one it would be. His father was getting his gun from above the fridge.

"I've tried to take care of you, too," Jeremy pointed out, but he'd spoken barely loud enough for those words to reach his own ears. It didn't matter what he said. His father was going to kill him. He had to leave *now*.

The keys on the side table drew his eye. They were right there, and his father was no longer in the way. All he had to do was scoop them up and go. And yet he couldn't move. His legs felt like unbendable wooden stilts from which he might topple at any moment.

His father came around the corner, blinked the sweat from his eyes and took aim.

But he didn't fire. Tears streaked down his face and his hands began to shake. Why? This was what he'd wanted for so long; he'd said as much.

"I'm sorry," his father whispered. It was

the first time Jeremy had ever heard him apologize. Or maybe it was the first time it had ever seemed real.

"I'm not a dog," Jeremy responded, and put up his arms to protect his head, but that didn't stop his father from pulling the trigger.

The blast drowned out all other sound.

Those first few minutes after Joe yanked her out of her car had been harrowing, especially when he hauled her into Peter's house and Peter blocked the door so she couldn't leave, but Claire was no longer frightened of the Kenyon brothers. They hadn't tried to hurt her. They'd restrained her until they could get her to listen to what they had to say, and then they'd promised they could prove their words if she'd just give them the chance.

What they'd told her hadn't been easy to hear. To avoid the way it made her feel, Claire told herself to withhold judgment until they found the metal box that was supposed to be buried here in the woods. But an emotional reckoning would, eventually, be inevitable. She already believed them, or she wouldn't have spent the past several hours digging in the forest.

Gasping for breath, she leaned on her

shovel. Her hole wasn't nearly as big as Peter's or Joe's but it would soon be the size of a shallow grave. Where the hell was that damn metal box? If she didn't find it quickly she wouldn't be able to lift her arms anymore. She'd never done this much manual labor.

"You *sure* this is the place?" She studied the trees towering around them as if they might offer her some sign.

Joe's shovel continued to scrape against the soil. "How many times are you going to ask me that?"

"Sorry. But it's been fifteen years. That's a long time. And this deep in the forest, everything looks the same."

"I know where I buried it," he said. "Or about where I buried it."

"It'll be here," Peter chimed in.

Claire was surprised Joe's brother had deigned to speak to her. He still wasn't happy that Joe had decided to take her into his confidence. He hadn't complained about it since the initial confrontation ended; it was a moot point now. But he thought that what they'd divulged was too risky, and he had a point. That risk was the reason Joe had kept his silence for so long. He had a lot to lose if this came out, and it *would* come out if it had any bearing on her mother's case.

Although Claire had been tempted to ask him about Leanne's tape and what had happened when Alana showed up at his place the day she went missing, she hadn't wanted to bring up that subject in front of Peter. She got the impression he didn't know about it, was pretty sure Joe had kept it from everyone. She didn't know if he'd handled it that way because Alana would've wanted him to or because Tug wouldn't give him any more work if he told or because he was simply that nice.

After the past few hours, she was willing to believe he was that nice. He hadn't *had* to come clean, even now, but he wasn't willing to keep secrets if doing so put Claire in harm's way. At least, that was what he said. After the incidents at her mother's studio and then her house, he was convinced he had to speak up. Having her appear on his doorstep this morning, and feeling that Carly was once again running off at the mouth about a relationship between him and Alana — those things had been the final straw.

She was glad he'd broken his silence. But what he'd told her wouldn't be worth much if they couldn't find the metal box to back it up.

"One of us will find the damn thing eventually," Joe added.

She just hoped the sun, and her strength, would hold out long enough. They were all damp with sweat, which meant they'd be cold once night came on. Pineview had beautiful summers with plenty of mild, warm days, but the air could get chilly as it grew late.

"What does the box look like again?" She was stalling, couldn't convince her aching arms to lift another shovelful of dirt.

Scrape. Plop. Joe kept at it. "It's a cash box."

"Right." Tilting her head back, she gazed up at the sky and cursed the growing darkness. She'd been away too long. Surely Isaac had returned from Myles's office in Libby and was wondering where she'd gone. She wished she had some way to call him, to relieve the concern he had to be feeling, but she'd never dreamed retrieving this evidence would take so long. Joe had said he remembered where he'd buried it.

Peter paused to look over at her. "You want to give up for today? We could always come back tomorrow after work."

He seemed to like that idea, and it was no wonder. He had nothing to gain by finding the box.

"We're not quitting." After all those hours of digging, they had to be close. . . .

A frown creased his face. "We'll have to quit soon. It'll be too dark to continue."

Joe wiped his forehead with the heel of his hand. "I can't believe we haven't found it yet. Maybe we're wasting our time. Maybe some animal dragged it away."

Claire bit her lip. No. That couldn't have happened, not after all the years she'd waited for Joe to speak.

"You think it's gone?" Peter asked.

"What would an animal want with —" she started, but Joe figured out where she was going with this and interrupted before she could finish.

"Depends on the animal. Maybe with erosion and whatnot it was uncovered. A bear could've come across it and tried to break it open. They're always looking for food."

"But it wouldn't smell like food." And she had to have *some* luck, didn't she?

"I'm just saying . . . something must've happened to it, because it was here."

"It's *still* here," she insisted. "Come on. Let's give it another hour." Summoning what remained of her energy, she positioned her shovel at the bottom of her hole and jumped on it so it would cut deeper into the soil.

About halfway in, it struck something hard.

23

Although he was still out searching, Isaac had been checking his messages every fifteen or twenty minutes. That was how he finally reached Claire. She said her car was banged up, that she had a broken window and a dented fender, but she was okay and waiting at his house.

He'd been so worried she'd met a grisly end, it took him several seconds to believe the nightmare was really over. He was standing at the pay phone he'd stopped to use, the one outside the Kicking Horse Saloon, his forehead resting against the cool metal long after they'd hung up, when he heard a voice behind him.

"You think you're so smart, don't you?"

Preparing himself for a confrontation — the tone of the man's voice certainly suggested there might be one — he turned to face Tug.

"Excuse me?"

"All that crap about David being killed." Tug looked strung out on stress — judging by the pallor of his skin, the hair that stood up and the way his hand kept twitching. "Don't you realize you're only making things worse?"

"Claire's fine. I just talked to her." Isaac thought that would handle the situation, but Tug's response surprised him.

"I heard. Myles spotted her as soon as she drove into town. He pulled her over and radioed for dispatch to call me. But it's no thanks to you that she's okay. You're getting involved in something that's none of your business. I suggest you let it go."

"I'd rather not have this conversation." Isaac pivoted and headed toward his truck, which he'd had to park in the overflow dirt lot because the bar was so crowded. He wanted to get home so he could hear what Claire had to tell him. She'd said to hurry — and he saw nothing to be gained by arguing with her stepfather.

"Maybe that wasn't a suggestion."

Isaac stopped. Did that make it a threat? "Do you have something to hide?" he said, turning back.

"I just don't like you meddling in my family."

"Is that what I'm doing?"

"You're not good for her. We've asked you nicely to stay away. Now I'm asking you not so nicely."

Isaac folded his arms. "Or what, Tug? You'll hire someone to kill *me* like you did David?"

His mouth popped open. "You son of a bitch! How dare you accuse me of murdering my own son-in-law!"

"Maybe it wasn't you, but it could have been. *Someone* hired him. There were at least ten calls between various pay phones in town and Les Weaver's home in Coeur d'Alene during the weeks before David's death. If you don't believe me, you can ask Myles. I went over the records with him today."

"So? Maybe he has friends here. Have you ever thought of that?"

"Not after he told me he didn't. Not after he said he'd never been here and knew no one in the area."

A man and a woman left the bar, but were so engrossed in each other that they didn't seem to notice the drama playing out near the pay phone.

"When did you talk to Les Weaver?" Tug asked.

"Just a few days ago."

"You're making that up."

"Check with Myles, like I said."

His hand plowed through his hair along the same well-worn path he'd obviously created earlier in the evening. "But . . . why would anyone want to hurt David?"

"You're really going to ask me that?"

"So what if he was looking into Alana's death! What are the chances he'd find anything? The police couldn't even figure out what happened to her." Closing his eyes, he shook his head. "Why can't we just leave the past in the past?"

"Because it has too much bearing on the present."

"It doesn't have to."

"The truth is coming out, Tug. If, for some reason, you don't want that, you need to be prepared."

"Stay out of it, Isaac. None of it concerns you."

"What's the matter? Afraid Claire finally has the support she needs to uncover the truth?"

He made a dismissive motion. "You have no idea what's best for Claire."

"And you do?"

"I know you're not the man for her."

"I think that's Claire's decision, don't you?" Isaac climbed into his truck, but he thought about those words the whole ride home and couldn't help wondering . . . was Tug right?

Just in case any of it ended up being crucial evidence, Isaac used tweezers to handle the objects spread out on his kitchen table.

Claire paced by the window, waiting for his reaction. "So? What do you think?"

The encounter he'd just had with Tug jumped into Isaac's mind. He hadn't mentioned it to Claire, hadn't wanted to make a bigger issue of the fact that her family disapproved of him. He hated acknowledging the conflict he'd caused, partly because he didn't want her to believe, as they believed, that he'd let her down, and partly because he feared they'd turn out to be right, despite his good intentions. Considering what he was sorting through, however, he now saw Tug's threats in a much more sinister light.

"I think your stepfather could be in trouble," he admitted.

A pained expression crossed her face, and she looked away, probably to hide how hard this was for her. Regardless of what Tug had or hadn't done, she loved him, couldn't stand the thought that he might have murdered her mother. But Isaac didn't know what else to make of the documents Joe had provided. A letter from Tug threatened to kill Joe if Joe didn't leave his wife alone. Another letter, written by Alana to Joe, confessed her love and the guilt she felt, which confirmed the rumors Claire had always denied. Then there was a ring made out of ribbon. Joe said Alana had teasingly made it for him one afternoon, and Claire acknowledged that her mother had made similar ribbon rings for her and Leanne when they were children.

Most incriminating of all were the pictures of Joe and Alana together. One strip of black and white photographs featured them kissing in the kind of photo booth typically found in a drugstore or old-fashioned grocery. They must've been in Libby or somewhere else when those pictures were taken. Pineview didn't have a booth like that — and they wouldn't have risked being seen.

Isaac felt awkward being privy to Claire's pain and all the reasons for it. Not only was she trying to cope with the gut-wrenching sadness of receiving confirmation that the man who'd raised her had a strong motive for murdering the mother she missed so badly, she had proof of her mother's infidelity. Then there were the calls between Coeur d'Alene and Pineview, and what Myles had found when he ran the background check on Les Weaver. Although Les had never been arrested he had ties to one of the most powerful Mafia families in New York — people who didn't bat an eye at murder for hire. Myles had even placed a call to the NYPD and learned that Weaver had lived in New York and was suspected of racketeering. They hadn't been able to prove it, but they were trying. That was probably the reason he'd moved west four years ago, when his brother got out of prison after being convicted of fraud and had also relocated to Idaho. It was his way of lying low.

Claire had winced when he explained all that.

"I'm sorry." That was hardly any comfort, but Isaac didn't know what to say.

She gave him a sad smile. "Thanks."

He watched her at the sink, staring out into the night. "Do you regret going after this?"

Shoulders hunched, she dropped her head in her hands. She'd been so physically exhausted when he arrived home, she could hardly get up off the couch, but now she seemed . . . pensive, unable to outrun the ghosts that were chasing her. "I'm not sure," she said. "Do you think it's possible that Roni was involved instead of my father? That maybe he . . . maybe he wrote that letter but never intended to hurt anybody? He threatens Joe, not my mother."

It was far more plausible that the tension between Tug and Alana had erupted into a fight, one with a very sad ending. But Isaac didn't *know* that had happened, so he didn't insist on it. "I suppose it's possible," he allowed, trying to be gentle. "There's nothing *here* to suggest Roni did it, but —"

"But I told you what April said," she interrupted.

"April has no proof," he reminded her.

"She knows something about Tug that very few people know. She and I might be the only two people left who are privy to that secret, other than his first wife."

"Still not enough to convince a jury."

Turning to face him, Claire gestured at the things she'd brought home with her. "But this is no better. It's all circumstantial. It establishes an affair, but not murder. We don't even have proof that my mother's dead."

"It creates motive."

"For Roni as much as Tug. And then there's what happened at the studio?"

"What about it?"

"The person who followed me there couldn't have been him."

Isaac cocked an eyebrow at her. "I thought

you didn't get a good look at the culprit."

She seemed to be gaining hope as she built a case in support of her stepfather. "I didn't, but . . . Tug's not in his prime anymore. He couldn't move that fast. And he would never hurt me."

If he'd been the reason her mother went missing and David was shot, he already had. "You're saying Roni could, or would?"

"No, the person at the cabin wasn't Roni, either. There must be someone else."

"Whoever pushed you didn't mean to hurt you, Claire. I think he was spying on you and panicked when you came downstairs earlier than he expected."

"I don't care. It couldn't have been Tug," she said. "He was at the fireworks show with Leanne and Roni."

But he could've claimed he had a headache and pretended he was going home early. Or said he was planning to meet a couple of friends for a beer. The culprit knew the back way to the studio, which Tug certainly did. "Have you asked them how long he stayed after you left?"

Sliding her hands in the pockets of her loose-fitting jeans, she smoothed the rug on the floor with one foot. "No. I never dreamed I'd need to."

"Then we'll check it out, okay? Hopefully,

he has a foolproof alibi — for then and the night someone was at your place, rummaging through everything."

Her forehead wrinkled. "He wouldn't destroy my pictures of David. Or that painting of my mother's."

Isaac didn't think so, either. That was the one thing that didn't fit. He could see Tug finding his wife's birth control pills and getting into an argument with her that quickly spun out of control. He could see Tug, if he was indeed guilty of murder, hiring someone to kill David to keep from being exposed. He had everything to lose — his money, his wife, his family, his standing in the community, his freedom. He could also see Tug following Claire to the studio to see if he had to worry about her resuming David's search. Hell, Isaac could even see him rummaging through her house for those damn files.

But why the destruction? What he'd seen at her house indicated extreme hatred, and he believed Tug loved her. "I'm impressed that Joe was willing to come forward with this, considering the damage it could do to his marriage," he said, hoping to change the subject.

"I'm bugged that he didn't do it sooner," she responded. "If he loved my mother, why wouldn't he want her killer to be caught?"

"He had his family to think about."

"He wasn't thinking about *them* when he slept with her."

"Maybe he kept telling himself that what they didn't know wouldn't hurt them. He was also afraid he'd wind up a suspect. Could be she tried to break off the relationship, and he killed her in the classic 'if I can't have you, no one can' scenario. I'm actually surprised he came clean at all."

Her teeth sank into her bottom lip as she considered his comment. "He said he did it because he still loves her, even after all these years. He told me he wasn't willing to sit back and let whatever happened to her happen to me."

"I'm liking Joe more and more," he said, and got up to cross over to her. "You ready for bed?"

She stepped into his arms and felt instantly better. "Yeah. I'm tired."

It was a mess. Jeremy had never seen anything like it, except in some horror movie. Instead of shooting *him,* his father had raised the gun and squeezed off a round that went into the wall. Then, sobbing like a child, even though he said only pussies cried, he'd fallen onto his knees, muttered that he wasn't worth shit if he couldn't do what had to be done and put the barrel in his own mouth.

Before Jeremy could stop him, he fired again, and now his brains covered the couch and part of the wall behind it. The rest of him lay sprawled on the floor next to the gun.

Jeremy had been sitting nearby, rocking back and forth and staring at what was left of his father, for hours. He kept asking himself if he should call Hank. But Hank was working, and Hank would go to the police. Anyone would. Which was bad. Jeremy knew what would happen if the police came. They'd take his father's body away, close up the house and put him in a strange place, a place that wasn't exactly a house and wasn't exactly a hospital in some town far away from here. His father had described it to him many times.

You'd better hope nothing ever happens to me.

He wouldn't have his car. He wouldn't have Hank, or his job. He wouldn't have his bedroom. And he'd never see Claire again.

Was Claire even alive? Maybe that was why his father was crying. Maybe he'd killed her. He'd never been the same since Alana.

Jeremy pictured the place where he'd be

sent, like the one in that *Cuckoo* movie his father had shown him. Then he imagined some other family moving into this home. What if that family had a boy who managed to remove the locks and went underneath the house? And what if that boy found the suitcase? The police would come to the sanatorium — that was what his father called it — and put him in prison, just like Don had told him they would.

"They're going to knock my block off," he whimpered. He'd been crying off and on. Didn't seem to matter now that his father wasn't around to yell about it. There was no one left to get mad. But he wasn't relieved about that. Not like he'd always dreamed. As mean as his father could be, Don had been there day in and day out. At least most of the time. Without him, a big hole seemed to yawn open right in front of Jeremy. If he moved an inch, he'd fall in. . . .

Oh, God . . . what should I do? He'd been asking himself that ever since his father killed himself, but he couldn't think of a good answer.

It was three o'clock in the morning before Jeremy came to his feet. He had a headache, his eyes burned and his nose was plugged, but he'd finally figured out that there was really only one solution to his problem. He had to bury his father. He had to get rid of the body and clean up the mess before anyone saw it. Only then could he go on living as he'd lived in the past. With the way his father had been drinking, no one would miss him. Not for a long time. If one of his friends called, Jeremy would make up some excuse. He could always say his father was passed out. No one would question that, no matter how many times he said it.

If that didn't work . . . he'd say that the same person who'd made Alana disappear had made Don disappear, too. That was true, wasn't it?

And if *that* didn't work . . . he'd go into the forest and never come back.

He vomited the first time he touched the body. Even after there was nothing left in his stomach, he continued with the dry heaves until he'd wrapped his father up in a blanket. From there, it wasn't so hard to carry him downstairs and around the corner. But getting him under the house wasn't easy.

Pushing and pulling, Jeremy managed to move his burden into the crowded space inch by exhausting inch until it was right next to the suitcase. Then he sat back and let himself cry some more.

"You've got company," he told Claire's

mother when he had no more tears to shed. Then he crawled into his bed. As strong as he normally was, he didn't have one ounce of energy left.

But it was okay. No one ever came to the house. He'd finish cleaning up in the morning.

Isaac's eyes popped open. It was dark and very late. If the moon was out, it couldn't be more than a sliver, or it was on the other side of the house, because he couldn't even see his hand in front of his face.

What had disturbed him?

Not Claire. She was sleeping soundly at his side.

He held still for several seconds, listening to the house settle above the sound of her steady breathing. Everything seemed fine, perfectly normal. He told himself he was just anxious about what had happened recently and snuggled closer to her warm body. But a thump, coming from outside, sent a charge of adrenaline through him.

What was that?

His mind reverted to the calls he'd seen on Les Weaver's phone bills. He believed Les was a contract killer, a person who was able to take someone out and not get caught. If Les knew he and Claire were making waves for him, he just might return to Pineview to be sure they couldn't continue.

Isaac's blood ran cold to think someone might have come to kill him or Claire or both of them. He'd been attacked by wolves and bears and wild dogs; he'd been bitten by a poisonous spider. But never before had he felt as if a *man* might try to kill him.

He slipped carefully out of bed so he wouldn't disturb Claire — Lord knew she needed the rest, and given the number of scavengers in the forest, this could easily be a false alarm.

After pulling on the jeans he'd been wearing earlier and his boots, he got his revolver from the top drawer. He didn't like guns. He was too much of an animal lover to enjoy hunting, didn't understand why it was considered such grand sport to kill when it was far more exciting to document life, but he kept a weapon handy in case of emergency.

The bedroom door creaked as he opened it. Claire stirred, but didn't wake. He waited until she'd settled again before creeping out into the living room.

Unfortunately, it was just as dark. Here in the mountains the stars were brighter than in the city, but with so many trees towering over his house that didn't help. The only outside lights Isaac had were the ones he'd installed himself — a flood, activated by a motion sensor, on each side of the cabin.

As he waited in the living room, one of those floods snapped on. An animal could've tripped the sensor, something as small as a rat or a skunk, but Isaac knew it could also be something bigger.

Crouching at the window, gun ready, he peered through the glass. He didn't see anything, but there wasn't much time to look before a shot rang out, shattering the light.

24

Isaac tried the phone first. He knew it wasn't likely that the police could make it to his cabin before whatever was about to happen went down. Lincoln was a sparsely populated county, with only a few small towns. Sheriff's deputies not concentrated in Libby, the county seat, were spread out. Myles lived closest, but even Myles's house was a fifteen-minute drive, and fifteen minutes sounded like an eternity when Isaac had Claire to worry about. It wasn't as if he could go one-on-one with whoever was out there. He had to keep her with him or risk losing her, and he wasn't prepared to let that happen. Fearing she'd been killed yesterday when he'd searched for hours and hadn't been able to find her was bad enough.

But calling for help wasn't among his options. The person who'd shot out the light had already cut the phone line.

"Claire?" He didn't speak loudly. The urgency in his voice would probably be enough to wake her — if the gunshot hadn't done so.

"I'm here." She stood in the doorway. "What's going on? What was that noise?"

"A gunshot. Get down and stay down. We've got company."

"Oh, God."

That was his reaction, too. He'd never expected anything *this* bold. He'd brought her here believing that would keep her safe.

"Do you have any idea who it is?" she breathed.

"I can make a good guess." She probably could, too.

"We should call Myles." The floor creaked as she moved closer, presumably to do just that, but he stopped her.

"Stay down! Phone's dead." He was afraid *they* would be, too, if this didn't go right.

Silence fell as they listened for more noises from outside.

Isaac couldn't hear a thing, had no way of knowing what their visitor was doing.

"What's next?" Claire whispered, beside him now.

His heart pounded against his rib cage as if he'd just run a forty-yard dash. "He can't shoot us from where he's at. He's got to get inside."

"Which way —" her voice shook but she paused, obviously attempting to control it "— do you think he'll come in?"

Isaac opened his mouth to answer, but the floodlight in back popped on and he hurried to the window instead. He hoped to catch a glimpse of the culprit, get some idea of what he was up against — at least establish whether he was facing one man or two. If he had to place a bet, he'd say there was only one, and it was Les Weaver. But he couldn't be sure.

No one stood in the clearing. The bastard was circling the cabin under cover of the trees, throwing pieces of wood or rocks to trip the sensors and make the lights switch on so he could shoot them out.

Within ten minutes, he'd destroyed all four.

Claire could feel the tension in Isaac's body. He'd rearranged the furniture to create various barriers and had her sandwiched, with him, between the leather love seat and the couch. But she didn't like waiting. She felt as if they were sitting ducks. With no help coming, they could be trapped for a long time.

"Maybe we should slip out into the forest. Make a run for it," she whispered.

"Too dangerous." His words, clipped and authoritative, brooked no argument, but she launched one, anyway.

"We know this area better than anyone else."

"I couldn't even make it safely from here to your mother's studio running in the dark. It's pitch-black out there. And we can't take flashlights without drawing him right to us."

He had a point, but it was so tantalizing to think of reaching the next cabin, where they could get help. "We might have more of a chance than in here."

"It'd be a gamble. At least here we have some cover."

"So what do we do?"

"I have a gun. We wait until I have something to shoot at."

"But *I* don't have a gun. Do you have a rifle?"

"No."

"Should I get a knife?"

"And give someone the chance to turn it on you? Forget it. You'll just have to rely on me."

In about any other cabin on this mountain Claire was willing to bet she'd find a whole stash of guns. But unlike most men in this part of the state, Isaac didn't care for that sort of thing. He owned expensive cameras and video equipment, which was probably the reason he'd bothered to install the floodlights — to protect the money he'd invested in his career, not to protect himself. Or her. If she had her guess he'd never expected he'd have to do either.

"You sorry we're friends yet?" she muttered.

"You told me you loved me. That's a bit more than friends."

She could tell he was teasing, trying to put her at ease, but there wasn't much that could relieve her fear with a gunman outside.

"You didn't say anything in return," she pointed out.

There was a slight pause during which he grew serious. "I care about you."

He spoke as if that was a major confession but she had to laugh at his hesitancy. "Thanks. That almost made me cry."

"You —" He stopped. Footsteps came across the wooden porch, moving toward the front door. "He's coming."

Claire squeezed her eyes shut — she couldn't see anything, anyway, and she couldn't do a whole lot without a weapon.

Isaac shifted. She sensed that he was turning toward the door, taking aim in case whoever it was managed to break in. But their assailant didn't even try. The footsteps stopped. Then they heard the kind of pounding done with a hammer.

"What the hell?" Isaac murmured. "Stay here." He got up and crept closer. Claire guessed he planned to get off a shot, if he could, but there was little chance that a bullet from a handgun would penetrate the solid-core door, as well as the outer screen, with enough force to injure the person on the other side. Not only that, but he'd already missed his opportunity. The footsteps had started up again, were moving away from them at a run.

"We could be in trouble," Isaac said.

What they heard a couple of minutes later — more hammering, this time at the back door — seemed to confirm it.

"Son of a bitch!"

"What's he doing?" Claire asked.

"He's not trying to get in. He's trying to make sure we can't get out."

"What?"

"Come here! Now!"

She scrambled toward him as he opened the front door. It swung in easily enough. The cool outside air gave her hope of escape and survival. Provided the man who'd shot out the lights was acting on his own, only the screen door stood between them and freedom, because they could hear their visitor was pounding elsewhere.

She hadn't expected to have any trouble with the screen door. It wasn't as substantial as the real one. But it wouldn't swing out.

"He hammered it shut," she said. It was too dark to see the exact problem, but she'd heard pounding and now the door wouldn't open. Still, she thought they should be able to break through. Isaac must've thought so, too. He threw himself against the screen door several times — with no luck.

"Damn it! He must've used a couple two-by-fours. Come on, we have to get out, even if it means taking him on." They made a dash for the only other exit. Suddenly it didn't matter that they might come face-to-face with a gunman. He was no longer their worst fear. Claire was beginning to guess what their visitor had in store for them — she could tell Isaac had figured it out, too — and knew they had only a short time to escape.

They reached the back door as the pounding stopped.

No! They were already too late. That screen door wouldn't open, either. And when their assailant took a shot at them while they were trying to bust it, Isaac pulled her to the floor and slammed the heavier door shut.

"A window?" she suggested.

"There's no way we can both get through fast enough," he replied. "He'll hear the breaking glass and be there to shoot us as we tumble out."

But they had to do something. She could already smell wood burning.

Isaac couldn't believe how quickly smoke was filling the cabin. He'd always known fire would be a very bad thing; he owned an all-wood house. The forest was in danger, too, but at the moment the trees he loved seemed like a lesser concern.

"I'm going to get this bastard if it's the last thing I do," he yelled, but he wasn't sure Claire even heard him. The flames crackled and popped, the noise far louder than he'd ever dreamed it could be, and she seemed entranced by the shifting light reflecting off the windows as the flames licked higher and higher.

Isaac smelled gasoline, knew it must've been poured all around the foundation for the fire to turn into such an all-consuming blaze almost instantly.

After shoving the gun in his waistband, he

grabbed two towels, thrust them in the bathroom sink and soaked them both. Then he gave one to Claire to wrap around her head and did the same as he pulled her to the ground and began to guide her to his bedroom. For all he knew, the flames were as bad or worse in there, but they had to choose a window before they died of smoke inhalation, and his bedroom was closest to where he'd parked his truck. He didn't have time to get his keys, but he kept a Hide-a-Key attached to the undercarriage. If they could get to that, they might survive. . . .

Claire didn't argue or try to resist. He'd told her they could be shot while coming out of a window, but she seemed perfectly willing to take her chances against a bullet if it meant avoiding death by fire, and he felt the same.

As they crawled through the smoke filling the house, he remembered thinking, when the first light had been shot out, that someone was trying to send them a message. *Back off. Leave the past alone.* The person who'd followed her to the cabin hadn't meant her any harm, or she wouldn't be alive today. Considering the destruction of her personal property, the person who'd ransacked her house — whether it was the same person or a different one — seemed more aggressive, but even then Isaac got the impression that he was more interested in recovering the files than anything else.

This, however, went well beyond a mere message. Whoever had set the fire wanted them dead.

Claire coughed as she hurried to keep up. His lungs burned, making it difficult to breathe, but he was fairly certain they'd have enough air to reach the window. Whether they could get out was the bigger question. If the arsonist was smart, he'd be out there, waiting. . . .

But you couldn't set a fire like that and assume it would go unnoticed, even in the mountains. From the outside, it had to look like an inferno. The speed with which the cabin had gone up had probably surprised even him.

Hopefully, fear of discovery had sent the son of a bitch running for his vehicle.

Picturing attorney Les Weaver losing his practiced calm as he barreled down the mountain, Isaac breathed too deeply and had to cough, but he urged Claire on. Either way, they were taking the chance that their assailant had left — because that was the only chance they had.

Claire's skin felt as if it would melt off. The

tremendous heat drove her back, made it all but impossible to continue advancing toward the flames. If Isaac wasn't so damn insistent, wasn't half dragging her, she would've faltered, doubted herself and searched for another way out, even though logic said this was their best bet. Considering how fast the cabin was turning to cinders, they'd probably have only one chance, and even that would depend on whether the surrounding trees had already caught fire. They couldn't bear the heat or the smoke much longer. . . .

Flames leaped as high as the window. She could see the flickering orange and gold through the glass, a wall of fire. Again, she wanted to find a safer exit, but Isaac yelled that the other walls were the same. They were hemmed in, surrounded, and the person who'd set this fire meant it to be that way. He'd left them no escape.

Claire wasn't sure how Isaac planned to break the window. He yelled at her to keep her head down, as close to the floor as possible. Then he let go of her for the first time since they'd found the back screen hammered shut.

Panic slithered down her spine as he disappeared into the smoke. She'd felt a sense of purpose as long as he was with her, but now she had the terrifying thought that she might never see him again. She lifted her head to keep track of him, if she could, and paid for it with a lung-searing intake of smoke.

"Head down! Head down!"

There was the sound of breaking glass, then Isaac grabbed hold of her arm. Dimly, she wondered if he'd been cut. He didn't act as though he'd been injured, but if his adrenaline was pumping like hers she doubted he would. As soon as he pulled her to her feet, he swung her into his arms and tossed her through the jagged hole he'd created in the window as if she was no heavier than a sack of potatoes.

She sailed toward the flames, thought she might land in the middle of them, but she didn't. She hit the ground with a bone-jarring thud that rattled her teeth, even stunned her for a few seconds. She lay there, blinking as the cabin continued to burn, distantly marveling at the blinding brightness — until the cool air brought her to her senses and she realized Isaac hadn't come out yet.

She sat up, waiting for him to leap through the window. He should've been right behind her. . . .

But he wasn't. She couldn't see him anywhere.

The sharp pain she'd felt when she'd first tried to move seemed to disappear as fear for his well-being overcame everything else. Shaking her head to clear it, she got to her feet and staggered closer to the building. If she was pregnant, this couldn't be good for the baby. The heat threatened to singe off her eyelashes and eyebrows, but she didn't care. Where was he? Why hadn't he made it out? Had he succumbed to smoke inhalation? Her lungs felt bloody and raw, and she wasn't the one who'd been doing the real work.

Tears streamed down her face as she imagined him crumpled on the floor inside. Was he still alive? Even if he was, how would she get him to safety?

"Isaac!" If the man who'd set this fire heard her screaming, she was a dead woman. But that didn't matter, either. All she cared about was seeing the man she loved.

The jagged rocks, pinecones and bristles that made the forest floor so unfriendly to bare feet cut into her soles as she ran to the right, then to the left, looking for some way to get back into the house. She was pretty sure their arsonist was gone. She didn't see anyone. But she wasn't looking into the forest; she was looking for Isaac. Her eyes remained fixed on the inferno in front of her as she tried to figure out how to rescue him.

She'd just grabbed the heavy rubber floor mat out of his truck and was beating back the flames at his bedroom window so she could climb through it when he jumped out, nearly tackling her as he landed.

"What the heck!" He coughed as he retrieved the computer tower he'd dropped. "What are you doing? Get in the truck!"

Bursting into a full-blown sob, she grabbed him. "I thought you weren't coming out!"

He gave her a squeeze, then he shoved her into the passenger seat, dumped his equipment in the bed of the truck and ran around to get behind the wheel.

The fire was beginning to spread into the forest.

"It's noon! Where've you been?"

It always frightened Jeremy when Hank glared up at him. Hank was small but he could talk and move very fast.

"I've been calling and calling your house," his boss went on. "I almost took off my apron and drove over there."

Jeremy couldn't look Hank in the eye. He hated disappointing him, tried to make sure that never happened, but this morning . . . everything had taken longer than he'd planned. Blood was the ickiest liquid in the world. He'd cleaned and dug and buried, but those tasks weren't even the worst of it. The worst of what had happened was the way Jeremy felt inside. Instead of being relieved that his father was gone, he felt . . . sick, lonely, lost. And knowing Claire might be dead, too, only made it worse. He wanted to ask if she'd been found, but he knew he wouldn't be able to make it through the day if she hadn't, so he kept his mouth shut. One thing at a time. Hank told him that whenever he got upset.

He pretended Hank had just said it now, but really he'd snapped his fingers. "Are you listening to me?"

Jeremy needed to respond, but he was having trouble forming sentences. They were all mixed up in his head. "Of course. I . . . I overslept, that's all. I'm sorry." With that, he tried to skirt past Hank, but Hank caught his arm.

"You were supposed to be here an hour ago, Jeremy, and you're never late. Are you sure everything's okay?" He lowered his voice. "You didn't get into another fight with your dad, did you?"

"Oh, no. He's fine. He's doing better. We didn't fight." Jeremy didn't like lying to Hank any more than he liked disappointing him. Because it was suddenly even harder to look at him, he stared down at his hands — and, to his horror, saw blood beneath his nails and around his cuticles. He'd been so worried about the wall and the couch, he'd somehow missed what was on his own fingers.

Shoving his hands into his pockets so Hank wouldn't see, he prayed that his boss would let him go. He had to visit the restroom and wash up, but Hank wasn't done with him yet.

"Let me take a look at you." He stared up into Jeremy's face, studying it closely.

All Jeremy could think about was his hands until Hank, at last, stepped back, seemingly satisfied. "You're a little pale but . . . I don't see any bruises."

"I'm fine," he insisted. Again, he almost asked about Claire but shied away. He didn't want to hear "no," didn't want to accept what "no" would mean.

"If you're really fine, I'm pissed off that you're late. Start flipping burgers. We're busy today."

Wincing at the "pissed off" part, even

though Hank hadn't said it as if he was serious, Jeremy apologized again.

"Forget it. I can't stay mad at you. That'd be like holding a grudge against my Saint Bernard."

Jeremy stopped him. "What'd you say?"

"Nothing. Get going before you cost me business."

"But I'm not Sigmund."

Hank had already turned away. "What?"

"Your dog."

"I don't know what you're talking about."

"I said I'm not a dog." The connection upset him. Why did this keep coming up?

"Of course you're not. That's not what I meant."

Then what *did* he mean? And what had his father meant? "Do you know Lennie?"

Hank's bushy eyebrows came together. "Who?"

"Lennie."

"Never heard of him."

"Me, neither," he said.

"Whatever, Jeremy." Smiling, he reached up to squeeze Jeremy's shoulder. "Work, remember?"

First, Jeremy went into the restroom. He wanted to wash his hands, but froze when he saw the image of himself in the mirror. He looked exactly like his father; he was just a bigger version. Everyone said it, but he could see it now, too.

His father was gone, and there was blood on his hands.

Someone pounded on the door, startling him. "Hey, come on! I gotta get in there!"

It was Millie, the girl who worked the register. Jeremy had once begged Hank to let him try being up front, taking orders, and had made a mess of everything. He hadn't asked since. He didn't want to fail. When Hank wasn't around, Millie teased him. Barely sixteen, she'd only started at Hank's Burger Joint the first of June while Jeremy had been working there for years, but she thought she was so smart.

"You big dummy!" she'd mutter, and roll her eyes whenever he made a mistake.

"Jeremy? Is that you in there?"

Her voice brought him back to the present. "Who else could it be?" he replied. Only four people worked at the burger joint. Hank, his wife, Reva, who did the "books," whatever that meant, and filled in when it got busy, him and Millie. If Hank and Reva were working, he had to be the one in the restroom, right? He felt like telling her *she* was a dummy, but that was mean, and he wasn't mean like her.

"Coming!" He turned on the faucet so he

could wash the blood away. But even with Millie right outside the door, he hunched over the sink and watched the water until it disappeared down the drain, taking the last of his father with it.

When he opened the door, Millie had her arms folded and was tapping her toe. "Took you long enough. What were you doin' in there, anyway? Jackin' off?"

"I would never do that at work."

"You're serious." Her eyes widened and she barked a laugh, but Hank got her moving again.

"Millie! We need you out here."

"Tell that to your friendly giant," she grumbled. "I couldn't get him out of the flippin' bathroom."

Afraid he'd upset Hank even more if he didn't get where he was supposed to be, Jeremy took over for Reva, who stood at the grill. "Sorry I'm late," he said.

She gave him a kind smile. She could get ornery with Millie. He got the impression she didn't really like Millie. But she never snapped at him. "That's okay, Jeremy. We were afraid you'd heard about the fire and were too upset to come in, that's all. You had us worried."

He blinked at her. "Fire? What fire?"

"Two fat boys, one skinny mama and a

bucket of fries," Hank called back.

Reva reclaimed the spatula she'd handed over and turned the burgers on the grill. She had ten half-pounders, or "fat boys," already coming and three "skinny mamas." "You haven't heard?" she said. "Isaac Morgan's house burned to the ground last night. It's the saddest thing. The fire destroyed several acres of forest, too. The fire crews are still up there, trying to put it out."

He'd been about to toast some buns but couldn't even do that. "Fire? But . . . how'd it get started?"

She lowered her voice so he could hardly hear her above the sizzle of meat. "It was arson, honey. In the middle of the night someone hammered two-by-fours across both doors so no one could get out, poured gasoline around the foundation and tossed a match."

But . . . Isaac could've died in there. "How do you know?"

Taking the buns from him, she dropped them facedown on one corner of the grill. "Isaac told the sheriff. But I bumped into Deputy Clegg at the coffee shop this morning. With all the activity in town, I could tell there was a ruckus going on, and he explained it."

"So . . . was Isaac in the cabin?"

"He was. And Claire, too. But don't worry, they both got out." She winked at him. "I know you're kind of sweet on her." She motioned to the deep fryer. "Can you put down a fresh batch of fries? We're getting low."

He didn't react to the request, couldn't process so many things at once. "Wait —" he grabbed her arm "— did you say Claire's okay?"

With a tolerant smile, she slid out of his grasp and put the fries down herself. "Yes, she had to go to the hospital to get checked out, but word has it they're both fine."

That meant his father hadn't killed her as Jeremy had feared. So why was Don so upset when Jeremy asked about her yesterday? Was he afraid Claire knew something that would bring out the truth, after all this time? Was that why he shot himself?

That sounded right. But then . . . who set the fire? If it happened in the middle of the night, his father couldn't have done it.

"Give me a mozzarella melt, another fat boy and some chicken fingers." Apparently, Millie was back at the register. She called in the order, and Reva acted on it because Jeremy couldn't.

"So where was she yesterday?" he asked.

"I hear she was with Joe Kenyon."

"But . . . they don't even like each other."

She handed him the spatula. "I guess they've worked out their differences. Are you okay here? Because you're not acting like yourself."

"I'm okay," he said. "I got it."

"You're sure."

"Yeah."

"Great, because I'm going to turn it over to you now."

He stared after her as she went into the small back room she used as an office. Claire wasn't missing. She'd almost died in a fire, but she'd gotten out. That made him feel better. Last night had been terrible. Today wasn't much of an improvement. But Claire was okay. . . .

"Who set the fire?" he called after Reva.

"No one knows yet," she called back.

But once Jeremy had a chance to think about it, he was pretty sure he could guess.

25

"At least they took out our stitches while we were at the hospital," Isaac said.

Claire slid her hand up his naked torso and pressed her lips to the steady beat at his throat. They were in bed at a motel in Kalispell, where they'd been for more than twenty-four hours. Isaac had insisted they not return to Pineview, said he wanted to get some sleep where he knew they'd be safe. He'd even parked his truck in the back, so it couldn't be seen from the street.

"That's not much consolation," she said. "Your house is destroyed. All your furniture, all your clothes. We don't even know how much of the forest went up."

"Last I heard they were getting it under control." He concealed a yawn, but it didn't come off as indifferent or uncaring. They were both groggy after a week of such intense emotion and so much loss. If Isaac was like her, he was just glad to feel safe for the moment. "It didn't reach your mother's studio," he added, "so it could've been worse."

"It took *your* house. That's bad enough."

"I'm not thrilled about losing everything. I'm even less thrilled about being displaced." He adjusted the bedding so he could pull her against him. "But we're alive, right?"

She laughed as he rubbed his cheek with its new beard growth against her neck. "Right."

He raised his head. "And everything was insured. My camera, my lenses . . ."

"What about the things money can't buy?" she asked, threading her fingers through his hair. "All your footage, the DVDs and negatives, your notes —"

"The really important stuff's in a safe. Provided that safe is as fireproof as I was told when I bought it, I'll be fine. And I managed to save my computer, which has my latest projects on the hard drive —"

"You saved it at the risk of your life." She scowled to show her disapproval. "And it still makes me mad. You have no idea how long those few seconds were when you didn't come out."

He grinned as he tweaked her chin. "I still don't know what you thought you were doing trying to get back inside."

"I wasn't trying to get inside. It just looked that way."

One palm cupped her breast as he leaned up on his elbow. "Tell the truth. You were coming back for me."

She gave him a saucy look. "No, I wanted to save that hippo print you said I could have."

He pecked her lips. "We'll get a new one printed."

"You're lucky your wallet was in the pocket of the jeans you pulled on," she mused. "Or you'd be depending on me for *everything*." She sort of liked that idea, at least as a temporary arrangement, but she knew he wouldn't.

"See?" he responded. "There's a lot to be grateful for."

She smiled at the way his hair stood up. They'd been sleeping for hours, had made love and then slept some more. She wasn't even aware of the time, didn't care how late it was. She was sure everybody in Pineview had heard about the fire, doubted anyone would expect her to be at the salon, including those who had an appointment. But she'd called Leanne and asked her to post a sign, just in case. "You're really okay with letting the rest go?"

"Like I said, it can all be replaced — except the picture of my mother. With some effort and money, I might be able to get a duplicate, but I doubt I'll try."

She smoothed the hair out of his eyes. "You had a picture of her?" Claire wished she'd seen it. Because he had no family, no roots, he was used to flying solo, which made it hard to become an integral part of his life. "That's not an easy thing to lose."

He ran his finger down her cheek. "It was a mug shot, so probably nothing I'd frame, anyway."

A mug shot. Claire had always known there was something wrong with his mother. "Tell me about her."

That muscle jumped in his cheek, letting her know he was as sensitive about the subject as ever, but at least he answered. "There's not much to tell."

"Who was she?"

He shifted onto his back. "Her name was Bailey Rawlings."

"And she was —" she snuggled close, resting her head on his shoulder "— a counterfeiter?"

"Nothing quite so glamorous." She could hear the dry note in his response to her teasing.

"A bank robber?"

"Far too creative. She was a hooker. And a drug addict."

Claire leaned up to look into his face. "Well, there you have it."

His lips pursed. "Have what?"

"Only something as powerful as drug addiction could make her do what she did."

"That's how you see it?"

"That's how I see it."

"You don't think that's too forgiving?"

The dry note was back. The anger he'd felt growing up had slipped deeper and deeper below the surface, but it was still there. "Forgiving her is the only way you'll be able to move on."

He studied her for several seconds, touched the end of her nose. "Does that go for you, too? If your stepfather killed your mother, will you be able to forgive him?"

She'd been thinking about Tug a lot — as they spoke to the police, as they drove to the hospital, as they waited for the doctor, as they checked into the motel and drifted in and out of sleep — and she kept coming to the same conclusion. "He didn't kill her."

Isaac adjusted his pillow. "Claire, I think you need to be prepared for the fact that he might've done just that. All the signs point to him. She was cheating. She'd inherited a lot of money, and he'd get to keep it. He loved her daughters and couldn't bear the thought of losing them."

"But whoever killed my mother also killed David. Tug wouldn't do that. He — he couldn't have lived *that* big a lie. I would've known it. Intuitively, if in no other way."

"Come on," Isaac said gently. "People surprise their loved ones all the time. He could do anything if he was afraid he might be exposed. My mother's drug addiction was powerful enough to make her abandon her five-year-old. Fear of life in prison could certainly motivate Tug to resort to murder. Whoever's behind David's death must've had a chunk of change, and your father fits the bill there, too. Contract killing isn't cheap. It's not as if Les is some hood who'd do it for fifty bucks."

"But that means he's also the one who tried to barbecue us the night before last!"

"Not necessarily. Les Weaver could've been acting alone on that one. He's tied into this now, too. If he's ever caught, his own life could be on the line. We live in a capital punishment state."

"What about Roni?"

"We're back to the evil stepmother being behind it all?"

"She's not evil. I mean, I've never viewed her that way." But it was true that Claire had a stronger bond with Tug and that his betrayal would hurt far more, because she'd actually trusted him as much as a girl could trust a father. She'd always been a little leery of Roni because, as good as she'd been, she could never compare to Alana. "I'm just saying she had as much to gain as Tug. And now she has as much to lose."

"You talked to Myles. He couldn't confirm that April ever came forward with her story."

"That doesn't mean she didn't. Myles didn't even live in Pineview back then. It was Sheriff Meade she spoke to."

"Then why isn't it in the files?"

"Because he either didn't believe her or —" she cleared her throat "— Roni paid him off."

Isaac seemed skeptical. "So now we're talking police corruption on top of everything else?"

"Not corruption, exactly. Just a favor for a friend he didn't believe was guilty. Maybe he got rid of his notes because he thought April was an angry teen out to malign an upstanding citizen."

"And in return Roni made a large contribution to his reelection campaign?"

"If you think things like that don't happen here, you're naive."

"I know they happen. I just don't think

you should rely on April's story without any evidence to back it up."

Claire frowned. "Okay, then, what about Joe as a suspect? Maybe my mother tried to break up with him and he wouldn't hear of it. They got into a huge fight that sort of . . . escalated, and he went too far." She could easily imagine her sister's claims that Joe had exposed himself as grounds for an argument. He might've killed Alana so she didn't label him as a pedophile, which could've ruined his business as well as his marriage and resulted in his own girls being taken away from him.

"You don't believe he spent all that time digging in the forest because he's worried about you, like he said?"

"By admitting the affair, he could be hoping to cast more blame on Tug. Maybe he was afraid we were getting too close to the truth."

"Or that could be the very reason he didn't come forward at the time."

"It wasn't until he saw me talking to Carly Ortega across the street that he changed his mind. Could be he was nervous about what she was saying to me and it convinced him that he had to handle the situation differently this time around."

Isaac made a clicking sound with his

tongue. "I don't know. . . ."

Because he wasn't aware of Leanne's part in what took place, and she couldn't tell him without betraying her sister. But . . . the more she thought about it, the more convinced she became. Joe had acted strange in the past. He hadn't even acted all that normal at Peter's. They weren't about to let her go until she saw what they wanted to show her. That had spooked her pretty badly. What would've happened if she'd acted skeptical instead of devastated by the knowledge that her mother had been unfaithful? Would she still be walking around today?

"His brother definitely didn't like that he was including me. He kept saying it was a risk. Like you said, he could've meant that more literally than I took it. Maybe Joe was making a last-ditch effort to throw us off-track."

"And here we'd decided he's so noble."

She nodded. This theory also offered an alternative explanation as to why he'd been so "kind" about keeping what Leanne had done to himself.

"Remember the inconsistencies David listed in the files?" Isaac asked.

Claire assumed he was about to bring up Leanne's absence from school. But he didn't. He'd never said much about it, probably because of what she'd already admitted to him. And Leanne was so young at the time he couldn't see her playing any meaningful role in the mystery.

"He mentioned Joe's lack of an alibi," he said.

He was talking about David. "See? Joe had opportunity. And he was working very close to our house that day."

Isaac rubbed his hands over his face. "I think it's time to call my P.I. to see what she's been able to uncover on Les Weaver. Hopefully, she'll have details that'll help."

"You're already expecting results? Have you given her enough time?"

"The way things are going, there might not be anything left of Pineview if she doesn't come up with answers soon."

Claire wanted to laugh, but it really wasn't funny. Her house had been trashed, many of her personal mementos destroyed. His had been burned to the ground. She was estranged from every member of her family and was losing money every day she didn't work.

Isaac was right. What would be left when this was all over?

With Claire out of town since the fire,

Jeremy didn't know what to do with himself. So many things were changing. He didn't like it; it frightened him, made him jumpy.

Usually after work he headed over to River Dell. These days, no one used the old park at the end of Claire's cul de sac. If he went in the back way, he could hide his car in the trees on the far side and walk along the bank of the creek until he reached her place. Because she didn't expect anyone to be looking in, and there were no roads with any traffic, she rarely bothered with blinds, except in her bedroom. She pulled those down every night, but he often got to see her finish work at the salon, eat, watch TV, maybe visit with her sister. Sometimes he even followed her to Laurel's or to the book group.

He'd gone to her place as soon as he left Hank's yesterday and today, but both times he'd found her house locked up and empty. He wasn't sure when she might return. The firefighters had finally put out the forest fire; it'd taken them most of two days. But Isaac wasn't around, either. Claire had to be with him.

If she was with me, I'd never bring her back. It's too dangerous here.

He drove through town a couple of times, then stopped at the store to spend the change someone had left on one of the tables he'd bussed at Hank's. Fortunately, he wasn't hungry because he didn't have much money and there wasn't any food at home. He'd been smart enough to have a burger for dinner, even though it was only four o'clock when he finished work.

He could afford a candy bar, but after he ate it he couldn't think of anything else to do. Tuesday afternoons weren't all that eventful in Pineview. Add to that the fire, and how worried everyone had been about it spreading — and the whole town was tired. Everyone seemed happy to go straight home, although it wouldn't be dark for four and a half hours.

Jeremy put on his brakes as he passed the Kicking Horse. There were a few cars in the lot. He could always come back later. Maybe things would pick up. But it wasn't a place he usually went. He'd avoided it in the past because he hadn't wanted to run into his father. He avoided it today because he didn't want to run into his father's friends.

That left him with no distractions. And he was running low on gas. Time to head home whether he wanted to or not.

"Hi, Dad," he called as he walked in. His father couldn't answer, but playing this game had worked last night. It felt better to pretend. Pretending meant he could be nice and his father would be nice in return. It also meant he didn't have to face what had really happened.

He kept that up for an hour or so, told his father all about his day and Claire being gone and the fire getting put out, but eventually he ended up pacing outside the door to the crawl space. He needed to go under there to make sure he'd done a good job burying the body. He'd tried to check last night, but it'd been too soon. He'd merely stood by the door and cried.

It was still too soon, but he couldn't let it go any longer. He also wanted to check that he hadn't left anything behind. His father used to say he'd forget his head if it wasn't attached to his body.

Gathering his nerve, he quit pacing, unfastened the locks and opened the door. But he barely poked his head inside. A quick peek was all he could stomach.

Fortunately, he couldn't detect anything other than the dank odor he smelled every time he went under the house. He figured that meant his father had enough dirt on top of him. He couldn't see much of a mound, either, even when he pointed a flashlight right where he'd done the digging.

He shifted his light to the suitcase. He should've buried Alana at the same time, but he'd been so tired. And he kept picturing her with empty sockets and clumps of hair falling off her scalp and feared he'd have nightmares about zombies if he disturbed her. The last thing he wanted was to wake the dead.

Breathing a tentative sigh of relief, he closed up the crawl space and went back to the living room. Everything looked okay here, too. He'd returned the gun to its cupboard above the fridge and cleaned up the blood. He'd scrubbed the living room some more last night. It seemed as if every time he sat down he spotted another drop of red somewhere, but he didn't see any now. The only thing that worried him about the living room was the bullet hole in the wall. He didn't know how to fix it. He'd tried to cover it with a picture, but he couldn't hang a picture so close to the ceiling. There wasn't room.

That hole's so small. Who's going to notice?

Eager to escape the living room almost as much as the crawl space, he climbed the stairs. He'd never been allowed in his father's room, not since his mother walked out on them. His father had made a habit of locking the door whenever he left, but

Jeremy had known how to pick that lock since he was twelve.

Tonight, the door stood wide open. No lock-picking needed.

With the owner of the house gone for good, Jeremy was tempted to move out of the basement, away from all the things he feared. He had his own little cemetery going, just like the one in town — without the headstones and flowers. But if someone found out he'd switched bedrooms, it could give his father's absence away.

He sat on the bed, staring at the clothes hanging in the closet, the hamper, the cast-offs on the floor, the bottle of cologne on the dresser, the messy pile of newspapers on the nightstand with the reading glasses on top. Jeremy had slept on the couch last night, but maybe he'd sleep here tonight. Just one night. He wanted to go through the photo albums hidden up in the attic above his father's closet. One of those albums contained pictures of his mother.

But he decided to rest until he felt more like himself.

Scooting toward the pillows, he was about to curl into a ball like he'd seen Claire do so often after David's death, when the loud jangle of the phone startled him.

He jumped off the bed, but he wasn't sure

whether or not to answer. He didn't want to talk to anyone.

Would that make whoever it was come to the house?

That was a risk he couldn't take. . . .

Rounding the bed, he snatched up the handset. "Good evening. Salter residence."

"Who's this?"

"Jeremy. Who's this?"

"No one you need to be concerned about. Where's Don?"

This wasn't how people normally acted when they called. Jeremy's hands were already beginning to sweat. "Downstairs."

"Good. Get him."

"I c-can't." Jeremy wiped his free hand on his jeans. "He, um, he's indisposed at the moment." His father had taught him to say that if he was in the bathroom.

"You mean he's shitfaced again?"

"Excuse me?"

"Oh, for God's sake, is he drunk?"

Jeremy didn't answer. He hated to actually *lie*. . . . "He can't come to the phone," he repeated. "But I'd be happy to give him a message when he wakes up, if you'd like."

There was a slight hesitation. "I'm not sure it would be worth my while."

"Why not?"

"Because you can't remember from one

minute to the next, can you?"

That wasn't nice. Why would anyone say that? Jeremy hadn't done anything to make this person mad, had he? "Who is this?" Jeremy asked again.

"You don't need to know. I'll call back."

But that voice. Jeremy was pretty sure he recognized it. "Deputy Clegg?"

There was no answer. A dial tone suddenly hummed in his ear.

26

Nancy Jernigan, the P.I. Isaac had hired, had discovered some interesting details about the incident in Les Weaver's office. Most notable was the fact that the dead man's wife, Shannon Short, claimed they'd been expecting a loan from her parents, which would've relieved the financial stress that had supposedly caused her husband, James, to take his own life. That, together with her insistence that Les had *asked* James to bring his gun to the meeting because he was interested in buying it, raised some questions. Les's motivation in the murder wasn't as clear, but Nancy felt James's business partner could've put him up to it. Apparently, Ted Abrams blamed James for the failure of their business and was determined to collect on the life insurance set up to protect him in the event of James's death.

"So James was worth much more to

Abrams dead than alive." Claire had lowered her window to enjoy the warm evening air while Isaac drove. The wind whipped her long curls around her face, but she didn't mind. Despite everything, she seemed happy just to be with him, and he felt the same.

"Exactly. And Les might've facilitated that. For a fee, of course."

"I'm shocked that he doesn't have a criminal record, that he's been able to skip out of everything he's suspected of doing."

"We'll get him eventually. Nancy's working on it."

"What about Weaver's wife?"

They'd been discussing what Nancy had told them almost the entire ride to Pineview. "What about her?"

"Maybe she'll talk if she realizes what he is."

"I bet she wouldn't believe it. He keeps everything from her. He didn't even want her to know I was at the door."

"But she can tell us whether or not he was home two nights ago."

"Let's wait and see what else Nancy digs up. Then we'll decide where to go next."

They passed Trudie's Grocery, which signaled the edge of town, but Isaac wasn't happy to be back. It'd been good to have a respite. He figured life could be worse than having Claire all to himself for a day and a half. In another four minutes they'd reach Big Sky Diner, where they were meeting the sheriff for dinner. Laurel had suggested they come to the house so she could see Claire, too, but they didn't want to talk about attempted murder in front of the kids, and Laurel had quickly conceded that it wouldn't make appropriate dinnertime conversation. This wasn't personal. They didn't need a friend; they needed a sheriff.

"Are we going to stay at my place tonight?" Claire asked. "The bedroom's been cleaned up."

"We'll be safer at a motel in Libby or Kalispell." And, after feeling so helpless to protect her when the fire started two nights ago, he was all about an ounce of prevention.

"That'll cost money," she pointed out.

"I don't mind." The insurance would probably cover it. He had to have somewhere to live until his cabin could be rebuilt. But even if the insurance wouldn't, he didn't care about the expense as long as it kept Claire safe.

"I don't want you to spend money if you don't have to, especially because of me."

"Quit worrying about it. If Myles is any

closer to making an arrest, maybe we'll stay," he said. "If not . . . we'll head out. Maybe we'll go as far as Big Fork."

She held the hair out of her eyes. "That won't give us much time in town. It's already six o'clock."

"You're the one who didn't want to let me out of bed." He added a wink since it had actually been the other way around. He'd been afraid everything would change once they left the motel, that the unity they'd felt during the past twenty-four hours would suddenly disappear. But it was still there, for now. It made him feel absolutely content and frighteningly unsure at the same time, which was the oddest dichotomy he'd ever experienced. She kept him so off balance. He was pretty sure that was why he tended to fight what she did to him. He'd never liked giving someone else the power to hurt him.

"You're incorrigible." She sent him a look of exasperation laced with tenderness. She'd stopped trying to hide her feelings, and he liked that, needed it. This morning when they'd made love she'd told him again how much he meant to her, and it'd enriched the whole experience, made him feel closer to her than he'd ever been to anyone.

He just hoped he could let go of his

reservations, his impulse to hold back. He wanted to give her what she gave him. "You're gorgeous, you know that?" he said.

Her lips curved into a cocky smile. "Yes."

Laughing, he took her hand. He loved her, all right. He might live to regret how much, but she made him whole.

He opened his mouth to tell her that this time things were different between them, that she could trust him, but the diner came up on their right and she distracted him by pointing out the window. "There's Myles."

The sheriff had beaten them to the restaurant. Isaac could see him waiting near the door. "Let's hope he has something to tell us," he said, and brushed his lips over her knuckles before letting go.

Myles looked tired, as if he'd put in a couple of very long days. Claire felt sorry for him — until Isaac sat next to her and Myles cast him a hooded glance that was just dark enough to convey his disapproval. Although Myles seemed to be making an attempt to separate his personal feelings from his job as the county sheriff — no doubt the reason he kept his opinion to himself except for that one glance — he wasn't having an easy time of it. Most likely he'd received an earful from Laurel about how terrible it would be if Claire went back to Isaac and agreed with her.

Claire wanted to reassure him, to tell him she sensed something deeper in Isaac than anyone had given him credit for in the past. But she knew that could be wishful thinking, an attempt to deceive herself as well as him — or Myles might take it that way. This wasn't the time for that discussion, anyway. For the most part, they were all hiding their personal feelings behind a businesslike facade.

The waitress appeared almost immediately to hand them laminated menus and rattle off the specials — meat loaf, mashed potatoes and green beans, with banana cream pie for dessert, for $11.99. Or a cowboy steak with pasta and grilled vegetables for two bucks more.

Everything sounded good to Claire. She was suddenly so hungry she could've eaten *three* meals.

They each ordered a soda. Then she selected the meat loaf and Myles and Isaac ordered off the menu.

"What'd you find at Isaac's cabin? Anything?" she asked Myles as soon as the waitress walked away.

"The fire started at the back door," he replied. "And whoever did it definitely used an accelerant. I'm guessing gas, but we won't have confirmation from that lab for days, maybe a couple of weeks."

"It was gas. I could smell it," Isaac said.

Claire settled her napkin in her lap. "What about tire tracks?"

"The firefighters pretty much obliterated any chance we had of recovering that kind of evidence. Whoever did this was either smart or very lucky. No one saw him, he used a common substance as the accelerant, so that it can't be traced back to him, and he created so much destruction with the fire and with the effort required to put it out that whatever evidence he might've left behind has been destroyed."

"He shot at me," Isaac said. "Shot the lights, too. What about the shells?"

"We're looking for them. We're also sifting through the ashes for the bullets. If we can find even one, we might be able to match it to the gun later."

Claire slid the salt and pepper shakers behind the napkin dispenser. "Did the Ferellas see anyone come flying past their house?" The Ferellas owned a mobile home on a couple of acres not far from the turnoff to Isaac's place.

He shook his head. "But Rusty was on duty, doing patrol. Fortunately, he saw the smoke and mobilized the fire department before you called in, which was probably the only reason we were able to put it out before it spread any farther."

Isaac rested his elbows on the back of the booth. "Shit."

He'd been hoping for more. So had Claire. "What about Les Weaver?" she asked. "Did you send someone over to see where he was when the fire broke out?"

"Jared Davis is one of my best investigators. He's originally from L.A., has lots of experience. He visited Weaver first thing this morning. Weaver claims he was home all that night and his wife backed him up."

"She's lying," Isaac said.

"A distinct possibility, but it might be hard to prove. We're checking with the neighbors to see if they saw him coming or going, but with the three-hour drive he would've left before it was unusually late and returned in the morning, especially if he stopped for coffee or breakfast after being up all night. Nothing that would make anyone question what he was doing."

"So that's it?" Isaac said. "This is going to end up another big mystery, like what happened to Claire's mother?"

Myles clearly didn't appreciate that comment, but his experience showed. He'd talked to other victims over the years, understood their impatience and anger. "Investigations take time, Isaac. I'm going to get this bastard. You have my word on that. And there is —"

The waitress appeared with their sodas. "Your dinners will be right out," she said, and hurried off again.

Myles went back to what he'd been about to say. "There is one other thing — an incident worth mentioning."

The seriousness of his tone put Claire on full alert. "What's that?"

"I got a call from Herb Scarborough yesterday."

Herb managed Mountain Bank and Trust — the only bank in town. "What does Herb have to do with anything?" she asked.

"On his way home from work, he saw a car weaving all over the road day before yesterday and followed so he could find out who it was. He planned to call and report the driver, but he was a bit surprised by what the guy did next."

"Which was . . ." Isaac prompted.

Myles's resistance to accepting Isaac became obvious again when he kept his gaze on Claire. "He went to the Petroglyphs Campground, circled around, found a site that was hidden from the others and lit a fire in the fire pit."

Isaac scowled. "Isn't that what a fire pit's for?"

At last, Myles shifted his attention. "This guy wasn't camping out. He wasn't going to eat. And it was only about four in the afternoon so he didn't need a fire for light."

"Why was he doing it?" Claire asked.

"He wanted to destroy something."

Isaac slid his Coke out of the way. "*Who* wanted to destroy something? Did Herb ever get a look at this man's face?"

"He did. He said it was Donald Salter."

"He didn't recognize the car? Both the Jeep and the Impala are distinctive."

"Yeah, but someone else could've been driving. He wanted to be sure."

Considering Don's drinking problem, Herb should've been able to figure out who was behind the wheel. "Don's an alcoholic. There's no telling what he might do."

"That's what I thought." Myles clasped his hands in front of him and leaned forward. "Until I heard the rest."

Claire stiffened in expectation. "Go on."

"Herb parked back in the trees and watched Don burn some papers. It seemed odd, given the time of day and everything, so after Don drove off, he went to see what, if anything, was left."

Isaac had been rubbing his chin as he listened, but at this point he stopped. "Did he find anything besides ashes?"

"The stuff in the pit was destroyed. But there were a couple of sheets that'd blown out before they were too badly burned. They were stuck in the trees. When Herb saw what they were, he brought them to me."

Claire could scarcely breathe. "And? What were they?"

Myles lowered his voice. "David's notes on your mother's investigation."

"That means they came from my house! So . . . did he steal them? What would he want with them? And why would he burn them?"

"All good questions," Myles responded.

Isaac had just pulled in to get gas when Claire's mother-in-law walked out of the mini-mart. Rosemary O'Toole spotted Claire the second she looked up, so there was nothing Claire could do, even though her first impulse was to avoid any interaction, at least while she was with Isaac. She already knew how Rosemary was likely to react. David's mother said she wanted Claire to move on, and would eventually be willing to accept someone else in Claire's life, but she didn't want another man to take her son's place too soon, especially a man as controversial as Isaac. That would cause a dramatic change in focus for the whole community, pushing David a little more decisively into the past.

Claire could understand why she'd feel that way. Claire felt the same loyalty to David, and even some fear of what might happen if she really let go of the one constant in the past twelve months — her pain at her husband's loss. She didn't need Rosemary's disapproval making all of it worse.

Isaac didn't seem to notice her sudden tension. If he'd seen Rosemary, he hadn't thought anything of it. He got out and started to pump gas while she approached Claire's side of the vehicle.

"Oh, boy," Claire breathed. They'd just left Myles at the diner. Her mind was completely preoccupied with Don Salter — whether or not he was the person who'd trashed her house and stolen those files, or if he'd come by them through a third party, which opened up a whole host of other questions. She didn't want to think about David. She'd spent a year crying over his death, was just beginning to come out of that dark period. The last thing she needed was an awkward or painful encounter with his mother.

But she stepped out of the truck, anyway, to give Rosemary a hug.

"Hi, Mom. How are you?"

Rosemary didn't return the hug. She suffered through it, then lifted her head, causing her chins to wag. "I'm fine. Except that you haven't been returning my calls."

Claire should've contacted her this week. Normally, she kept in close touch. "I haven't even received your messages. My life's been crazy. First, there was that incident at the studio. I'm sure you heard about that. Then someone broke into my house. We still don't know who or why. And the fire . . . I don't know what's going on."

Rosemary's eyes cut Isaac's way. He now realized she was there. Claire knew because he was looking over at them. "Maybe it's the company you're keeping," Rosemary muttered.

Here we go . . . "Isaac has nothing to do with what's happening," she said. "As a matter of fact, he saved my life."

"But he wouldn't have had to do that if you hadn't been at his place, sleeping with him, to begin with."

This was turning out to be a frontal assault; Claire hadn't expected it to be this bad. She'd seen David's mother upset before, but never so livid her lips quivered and her voice shook. “Rosemary —”

“I was Mom a moment ago.”

“You were Mom until you started acting as if you don’t care about me,” Claire snapped.

“I wouldn’t have said anything if I *didn’t* care. Someone needs to talk some sense into you. If you won’t listen to your own parents, or your sister, who else is there? Do you think David would want to see the woman he adored with a man like *him?*”

The fact that she’d used David to shore up her side of the argument stung, even though Claire should’ve seen it coming. “David’s not here to give his opinion,” she said.

“But you can’t really be satisfied with someone of *his* moral character —” she motioned to Isaac “— after being married to my son!”

Claire thought of when she’d told Laurel she’d never really liked Isaac. She’d regretted making that statement ever since, and not only because it was a lie and had possibly hurt him. She was a coward. Maybe he’d never be able to love her the way she loved him. Maybe they wouldn’t wind up together, as committed as she’d been with David. They were just beginning whatever their relationship would be and couldn’t predict the future. But she was going to have the guts to own up to what she felt, regardless of how it all ended.

"David was a good man," she said. "I miss him so much and I'll always love him. But Isaac is just as good. And I love him, too."

Her mother-in-law's eyes nearly bugged out of her head. "Love him!" Everyone within earshot turned to look.

Claire felt herself flush but stood her ground.

Isaac left the nozzle in the gas tank and walked over, but he didn't get involved. He stood behind her, a silent support.

"That doesn't mean he's going to love you back." The gleam in Rosemary's eyes challenged either one of them to contradict her. "He's not someone who —"

Claire interrupted before she could go on. She didn't want Isaac to hear any more of this. Some people might say he deserved his reputation, but who were they to judge? His psyche was so complex *he* probably didn't understand why he'd done half the stuff he'd done. "You're right. It doesn't mean he gives a damn," she said. "But he doesn't have to."

The tension left Rosemary's spine, making her look fat and deflated. "And you're okay with that?"

"Yeah, I'm okay with it," Claire replied, and got back in the truck.

Isaac finished getting gas, then climbed behind the wheel. "I've always loved you," he said softly, and started the engine.

27

Although Isaac and Claire had gone over to the Salters' house three different times since their conversation with Myles at the diner — had called, too — they hadn't been able to rouse Jeremy or his father. According to what Myles had said at dinner, the county investigator, Jared Davis, had also been trying to reach the Salters.

Claire wasn't sure where they could be. As far as she knew, other than working at Hank's — and his shift had already ended — Jeremy didn't have a lot of places to go. He had no friends, no other family. His father wasn't working these days. And, strangely enough, both vehicles were parked in the garage. . . .

"Why do you think Joe was with Don?" she mused. They were at her place, cleaning, but they'd been analyzing the situation while they worked. It had felt strange to see Joe in Don's car, but the fact that they were together recently seemed even more suspect now.

"Maybe Joe did this —" he gestured at the glass he was sweeping up in the kitchen "— and had just passed the files off to Don when you saw them. Because I can't imagine any other reason for the two of them to be together."

"Neither can I. But why would Don want the files?" They'd cleaned her bedroom and bath the other day, but much of the mess in the kitchen and living room remained. Holding a big garbage sack, she picked through the rubble, throwing away what was too damaged to keep. "There are various names associated with my mother's, but Don's has never come up."

"On our way back from the diner, you said he was good friends with Tug."

"That was a long time ago. They've been mostly estranged for years, ever since my father remarried and Don's wife left town. I think Don's been bitter and jealous of Tug's happiness and money. At least, that's what my father's had to say about the rift. And they've had words over the way Don treats Jeremy."

"Jeremy would be a challenge for anyone to raise."

Claire felt a little protective of her old biggest fan. He'd had a hard life. "He's a nice kid."

"He's not a kid anymore. But I didn't say he wasn't nice. I said he'd be a challenge."

Planning to see if she could find its match, she fished an earring out of the pile of junk on the floor and set it on the coffee table. "Hank does pretty well with him at the burger stand, but his father is . . . having some serious problems of his own. I don't like the way I've seen them interact."

"Maybe we should —" Isaac lifted his head.

"What is it?" she asked, but he didn't answer. He dropped the broom and rushed over to yank her behind the couch with him, then pulled the gun that'd been wedged in his waistband.

"Listen." He pressed a finger to his lips to indicate silence.

Claire held her breath as she waited for whatever had alarmed him. But then she heard the sound — and recognized it. Leanne's wheelchair. "It's okay. It's just my sister."

Sure enough, Leanne's voice rang out a few seconds later. "Hello? Can I come in?"

Claire raised her eyebrows at him. "Should we let her?" she teased.

Isaac didn't respond to her question. He

stood and returned his revolver to his waistband. "Man, I'm jumpy," he muttered, and went back to work, leaving her to answer the door.

She did, but a bit reluctantly.

"Hi." She summoned a pleasant expression even though, after the past week, she had no idea what to expect from her sister.

Leanne studied her. "Hi."

Claire hated how awkward it was between them. "Did you need something?"

A frown appeared on her face. "I have to need something to visit my sister these days?"

In case she hadn't noticed, they were no longer on the best of terms. "Look, Lee, my life is out of control at the moment. I can't be the same person I've always been for you. I need some time to —"

"You don't want any more grief about Isaac, and I get that," she cut in.

They had other problems, but they could start with that. "So . . . why'd you come?"

"I want to help."

Claire had never heard those words from Leanne. "You mean . . . clean up?"

"Whatever you need. Talk about Mom. Tell you what I remember." Her gaze fell to the floor as if what she had to say next wasn't easy. "Everything that's happened, especially the fire, really scared me, Claire. I know I haven't been the best sister in the world. I've got . . . issues I need to work on. We both know that. And I plan to make some changes. But —" she seemed to be struggling with tears "— I didn't hurt Mom. I swear it. What I did with that tape and Joe — it was stupid and I'm embarrassed. That's why I reacted the way I did." She looked up. "I don't want to lose you."

Claire bent to give her a hug. "I'm not going anywhere."

She sniffed, confirming the tears Claire had heard in her voice. "And if I'm jealous of your hot boyfriend, well . . . who isn't?"

Blocking Isaac's view of them with the door, Claire gestured toward the kitchen. "He can hear you," she mouthed.

"It won't be news to him," she said, but then her grin instantly faded. "I owe you an apology where he's concerned, too."

Claire's stomach muscles tightened. "I don't know what you mean."

"If you don't it's because he's too good a guy to make me look bad. But I'm sorry all the same. Sometimes I . . . I have no idea why I do the things I do. Life just gets me down, and I make it worse. It's . . . illogical but . . . it's me."

Claire felt the tension in her body begin

to dissipate. She understood, because she'd watched her sister struggle through life almost from the day she was born. Claire could certainly forgive her; she'd been forgiving her for years, but she'd rather have it that way than cut her younger sister out of her life. She was grateful that, for once, Leanne had something kind to say about Isaac. The acknowledgment felt great.

Stepping back, Claire opened the door for her sister's wheelchair. "Come on in. We're just sorting through stuff and trying to get it in order."

"At least I hung out with you enough before all this to know where everything has to go. That makes me a *little* more valuable than Isaac."

"I love you both," Claire said.

Leanne gaped at the admission. "I knew you loved *me.* You're supposed to love me. But *him?* Really?"

She was asking about David, but Claire didn't want to address the subject, so she shrugged it off with a joke. "Shh, it'll go to his head."

"That happened fast."

Claire smiled at the memory of the six months she and Isaac had spent together ten years ago. Their feelings for each other had been simmering a long time. "Not really."

Leanne sobered. "I'm happy for you," she said, and seemed to mean it.

"Thanks." Realizing that this might be the best opportunity to ask her sister the hard questions she still had to ask, she motioned her into the back bedroom and closed the door. "I do have some questions about Mom and . . . and what happened . . . with Joe."

Leanne shifted in her seat as though bracing for the worst. "I hope the fact that you brought me here means you haven't told Isaac about that."

"No." And now Claire was glad because her sister could truly forget that mistake. "But . . . did Joe really . . . expose himself to you, Lee?"

They could hear Isaac still cleaning in the kitchen. Claire wondered what he thought about this private moment, but she doubted he'd mind.

Leanne's cheeks went pink as she shook her head. "No. It was all me. I just . . . I was so mortified when he went to Mom that . . . I had to come up with some reason for what I did."

Claire crouched at her side. "That lie could've ruined his life, Lee."

Fresh tears hovered in her sister's eyelashes. "Sometimes I'm afraid it did."

"What are you talking about?"

"I didn't hurt Mom. But —" her chest rose as she drew a deep breath "— I'm afraid what I said got them into a fight. That he killed her and I'm to blame."

No wonder she hadn't wanted Claire searching for answers. No one would want that to come out. Her guilt explained why she'd been drinking, too, and some of her other self-destructive habits. "That's a lot to carry around, Lee."

Tears streamed down her face. "Too much. Sometimes I . . . I have to dull the pain."

With sex and alcohol. Claire squeezed her arm. "It's off your chest now. Let it go. Even if Joe killed Mom, you're not to blame. What you did was bad, but you were only thirteen. Kids make mistakes. And causing a fight isn't murder. If he made that choice, he's responsible for it."

Self-recrimination caused Leanne to wring her hands. "But I'll always feel like she'd still be with us if only I hadn't . . . done what I did."

"Where on earth did you get the idea of creating that tape?" Claire asked.

"Katie's older cousin was . . . sixteen. He

introduced us to . . . certain things."

"He didn't molest you, did he?"

"He had sex with both of us. More than once. Katie thought she loved him. I thought I loved Joe."

Claire felt her own eyes burn with tears. Her little sister had been so young. "Mom and Dad didn't know?"

"Of course not! Neither did Katie's parents."

"Where's this cousin now?"

"Who cares? I never want to see him again — or Katie, either."

So that was why they'd lost touch. It all made sense now. "But what if Joe *didn't* do it?" Claire asked.

"He *has* to have done it. He and Mom were so upset that day."

Claire thought of Don Salter burning everything in their mother's case files. "Can you name one reason Don Salter might have any interest in our mother?"

Leanne blinked several times. "Did you say *Don Salter?* No. Except . . . he and Dad used to be close. Have you asked Dad about him?"

"Not yet." But it was interesting that Don had a stronger tie to Tug than he did to Joe, at least back then. "Do you know if Joe and Don are or were ever friends?"

"They weren't before, but . . . these days Joe and I pretty much avoid each other, so I have no idea who he might be friends with. Why?"

"I found a copy of our mother's case files in the studio the night I was attacked. David had them. His handwriting was all over the interviews and stuff. I brought them here, but they went missing during the break-in. Don was seen burning them the day of the fire."

Leanne's jaw dropped. "So you think . . . Don Salter did this?" She waved at the door to indicate the wreckage beyond it.

"We don't know. We only know that he burned the files."

"I can't tell you any more. Jeremy's the only Salter I'm really familiar with, and that's mainly because he has one heck of a crush on you. He's been stalking you for so long I don't even notice him anymore. But I bet, for five minutes of your time, he'd tell you anything you want. You should give him a call."

Claire glanced at the clock. "Maybe in a little while. He's not there, but he has to come home sometime, right?"

The phone kept ringing. The doorbell, too. So far Detective Davis, Sheriff King, Deputy

Clegg, Tug, Joe, Isaac and Claire had all come by. The noise and the threat of someone barging in and finding that he wasn't really gone made Jeremy's head swim. He couldn't even come out of his father's bedroom for fear someone would knock at the door. Or the phone would start up again.

Did the police know his father was dead?

They couldn't. People who'd come had called out for Don as if he was alive. But why did they suddenly want to talk to him? Jeremy's father hadn't had this many people come to see him in years.

Covering his ears, Jeremy mumbled, "They can't know. They can't. How could they?" Maybe he wasn't the smartest person in the world, but Mrs. Hattie was his closest neighbor, and she lived clear down by the highway. No way could she have heard the gunshot. Jeremy helped plant her garden every spring. At eighty-one, she couldn't hear him talking even when he was standing right beside her.

So maybe it wasn't that they thought his father was hurt or . . . or worse. Maybe they planned to ask about something else — like the fire. Was Detective Davis trying to reach him about that? Because Don couldn't have set it. He was dead before it started. Jeremy got confused sometimes, but he was sure of that.

Unless he did it as a *zombie . . .*

No, Jeremy had to remember what was real and what wasn't. Zombies weren't real. His father had told him that. And something not real couldn't set fires.

Which meant someone else did it. But who? The same man his father had hired to kill David?

Just thinking about the possibility that David's murderer was back in Pineview made Jeremy curl up even tighter on his father's bed. What his father had done was bad. Really bad. What made it worse was that he said he'd done it for Jeremy. Because that couldn't be true.

"You're a liar, Dad. Liar, liar, pants on fire." He'd *never* wanted anyone to get hurt.

There was another knock at the door. Hugging a pillow to his chest, Jeremy squeezed his eyes closed. "Please go away," he whispered.

"Don? Don, you there?" It was a man's voice. "It's Detective Davis. I'm here on official business."

Again! Davis kept coming back!

"I'd like a word with you, please." *Bang, bang, bang.* "Don? Come on now. I see your car's in the garage."

How'd he get into the garage? Had he

opened the side door?

"If you're in there, open up."

Jeremy held his breath, waiting to see if Davis would bust in like he'd seen the cops do on TV. He knew he should probably answer and tell the detective that his father wasn't home. But he couldn't think of a good reason for him to be gone. He'd had one but he couldn't think of it right now. He was too scared. And what if the detective didn't believe him? Or . . . or what if Jeremy started to cry when they were talking?

He felt like crying already. He wasn't himself. He couldn't talk, couldn't say what needed to be said. He'd never been so miserable, even after his mother left. "Go away," he whispered again.

The detective knocked some more. He yelled again, too. Then finally . . . silence.

After what seemed like a very long time, Jeremy lifted his head to see the clock. Eleven-thirty. That was late. No one was supposed to be coming over during "late." His father told him it was rude to bother people after ten o'clock.

Why was everyone being rude?

It was the fire. Because of the fire they'd keep coming and keep coming until they eventually broke down the door. They wanted to know how his father started the fire. But he didn't! They wanted to blame it on him. Why were they coming here? Had his father hired Les Weaver again? Had Les told them that?

It was all so confusing. . . .

Another fifteen minutes ticked past before Jeremy got up the nerve to climb off the bed and creep down the stairs. Was someone on the other side of the front door, listening for noises coming from inside?

The idea of that made his stomach hurt, especially when he imagined Detective Davis or Deputy Clegg at the window, watching him through the cracks in the blinds. It was easy to spy on someone. He knew because he'd been spying on Claire since he was a kid.

"Detective Davis?" He rested his forehead against the door as he waited for a response, but there wasn't one. The detective had left. He cracked open the door, just to be sure, and saw something white flutter to the ground. When he stooped to pick it up, he realized it was a business card.

"J-Jared D-a-v-i-s. L-Lin-coln C-Coun-ty In-ves-ti-ga-tor." He had to sound out the words. The note on the back was even harder to read because Detective Davis had written it in cursive.

"I have . . . to . . . t-talk to . . . you. It's im-por-tant . . . Call me."

The fire *was* important. That meant they'd keep coming back.

"What do I do?" he breathed. Tilting his head back, he stared up at the bullet hole in the wall, which suddenly seemed so big, so obvious, that he was sure anyone who walked in would see it.

He had to leave. He had to gather all his survival gear and head into the mountains. That was the only answer, the only way to avoid prison and the cuckoo place.

Even after all his planning, all his dreaming, the idea of being alone out in the wild terrified him. But if Claire wasn't safe in Pineview, maybe she could go with him.

28

The house was finally as restored as they were going to get it, at least until the insurance kicked in to replace what had been broken, but Isaac wouldn't hear of spending the night. He said he wouldn't sleep anywhere he couldn't adequately protect them.

Claire didn't want to stay, either, but Libby was a thirty-minute drive, and it was already midnight.

"Aren't you tired?" she asked.

"Not tired enough to close my eyes while there's a killer running around," he replied, and she had to admit he made a good point. She hadn't forgotten the fire. If they stayed, whoever had tried to kill them might try again. And a fire at her place could endanger Leanne, too. Claire couldn't even imagine how hard it would be to get her crippled sister out of a situation like the one they'd been in two nights earlier.

"You're right." She yawned. "But do we have to go all the way to Libby?"

"You have a better suggestion?"

"It's summer and sort of warm. We could camp out."

"Sorry. I don't think sleeping under the stars would make us any less vulnerable."

"Even if no one knows where we went?"

"I vote for the security of four walls and a locked door. I'll drive. You can sleep in the truck."

She felt bad about giving out on him. He had to be tired, too. But she leaned against him and dozed off almost as soon as they'd left Pineview and would've slept the whole way if Isaac hadn't suddenly let up on the gas.

"You've got to be kidding me," he said.

Claire lifted her head from his shoulder. His gaze was riveted on the rearview mirror. Sitting up, she twisted around to see what was going on, but she could find no obvious reason for him to be concerned. A pair of headlights cut through the dark several car lengths behind them, but why would that be a problem? "What is it?" she asked, still groggy.

"Someone's following us."

The grogginess fell away. "How do you know?"

The highway was the most direct route to Libby, and it wasn't unusual for two cars to travel in tandem for the whole thirty minutes.

"Because this is someone who never leaves Pineview."

"You know the driver?"

"It's Jeremy Salter."

She twisted around again. "Are you *sure?*"

"A few seconds ago, he came up close enough for me to see the make and model of the car. If that's not his Impala it's one that's identical. And his is sort of distinct."

Claire wasn't upset by this. Jeremy had been part of her life since she could remember. His showing up actually seemed sort of fortuitous, since they'd been looking for him, anyway. They'd stopped by once more before leaving town to see if he was home yet. "He must've followed us when we left his house. I *thought* someone was there."

"The question is . . . why wouldn't he answer his door?"

"Who knows? With Jeremy, nothing's ever very clear." Except his devotion to her, which was a constant she'd often felt she could live without. "Does he want us to pull over?"

"He hasn't flashed his lights or done

anything else to indicate that."

She thought of all the small gifts he'd brought her over the years, how excited he was to have her cut his hair, how he seemed to appear almost everywhere she went. "Pull over. Let's see what's going on."

"Not yet. I want to wait until we get to Libby, just in case."

"In case he's dangerous?" she asked. "Jeremy wouldn't hurt a fly."

"In case it's someone else, someone who might not be as harmless. His father could be driving his car."

It could easily be Don. She'd seen him behind the wheel of Jeremy's Impala at Joe's place, hadn't she?

"This is so weird," she murmured, and waited nervously through the next fifteen minutes, until they reached Libby.

All the businesses were closed, but Isaac found a well-lit service station and pulled in. "Hand me my gun." He'd stuck it under the seat so it wouldn't be in the way and she could sleep against him.

Claire did as he asked, then watched her side mirror as the Impala pulled in behind them. "Is it Jeremy?"

"Yeah."

She let her breath go in relief, but Isaac didn't put his gun away. He waited until

Jeremy got out and they could see that he was unarmed.

Isaac lowered his window, but Jeremy trudged up to her side instead. Claire wasn't surprised.

"Claire, I'm so glad I found you."

"What's wrong?" she asked. "What are you doing out so late and so far from home?"

He ignored Isaac just like he had at Hank's. "Something's happened. Something terrible. I have to leave Pineview. It's not safe there. You can't go back, either."

"What are you talking about?"

"My father's missing. Just like your mother."

She wasn't sure whether or not to take him seriously. "What do you mean . . . *missing?*"

He scratched his big head, seemed to struggle with the answer. "He's gone."

"Where?"

"I don't know. I've been waiting for him, but he doesn't come home. I haven't talked to him in days."

"Where were you earlier?"

"At home. Waiting for him," he repeated.

"But we stopped by. Why didn't you answer the door?"

"I didn't dare. I thought maybe . . . maybe

it was a trick. The person who killed your mother. Or the person who set the fire. You never come over." For the first time, his eyes darted toward Isaac, giving Claire the impression that it might've been Isaac's presence at his door that had made Jeremy shy away. Jeremy didn't trust him.

"Your father's probably over at the Kicking Horse," she said. "He spends a lot of time there."

"He's not at the Kicking Horse." He screwed up his face as if he was about to cry. "The police are looking for him and everything."

The police were looking for him so they could ask why he'd been seen burning her mother's files. But if word of Myles's interest in Don had gotten out, maybe Les Weaver had killed him to make sure he couldn't talk. Or maybe someone else had a vested interest in keeping him silent.

She turned to Isaac. "Are you thinking what I'm thinking?"

"Unfortunately, I believe I am." Isaac leaned toward the steering wheel so he could see around her. "Has anything else happened that makes you feel your father might've been hurt?" he asked Jeremy.

A *V* formed in Jeremy's forehead. "You mean besides the bullet hole?"

Claire gripped the window ledge. "What bullet hole?"

"The one in the living room. It wasn't there before. It was only there the day my father went missing."

"And when was that?" Isaac pressed.

"The night the fire started. I saw blood that night, too. S-some speckles on the wall." He hugged himself, no doubt to control the shaking that had set in. "I think someone t-tried to clean it up. The — the cleaning smell makes me sick. I don't like it."

"Holy shit," Isaac mumbled.

Claire was horrified. Poor Jeremy. He'd had so many things go wrong in his life. "Do you know of anyone who might want to hurt your father?" she asked.

"Has anyone been calling him lately? Anyone you don't normally hear from?" Isaac chimed in.

"Just Tug," he said.

Claire's blood ran cold. "My stepfather's been calling?"

Jeremy nodded.

She swallowed hard. "Does he usually call?"

"Not usually. He said it's important. But I don't think my dad will be calling him back."

■ ■ ■ ■

Isaac hated to leave Claire, but he was convinced something was going on — something involving Don Salter and possibly Tug. Someone needed to go back and take a look at the bullet hole and the blood Jeremy had mentioned, before the police figured out that Don was missing. If it *was* a crime scene, the Salter residence would be taped off, and he and Claire would be denied access. As civilians, they'd be excluded from most of the information gathered by the police, too. Just like before, when Alana disappeared.

Isaac wasn't comfortable allowing that to happen. He respected Myles, and he understood the police worked that way for a reason, but he felt responsible for protecting Claire, and he wasn't about to let information slip past them that might answer her questions about Alana or help eradicate the danger.

On top of his concern for her, he felt he owed it to Jeremy to help right his world, if possible, simply because Jeremy was incapable of coping with such unusual events on his own. Isaac had once been that vulnerable. He'd been five at the time, but what would he have done without Tippy? Where would he be today?

"Are you okay with staying behind?" he asked Claire before he left.

He could tell she wasn't happy about it, but she nodded. "I guess."

"We can't leave Jeremy alone. He's too agitated."

"I know. It's just that . . . I want to ask my father why he's been calling Don. And I want to see his face when he answers."

Isaac wanted the same thing, too. But why drag Tug from his bed? "He's not going anywhere. It can wait until tomorrow." Right now, Isaac needed to take a look at the Salter home, and he preferred to do it at night, when he had a better chance of going unobserved.

"Okay," she agreed. So he left her and Jeremy in separate rooms at the Cabinet Mountains Motel and headed back to Pineview.

Jeremy paced the motel room Isaac had rented for him. The lights were off, but he hadn't removed his clothes because he didn't plan on going to sleep. He couldn't stay the whole night. He had to leave, go as far into the wilderness as possible — someplace no one would find him.

But he couldn't go alone. That would be too frightening. He'd heard about Isaac's bear story, seen the scars on his arm. Everyone asked to see those scars whenever Isaac came into the Kicking Horse. His father had told him that.

Jeremy imagined himself trying to fight off a wild animal, but he didn't think he'd be able to. He wasn't good at fighting, not like Isaac was. That meant someone had to go with him, and he didn't want anyone except Claire. She'd shoot anything that tried to hurt him, and he'd do the same for her. He'd brought his father's gun from above the fridge and everything.

Pivoting at the foot of the bed, he went back toward the closet. How was he going to convince her? She wouldn't leave Isaac behind, not willingly. He'd seen the way the two of them kissed when Isaac left the motel, heard the way she'd asked him to be careful.

She was in love.

But she couldn't be all *that* much in love. She'd forgotten him once before, when she got back together with David. Isaac was just a stand-in for her husband. And why should he get David's spot? Jeremy had loved Claire longer than anyone. He'd only been in second grade when some other boy pushed him off the swings and she came over to help him to the nurse's office. Ever since then, he'd lived for her smile, her touch, even the sound of her voice.

If she went back to Pineview, she'd be killed, anyway. It wasn't safe for her there. Look what had almost happened in the fire.

Jeremy couldn't let her get hurt. He'd promised her mother he wouldn't. He couldn't stand the thought of it himself.

But if he took her with him, Isaac would come after them. Isaac wouldn't let her go. And Jeremy would never be able to fight someone like Isaac. He'd seen what Isaac had done to anyone who bothered him, especially when they were in high school.

So — Jeremy returned to the window — what if Isaac *couldn't* come after them? What if Les Weaver got rid of Isaac like he got rid of David?

Jeremy had heard his father on the phone, pleading with Les for it all to be over. He'd said he didn't want anyone else hurt. But it didn't matter what his father said because Les started the fire, anyway. He didn't want to go to prison. He didn't want to have his block knocked off, either. So he'd do anything. Even kill Isaac.

Jeremy understood. Because *he'd* do *anything* before he'd be raped in the butt — or dragged off to the cuckoo hospital. His father had told him too much about both places.

He'd do anything before he'd lose Claire, too.

He needed to call Les and tell him where Isaac was. That was what his father would do, wasn't it? Yes. He'd done it before. Jeremy wasn't sure Les would be close enough to fix anything. He lived far away. But if he set the fire, maybe he wasn't so far away right now. Maybe he could get to Pineview in time.

Taking a deep breath, Jeremy crossed over to the phone. He had a lot of numbers in his head from all the messages he'd taken in the past week. But he knew one of them belonged to Les. And he knew which one. It started with three extra numbers.

A man picked up almost immediately.

"Is this Mr. Weaver?" Jeremy asked. He figured that was more polite than calling him Les.

"Who is this?"

He hadn't spoken very clearly. He had his fingers in his mouth, chewing on his nails. He forced himself to stop. "Jeremy. Don Salter's son."

"What do you want? Where's Don? I've been trying to reach him."

Jeremy wondered if he had the right Mr. Weaver. "Are you Les?"

"Yes."

"You're sure?"

"Yes! Where's Don?" he asked again.

His impatience reminded Jeremy of his father. "He's dead."

"What? How?"

"He killed himself. With a gun. But I have a message for you."

"What kind of message?" He didn't seem to care that Don was dead. He didn't act all that surprised or ask any more about it. That didn't make him a very nice friend.

"Isaac Morgan will be at our house soon. And he'll be alone."

"What's that supposed to mean?"

"He owned the cabin you burned down."

"*I* didn't burn anything down!"

Maybe he didn't. Maybe he only shot David. Jeremy didn't argue. He was getting too nervous. "Okay, well, anyway, no one else will be home."

There was a long silence. "Are you kidding? This is like taking instructions from a ten-year-old! How can I trust you?"

"I'm just trying to help," Jeremy said.

"Fuck!" he screamed, and hung up.

"That's a bad word," Jeremy said, but there was no one to hear him.

By the time he put the receiver down, he was breathing hard. He didn't want Isaac to be shot, to have his brains all over the wall Jeremy had just cleaned, but . . . he wouldn't think of that. It would all be over soon. Then Isaac would be buried and he wouldn't have to worry about anything anymore. Jeremy had no choice. He had to leave *now.* Claire would get over Isaac. Once she understood that Isaac was dead, she'd have to get over him just like she'd gotten over David.

"Don't worry. I'll be your sweetheart," he whispered.

The thought of finally touching her, of kissing her with his mouth open like Isaac, made Jeremy's whole body tingle.

He'd only been able to dream about kissing her in the past. Now it would be real. And they'd be together forever.

He wouldn't let her leave him like his parents had.

Claire sat up straight, feeling as if she'd been wide-awake all along. She heard a noise at the door, thought maybe it was Isaac. Even while she slept she'd worried about him, kept dreaming that he was in a car chase or a gunfight or lay bleeding somewhere and she couldn't get to him.

"Isaac?" She was so eager to have him

back with her, she got up and went to the door, although she knew he'd taken a key card.

"It's me." Jeremy. She frowned as she recognized his voice and peeked through the peephole to see a somewhat distorted view of his head.

What did he need *now?* He'd had such a hard time going to his own room when Isaac left. He hadn't wanted to be alone, but Isaac wouldn't let him stay in their room, and she was glad. He was acting so strange; it was starting to creep her out. The way he stared at her, how quickly he agreed with anything she said, how loudly he laughed at any joke, no matter how lame, she could usually tolerate. But something had changed. . . . Still, Alana and Roni, as well as her father, had warned her not to mistreat him, even when she didn't want him following her around, and she heard their voices in her head now. His life was hard enough, especially with some of the other kids' cruelty. She didn't want to be unkind.

"What is it you need?" she called back.

"Can I come in? I — I can't sleep. My father's dead. I know it. He's buried under the house. There was blood. Everywhere."

"He's buried *where?*" That part sounded a little too definite for comfort. What would make Jeremy say something like that?

"Right next to your mother. I'll tell you where she is if you'll let me in."

No way could Jeremy know what he was talking about. It was pathetic how far he'd go to avoid being alone.

Claire rubbed her face while trying to decide what to do. She didn't want him to disturb any of their neighbors by continuing to knock on her door. She was afraid the manager would come down to shoo him away. Then what would she do? She'd have to take him in because she was pretty sure Jeremy wouldn't be able to handle that, and she felt responsible for him.

"Look, Jeremy, I'm tired. I understand you want to help me, and I want to help you, too. We're friends. But you can't tell me where my mother is because you don't know."

"Yes, I do. I swear. She's in a suitcase under the house. My father killed her."

If not for the mention of the suitcase, Claire might've passed this off as a fanciful invention. That a piece of luggage had gone missing from the house the same day as her mother wasn't one of those details the police had kept under tight wraps, but Jeremy was talking about an incident that'd happened fifteen years ago. How come he remembered the suitcase?

A chill went through her as she envisioned what he'd told her. She didn't like what he was doing to get her to open the door, but she couldn't hold it against him, either. He was frightened and desperate and probably had no clue how hard it was for her to hear things like this, how gruesome imagining her mother's body in a suitcase would be.

On second thought, it wasn't all that surprising he'd remember the suitcase. He had an incredible memory for odd facts, unusual details, numbers. He never had to write down a phone number. He could rattle off any one he'd ever called, even if he'd only dialed it once. The kids at school used to jabber off a bunch of numbers just to see if they could stump him.

"Claire?" He knocked again. "Did you hear me?"

"I heard you." She just didn't know how to respond.

"Do you believe in zombies?" he asked.

"No, Jeremy. I don't. There's no such thing." This confirmed it. He was completely out of touch with reality.

"I'm afraid my mom and your dad are going to come alive and — and hurt me if I don't take care of you. I promised your mother I'd keep you safe. Did you know that?"

"No, but it's . . . sweet." *In a revolting sort of way . . .*

"So will you let me in?"

She rested her head against the door. "Jeremy, I was asleep. . . ."

"Please? I don't like it out here."

"Can't you just go back to your room?"

"No, there are zombies in my room!"

"Oh, God," she muttered to herself, but she pulled on her jeans under the T-shirt she'd worn to bed and opened the door.

Jeremy stood in the puddle of blue light shed by the energy-conservation bulb in the fixture closest to her door, looking even more distraught than when he'd gone into his room fifteen or twenty minutes earlier. He'd really worked himself up.

Claire felt sorry for him, but with Isaac gone she might still have insisted he go back to bed. His babbling unnerved her, even if he didn't know what he was saying. *He* unnerved her. But there were tears running down his cheeks, and the memory of how she'd felt in the days following her mother's disappearance wouldn't allow her to be that hard-hearted. At least she'd had her stepfather to rely on. If Jeremy's dad was really gone, and he wasn't coming back, Jeremy would have no one.

"Don't cry," she said. "Come on. You can sleep in the other bed while we wait for Isaac."

He stepped forward as if he'd brush past her but grabbed hold of her instead.

"Jeremy, don't —"

Clamping a hand over her mouth, he pushed her to the ground.

Claire struggled, but he was freakishly strong. She'd just begun to realize he wasn't joking, that he wouldn't stop this unless she *made* him understand he had to let her go, when he leaned in close.

"Don't scream," he whispered in her ear. "Please, don't scream. I don't want to have to shoot you. I love you, Claire. I've always loved you."

That was when she felt the hard muzzle of a gun between her shoulder blades.

29

The drive went by fast, probably because Isaac was no longer tired. He was too busy considering what might've happened to Don. Even though he was already expecting the worst, what he found when he arrived still surprised him.

The door was unlocked, and he didn't have to step all the way across the threshold to smell the bleach. Jeremy had been right. A "cleaning smell" pervaded the whole house. And the couch and a big section of carpet were damp — again, just like Jeremy had said.

The odd thing was the bullet hole. It wasn't anywhere near the place where the violence seemed to have occurred; it was on the opposite wall.

"What the hell happened here?" Isaac muttered.

Maybe Don had some dangerous company and attempted to defend himself. If so, he was either a terrible shot or he was drunk.

More likely he was drunk. . . .

"Poor bastard." Isaac felt as sorry for him as he did Jeremy. Don hadn't had an easy life, either.

Myles checked the garage. Don's Jeep was parked inside it. So where was he?

The evidence suggested he might be dead. Or hurt. It didn't look good. Isaac needed to get out as soon as possible and call 9-1-1. But first he wanted to go through Don's phone records to see who he'd been calling and if any of those calls corresponded to a number associated with Les Weaver. He also wanted to find Don's bank statements. If Don had been hired to trash Claire's place, maybe there'd be a corresponding deposit Isaac's P.I. could trace back to the source.

It took nearly an hour for Isaac to come to terms with what he'd begun to suspect shortly after he started searching — he wasn't going to find much in the way of documentation in Don Salter's house, certainly not *paid* bills. The man didn't have a filing cabinet, didn't seem to keep any records at all. Isaac couldn't find a single bank statement.

He did come across a big stack of outstanding bills shoved into a kitchen drawer, however. Most were overdue. And right there, near the bottom, he found Don's most recent telephone bill, which showed several calls to Coeur d'Alene in Idaho.

"*That's* what I want."

Feeling he was finally getting somewhere, Isaac grabbed a dish towel to pick up the phone, so he wouldn't leave any prints. He wanted to see where the Idaho number went, see if Les Weaver answered. If Les was used to accepting calls from Don's house, he'd recognize the number on caller ID and might pick up, despite —

But before Isaac could dial, he heard a noise that made him freeze.

Someone had just come through the front door.

Claire couldn't feel her hands or her feet. Jeremy had ripped out the cords of the lamps in her motel room and used them to tie her up until he could get some rope from his car. Then he'd used that instead. He'd gagged her, too, with a strip of fabric he tore from the motel sheets. He said he couldn't think with her begging him to let her go. He also said she'd be happy he'd done this in the end.

She couldn't imagine that. But without the use of her limbs, or even her mouth, she couldn't get free. Her wrists were already raw from trying. She wasn't sure where he'd gotten the rope but it was the worst kind, so scratchy it hurt even before she'd rubbed the skin away. At this point, the slightest movement brought pain. There was nothing she could do except lie on the backseat of his car in a sideways crouch with her cheek pressed against the fabric of his seat, which smelled like dirty socks. She tried to brace herself against the jostling of the car, but even that became impossible once he turned off the highway.

The suspension in his old car wasn't the best for such rough terrain. The vehicle bounced as he drove through potholes and rocks and ruts. He seemed to be taking her up into the mountains on one of the many fire roads that led to remote hunting or fishing destinations. She couldn't tell if he'd chosen it at random or he'd been here before, but he rarely left home so she doubted he knew what he was doing or where he was going. She also had no idea how anyone would ever find her out here — or how, if she managed to get free, she'd reach the highway.

As the minutes dragged on, tears slipped from her eyes, but they weren't tears of sadness or fear as much as anger and frustration. She'd tried to be so good to Jeremy. For years she'd put up with him and endured the teasing his devotion had inspired among her friends, the discomfort of his inappropriate remarks, the awkwardness of his constant and invasive staring, the lecturing from her parents about the less fortunate. And *this* was how he repaid her?

"I'm sorry I have to do this," he said at length.

He was crazy. She was beginning to understand *how* crazy. She'd thought he was just slow and rather sweet. Someone who'd always been bullied. That was the whole reason she'd been willing to tolerate him. But he'd been telling her how his father had shot himself the night of the fire, and instead of calling the police, he washed the blood and brains off the wall and buried him under the house.

She didn't know whether or not to believe him, especially when he insisted that her mother was down there, too. How could that be? Jeremy claimed his father had murdered her, but Don Salter had no connection to her mother. Except for the fact that he was seen burning the files, and the fact that Don had once been her father's friend.

If what Jeremy said was true, Tug had to

be behind her mother's death.

She wanted to ask for details, proof, but she couldn't even talk.

"You believe me, don't you?" he asked.

He sounded childlike again. Harmless. And that made her angriest of all. He'd taken everyone in — everyone but his own father, perhaps. She now realized that the whole town had probably misjudged Don, at least when it came to his son. It was a miracle that he'd cared for Jeremy all those years. They'd all been so afraid Jeremy would end up in a sanatorium, but she was pretty sure that was exactly where he belonged.

He slowed to a stop, but she got the impression that they hadn't yet reached their destination. "You can grunt if you believe me."

She did nothing. She was beginning to hate him. If he'd known where her mother was all these years, why hadn't he told someone? Maybe he wasn't the smartest person in town, but he'd been fully aware of how long she'd been searching for the truth and how much it would mean to her to finally know. He'd mentioned the situation quite often.

I hope you find her, Claire. . . . He used to say that all the time. If he loved her like he claimed, why hadn't he taken pity on her and told her the truth years ago?

"You're not being very nice," he said when she maintained her silence.

That statement alone proved he was unbalanced. *She* wasn't being nice?

He started driving again, but slowly. He was obviously more interested in talking to her. "I hope you're not mad. You'll be fine. I don't want you to worry. I'm going to take care of you. Just like David did."

He didn't have the ability to take care of anyone, even himself. But that wasn't what she focused on. She was thinking about David. She had so many questions. If Don had killed her mother, was he also the one who'd hired Les Weaver to shoot David? Or had Tug handled that?

Fresh tears slipped from Claire's eyes. *Dad, could you really have done this to me? Taken away two of the most important people in my life?*

Her heart said no. But everything else said yes. It had to be him or Roni. Jeremy had told her they'd been seeing each other well before her mother went missing, just as April had said. He'd been watching her for so long, he knew almost as much about her family as he did about her. Isaac believed her stepfather was behind it; she could tell by the way he'd approached their talk about forgiveness.

Dad, how could you? Those words went through her mind again and again, but she supposed that anyone who'd had a loved one do something like this felt the same. As horrible and unfair and unthinkable as it was, it happened. There was no way of understanding it. There was only the bitter taste of betrayal — by Tug, the man she'd accepted as her father, and by Jeremy, the boy she'd stood up for all her life.

Soon the jostling took its toll. Her body ached from being unable to change positions. Her head pounded from lack of sleep, a surfeit of emotion and the gag cutting into her jaw. Yet Jeremy drove on.

Did he even know where he was going? Did he have any kind of plan?

He'd said his father had killed himself. Was that true, or had Jeremy shot him? He had a gun. . . .

Either way, Jeremy had nothing to go back to. No family, no friends. After this he wouldn't even have his job at Hank's.

So what could he have in mind? They couldn't survive out here, not for any length of time. She doubted they had enough food or water for twenty-four hours. They hadn't stopped anywhere; nothing was open this late. And she wasn't sure Jeremy had come prepared.

Maybe survival *wasn't* what he had in mind. Maybe he only wanted to escape the consequences of what he'd done long enough to spend some time with her, after which he might let her go.

Or he might kill himself and take her with him.

"Isaac?"

Isaac released his breath and stuck his gun back in his waistband. He'd been sure it was Les Weaver, coming to finish what he'd failed to do when he started the fire. But this was a much more familiar voice. It didn't belong to someone he particularly liked, but running into a man he didn't like was better than running into a contract killer.

"In here."

Rusty Clegg came around the corner and eyed him from head to foot.

Isaac didn't appreciate his condescending expression. "Did you have something you wanted to say to me?"

"I thought that was your truck parked off in the trees." He clicked his tongue as he shook his head. "You just don't know how to stay out of trouble, do ya?"

"Excuse me?"

He hooked his thumbs in his utility belt and puffed out his chest — to show off the badge on his uniform or make himself seem bigger and tougher, or both. "What the hell are you doing here?"

"Probably the same thing you are. I'm looking for Don."

"By going through his stuff?"

"I'm hoping to find something that can tell me why he hasn't been seen for two days. And whether or not he's had contact with someone in Idaho."

"That's not your place! You're not a deputy!"

Isaac raised his eyebrows. "Maybe if you were doing your job I wouldn't have to be doing it for you."

His eyes glittered. "You could be arrested for interfering with a police investigation."

"Last I heard, this wasn't an official investigation."

"But if Don's missing —"

Isaac broke in. "In case you haven't figured it out yet, Don's not just missing, *Deputy* Clegg. He's *dead.*"

This took him aback, wiped the contempt from his face. "How do you know?"

"Let's call it an educated guess. First of all, Jeremy's freaking out because he hasn't seen his father for two days. Don's never taken off like this before, especially when his car is in the garage. There's a bullet hole in the wall out there —" he gestured toward the living room "— and a big wet spot on the carpet, where someone used a hell of a lot of bleach."

"That's not like finding a body," he argued.

Isaac propped his hands on his hips. "It's enough that someone should start looking for one."

What was left of Rusty's bravado disappeared and his shoulders slumped. "But . . . who would want to kill Don?"

"Someone convinced he knows too much. Someone who saw him as a weak link."

"Based on your theory that Les Weaver shot David on purpose."

"He did. And I'm going to prove it."

"Shit." He ran three fingers over the distress lines in his forehead. "I was there. I was with him. It seemed legit. Weaver was *so* upset." A little of his former belligerence returned. "And there was no motive. Weaver was a total stranger, an upstanding citizen from out of state. You wouldn't have suspected anything, either!"

"That 'upstanding citizen' has ties to the Lucchese family."

"Who the hell is that?"

"One of the most powerful organized crime syndicates in New York City."

"How do you know?"

"I asked Myles to check. It was that simple." Heck, even Leland Faust had an uncomfortable feeling about how smoothly that day's events had been explained and accepted. If Rusty hadn't taken the easy road, the one Les Weaver had paved for him with his good looks, charity work and attorney trappings, the truth might've come out a year ago. And if that had happened, maybe Isaac's house wouldn't be in ashes. "I've got to be honest with you, Rusty. You should've asked a few more questions."

Crimson suffused the deputy's face as his lips pulled back to show his teeth. "You're so full of bullshit, standing there like you know everything. Big Isaac, who swoops in at the last minute to steal *my* girl."

So it wasn't all about Les or David. "*Your* girl? Claire's never been yours." In one way or another, she'd always been *his* — she'd known it and he'd known it — even when she was with David.

"Without your interference, she might've been. She asked me out last week. That was a start. Then *you* got involved."

"She wasn't really interested in you,

Rusty. She just wanted to get out."

"You don't know that. You don't know shit. And you have no proof Les killed David on purpose. You're just trying to make me look bad so you look better." With that he left the kitchen and started going from room to room, calling for Don and Jeremy.

"Jeremy's with Claire in Libby. So don't waste your breath yelling for him," Isaac said. And if Don was home Isaac would already know it, but . . . Rusty didn't respond.

Isaac listened as the deputy marched upstairs; when he came back and headed down to the basement, Isaac followed.

"Are you satisfied yet?" he asked when Rusty stood staring at Jeremy's empty room.

Again, he didn't answer. He was gaping at a wall covered in pictures of Claire and embellished with poems and dried flowers and drawings of hearts. "What the hell is this?"

Isaac had seen it earlier. He'd found it a bit unsettling but not surprising. "What does it look like?"

"That little creep has it bad."

So did Rusty. He'd been trying to get together with Claire ever since David was killed. "Creep? You probably have a shrine in your house, too."

"Screw you."

Isaac had provoked him so he let it go. They needed to put aside their differences and get to the bottom of what was going on here. "Look, something's not right. Don't you think you should call the sheriff and have him send over some forensic techs?"

The stubborn set to his jaw hadn't lessened. "Hell, no. I've seen no sign of a struggle. No forced entry. No blood and no body. Nothing but a little cleaning solution that could've been spilled and a bullet that could've come from Jeremy messing around with his daddy's gun."

"Then where's Don?"

"Who knows? He's an adult. Maybe he took off for a few days. He'll turn up."

"Dead." Isaac had heard enough. He was done with Rusty. "That's it. I'm calling the sheriff myself." Whirling around, he started up the stairs.

Rusty began to trail after him but stopped. "Wait a second!"

It was the tone of his voice and not his words that made Isaac pause. "What is it?"

"Look at this."

Rusty had snapped on the flashlight he carried on his belt and was aiming its beam into the shadowy area below the stairs, but Isaac couldn't see what he was referring to.

"Look at what?"

"The crawl space. It's been locked."

Isaac hadn't even noticed. The dim glow of the single bulb dangling over the laundry area didn't extend to the corners of the concrete basement, and he'd been searching the finished parts of the house, looking through drawers and in closets for bank statements, bills and other documentation. "Is that unusual?"

"One padlock wouldn't be. But *six?*"

30

This wasn't how Jeremy had imagined it would be. It was too dark to see beyond the headlights of his car, so he couldn't find a good spot to set up the tent. And he was hungry. It'd been a long time since he'd had that burger at Hank's. There was a cooler at home he could've used, if he'd had some food to put in it. But he hadn't, so he'd left it behind. He'd been so rattled when Claire and Isaac showed up at the house that last time he hadn't even remembered to bring water. He'd known they probably wouldn't come back — it was too late — so he'd jumped in his car, which was only half-packed, and followed them. He couldn't bear the thought that Isaac would take Claire out of town again, where he couldn't find her.

As usual, she was all he'd been able to think about. Now he had her with him, but even that wasn't what he'd hoped. She'd somehow managed to get the gag off, and kept saying the same thing, over and over. "Jeremy, you have to turn around and go back. This isn't right and you know it."

But he *couldn't* go back, not after telling Les Weaver where he could kill Isaac. Isaac was probably lying on the floor, blood pouring onto the carpet, maybe right on the spot Jeremy had already cleaned. If that had happened, the police might be there. And that meant it was just a matter of time before they found his father and Alana under the house.

"I c-can't," he mumbled. He could only try and do what he'd always told himself he would. His father had laughed whenever he mentioned his great escape, said he'd never survive in the woods, but Jeremy didn't believe him. *Wouldn't* believe him. This was where he'd find peace and happiness — someday.

That day was today.

But coming here didn't seem so happy right now. Jeremy was getting more upset by the moment. If only it would get light, then everything would be better. The dark made him think Alana had climbed into his trunk, that he was actually bringing her with them just when he figured he was finally going to get away from her.

"What if you run out of gas, Jeremy?" Claire interrupted his thoughts. "We'll be stranded out here. Do you know where we are? Or where we're going?"

There's no such thing as zombies.

"Are you listening?"

He had to say something or she'd keep asking. "Sh-shut up. I c-can't think." He didn't like talking to her that way, but she was making everything worse. She didn't like him anymore; he could hear it in her voice. She sounded more like Leanne than Claire.

And what if she was right about gas? He'd been pretty low to begin with and he hadn't brought any extra. Not only that, but his stomach was already growling. What were they going to eat? He'd watched TV shows where people disappeared into the wilderness but he couldn't remember what they ate, other than game, and he wasn't much of a hunter.

He thought of the huckleberries that grew wild in the area. Tourist stores in Kalispell, Pineview and Libby sold huckleberry jam, huckleberry lotion, huckleberry chocolate, even huckleberry fudge. That meant there had to be a lot of berries. But would they be able to find them? What if the bears had eaten them all?

And what if those bears were still hungry?

The scars he'd seen on Isaac's arm popped into his mind. *Don't think of bears. Don't think of Isaac, either. Isaac's dead.* But Jeremy didn't really want him to be dead. Isaac had been nice to him. In school, he'd stopped other people who were saying mean things and pushing him.

"Jeremy, please," Claire said. "If you care about me, take me home. I want to go home."

"You can't go home." This much he knew. "It's not safe. I'm doing you a favor. I'm trying to protect you."

"From what? Or whom? Why isn't it safe to go home?"

She had that irritation in her voice, the kind his father used to have. He hated it. Did he hate her, too?

No! This was Claire. He loved Claire.

He hit the steering wheel and the pain actually felt good because he could tell it was real when nothing else seemed to be. Was he having a bad dream? Would he wake up any second?

He prayed he would.

"Jeremy?"

He swallowed. "What?"

"Why isn't it safe to go home?"

"You know why," he said. "My father

killed your mother. Then he hired Les Weaver to kill David. You don't want to be next, do you?"

"Is he the one who attacked me at my mother's studio?" she asked.

"Attacked you?"

"Pushed me down?"

"No, that was me. I — I didn't mean to hurt you. I just wanted to see what you were doing. And I said I was sorry."

"You said — Oh, I remember. You apologized at Hank's." She made a funny laugh, but she was right. He *had* apologized there.

"See?" he said. "You do remember."

"Have you been following me a lot?"

"Whenever I can."

"That's a little too honest to make me feel better."

"How can it be too honest?"

"Never mind. I sort of knew. You show up wherever I go. It just happened so often and for so long I quit paying attention."

After a few seconds, she laughed again.

"What is it?" he asked.

"This is unfair. You know that, don't you?"

"My dad says nothing's ever fair."

"You told me your father's dead, that he killed himself. Is that true?"

"Yes."

"What about Les Weaver? Do you think

he could've killed your dad?"

"No. I saw what happened. He pulled the trigger right in front of me. Most of his head flew off and hit the wall. He was going to kill me instead. I don't know why he didn't."

This unemotional reporting added to Claire's discomfort. "But why would he take his own life?"

"Someone named George told him to do it."

"George who?"

"I've never met him. It's someone who killed his own dog. Not a very nice person."

There was a brief silence. Then she said, "Could it be that *you* were holding the gun?"

"*Me?* Oh, no. *I* didn't kill him." She kept asking about that. Why?

"And there's no way you could be mistaken?"

Jeremy was getting confused again. "No. George told him to do it, like I said. I saw it." He hit a rut, which pulled the car hard to one side. He screamed but managed to stay on the road. Then he slowly crept forward because he didn't want to get into a wreck. What Claire had said about running out of gas worried him, too. But he wouldn't need gas if they were going to live here, would he?

He didn't think so. Maybe he *should* run out of gas. Then Claire couldn't leave him while he was sleeping.

Turning onto yet another dirt road, this one even rougher than the ones before, he maneuvered as best he could while pine trees scratched the sides of the car.

"Why would your father kill my mother?" she asked.

"I don't know. It was a long time ago."

"Okay . . . if he paid Les to kill David, where'd he get the money?"

Jeremy struggled to come up with the answer, but his father didn't tell that part. His father got mad whenever Jeremy asked about Les.

But then it came to him. All the calls he'd overheard. His father pleading for a loan, saying he needed it to save their house from the bank — although Jeremy wasn't sure how a bank could come after a house. "Your father gave it to him."

"Tug? He wanted David killed?"

"No. Why would he want that?"

"To hide the fact that he'd killed my mother."

"But he didn't kill your mother. *My* dad did."

"You said Tug and Roni were having an affair."

"They were."

"So why did your dad kill David? Because Tug told him to?"

All the questions were giving him a headache. "No . . ."

"You're not making any sense, Jeremy."

"I'm trying to be nice, Claire. I'm trying to tell you what I know." Even though he was so hungry and tired he couldn't think straight. "You want me to tell you what I know, don't you? I've wanted to tell you for a long time."

"Of course, but . . ." She seemed to be having trouble talking — that gag was still on her face. "Just answer one question. Was my father behind it all?"

He didn't think so. Don had always told Jeremy they couldn't tell Tug about the suitcase or anything else. But if he wasn't making any sense, he had to be wrong. "I guess."

The locks presented no problem. Whoever had attached them to the flimsy door hadn't realized that the hinges could be pulled out with the claw side of a hammer, so the size and strength of the locks didn't matter. They weren't going to stop anyone who really wanted to get inside.

It took Isaac and Rusty less than ten

minutes to remove them.

"This looks like Jeremy's handiwork to me," Rusty said as he shoved the last lock to the right so he could open the door.

Isaac had to agree. Surely if Don wanted to secure his valuables he would've done a better job.

Rusty turned to look back at him. "What do you think the big deal is?"

"Jeremy's probably trying to protect some possession he's afraid to lose, like that survival gear he's always talking about."

Rusty opened the door. "Or maybe it's a blow-up doll he doesn't want his father to know he has."

They didn't find any of those things. But once they poked through a few boxes filled with old bedding and household items that'd been stashed near the door, they discovered a suitcase shoved into the far corner, behind the furnace.

"I think you'd better get the sheriff," Isaac said as soon as he saw it. There was no reason for it to be where it was. The color and style suggested that it belonged to a woman. And he remembered that Alana's suitcase had gone missing the day she did.

But Rusty had come this far; he wasn't about to stop before he'd had a look. He laid the suitcase on its side and popped the locks.

Inside, just as Isaac had feared, they found a skull and human bones, plus ragged shreds of cloth, sitting in some nasty-looking liquid inside a clear garbage bag.

"Oh, God!" The deputy drew back in disgust.

"It's Alana." They'd found Claire's mother. The police would have to use dental records or some other way to identify her, but there was no question in Isaac's mind.

"What's she doing here?" Rusty wanted to know.

Isaac had no idea. But it made him uneasy. He'd left Claire with Jeremy in Libby, and it was clearly Jeremy who'd put all those locks on the crawl space door. Which implied that he had a pretty good idea of what was under the house.

A sick feeling settled in the pit of Isaac's stomach. "You don't think Jeremy's capable of this kind of violence. . . ."

Rusty couldn't seem to remove his gaze from that bag. "Oh, hell, no. Jeremy would only have been sixteen when Alana went missing."

Isaac had thought of that. But he'd always been big for his age. Strong as an ox, too.

"He never even fought back when he was

picked on at school," Rusty added. "Remember?"

Isaac remembered, all right. He'd had to fight Jeremy's battles for him. Or Claire or David would threaten to go to the principal if the ridicule didn't stop. Isaac couldn't recall Rusty getting involved, but he'd never been much of a focal point for Isaac.

"So now that you've seen this, where do you think Don is?" Isaac asked.

The sight of those remains seemed to be getting to Rusty. A bead of sweat rolled down his face, even though it was cool under the house. "He could be on the run. We've been looking for him in conjunction with the break-in at Claire's house. Maybe that spooked him."

"What about the bullet in the wall?"

He wet his lips before answering. "I told you. That bullet doesn't necessarily mean anything. Someone could've been cleaning a gun when it accidentally went off. It hit too high to have injured anyone."

"You've seen this —" Isaac pointed at the suitcase and what was inside it "— and you're still saying you don't think what we saw upstairs is worth worrying about?"

"I'm not sure," he admitted.

Isaac grabbed his flashlight and angled it into the corners. His breath caught in his throat when he spotted an area where someone had been doing some digging. "Look at that."

Rusty glanced over and grimaced.

"Looks like a grave to me," Isaac said.

"I don't feel so good. I gotta get out of here." Rusty hurried for the entrance but got only as far as the boxes by the door before throwing up. "I've never seen anything like that," he mumbled, presumably talking about the body in the suitcase. He wiped his mouth. "I'll never forget it."

Isaac knew he wouldn't, either. He was afraid they'd find an equally ghoulish sight if they did a little excavating. But he was too worried about Claire to start digging. He kept telling himself that Jeremy was as childlike and innocent as he seemed. . . .

Regardless he wasn't sticking around. He was heading back to Libby. Rusty was right; he wasn't a sheriff's deputy. Lincoln County's finest could take over from here.

The smell of bile completed what Isaac knew would be one of the worst moments of his life. He gagged and thought he might be sick, too — until Rusty distracted him by calling from the stairs. The deputy said something like, "You coming? How can you stay under there?"

But Isaac never got the chance to answer.

A gunshot rang out above.

"Rusty?" Isaac yelled.

There was no answer. He heard a *thump, thump, thump* as if someone had just fallen down the stairs. Then silence.

"You have to untie me." Claire had been trying her best to make mental notes about how long Jeremy drove and in which directions. But without being able to sit up and see any landmarks, she'd probably only confuse herself if and when she had the opportunity to navigate her way out.

Her best bet was to convince him to turn around. Except that she wasn't sure he knew how to get back. He'd been driving randomly, and he was becoming more unhinged as the minutes ticked by. He was almost delusional at this point, mumbling about zombies and bears and her mother waiting to get out of the trunk.

The most coherent thing he said was that they were going to get married and live together out here in the wilderness. But he couldn't tell her what they'd eat or drink — apparently, he had no food or water, even for the short-term — or what they'd do for heat in the very cold winters. He was living in his own little world, and if she couldn't get him to see reality, they'd both wind up wandering around in the forest until they died of hunger or thirst or fell prey to some wild animal.

"Jeremy, are you not going to answer me?"

He'd quit talking to her maybe fifteen minutes earlier. He said her words confused him. Now he tuned her out by humming or singing to himself, or jabbering on about how his father had been crying — even though he *never* cried — when he fired the gun.

"Jeremy!" Claire spoke loudly in an attempt to cut through all the babbling, and he broke into sobs.

"You don't love me!" he shouted. "You don't want to be here with me."

"Because I want to go home. *You* want to go home, too."

"But we can't go home. Isaac's dead. Les killed him."

"What are you talking about?" she asked.

"He's dead. That's what I'm talking about."

That couldn't be true. Claire refused to believe it. Isaac was perfectly safe. Jeremy had no way of knowing he wasn't. "No, he's not."

"He is! I'm all you've got. You *have* to love me. You *will* love me."

All the anger Jeremy had ever suppressed

seemed to be rising to the surface.

Claire closed her eyes. He sounded so bizarre, so unlike the person she'd thought he was. His craziness scared her, forced her to realize just how little control she had over this situation and how much her life depended on what he did in the next few hours. She didn't think his mental state could hold out much longer. No way could he keep it together for days. Already he'd been telling her about the food he liked to eat at Hank's. He'd never have another hamburger there, he said. But giving up Hank's was better than having someone knock his block off.

Who he thought was going to do this he wouldn't say. She tried telling him that Isaac wouldn't hurt him if he'd just turn back, but he seemed absolutely certain that Isaac was dead.

"If we return to Libby, we can eat," she said. "I know you're hungry. I've got money at the motel." He'd carried her off in her jeans and T-shirt. She didn't have her purse, didn't even have shoes.

"Nothing's open," he grumbled, but at least he'd responded. She preferred that to silence. When he wouldn't talk, she imagined him thinking all kinds of insane thoughts about dying together in the woods.

"By the time we reach Libby it'll be morning." She softened her voice, trying to entice him. "The restaurants will be serving coffee and eggs and toast. Waffles and pancakes. You like waffles, don't you?"

He didn't answer the question. "My dad's gone. My dad's not coming back," he said.

"But we'll find a safe place for you. One that you'll like. I promise."

"You're lying. I know what you're doing. You're going to call the men in white coats. My dad said the men in white coats will take me away and operate on my brain."

His father had obviously been telling horror stories, maybe to make him behave. She didn't think she could convince Jeremy that the men in white coats were there for his own good. So she tried to get him to trust her. "I would never do that. I bet . . . I bet Hank would take you in." She hated that she was doing exactly what he'd accused her of — lying. As desperate as she felt, there was something so sad about what was happening to him, something sad about his whole unhappy existence. But she had to do whatever she could to survive.

"Yes, you will."

She'd just opened her mouth to continue trying to persuade him when the engine sputtered and died. Had he turned it off?

She thought maybe she'd been successful at convincing him to stop, but when he tried to start the car again she realized it was engine trouble. Or they were out of gas, as she'd predicted.

"That's it," he said. "No more car. It's just you and me now."

"You and me doing what?" Claire asked.

He turned around to look at her. "You could kiss me like you kissed Isaac."

New fear charged through her. She fought with her bonds, trying again to get free despite the pain. "Let me go, Jeremy. I don't want you to touch me. Ever. Do you understand?"

He didn't respond right away.

"Do you understand?" she repeated.

"You're like Leanne," he replied. "She's mean, too."

"I'm not mean. You had no right to do this to me. This is called kidnapping. It's illegal."

"Would you rather die?"

"What'd you say?"

He picked up the gun and dangled it over the seat. "I'm giving you a choice."

She stared at the glint of moonlight on metal. Was he serious?

Something told her he was. But if it came

down to an either-or scenario . . . she knew what her answer would be: she'd rather die.

31

Rusty lay at the bottom of the stairs in a crumpled heap. Isaac was pretty sure he was dead. He couldn't see any blood, not from where he crouched, but the deputy didn't seem to be breathing. Isaac wanted to check, to get help, but he couldn't come into the open in case whoever fired that shot was still at the top of the stairs.

Hoping to hear footsteps that might tell him more precisely where the shooter was, he paused to listen — and heard nothing. He was tempted to believe the person had already run off, but he knew better. It had to be Les Weaver, and Les Weaver was a cool customer. He'd left too soon when he torched Isaac's cabin; he wouldn't make the same mistake twice.

That meant Isaac had to be careful and not make a mistake himself — or he'd end up on the floor like Rusty.

Pulling his gun from his waistband, he

peered around the corner and saw only darkness. Whoever it was had turned off the upstairs lights. Was he sitting there, waiting for Isaac to come out so he could pick him off?

Probably. But if he was going to be trapped in the basement, he had to get behind something that might block a bullet or two and allow him at least a limited view of the stairs, since they were the only exit. Jeremy's room provided his best option, but to get there he had to cross the laundry room.

Reaching around the wall, he switched off the light, plunging the basement into darkness, too. He couldn't let Les see him; he'd be a dead man if he did.

Now!

A gun went off as Isaac charged past Rusty and dived through Jeremy's open door. Les had fired on sound alone.

Isaac didn't feel any pain, but he was so rattled it took him several seconds once he'd scrambled up against the inside wall to ascertain that he wasn't injured. The bullet must've gone into a wall or the bed.

Thank God . . .

"Les?" he called. There was no answer, but he kept talking. "If you're smart, you'll get the hell out of here *now.* You just killed a sheriff's deputy. The police catch you, you'll get the death penalty for sure."

Again, no reply. Les was hedging his bets, trying to kill and get out while concealing his identity, just in case Isaac — or even Rusty — somehow survived long enough to finger him.

"Rusty radioed the sheriff. He'll be here any minute," Isaac yelled. He wanted to believe that was true; Rusty had been about to contact Myles but no way could he have had time.

Maybe if he stalled, the police would arrive even without Rusty's having called.

No, that wasn't likely. He had to be realistic. Someone might eventually come looking for the deputy, when dispatch realized he hadn't checked in for a while, but that could be an hour or more away.

"Les? You listening? We found Alana O'Toole in the crawl space. Probably Don, too. The game's up."

"Not yet it isn't!" A rapid succession of gunshots rang out as someone came running down the stairs.

It was a fast, bold and confident move — so fast, bold and confident it took Isaac by surprise. In that split second, he wasn't sure whether to dash into the open, like his adversary. With bullets going everywhere, he could easily be hit. But if he waited, he'd get pinned in Jeremy's room.

Heart pumping so hard he could almost hear it above the gunfire, he froze in indecision. If he didn't act fast, he wouldn't get out alive. Les was almost on him.

He thought of Claire. They had something — something worth fighting for. He wasn't going to let it end this way.

Dropping to the floor, he rolled into the center of the doorway, did what he could to steady his hand and pulled the trigger.

The random firing stopped; it sounded as if his opponent fell.

Rolling back behind the cover of the wall, Isaac waited a few seconds to see what would happen next. But nothing happened. He could hear heavy breathing and the grunts of someone in pain, so he got up and turned on the light.

It was Les Weaver, all right. He'd fallen over Rusty and landed on his face. When the light came on, he managed to roll onto his back. He even attempted to lift his gun. "I'll get you, you son of a bitch!"

Isaac wasn't too worried. Blood poured from the man's chest, and he was shaking too hard to control his hand. When he finally managed to take awkward aim, Isaac merely kicked the gun away and stepped on his wrist. "I think you should've taken my advice and left."

Les's demeanor changed instantly. Clutching his chest with the other hand, he winced. "Help. G-get help!"

Isaac felt drained, weak. The adrenaline — and the fear, anger and shock — were taking a toll. He almost made himself stumble up the stairs to the phone, but Rusty hadn't stirred or moaned or done anything since he'd been shot, even when Les fell over him. He was dead. The only person at risk here was the person who'd killed him, and Isaac doubted Les was in as much mortal danger as he thought. The way he kept gasping, the bullet had probably punctured a lung, but the hole wasn't very close to his heart.

"First you're going to help *me.*" Because this was his only hope. Once Les went into police custody, he'd lawyer up and they'd never get the real story. He'd deny having shot David, setting the fire, ransacking Claire's house, killing Don — whatever he'd done.

Isaac figured Les owed him and Claire a few minutes of his time, but Les's eyes widened as if he couldn't believe what he'd just heard. Apparently, despite how cold-blooded and calculating he'd been, he expected nothing but compassion in return. "I — I'm dying!"

"Tell that to Rusty over there. I'm sure he'll feel bad for you."

"How — how can I . . . help you?"

"By telling me why. Why'd you do it?"

"I don't . . . know what you're . . . talking about —"

Isaac pressed harder on his wrist. "Are you really going to play dumb? In case you're not aware of it, your ass is already beyond saving."

"You — you're crazy. Just . . . just get the helicopter!"

Isaac didn't move. "Maybe I am crazy, but after everything you've done I consider Life Flight an unnecessary waste of taxpayer dollars."

He blinked rapidly. "So . . . you— you're going to let me . . . *die?*"

"Unless you tell the truth."

"You — you'll go to . . . prison . . . yourself."

"I doubt it. This was self-defense, pure and simple." He bent to press the muzzle of his gun to Les's head, just to put him at even more of a psychological disadvantage. *"Were you hired to kill David?"*

He struggled for breath. "Yes, okay? Now will . . . will you call for the helicopter?"

"Tell me who hired you."

"D-Don."

"Where'd he get the money?"

"How should . . . I know? I never . . . asked."

The bloodstain on his black T-shirt was spreading fast. Isaac wondered if he should feel sorry for him, because he didn't. It wasn't easy to take pity on a cold-blooded killer. "And Alana? Did you murder her, too?"

"No."

"Who did?" Isaac thought he knew. He assumed it was Tug, or that Tug had put Don up to it, but he wanted to hear the answer straight from Les's mouth.

Shaking his head, Les licked his lips and gasped for more air. "His — his son."

The blood seemed to freeze in Isaac's veins. "*Jeremy?* That can't be true. He was only sixteen at the time," he said, but the memory of all those locks on the crawl space door seemed to give credence to Les's words.

Chest rising and falling in violent spasms, Les tried to explain. "All I know . . . is — is what . . . Don told me." *Gasp.* "He . . . he said his boy . . . didn't mean . . . to do it. Alana caught him . . . in her daughter's room . . . when he was supposed to be at . . .

at school." *Gasp.* "He was . . . going through Claire's . . . drawers." Closing his eyes, he slumped back as if he couldn't say another word, but Isaac wasn't finished with him yet.

"Tell me more!"

Les cried out as Isaac shook him but seemed to rally. "He — he tried to get around her —" *gasp* "— but she cut him off."

"And then what?"

"God, can't you . . . imagine? She — she said she . . . was going to call the police."

"That's why he killed her?"

"He panicked! He just wanted to shut her up . . ." *Gasp.* "She was screaming and crying . . . so he put his hands . . . around her neck . . . and . . ."

"Strangled her."

Les nodded.

"How did Don get involved?"

"He — he helped get . . . rid of the body but —" Les swallowed hard "— last year David started figuring it out. Don couldn't . . . let that happen . . . couldn't go to prison . . . or allow his son to go to prison over a . . . a stupid accident. He said Jeremy was . . . like Lennie in *Of Mice and Men.* Jeremy even convinced himself that . . . he didn't do it."

Isaac had read Steinbeck's novel in freshman English and always hated the ending.

"*Now* will you help me?" Les gasped. "This bullet . . . My chest feels . . . like it's on fire."

Which reminded Isaac . . . "Did you set the fire at my place?"

"No!" he said, but the fear in his eyes gave him away.

"Did you?"

Tears slipped down his cheeks, but they were the result of pain, not remorse. Isaac didn't think Les was capable of feeling remorse. "I — I had to. You — you and Claire . . . wouldn't leave this . . . alone. You . . . showed up at my . . . house, for crying out loud. Right in front of my wife!"

"You didn't have to do any of it," Isaac said, but he stooped to pick up Les's gun and ran upstairs for the phone. He had to call for the helicopter before Les lost any more blood. And he had to get back to Claire.

He called 9-1-1, then tried the motel. He had to reach her, had to warn her that Jeremy could be dangerous.

The phone rang and rang and rang. No answer. So he hung up and called again.

This time, he asked for Jeremy's room, but Jeremy didn't answer, either.

■ ■ ■ ■

"I have to go to the bathroom." Claire had tried everything to get Jeremy to untie her; nothing had worked. She'd been afraid to use this ploy because she didn't want him to say he'd help her, was afraid it might give him ideas. The things he kept saying about the way she'd kissed Isaac — *with her mouth open* — frightened her, but she couldn't think of anything else that might persuade him to untie her.

This seemed to give him pause.

"You don't want me to go in your car, do you?" she pressed. "I don't have any clothes to change into. How will we wash these?"

Since running out of gas, they'd stayed in the car, waiting for God only knew what. Jeremy had locked all the doors as if he was afraid someone or something, maybe the zombie he kept talking about, might come after them. But he hadn't explained what he planned to do from now on; he hadn't so much as helped her sit up. He remained behind the wheel while she lay in the back-seat. They were deep in the woods with no food or water, not even a working vehicle.

Thank God it was summer. As chilly as it was — she could almost see her breath —

they would've frozen to death if he'd done this in winter.

"But you don't want to get *out,* do you?" he said as though he couldn't believe she'd even consider it. "There are bears out there."

"We have to get out sometime. We have to go to the bathroom and we have to find food and water."

He dropped his head in his hands. "Can't you wait until morning? Your mother could be in the trunk."

She wished he'd quit talking about her mother. Her heart ached enough right now. "She won't hurt me. But she might hurt you for kidnapping me. So untie me, and I'll go by myself."

His voice fell. "You think she's angry?"

"Wouldn't you be angry?"

"But I'm just trying to protect you."

He was trying to protect himself. "I'm going into the trees over there for a few minutes. Then I'll come right out."

"How do I know you won't leave me?"

She heard panic in that question, panic she quickly tried to relieve. "Where would I go? I don't even know where I am. Do you think I want to get attacked by a bear? They forage at night."

Head still in his hands, he nodded. "We

can't leave any food in the trash."

"See?"

"Okay," he said, but he obviously didn't like the idea. He rubbed his head some more, sighed, sniffled a little and began to whine. "I want to go home."

"Then let's go home."

"I told you! We can't!"

The anger that flashed in his voice frightened her even more. She'd never seen him act volatile or unpredictable. He'd been pushed so far beyond his ability to cope she had no way of guessing what he might do. "It's okay, Jeremy. We'll figure it out together," she said. "But first, let me go to the bathroom before I have an accident."

"That'd be gross," he muttered, sniffling again.

"Not to mention unnecessary. It won't take me long. You can tie me up again afterward."

"If you run away you'll get eaten by a bear."

"Which is why I'm not going to run away. Like I said, we'll figure this out together."

Getting up on his knees, he twisted around. With his big body hunched, head and shoulders pressed up against the ceiling, he stared through the windows as if he was ten years old and imagining all kinds of terrible dangers lurking out there, cloaked by darkness.

In that moment, Claire was able to feel sorry for him again. He didn't know what he was doing; he was just trying to deal with the loss of his father, his fears and basic survival. Even innocuous animals in that type of situation could be dangerous.

"You don't have to get out with me," she said. "Reach over and untie this rope. It's cutting into my wrists and ankles."

He wiped the tears from his face and did as she asked. His thick fingers struggled with the tight knots but eventually he succeeded and blood began to flow back into her hands and feet.

However, that wasn't an immediate improvement. The burning sensation hurt so much Claire couldn't even move.

"I thought you were going to get out," he said.

She considered explaining to him what the ropes had done, but why confuse him further? She couldn't tell how he might react to more guilt or pressure. "I just . . . I need a minute to . . . to think about how to do this."

"What's wrong?"

The strain in her voice had given her away. "Nothing," she lied.

"Are you scared, too?" He seemed relieved to think he might not be alone in that.

"A little," she said. "That's why I —" she drew a deep breath as the prickling in her feet intensified "— I'm going to make it . . . really quick."

"Okay. I'll leave that door unlocked so you can get in. But I'm going to lock the rest."

"Good idea," she said, playing along. No matter what Jeremy had done, he was as much a victim in all of this as anyone else. He didn't understand enough about life and people or what was right and wrong to avoid the many pitfalls. She just happened to be something — like a shiny bauble — that'd caught his attention and captured his heart. Lucky her . . . But she was still better off than he was. Despite what she'd been through, what she might still lose before this was over, she'd had a keen mind, good health and people to love, including Isaac. After what he'd said in the truck — that he'd always loved her — she had such hope for the future. She wanted that future, a future with him. She was almost certain she couldn't be pregnant, but if she was, she wanted Isaac's baby, too.

The pain hadn't eased but she didn't dare delay any longer for fear Jeremy would change his mind. He wasn't smart, but he was physically intimidating. If, for some reason, he got spooked and decided to restrain her again, he'd have no problem getting the job done. Her best option was to get away from him as soon as possible and hide until morning, then try to find help. If she was fortunate enough to make it, and careful enough to remember her route, she could take someone back for him.

She'd barely climbed out of the car when he surprised her with the reversal she'd feared.

"Wait! Don't go! You'll leave me. I know you will." He scrambled out of the car even though she'd thought his terror would keep him inside, and tried to grab her.

Her feet felt as if a million needles were stabbing into her soles at once. To make it even worse, they were still sore from the night of the fire, when she'd been running without her shoes.

The pain was unbearable and she screamed, but that only frightened Jeremy more. She could tell by the look on his face that he was suddenly determined to stop her.

He reached out, but if he got hold of her, she might never have another chance to escape. They'd die together in that car.

Run! her mind ordered, but she couldn't.

Her feet wouldn't carry her. Instead of darting off into the trees, as she'd planned, she stumbled and fell.

32

Isaac drove as fast as he could all the way to Libby. He wanted to believe Claire was there and had simply been sleeping too deeply to hear the phone.

But he already knew that couldn't be the case. When he couldn't rouse her or Jeremy, he'd contacted the manager and had him check. Both rooms were empty, and Jeremy's car was gone.

Where could they be?

Isaac had no idea. But the images Les had painted of Jeremy flying into a panic and strangling Alana kept coming to mind. Jeremy had plenty of strength. If he got his hands on Claire, there'd be nothing she could do.

Surely he wouldn't hurt her. He loved her, had always adored her.

But he probably hadn't disliked Alana. And he wasn't himself right now. Depending on what had happened in Don's house, there was no telling what Jeremy had seen or done or suffered this week. If he was spinning out of control, he could strangle her like he had her mother, without even realizing he was doing it. Les had said Jeremy didn't believe he'd killed Alana. He'd completely blocked it out.

Isaac wished he could use his cell phone. He would've had service once he reached Libby, but he didn't have the phone itself anymore. It'd been destroyed in the fire, along with all his other belongings. He'd called Myles before he left Don's house, while he still had a landline, and told him what was going on. Myles was on his way, and he was sending several deputies, leaving Jared Davis to meet the coroner, who was coming to collect Rusty's body, and the paramedics, who were going to take Les Weaver to the hospital in Kalispell.

But that was twenty minutes ago. Isaac wanted an update, wanted to stay in touch. He knew he wouldn't be nearly as effective at searching for Claire if he couldn't coordinate with others making the same effort. All he could do was drive around, hoping to spot Jeremy's car, even though he doubted Jeremy and Claire were still in town. It was dawn. Isaac had left Libby seven hours ago, and they could've left shortly after. . . .

He went to the motel first. The manager had gone in, but he had to see with his own eyes that Claire was really gone. He also wanted to look for any hint as to where Jeremy might've taken her. But it was far from obvious. He found Claire's overnight bag, the shirt and bra she'd removed when she dressed for bed and her shoes.

He also found a torn sheet, electrical cords that had been ripped from the lamps and proof of a struggle.

Claire wasn't sure she wanted it to get light. She'd kicked Jeremy in the face and then the balls when he tried to grab her, which had dropped him to the ground and given her just enough time to steady herself and run into the forest. But he'd come after her. For the past hour, she'd heard him searching through the trees, sometimes very close, alternately calling her name and throwing a temper tantrum when she wouldn't respond.

The darkness had worked in her favor. All she had to do was stay still and let him be the one to thrash around. As daylight approached, she had to risk moving — without any shoes. Considering that her feet were already so cut and bruised, she'd have no chance if it came to a footrace. She wasn't even sure she'd be able to limp very far. . . .

"How could you do this to me?" Jeremy wailed.

The words bounced against the surrounding mountains, creating an echo. *Do this to me . . . do this to me . . . do this to me.* She hated the sound of it, hated his voice, hated his distress and what he'd done to her. But hating didn't help. And neither would answering. She couldn't reason with him. He wasn't capable of it.

Ignoring the fatigue that overwhelmed her, she began to pick her way through the rocks and trees as quietly as possible, moving in the direction from which they'd come. That dirt road had to lead somewhere. She planned to follow it as much as possible.

He'd been pretty out of it since they'd left the motel, but he seemed to be moving in the same direction she was. "Claire! Your mother's in the car. She wants you to come back."

God, help me get out of here. She saw no way to make it. Any real exertion would require water, or she'd become dehydrated and unable to think clearly herself. As cold as it was at night, it could get very warm during the day, which meant she'd sweat, and that would compound the problem. But staying here and hoping help would come to her wasn't an option. She couldn't trust Jeremy, couldn't even guess what he might do if he caught her. He'd been acting so bizarre; in the past hour he'd even started firing his gun. She didn't know if he was trying to hit her, or some imagined zombie, or simply dispel his frustration, but it scared her. . . .

Knowing it could take hours to get anywhere — she had no idea how many miles they'd driven or what, if anything, was in the area — she forced herself to pick up the pace. She didn't want to spend another night in the forest, even without Jeremy.

She walked for what seemed like hours. After a while, she could no longer hear him. He'd fired off a shot fifteen minutes or so earlier, but that was it.

She heard other noises — scurrying, scuffling, rustling, a crack, an odd echo — and couldn't tell if she should worry that he might jump out from behind one of the trees.

Where had he gone? What was he doing? Had he given up? Was he letting her go? Or was he still following her?

She knew she should strike out, deeper into the forest. Staying so close to the road risked letting him catch her, but she couldn't abandon the only lifeline she had. Her feet hurt too badly. She was almost ready to crawl just to give them a break —

A twig snapped. *Very* close. And it sounded as if something large had broken it.

She froze as she tried to figure out if she had fresh cause for alarm. She listened but couldn't hear anything except the caw of a bird. And when she turned to look behind her, she couldn't see anything except pine tree after pine tree and the dappled sunshine that filtered through the branches.

Was it Jeremy? Was he close? If not, where had he gone? And why had he stopped screaming for her?

It didn't matter. Once she was safe, she'd send someone back.

Keep moving, she told herself.

She took a step before looking up and ran smack into the barrel of a gun. There was a man holding it, and he didn't seem pleased.

"What are you doing, wandering around my property? And what have you been firing at?"

He was tall, wiry and approaching fifty, but she'd been so sure it was Jeremy, Claire sagged to her knees.

"Are you all right?" Realizing she didn't even have shoes, let alone a gun, he lowered his weapon.

"I need help," she whispered, and he offered her his hand.

Her feet cleaned and bandaged, Claire had a blanket around her shoulders and a hot cup of coffee in her hands as she sat in the sheriff's office in Libby. Isaac sat next to her, his expression grim. Myles, behind his desk, didn't look much happier. They'd just received the news that Jeremy had been found by the son of the man who'd helped her — but he hadn't been found alive. That last shot she'd heard had been the one he'd put through his own brain.

Claire felt bad about that. It made her wonder if all those other shots had been Jeremy preparing to end his own torment. She couldn't help thinking that if she'd stayed with him, she might've been able to calm him enough to save his life — and survive. But it was those gunshots that had brought help, and he might not have fired them if she hadn't run away. They could still be sitting there together, in his old Impala, going hungry and talking about zombies. The ranch on which they'd inadvertently trespassed was so large the owners themselves admitted they probably wouldn't have come across that car for days.

Or maybe, as Isaac had pointed out, if she'd stayed, he would've put a bullet in both of them. It was a chance she couldn't have taken, even if she had to do it over again. Both Myles and Isaac agreed on that.

"Maybe what he did is for the best," Isaac said, taking her hand.

"The *best?*" she repeated, a little shocked.

"I can't imagine him being happy anywhere except Pineview, can you?"

She shook her head. She couldn't imagine *any* of them being happy anywhere except Pineview — even her, and she'd wanted to leave for so long.

"No," Myles said. "And the law wouldn't have allowed him to stay. For obvious reasons."

Because he was a danger — not that he'd ever meant to be. That was the sad part.

Isaac had told her what Les had said. He'd also told her about the suitcase he'd found in the crawl space of Jeremy's house, and what was in it. "So you think it's true?" she asked. "You think Jeremy killed my mother?"

"I do," Myles said. "It checks out."

"We all thought Don didn't love Jeremy. But he loved him enough to kill for him — to have David killed."

"Don knew what would happen to Jeremy

if the truth ever came out."

Claire adjusted her blanket. "So Tug and Roni, they had nothing to do with it?"

"No. Tug gave Don the money, but he thought he was lending it to save the house from foreclosure. Don was supposed to be working it off, but he didn't follow through."

"What was he supposed to do?" she asked.

"A lot of things. Most recently he was supposed to help Joe and his brother remove some trees from the old Bentmore property."

"That's why he was with Joe!"

Myles nodded. "Tug thought providing Don with a purpose might help him regain control of his life, which would help Jeremy, too."

Claire sipped her coffee. "Jeremy told me where his father's buried."

"Is it under the house?" Isaac asked.

She nodded. "You knew that, too?"

"I saw what I thought might be his grave."

"We're on it," Myles said.

"Do the doctors know whether or not Les is going to survive?" Claire asked.

"He's in intensive care, but they've already removed the bullet. His prognosis is good."

"So he'll stand trial."

"You bet he will," Myles said. "For killing David. For killing Rusty. For arson. And probably for killing the man who died in his office. I received a message just a few minutes ago that the police in Coeur d'Alene have found evidence of at least five calls between that man's business partner and Les Weaver."

"Let me guess. The partner was after his life insurance," Isaac said, and Myles nodded.

"I'm glad they discovered that." The dead man's wife deserved justice and answers just as much as Claire had deserved justice and answers. "So is Les the one who trashed my house?"

"We don't think so. We're pretty sure it was Don."

Claire frowned into her coffee. "But why would Don destroy all my pictures of David, when he'd already killed *him?* Wasn't that enough to take from me?"

"We may never know the answer," Myles replied. "I'm guessing he blamed David for forcing his hand. It wasn't as if Don was a killer at heart, any more than Jeremy was. He just felt he had no choice. He was acting to protect his son. I'm even wondering if Don might've been the person who followed you to your mother's studio."

"No." Claire shook her head. "That was Jeremy. He admitted it."

"Then how did Don know you had the files?"

"We weren't keeping it a secret. Leanne knew. My father and Roni did, too. Tug might've mentioned it to Don when they spoke about the tree work."

"Let's take you home," Isaac said. "You need some rest. And then we have to start shopping."

That last part took Claire by surprise. "Did you say shopping?"

"I need to replace all the things I lost in the fire. You need to replace what was broken. We'll make your house comfortable while we rebuild mine, then we'll decide where we want to live."

"We?" She waited for the resistance she'd experienced earlier that had made her hesitant to accept Isaac into David's house, but it was gone. Instead, she felt as though David was standing in the room, nodding his encouragement, relieved that she was finally happy again. "Together?"

Isaac's mouth twisted into a crooked grin. "Isn't that what married people do?"

She was feeling better already. "I think a big diamond ring comes first," she teased.

He winked at her. "Like I said, we have to go shopping."

Myles had been watching them with a half

smile. She could tell he was warming up to Isaac. Her friends just needed to know his intentions were honorable, and he was proving that now. "I think I'm getting my second wind."

They started to laugh but a noise at the door interrupted. Claire looked around Isaac to see Tug and Roni come rushing in, flustered and worried.

"Claire!" Roni cried.

"I'm so glad you're okay, honey," Tug said.

Claire let Isaac take her cup as she hugged her stepmother, then fell into her stepfather's arms. "I'm sorry I ever doubted you," she said. "I love you. I love you both."

The employees of Thorndike Press hope you have enjoyed this Large Print book. All our Thorndike, Wheeler, and Kennebec Large Print titles are designed for easy reading, and all our books are made to last. Other Thorndike Press Large Print books are available at your library, through selected bookstores, or directly from us.

For information about titles, please call:
(800) 223-1244

or visit our Web site at:
http://gale.cengage.com/thorndike

To share your comments, please write:
Publisher
Thorndike Press
10 Water St., Suite 310
Waterville, ME 04901